A SCENT OF BLUEBELLS

Also by Meg Henderson

FINDING PEGGY: A GLASGOW CHILDHOOD
THE HOLY CITY
BLOODY MARY
CHASING ANGELS
THE LAST WANDERER
SECOND SIGHT
DAISY'S WARS

A SCENT OF BLUEBELLS

Meg Henderson

HarperCollins*Publishers*

This novel is entirely a work of fiction.
The names, characters and incidents portrayed in it are
the work of the author's imagination. Any resemblance to
actual persons, living or dead, events or localities is
entirely coincidental.

HarperCollins*Publishers*

available from the British Library

ISBN-13: 978 0 00 719660 9
ISBN-10: 0 00 719660 1

Set in Bembo by Palimpsest Book Production Limited,
Grangemouth, Stirlingshire

Printed and bound in Great Britain by
Clays Ltd, St Ives plc

This book is proudly printed on paper which contains wood
from well managed forests, certified in accordance with
the rules of the Forest Stewardship Council.
For more information about FSC,
please visit www.fsc.org

Mixed Sources
Product group from well-managed
forests and other controlled sources
www.fsc.org Cert no. SW-COC-1806
© 1996 Forest Stewardship Council
FSC

For G. G.
Over and out, old bean.

Acknowledgements

This is always the hardest part of a book. My approach to research is to interrogate everyone I meet on a daily basis on whatever subject I'm interested in, they don't have to have any knowledge or be involved in any way, they just have to cross my path. This scattergun approach always produces multi-duplicated results and information I already have, as well as enough very welcome red herrings that have to be traced to source, thereby keeping me from actual work. However, this inevitably means that there are always people who read the acknowledgements when the book finally comes out and say 'I told her that!' convinced that it was exclusive information and are hurt at not being mentioned. To those who may feel like this, I hope this explains why.

Having said that, my thanks to Jess Sandeman of Rothesay, who gave me a great deal of background information about the Isle of Bute in past times, and to Deaf Connections in Glasgow, especially their Archivist, Robert J Smith, who generously answered the many questions that cropped up at various times. His excellent book, *City Silent* (published by Douglas McLean/Forrest Books), about the historical difficulties facing the deaf in Glasgow over the years, should be compulsory reading in all schools.

Here, I should have been able to thank one Alice Lutyens, a Literary Assistant who works for my agent, but I can't. Alice was born deaf, so the least an author writing a book containing a deaf character should've been able to expect was a lengthy and detailed list of problems encountered and overcome, but she proved to possess none of these. Born to parents who saw no reason why she should not attend mainstream schools and should achieve no less than other children, that's exactly what she did. As a result she holds down a job that involves dealing with difficult authors, even more difficult agents (as all authors know) and a mixture of bizarre egos (exclusively agents, as all authors again know). It wasn't that I didn't ask the right questions of Ms Lutyens, it was that she didn't recognise the difficulty I'd asked about, though I have to warn any well-intentioned person touching her shoulder to get her attention, that it 'scares the hell out of me' and she has been known to bite in retaliation. Quite scurrilously, in my opinion, she has confessed to using her deafness for her own advantage at times. For example, various innocent policemen who have had occasion to question her parking have been met with the tears of a damsel in distress who can't hear and is therefore unable to communicate. Young girls today, honestly, my generation wouldn't have thought of such dishonesty, and I urge the Metropolitan Police to be on their guard against her nefarious ploys now. So Alice Lutyens is an example of an *un*-acknowledgement, someone I had every right to depend upon for information and who produced very little, and most of that unprintable. A compliment to her parents, of course, but a huge disappointment to an author, and I hope she will be decent enough to hang her head in shame, though I have no confidence of that.

The next lot I have to thank have quite won me over, however. Over decades we've read about Northern Ireland and we've seen a great deal about the Troubles on TV, but in doing this book I've discovered a whole other side to the place. I have to explain that getting information is not always easy, there is sometimes a perception among museum people, especially volunteer museum people, that the whole idea is to give them a job they like doing, it's their information and they don't want you to have it. There are honourable exceptions to this, but the 'I'm not telling you' attitude isn't entirely unheard of. I was once physically barred from leaving a certain maritime museum which shall remain nameless - a wee woman stood against the door and wouldn't let me out, I kid you not! - until I gave an undertaking that I would not use information from a reference book already in the public domain that they had deigned to let me consult in their library as they stood over me. I didn't give the undertaking, neither did I give them a mention in the acknowledgements of that particular book, but the memory of my escape to freedom still makes me laugh. However, Northern Ireland isn't like that. I've never come across friendlier, warmer, more helpful people in my life, all happy to pass on their knowledge and to find out whatever minute detail someone else might have. The Northern Ireland Tourist Board went out of their way to provide whatever I needed, and the staff of the Ulster Folk and Transport Museum in County Down have been especially wonderful. Not only were they happy to pass on their knowledge, but they were more than willing to find people to answer obscure questions that fell outwith their own expertise, to photocopy documents and make helpful suggestions, and I thank them for that. Elaine Hill, Curator of Craigavon Museum Services in County Armagh, without being asked, even visited a particular cemetery on Lough Neagh-side to confirm the view and, like all her colleagues, put herself out to find whatever I wanted to know, and was always available for a chat. And the staff of the Botanic Gardens in Belfast were just as helpful, passing on anecdotes and facts about bluebells, beech trees and anything else I dreamed up, then calling back with stories they remembered that might be of use to me - like the chap who heard about my questions and called to say he knew precisely when bluebells bloomed on the Banks of the Laggan, because he was born in early May and his mother always told him that when she took him home from hospital a week later they passed the bluebells in full flower. For me dealing with everyone I encountered in Northern Ireland has been a joy, and it taught me to view those pictures in the media in a different light. I will also miss their easy friendliness and the chat now that the book is done, talking to them over the months was such a pleasure. Included in this are my sons-in-law, Kenneth and Maureen Davidson from Bangor, County Down, who set me off on the right routes and gave me a far better understanding of the Northern Ireland situation than I had before. While I was working on the book I coincidentally discovered that three quarters of my family in the near past came from Belfast and Omagh, County Tyrone. Once this would have been no more than an interesting genealogical fact, but that connection to Northern Ireland is something I feel quite pleased about now.

Thanks, too, to Caledonian MacBrayne's Company Historian, Ian McCrorie, for background as well as specific information on the Clyde Steamers of yesteryear so beloved of Glaswegians, and to Terry F Mackenzie, Museum Officer with South Lanarkshire Council, for passing on his knowledge of both wars, and the Cameronian War Diaries Teams of South Lanarkshire's Family History Society, for access to the WWI battle diaries they had transcribed with such care.

Apart from those above there are the perennials, my family, who once again put up with the odd hours, the obsessive talking about the book and the frequent tantrums when the computer didn't do what I wanted it to do and insisted on doing what I didn't want it to do. What was wrong with pen and ink?

Lastly, I want to acknowledge my uncle, George Clark, who died in 2003 aged 87. As a young man in WWII he served with the Argyll and Sutherland Highlanders. He was of a generation of men who didn't talk about his experiences, though the family never gave up trying to persuade him to do so. After his death, however, we found a pile of notes painstakingly written in pencil, about his war, together with a letter explaining that he never talked about it because he still had nightmares and he thought people would think he was stupid because of that. What none of us had known was that he had been a marksman, and the story that haunted the character of Matt in the book, of the young German girl with a baby in her arms, found riddled with bullets one Christmas Eve, was true. Even though he had been separated from his family for years fighting the Germans and had witnessed his comrades being blown to bits in front of him many times, the that act of brutality appalled him, and he felt no remorse about tracking down and killing the Pole who had murdered the defenceless girl and baby, 'He was a bad man,' he said in his notes. George Clark was nothing like Matt, quite the reverse, he was the most decent, honourable man I ever knew, my mother thought the world of her big brother, as I did and still do. It's sad that all the years I knew him he secretly carried the awful memory of that event and that it continued to haunt him until he, too, died on a Christmas Eve all those decades later, but it also says much about the man and his humanity.

PROLOGUE

What were they saying? She smoothed the hair from over her ear, pushing it quickly back into the plait round her head, as though a few strands of grey could muffle the sounds coming through the door and leaned into the wood panels, holding her breath so that she could hear more clearly. The upper third of the door was inlaid with six panes of frosted glass, but, slightly crouched, she didn't reach that high, so they wouldn't even see a shadow, would have no idea she was there. They were whispering. Two voices. She even knew whose voices they were, the lassie from up the stairs and her latest man. Sadie? Aye, Sadie. Sadie Duffy. His name didn't matter.

Alice had watched them from behind her curtains in the last few weeks. It did no harm to keep tabs on what was going on in the streets of Inchcraig, and she had more reason to be alert to every sound, every movement, during these endless days. She had noted the excitement on the lassie's face, the expectation on his, and vaguely registered that at least this one was out of uniform, wondering just as vaguely how long it would be before Sadie was arm in arm with a new man, both with the same expressions. That was the problem with the lassie, so her mother said. Sadie liked the excitement of those first few weeks, the thrill of the chase, but once that was over she lost interest. To add to 'the problem', she had grown accustomed to the thrill of being chased by a great many servicemen from all over the place. It had become a way of life for Sadie during the war years, though Sadie wasn't alone in that. But now that the war had drawn to a close, the lassie would find it hard to become accustomed to peacetime morality; everyone knew her reputation would be hard to live down. Maybe, she thought with a smile, Sadie knew this herself but couldn't care less. 'If she wants a man tae marry her,' the local women muttered, though it was by no means certain that Sadie did, 'she'll find people have long memories hereaboots,' quickly followed by; 'an' if she knows whit's good for her, she'll keep her mitts aff ma laddie!'

'Ah'll have her for life,' Marie Duffy had sighed. 'She'll die an auld maid.' Then, realising what she had said, she quickly added, 'No' that there' anythin' wrang wi' that, like, if it's whit ye want.' With no reply forthcoming she had panicked. 'Ah mean, no' everybody's suited tae married life, are they?' and she had laughed a little too shrilly, eyes darting about in embarrassment. 'Ah sometimes think if Ah had my life tae live ower again Ah might no' bother, Ah sometimes think Ah would've been a helluva lot better aff in fact.' Another troubled cackle.

She pressed her ear closer to the door. That was the trouble with whispers, they made you listen even if you had no real interest; the very fact of the implied secrecy made you feel there was something there you had to hear, or else why whisper at all?

The war had finished months ago, and the daily anxiety of families for the safety of their menfolk had given way to excitement and celebrations at first. Then another anxiety had taken over as they waited for husbands, sons and brothers to be demobbed. What would they be like? Would they have changed?

As though a gap of six years would leave anyone unchanged, never mind six years of fighting and killing and waiting to be killed. 'I'll be home any day now,' Matt had written, but 'any day' wore on into weeks and the weeks dragged into months and then a year that appeared to stretch in time with your nerves, she often mused. In the aftermath of Germany's surrender everyone wanted their men home on the next boat or plane, and it seemed like she had already waited longer than the war itself for the heavy tramp of his boots on the stairs, jumping out of her chair by the range, out of her bed in the middle of the night even, and rushing to the door at every sound. Just like now, it was never him. From the moment he went away it had been like going back in time, the feeling was the same. The way waiting took up your entire life, made you live each moment preoccupied with what might or might not be happening in some foreign land. Your heart tightening in your chest every time you saw the telegram boy in the street, and the dizzy relief when he passed by your door, quickly followed by guilt, because he had brought some family the news you didn't want to hear. Not again. Her hands almost went to cover her ears, a familiar gesture laden with meaning if you knew Alice McInally, or who she had been. Once. She checked herself and placed them softly either side of her head as she leaned against the door again.

She had known it wasn't Matt coming home. She'd only jumped out of her seat because she was snatching at any chance, no matter how unlikely, quite prepared to go along with fooling herself. It was courting talk, she had recognised that from those first fumbling noises that had caught her attention before the whispering began. Sadie, for all her wayward morals, respected the decorum of not doing her courting outside her own house on the top flat of the tenement, where her mother could open her door and see what was going on, so she conducted her amorous adventures on the landing below, even though her mother knew perfectly well what was going on down there.

'Stop it!' Sadie was saying, not altogether convincingly. 'She'll hear ye!'

'Who will?' he whispered back, playing for time, his hands continuing with what they were up to.

'Auld Nally!' the girl hissed. 'Ye don't want tae upset her or he'll see tae ye!'

From behind the door she sighed and drew back, all interest lost, and, even if she found it again, she knew she had missed nothing, the same scene would be re-enacted shortly between Sadie and some other man on the make, uniformed or in mufti. They all knew about Sadie, and not just the women, she was pretty sure of that – pretty sure, too, that Sadie knew it. She was the talk of the local as well as the international male fraternity. She was 'a sure thing', a bit of fun that you would never have to marry, because Sadie wasn't interested in marriage, just in having her bit of fun, and that was so unnatural that you wouldn't marry her anyway, even if she wanted you to. Especially if she wanted you to. There was one law for men and another for lassies, and lassies like Sadie Duffy broke the women's law. To the men of the area she was a whore, easy, a tramp, though Alice wondered what it said about them that they went with her so enthusiastically. 'A right cow', that was another of their insults – one that stuck in Alice's mind because she had once been a country girl, during the summer at least, and she liked cows, could see nothing about them that anyone could use as an insult.

Sadie Duffys had been around as long as creation. There was nothing especially good or bad about the lassie herself, she was just a product of her time. She was the kind of female mothers had disapproved of through every century, and men welcomed, temporarily, at least. But then Sadie had only herself to consider – apart from her despairing mother. Sadie wasn't deceiving a husband and had no children who might suffer as a result of her lifestyle. The Sadie Duffys of the world might have been created with wartime in mind – any wartime. And 'he'll see tae ye', that was what the lassie had said. Well, 'he' would, that was true, if she asked him, which she wouldn't, but no one knew that. And it was all to the good that they didn't, it kept them on their toes, made them watch their step, and if you lived in Inchcraig that was no bad thing. Everyone in Glasgow knew what Inchcraig was like, or thought they did: a tough place, a rough place, full of people who were the same. But still, Sadie's remark made her feel slightly uncomfortable. Standing in the hallway, staring down at the patterns on the lino, left arm across her ample chest, the right bent upwards so that her hand held her throat, she pursed her lips as something between a shrug and a shiver ran through her body. Behind her she heard Beth's footsteps and turned to see her sign with her hands 'Not Matt?' Alice signed back to her, mouthing as she did so, 'No. Just Sadie and her latest.' Beth nodded silently and smiled knowingly, then signed back, 'Cup of tea?' Auld Nally nodded and her niece moved towards the kitchen, leaving her alone again to pick out shapes on the lino.

In the small kitchen Beth filled the kettle from the tap, feeling the surge of water rippling up her arm as it filled. Then she placed it on the range and waited, watching her aunt from the corner of her eye, because she knew Alice didn't like people observing her, strange in someone who watched other people. It wasn't out of nosiness, Beth thought, rather it was the sign of a life lived for others.

Alice would take up her normal position whenever there

was a knock at the door. First she would look through the keyhole to see who it was, then she would think for a moment before getting Beth to answer it as she scurried back to the sitting room. If the visitor was welcome that was – if not, the door wouldn't be answered; and everyone in Inchcraig knew what that meant. By the time Beth had conveyed them into her aunt's presence, Alice would be sitting in her chair by the range in the sitting room, facing the door but not looking up, her hands folded calmly in her lap, waiting.

Beth laughed quietly: none of the visitors who went through the performance knew it was one, except her, of course, and perhaps Aunt Alice, though she wasn't sure about that. Usually the visitors were looking for money, or paying a little back, but throughout the transaction Aunt Alice would be almost silent, for she rarely uttered a word, far less cracked a smile. If a loan was being requested, Alice would listen intently, gazing into the fire, her hands never leaving her lap, and then she would nod to Beth and hand her the key she kept in a dark recess somewhere about her waist. Beth would unlock the press, the cupboard across the corner of the room, and withdraw a locked box that was carried to the kitchen. When she came back to the sitting room Aunt Alice would nod again to Beth, a sign that she should remain with the visitor while the box was opened in privacy, an entry made in a book and replaced inside. The requested sum of money would then be counted out and placed on top of the coal bunker, to the left and just inside the kitchen door. Returning to the sitting room, Alice would hand the box to her niece to be replaced in the press, then take possession of the press key once more. Another nod and Alice would sit down again, giving a curt, almost shy glance of dismissal to the visitor. On the way out, Beth would lift the counted notes from the top of the coal bunker and hand them to the visitor before opening the door and seeing them off with a wordless smile, just restraining herself from bowing.

The whole thing was like a stately dance, every movement worked out in advance, the dancers performing the steps precisely as laid out and progressing to the bow at the end, the one that Beth managed not to give. She looked up, saw the steam from the kettle and made the tea, then carried the tray past her aunt, still standing by the door in the hallway, and into the sitting room. Alice was thinking about Matt, she knew, for her aunt always thought of Matt, he was her favourite. Nothing wrong with that, Beth told herself, trying to convince herself that she didn't feel second best to her younger brother. Aunt Alice had done well by both of them, cared for them when there was no one else prepared to do it, sacrificing her life and marriage, too, probably, because what man would take on a woman plus her orphaned niece and nephew, especially when one was a deaf mute? No, she was grateful for what she had, and why wouldn't Matt be the favourite, when he could hear and talk and laugh, and take part in everything? Besides, he was a charming companion, her brother, and good-looking too, blue-eyed and fair-haired as she was herself, but differently laid out in some indefinable way, and when he smiled he made you laugh, cheered you up. When you looked at pictures of Granny McInally, the grandmother Beth didn't remember, Matt's resemblance to her and to Harry, Beth and Matt's father, was striking in a way that Beth's wasn't.

So Matt probably reminded Aunt Alice of her family, and he made her laugh, too, and if anyone deserved to laugh it was Aunt Alice, after all she'd done for them both, was still doing. Beth had understood it less when she was a child, of course, and had sometimes felt left out, but life had contributed to that, she could see it clearer now that she was older. It was no

7

one's fault that she had been born deaf, and the deaf always felt isolated just by being deaf. At least she had a roof over her head, a warm home where she had no worries over where the next meal was coming from, and an aunt who made sure she could look after the house and herself.

As Beth passed, after taking the tea things to the sitting room, she looked at Alice, standing in the hallway, staring down in thought, and smiled. It was a scene she had become used to, as their daily life revolved around waiting for Matt's footsteps on the stairs.

Beth didn't know about the shapes, to Beth the lino was plain mottled brown. She had no reason to suspect that there was a bunch of grapes up on the right there, if you looked hard enough, Winston Churchill just below and on the other side, half a woman, her right hand cheekily on her waist and her hair flicking out. Beside her, the shape of Shaw's Bridge, something Alice had once known well. No bluebells that she could see, but the image stirred her heart each time she looked at it so that she could smell the bluebells without seeing them. She had loved the bluebells on the banks of the Laggan. Once. She had pointed out the bridge in the lino to Matt when he was a child and he had laughed, though she hadn't explained its significance, but she had never shared the imaginary shape with his sister. Maybe the shape wasn't there at all, she had often thought that, maybe she had truly made it up, but when she looked again she always saw it, and Matt had seen a bridge, too, and somehow that made her feel better.

She had concentrated on the practical with Beth, on giving her no-nonsense skills. God knows, she would need them, life would always be more difficult for Beth and without a doubt no man would take her on: she, too, would 'die an auld maid',

8

though for different reasons than Sadie Duffy, or Alice herself for that matter. In a world that could hear and talk she had managed to have Beth taught to communicate by lip-reading and by signing with her fingers, and that was fine between themselves, but few outsiders knew that language. She could read and write, too, of course, a battle she was proud of winning, but no one in Inchcraig understood any of that. To them she was 'a dummy', an idiot, or would have been, if her aunt hadn't been 'Auld Nally' and had 'him' behind her.

Suddenly Alice felt angry, though she didn't really know what she was angry about. Life, maybe, and how she had ended up here, the way she was regarded by the neighbours, Sadie Duffy and her men, all of it rolled up in the frustration and anxiety of waiting for Matt. She threw open the door with more force than it needed.

'Sadie, will you for God's sake either pack it in for the night or go to the landing below for a change!' she shouted. Sadie giggled and her latest looked shocked. 'And could you,' she said, glaring at him, 'take your hands out of there, while I'm talking at least?'

Alerted by the noise, Mrs Duffy, who had been on guard upstairs, shouted down, 'Sadie, will you come up here this minute!', just as Alice had known she would, and the giggling Sadie extricated herself from the hands of her beau and climbed the stairs, leaving him standing alone, looking particularly stupid.

'You'd think you might at least have had the decency to listen to her while you were exploring her,' Alice said to him solemnly. 'Didn't she tell you, you don't want to annoy me?'

As he took to his heels she shouted after him, 'And don't let me find you outside my door again, do your dirty work somewhere else in future!' She moved to shut the door then opened it again. 'And another thing – wash your hands after where they've been tonight!'

When she turned, Beth was laughing and dabbing her eyes. 'What's got into you tonight?'

'I don't know,' Alice laughed back. 'Just in a mood, tired of waiting for Matt, I suppose.'

'Auld Nally.' She knew they called her that. It wasn't the first time she had heard it, she thought darkly. 'Auld Nally the moneylender.' Not to her face, of course, but between themselves. And it wasn't intended as an insult, they said it in the way people do when they're talking about a familiar object in their lives, something that's been there as long as anyone can remember. If they were giving directions to someone they might say 'Go straight till ye come tae the bend in the road, then go alang past Auld Nally's hoose an' turn right, then . . .' Like the bend in the road, she was something familiar that they 'knew' but had no feelings for or about. Except a little caution in her case, perhaps, a little fear, which was fine. That was how she wanted it; after all, she preferred to be an object in the background of their day-to-day existences rather than a person with a life of her own they might try to connect with and pry into. The picture they had of her was the one she had set out to create. So they didn't know – how could they when she made sure they didn't? – that once she had been Alice McInally, a Belfast girl with bright, dark eyes and a long, thick plait of auburn hair falling down her back, a girl who laughed and sang and danced, who walked along the banks of the Laggan hand in hand with her young man, pausing on Shaw's Bridge to kiss in the shadow of the beech trees, their reflection borne along by the Minnow Burn flowing below and carried on the cheerful, burbling water to the River Laggan and on out to sea. She had loved in her time, not as often nor as fleetingly as Sadie Duffy, perhaps, but she had been young, too, once, and she had loved. There was no one in Inchcraig who had known Alice McInally, but deep inside 'Auld Nally' she was still there, along with her memories.

The days kept the pattern of too many that had gone before. It was the incessant waiting that did it, she knew that, remembered it well from past experience, but still, she was annoyed with herself for letting it happen. Your mind shrank, that's what happened. It became concentrated on the event you were waiting for and, gradually, without your realising, it couldn't take any other thoughts.

She looked up at Beth standing by the door.

'Do you want anything to eat yet?' Beth signed.

Alice shook her head.

'You have to eat something.'

'Later.'

Beth stood her ground, arms crossed, looking at her disapprovingly.

'Will you stop that?' Alice signed.

Beth shrugged.

'You've got your telling-off face on. I know whether or not I'm hungry, I'm not a child, you know.'

'No, but you're behaving like one. The way you're going, the minute Matt steps over the door you'll drop dead of starvation. Some homecoming.'

'If it'll stop you nagging,' she signed, 'I'll have some chicken soup.'

Beth nodded happily and went to the kitchen, smiling, returning minutes later with a bowl on a tray with some bread.

'You were quick with that,' Alice signed, with a sceptical look.

'Yes, I'm a sneaky cow,' Beth responded. 'I had a pot of soup on the stove all ready, I'm a right bad lot. And what's more, I was prepared to force-feed you.'

And that's when it happened, of course, when she was sitting there, mouth full of thick soup and soggy bread. All those weeks waiting for the sound of his boots on the stairs and she missed it, the first thing she heard was the pattern of cheery little raps Matt always used when he knocked on the door. She stood up, the tray with the bowl smashing on the floor, her feet skidding on the spilled soup as she made for the front door. Beth looked at her, her eyes alarmed. 'Matt!' Alice shouted. 'It's Matt!' And though Beth couldn't hear her, she knew what Aunt Alice was saying.

Alice opened the door and saw Matt standing there, thinner, older, the smile just the same, but, ah, the eyes! The eyes, there it was again, that awful mixture of feelings and terrors she instantly recognised because she had seen it before, and the next thing she knew the mottled brown lino with the imaginary pictures was coming up to meet her.

'What the hell happened?' Matt was saying, as he and Beth lifted Alice from the floor and struggled with her into her bedroom.

'She's seen you again,' Beth mouthed, using the voice she had no need of and so rarely used, because her hands were too full of her aunt to sign.

They laid her on her bed and she began to come round.

'I'd just been telling her she'd faint from starvation, the way she was going on, didn't really think she'd do it, though,' Beth signed. 'She hasn't been eating much, been jumping up and down at the slightest sound outside for months now, in case it was you.'

Matt shook his head, thinking it was all very well to be anxious, but this was ridiculous.

Beth looked at him. 'Welcome back, wee brother,' she signed.

'Aye, aye,' he smiled. 'But are you sure she's OK?'

'Of course I'm OK,' Alice muttered. 'I moved too quickly, that was all. Not as young as I used to be.'

'Oh, aye, you're really ancient,' Matt said dryly. 'What are you now? A hundred and ten, is it?'

Alice glared at him, then began laughing. 'I can still dish out a slap about the ear, and don't you forget it!'

Then they hugged and laughed and talked too much for any of it to go in, and once again Beth was on the outside, watching, the conversation too fast and intensely meaningless for her to follow or for Alice and Matt to sign to her. That was the hardest part of being deaf, not that she even understood what being deaf was. Her situation was entirely normal for her, she had nothing to compare it with. The problems stemmed from the fact that other people were abnormal as far as she was concerned, they had this other sense, whatever it was. She could hear to a small degree, but only on a certain level, so it amounted to very little and wasn't something she could use. It didn't even occur to her that it was usable, but there had been a time, though she couldn't pinpoint it exactly, when she understood that the sound she heard was obviously different from what other people heard. Throughout her childhood it had seemed to Beth that Matt and Aunt Alice spent a great deal of their time talking to each other, laughing and joking, and when she asked what was going on, Alice would sign that she would tell her later. The trouble was that when later came, the explanation often amounted to a couple of minutes, yet the conversation had taken perhaps an hour. That was what she missed, being part of things, being involved in this other world of hearing that took up so much of their time, time when she was excluded. Eventually Alice and Matt would calm down, see her standing there, observing, and remember to slow down and include her. She knew that all she had to do was wait till their excitement had peaked and they were exhausted with talking, but it meant that she was never part of their excitement.

Matt had brought them back presents, which Beth found strange, gifts from the war, as though he had just returned from a world tour. He gave her a gold ring set with a single large ruby, and a pink silk handkerchief edged with heavy lace. In one corner there was a little pocket and, inside, a powder puff attached with a silk cord, and in another corner the embroidered crest of the Argyll and Sutherland Highlanders. Alice was given a brown leather bag, with a scene of ancient Egypt painted on the flap in bright colours and lined with silk, and a rose-gold locket with an emerald in the centre and room for two small pictures inside. He had also brought back a *kukri*, the long, curved knife carried by Gurkha soldiers from Nepal, and a set of arab robes complete with headdress. He put these on and then walked about to make them laugh. That seemed to be his main objective, as far as Beth could make out, to make them laugh. War must be a very funny thing.

I

Liam. That was his name, the other young man Alice had waited for to come home from a war. Liam McCann, whose family wealth had started three generations before his birth with a piglet, a 'jarrie', as the runt of the litter was called in Ireland, the one that didn't have a teat to suck on and was therefore bound to die. It was his great-grandfather who had taken on that first 'jarrie', fattened it up and bought another two, bit by bit ending up with a small empire. When the Irish Potato Famine took hold in the 1840s and mass emigration gathered pace, Old Man McCann had somehow held on, managing to buy up what good land existed around Lough Neagh, thereby becoming a self-made man of means. He never forgot his debt to the pigs though, and was fond of them all his life, knowing every one by name, even if that fondness meant breeding them, fattening them up, then slaughtering them, which he always did himself.

'But why did he kill them if he liked them?' Alice asked, watching her father as he effortlessly jointed the salted pig carcass before him. Henry McInally was always immaculately turned out, three-piece suit over pristine white shirt, discreet dull striped tie holding a stiff collar in a tight stranglehold, and a heavy chain across his waistcoat attached to a gold watch that lived inside his pocket. Not actually dressed to be messing about with pigs, alive or dead.

'What did you say, Alice?' he asked, pulling himself up to his full five foot two, his little black moustache bristling with annoyance, the sunlight streaming through the window bouncing off his black, slicked-back hair.

'Well, if he liked his pigs so much,' Alice said with innocent logic, 'why didn't he keep them as pets? Why did he kill them?'

'How many times have I explained this?' Henry demanded. 'He didn't trust anyone else to do it,' he said slowly, irritated by her lack of understanding of things chivalrous and admirable, forgetting that he was talking to a child, as adults always do. 'It was his work, same as this is mine, but he didn't trust anyone else to do it right, and because he did like the pigs, he wanted it done right, didn't he?'

Alice nodded uncertainly, a quizzical glance sideways at her older brother Harry, who grinned back. Harry always understood. He had been there two years before she was, so Harry knew things she didn't and she wondered if she ever would. Harry always did and said the right thing. He was so clever. She had been about to point out that people had always slaughtered pigs, still did, there was nothing much to it. Even now, when you went back to Lough Neagh during the long summer holidays, you would see it being done all the time, so she didn't understand why Old Man McCann thought he was the only one who could do it right. Beside her, Harry's eight-year-old elbow nudged her to say no more and she bit her lip into silence instead. It was true, though, that the process hadn't changed a great deal in the country areas. The pig would be stunned by a blow to the head with a sledgehammer before its throat was cut. Sometimes the blood was allowed to flow away, but most people collected it in a bucket and mixed it with oatmeal to make black puddings. In poor areas nothing was wasted, but that sight had put Alice off black pudding all her life. Then the coarse hair would have to be removed with scalding hot water and a sharp knife, before a cut was made from throat to rib-cage, and the chest jacked apart with wooden staves. Once it had been hoisted to head height, another cut was made from the back legs to meet the open chest so that the entrails would fall out, giving easy access to the organs, the offal. The heart and liver were sold to the butcher, who sold the hearts on to Russia, where they were said to be a great delicacy, and the small intestine was kept for making sausage casings. The large intestine was rendered down to make grease and the head sold to whoever wanted it, because there was good eating in it, then the carcass would be hoisted even higher to keep it away from hungry cats and dogs and hung for two or three days, before the salters came. Alice's family, the McInallys, had been salters in the Derryhirk area of Lough Neagh since before Old Man McCann had bought his first 'jarrie', travelling from steading to steading to cure the hanging pigs.

'Before your great-grandfather arrived,' her father Henry would say, 'everyone would have been up at four in the morning to light the boiler so that there was an endless supply of hot water. As a wee boy I used to go with him on his travels, watching him mixing salt, cream of tartar, saltpetre and brown sugar, and rubbing it into every crevice of the carcass. That's what everyone used, but he had his own recipe and ways of mixing, that's what made him special.' He'd stop to wink theatrically at his children. 'He was a wee man, but he had powerful arms and great big hands like shovels, skin like leather.' Here his children would duck slightly just in case, as, knife in hand,

Henry McInally threw his arms outwards with reckless abandon to demonstrate the gigantic and unlikely proportions of the 'wee man's' arms. 'But the mixture still found wee nicks to get into, and if you ever had that stuff on even the tiniest bit of raw flesh you'd know all about it. The finest bacon it was,' he'd continue, his eyes misting over, as everyone's does about their childhood, good or bad, the sharp knife nestling incongruously against his chest, 'cut thicker than now, and no rind left at all.' Here he'd pause to sniff disapprovingly, unaware that Alice and Henry sniffed with him right on cue, exchanging muffled giggles. 'It's still the tastiest bit, if grand people' – always said with extreme distaste, to prove that Henry McInally was a man of the common people, which he was not – 'did but know it, and afterwards we'd fry eggs and potato bread in the fat left in the pan.' He'd sigh, give himself a shake and return to the task in hand. 'My father never wanted to do anything else than follow my grandfather, and I wanted nothing more than to follow him either, till Old Man McCann was dead and his son made my father the offer.' About that point Harry would nudge his younger sister again to remind her not to point out that their father was not a common or garden salter, in fact he never had been. He had learned the salter's skills many years ago from his grandfather and father, but he never used them in earnest. He was a Belfast businessman who liked to pretend he was a horny-handed son of the soil. She didn't know these exact words then, but she was a child, she knew play-acting when she saw it.

'The offer.' Henry McInally's voice rose and swelled as he said the words, so that they resonated with such importance that you could almost hear a trumpet fanfare in the background. It had changed the lives of the McCanns and the McInallys for all time, so maybe his reverence was understandable. It had transformed them from country-dwellers, from peasants, to city folk of some means, though the McCanns would remain of higher means than the McInallys. In the 1850s it took them from Lough Neagh to the suburbs of fast-growing Belfast, making them, on visits 'home', outsiders to where and who they had come from. It taught both sides, if truth be told, to look down on each other because they didn't understand each other, and that lack of understanding inevitably bred a feeling of slight distrust. The children knew this without being able to explain it, felt it without being able to understand it, so that even when they played with the local children, the Belfast McCanns and McInallys did so together. All Alice's life it had been like that, though no one ever put that slight distance into words. All through the summer escape from Belfast, Liam and Brendon McCann were inseparable from Henry, Alice and, eventually, Isabel McInally, complete in themselves when there weren't any local children to play with, when even their country-dwelling cousins didn't play with them. It was hard to work out who you were or where you belonged when your own family saw you as an incomer, and you saw your own family as strangers, even if you didn't say that out loud. The local children spoke differently, too, they had a rougher, deeper accent that they would first find hard to tune into; but once they had picked it up themselves they found it harder to tune out of when they returned to Belfast.

In the days leading up to the twenty-three-mile journey 'home' from Belfast, and for the first few days at Lough Neagh, the children felt hugely excited, but after that, being accustomed to the more diverse delights of the big city, they became slightly bored – apart from Liam, that was. They hoped their country relatives didn't know this, which, of course, they did. A bored and out-of-sorts visitor from Belfast was a thing of embarrassment to his or her parents. 'Tired out,' a mother would say, almost guiltily, 'not used to all this fresh air!' and all the adults would smile, colluding together to hide what they all knew better. By the end of the summer they were usually ready to return to Belfast – apart from Liam once again – though they were well-warned not to show it, to pretend to be desolate instead: though, again, everyone knew better. They were the first generation of each family to have been born in Belfast, and so they hadn't the strong, visceral connections that led their fathers and mothers to regard the Lough Neagh area as 'home' in the truest, most instinctive sense. Even before the children were born in the 1890s, both families were living in luxury compared with their Lough Neagh beginnings, and forever separated by more than distance. The McCanns lived in some splendour, and the McInallys in slightly less splendour, in North Belfast. Bridie McCann had a maid and a cook, for instance, whereas Victoria paid a cleaning girl who came in twice weekly and did all her own cooking, whether from lack of funds or her own obsession with cooking no one questioned. And though the houses were constructed of locally made red brick, there being no native stone in Belfast, there were ways, as there always are, of demonstrating wealth and position, even with identical red brick. The McCann house had bay windows, odd patterns in the brickwork, and a large walled garden with a driveway at the side, little extras that Victoria McInally envied in a genteel way, but envied just the same.

To Liam and Brendon McCann and Harry, Alice and Bella McInally, Belfast was where they had been born and raised, and Lough Neagh was 'home' simply because their parents called it that. For Liam it eventually became different. Lough Neagh was where he discovered boats, so it was always special to him and he hated leaving. 'Life in Belfast' he used to say was 'just time spent between visits to Lough Neagh.'

'The offer' came from Old Man McCann's son, known all his days as Young McCann. His father had been content with his life, where he had made his fortune – a fortune in Lough Neagh terms at any rate. Old McCann tended and killed his pigs, and he looked after the land and cattle he had, employing people he had known all his life to help him. When he died he was buried in the family plot in Derrytrasna Cemetery, close to the southern shore of the Lough, with all the McCanns who had gone before him, leaving behind Young McCann, who had grown up knowing a different life and a better standard of living than Old McCann – thanks to his father. Unlike Old McCann, he had been educated, and that had inevitably resulted in him having ideas. One of those ideas was that he didn't like being a peasant, even a relatively well-off one. Young McCann felt he was better than the people his father identified with; his father had embarrassed him. The old man had been proud of knowing every pig's family history and could recite the names of every porcine ancestor, indeed he often did as his son cringed by his side. Young McCann wanted away from pigs, he wanted away from Lough Neagh and for his children to become respectable businessmen. Maybe, being the first generation born after Old McCann became a man of means, his son could see only too clearly where the family had come from. He had been removed from that life by his father's hard work and wealth, but he was still close enough to understand how easy it would be to lose it all and accustomed enough to his standard of living not to want to. Perhaps that was what made him determined to leave his roots as far behind as possible, and seek higher, better, richer lives for his children, or perhaps he was just a different man from his father.

Belfast was expanding rapidly and Young McCann saw a chance, a way out. He may have hated having a father who loved every pig he had ever owned – and slaughtered – but he was realistic enough to know that for the time being his family's fortunes were tied to the beasts. He would, he decided, move his family to the city and set up a bacon-curing business, a commercial enterprise that would grow in time and lead to better, non-pig-related opportunities. He wasn't a particularly bright man, only educated, so the details took him some time to work out, but if his education had taught him anything it was that to succeed he had to use the skills of others. That was how men of means became wealthy men of means. Eventually he had approached Henry McInally's father and offered him the chance to manage the business for him. It meant moving out of Derryhirk and becoming city dwellers, but it also meant a huge step up from being a travelling salter, and it gave the McInally family, too, the chance of a better life and future. From then on the Catholic McCanns and the Protestant McInallys were closely linked, and it didn't matter to any great extent that their religions were different. There were simmering religious and political issues in the country – the two were intertwined as far as Ireland was concerned – but the families had lived perfectly amicably 'at home' for generations without it ever being a problem for them, after all. And though the children of the families went to different schools in Belfast, what united them – a shared background, money and business – was more important than what divided them, especially when they went 'home' together as incomers every summer.

By the time Young McCann had joined his forebears in Derrytrasna, his son Dermot had taken over ownership of McCann's, just as Willie McInally had taken over its management from his father. One day Seamus McCann would succeed Dermot, just as Henry McInally waited in the wings, learning the ropes, and after them Liam and Harry would take over, that was the accepted wisdom. The plan was already working out well, the curing business down by the docks had expanded and led to better things. At first the pigs were still slaughtered on the smallholdings around Lough Neagh and brought to the sheds for curing by horse and cart; then agents appeared, who bought them and brought them live to the new abattoirs in Belfast for slaughter, and from there an export business was built up, gradually taking Belfast Ham all over the world.

However, it wasn't ever a major part of the area's commerce. It was a minor player in the business life of Belfast: ham-curing never reached the heights of linen or shipbuilding, for instance, and it was dependent on the vagaries of public taste and fragility of livestock prices, which moved up and down seemingly without reason. The McCanns understood the need to diversify and built their own ice factories, to supply the high amounts of ice needed for the Wiltshire Cure, which had changed the curing business forever. Then they moved into grocery provision and bought up a few pubs, always a lucrative business.

Over the years the master plan adapted and evolved to take in wider horizons, with visions of future McCanns being involved in banking and the law, and by the time Seamus took over in the 1890s the family was part of the business fabric of the city. The McCanns were well set up, and as well-removed from the Lough Neagh days. There was a confidence born of success and wealth, an arrogance perhaps, that there would always be sons in both families to take over the ownership and the management of the business, in time the businesses, even if they didn't express much enthusiasm as children, just as Liam didn't – but that, Seamus hoped fervently, would pass, as it was made to pass for him.

Seamus wanted his eldest son to be the first lawyer in the family. He certainly had the brains for it, but the trouble was that Liam loved boats. Loved them with a passion, loved the process of building them, selecting the wood, persuading it to take on the shape you wanted, balancing the craft. He exulted in the lines, the beauty of the creation, the way it handled on the water. It was the fault of those summer holidays, his father would fume in later years. He should never have allowed his sons to run wild with the natives. Seamus wasn't as driven as his grandfather had been, he was safely removed from all the terrors that had prompted Young McCann to leave the countryside and head for the city, he was secure in his prosperous Belfast life, but he still expected his sons to take over when he was gone. The younger boy, Brendon, would oversee the businesses while Liam would take the family's standing another rung higher up the social scale. It was the natural way of things to improve and drive upwards, after all, the natural order.

Only Liam seemed hell-bent on ruining everything. It seemed that he delighted in causing his father more worry and concern than dealing with all the businesses put together, and now they'd had another run-in that had left Seamus enraged, which was normal these days. He tried to go back to his work, but this was too much. This time the boy had pushed him so far over the edge that he'd been unable to concentrate on anything else. He got up and left the office early, heading for home, heading for Bridie to make it better.

Bridie McCann was sitting in her parlour concentrating on her needlework when Seamus arrived unexpectedly.

'Seamus! You're home early, it's not more than three o'clock. Are you ill?'

'What is it with the boy?' Seamus demanded of his wife, ignoring her concern.

Oh, so it was Liam again, but then it always was, so no surprise there. Bridie, busy with her latest embroidery, made herself even busier. 'What's he done now?' she asked amiably.

Her tone infuriated Seamus; she never took these things seriously.

'Well, we won't even start with his complete lack of interest in a career in the law,' he seethed. 'And you know that as it is he rarely graces us with his presence at the office?'

Bridie saw Seamus from the corner of her eye, standing stiffly, one tightly fisted hand on the back of his armchair. She didn't need to look at him to see his blue eyes blazing, she could almost feel the fire from across the room. Bridie kept her counsel. A particularly difficult stitch needed her urgent and full attention, she decided.

'He came to me this afternoon and informed me – informed me, mind you – that he will be taking the next month off to help old Jimmy Devlin build a fishing boat on Lough Neagh! I said to him, "What about McCann and Son?" and he replied, "You've got a son, Brendon." I said to him, "What about university? You want to be a lawyer, don't you?" and he shrugged his shoulders – you know the way that he does – and said, "Well, that's what you want, Father, but I haven't got time to discuss it, Alice is expecting me for a picnic."'

Bridie put her head down and concentrated hard. She could see it, hear it – it was pure, unadulterated Liam. She said nothing, knowing there was more to come from his father.

'Why am I shocked? Answer me that? As I said, we rarely get to bask in his company these days for more than three days out of every week. It's hard to say whether he's late after one weekend or early for the next.' Seamus stared at his wife. 'Well, say something, Bridie! Aren't you shocked to your toes?'

'Um, what did you say to him?'

'I told him it was out of the question, pure and simple, that was all. What else was there to say? When I could talk at all, that was. I was so shocked that it took me almost ten minutes to get a word out!'

Bridie doubted that. 'Calm down, Seamus. Why must every conversation in this family be conducted through a megaphone?' Though she knew why: Seamus and Liam.

'Calm down?' he yelled back, repeatedly slapping a rolled-up newspaper into his hand. 'Calm down, is it? Is it some sort of rebellion against me, do you think? And if it is, what have I done to him?'

'Maybe,' Bridie suggested gently, smiling at her irascible husband, 'he just wants his own life.'

'What kind of talk is that? He has no right to a life of his own!'

'Seamus!' Bridie put her embroidery down in her lap and looked at him accusingly.

'You know what I mean, Bridie, and don't say you don't!' Seamus turned and paced about their large, opulent parlour, finally stopping at the big bay window and looking out without seeing anything but his red fury.

Bridie looked at him, a tall, handsome man in his forties, an older version of Liam in every way, though he would have none of it. To hear him talk, or shout, their eldest son might have been found in a basket in the rushes, like Moses, but there was no mistaking the build, the blue eyes, the fair, reddish hair and the stubborn intensity that made them circle each other like prize fighters. Brendon took after Bridie, as Seamus admitted: he was smaller with dark hair, hazel eyes and a pale complexion and, more than that, he was a calm boy, not given to Seamus McCann's emotional explosions; a boy who would exchange amused, despairing glances with his mother at the antics of his father when it came to his brother. In the middle of yet another disagreement, Brendon, from his earliest years, would send a look to Bridie that said, 'Here we go again. What can you do with them?'

'Where would any of us be if we'd followed our dreams?' Seamus demanded. 'If I had done that he and his brother wouldn't have the life they have.' He threw his arms out again to encompass the grand house and all that it signified. 'He has a duty to do the same for his children. Instead, what do we get?' He turned furiously and glared at his wife. 'We get business taking second place to boats, we get business being fitted in around boats. What future is there in that?'

Bridie shrugged diplomatically, thinking, as she returned to her embroidery, that Jimmy Devlin and his boys did all right.

'And when he is here we have to fit any work he's prepared to do around whatever plans he has with Alice. That's another thing, how is he ever going to meet anyone suitable if he insists on spending every moment with Alice? I can just see him standing at the altar, and when the priest asks if he takes this woman, he'll say he has to check with Alice!'

Bridie fought to hide her laughter, though the Alice situation was concerning her slightly, too, as it was the McInallys. Once or twice she had caught a certain note in Victoria's voice as she mentioned the ongoing friendship. What was that last remark she had made at tea the other day? 'I was just saying to Henry, it's hard to tell where one ends and the other begins, they're hardly ever apart,' followed by a gentle little laugh, but Bridie caught her meaning.

'Yes,' Seamus continued, 'he's quick to turn his nose up at spending any time working in the business, but happy enough to live off it!'

'Now, Seamus, that's unfair,' Bridie said quietly. 'It's a father's business to provide for his children, but when does any child have a say in what that business is? Liam – and Brendon, for that matter – are no different from other children in that.'

'There you go! You indulge him, you always have!'

'Now it's my fault, Seamus?' Bridie laughed. 'First it's letting him run wild at Lough Neagh, now it's my fault? Just how do you make that out?'

'You're . . .' He whirled about, his arms flying upwards in the air like a fisherman casting a net, trying to pull sense from it. 'You're too accommodating, too calm, that's how!' he finally shouted, and Bridie laughed even more, which infuriated him, because he knew she was laughing at him; knew, furthermore, that she had every right to.

'It wouldn't matter a damn what the boys wanted to do – they could come in here and announce they were off on the next boat to Paraguay, or they were planning to grow wings and fly, and you'd just smile at them and tell them they're wonderful.'

Bridie was struggling to convert her laughter into a more acceptable smile that wouldn't feed Seamus's fury. She tried to imagine Brendon ever suggesting such a thing, but decided not to pursue the thought because it would make her laugh out loud again. 'That's probably very true, Seamus,' she said quietly. 'But you see, I take the view that banning children from even thinking such things would only make them more likely to do them.' She looked up at him kindly. 'Don't you think so, Seamus? Really? I mean, what actual good does shouting at them do?'

'Oh, I see!' Seamus threw back at her. 'So it's all my fault then, you're saying I'm a bad father now?'

Bridie put her needlework down, got up from her chair, crossed to the window and put her arms around her husband, stroking his arms as though he were a huge, excited bird flapping his wings and putting his feathers out of kilter. 'I won't talk to you when you're like this, Seamus,' she said quietly. He tried to stop himself giving in to her embrace and she shook her small, dark head. 'You see?' she smiled. 'Now where do you think Liam gets his stubborn streak from?'

Seamus McCann relaxed, slipping his arms around her waist. 'It's not the boys,' he said resignedly, his chin resting on top of her curls. 'I know that. It's just Liam.'

'That's because you expect so much of Liam,' Bridie told him. 'It's that eldest son thing, Seamus. Try to think for yourself a moment, rather than as a McCann. You know perfectly well that Brendon loves the business world.'

'Yes, I do know that,' he said, pulling back to look at her. 'But why would that stop Liam reaching beyond that? That's all I want, for him to make progress while the businesses are taken care of.'

'But just because you want it doesn't mean it has to be or will be, Seamus,' she protested. 'You're a smart man, but your head's still in a time when a father could tell a son what to do with his life. Times are changing, the old traditions are changing.'

'It's the way it's always been,' he replied in a puzzled voice. 'And it's always worked well, why change it now? Why does he want to destroy all that tradition?'

Bridie held him silently for a moment, thinking. 'Everyone's different, Seamus. You know perfectly well that Brendon might've been made for business. It suits him and he suits it, you have no trouble accepting that. Isn't that true? Why can't you accept that he and Liam are very different?' she said quietly. 'Brendon's like me, but —'

'No!' Seamus protested, laughing despite himself. 'I know what's coming next! Don't say Liam's like me!'

'But he is! That's why you find him so infuriating. Granted, he's not quite as, well, excitable, but he has his opinions and holds them strongly, as you do. You know your father never gave you any choice in the life you have, so you don't want to give Liam any, and you know what that feels like. You're not angry at Liam, you're angry because you're doing to him what your father did to you, and you know you shouldn't do it.'

He pulled away from her and took up a position in the other corner of the room. This, she thought sadly, is what Liam sees.

'There it is again, Bridie McAlinden!' he shouted. 'You always side with Liam against me!'

'That's simply not true!' she shot back at him in a hurt voice.

'You're siding with him and saying I'm a cruel father who denies his son his dreams because my father denied me mine!'

Bridie sighed and shook her head, turning away from him.

'Well that's what you mean, Bridie!' he persisted, angry again.

'No, Seamus,' she said evenly. 'It's what you hear, what you want to hear.' She stared at him meaningfully for a long moment. 'Maybe you should ask yourself why that is. Now I'm going out into the garden, I can't bear your noise and nonsense a moment longer.'

By retreating from the pointless fray to walk round the garden inspecting the roses she was depriving him of a target for his rage, so he would sit down in his chair with his now mutilated newspaper, then one of the pages wouldn't fold properly and he would throw it as far across the room from him as he could, before finally subsiding into the calm after the storm. She knew him so well. When she was sure it was over for now, she went back in, picked up the scattered pages of the disobedient newspaper, then sat down quietly at the other side of the fireplace and resumed her needlework. As she sat down he looked at her sheepishly and said, 'What he needs is a wife.'

'Oh, Seamus, of course he doesn't! He's far too young!'

'Well, that's what the church tells us, isn't it? Marry them off young to keep them out of trouble? I mean it,' Seamus sighed. 'Some nice Catholic girl to fill his mind and his time with lots of babies, that's just what he needs. That would settle him down.'

'Marriage doesn't solve everything, Seamus.'

'It did for me,' he smiled.

'Oh, Seamus!' she teased, glancing up from her work, because she knew that was the response he wanted. Because marriage hadn't solved all his problems, she knew that as well as Seamus did.

'It's the fault of bloody Lough Neagh, that's the truth of it,' he said thoughtfully, as he always did eventually, 'of letting them run wild there for months at a time when they were children.'

He was right about that. Bridie knew that Lough Neagh was the very place for a boy who loved boats. Especially a boy quietly shunned by the local children but tolerated by the local adults because of who his father was, so even when the others were bored, Liam never was, he always had the boats. And Alice, of course: he always had Alice.

At the very moment his mother was trying to calm his father, Liam and Alice were walking towards Shaw's Bridge, their favourite destination when trouble brewed at home.

'So what is it this time?' Alice asked, smiling; she rarely took the arguments between Liam and his father seriously, it was just how they were.

Liam was fiddling with his newest acquisition, a camera he had bought to take pictures of the boatbuilding at Jimmy

Devlin's. 'He's had a screaming fit because I want to go off to the Lough for a month,' Liam said, shrugging his shoulders to emphasise the silliness of Seamus's reaction.

'What does he want you to do?' she asked, handing him a blanket to spread out for their picnic.

'Work,' he replied, 'his kind of work, the boring sort.'

'I've found that all parents expect that,' Alice said with mock-seriousness. 'Most unfair, I call it.'

Liam laughed. 'You know what I mean. Have I ever shown the slightest interest in his kind of work? Have I ever said I wanted to do anything other than build boats?'

'No,' Alice grinned, emptying the contents of the hamper bit by bit. 'I'll give you that, you've never left him in any doubt. Here, gnaw on a chicken leg, might take some of that resentment out of you.'

'Careful! I don't want to get grease on the lens.' He wiped the camera carefully and placed it safely out of reach. 'I just don't see why he's got to make such a drama out of everything,' he sighed, savaging the chicken leg. 'Why can't he just say very calmly, "No, Liam, I'd rather you stayed here"'? Why does he have to go ten shades from red to purple and scream till the veins stand out on his forehead like that?'

'And you'd accept that, would you? A calm "No", I mean?'

'No, of course I wouldn't, but I don't accept it if he screams either.' He looked up at her. 'And why are you taking his side anyway?' he demanded.

'I'm not,' Alice laughed, settling down beside him with a quiet smile. 'I suppose I'm trying to introduce some spice into the boring monotony of yet another McCann battle, that's all.'

He reached over and hit her softly on the head with the half-eaten piece of chicken.

She slapped his hand away and reached up to her hair, grimacing. 'Yes, that's bound to get me on your side, isn't it?' she demanded. 'I'll have to wash my hair to get the smell and the grease out of it.'

He shrugged again. 'So wash it,' he said simply.

'It's all right for you, you have no idea how long it takes to dry!' She made a lunge for him, but he knew her too well and body-swerved out of her reach, so she lifted a piece of chicken from the basket and threw it at him, and when he got up and ran she went after him, her arm raised, giggling. After a brief struggle they settled down again to their meal.

'You see?' he said contentedly. 'We've just settled a differ-ence of opinion by throwing the odd piece of chicken. Why can't my father do the same?'

Alice laughed out loud at the thought of Seamus throwing chicken instead of a fit. 'So what are you going to do?'

'I'm going to Lough Neagh, of course!' Liam replied. 'What else?'

'So we'll be having a similar conversation very shortly then?'

'What do you mean?' he asked her, puzzled.

'Well, it's not the first fight you've had with your father, is it? And it won't be the last; but they always blow over, don't they?'

'Till the next one,' Liam sighed, 'till the next one. Living with my father is like living on the edge of a volcano.' He was quiet for a while, so that the sound of the Minnow Burn was very loud and comforting. 'Are we still planning to see that new film tomorrow?' he asked.

'If you're sure the volcano won't lock you in your room tonight,' Alice replied.

'Don't think he hasn't thought of it,' Liam muttered. He wiped his hands and picked up his camera. 'Smile,' he said.

'Go away! I'm not having my picture taken! Take one of the bluebells while they're there.'

'Well, it would only technically be of you,' he said, his attention on the camera. 'I'm just trying it out, you're incidental, you just happen to be here.'

'Of all the cheek!'

Liam was unfazed.

'Why do the bluebells last such a short time, do you suppose?' she asked, breathing in the scent. 'Two weeks at most and then they're gone.'

'It's the trees,' he muttered. 'Once the leaves come out they form a canopy that cuts out the sunlight, so the bluebells die.'

'And you can't pick them,' she mused, 'they die before you can get them home.'

'It's the stems,' he said.

'What do you mean?'

'God, you really are dense! Can't you work it out?' He looked up at her. 'Think of rose stems.'

'I don't want to think of rose stems, we're talking about bluebells, fool.'

'Rose stems are hard and woody, when they're cut they retain moisture,' he explained, his voice deliberately weary to annoy her. 'Bluebell stems are succulent, they're soft, they don't retain moisture, so they die quickly. Now do you understand?'

'You think you know everything, Liam McCann,' she said archly. 'No wonder your father yells at you!'

'I don't know what I'm doing with this damned thing,' he complained. 'I'm having trouble working out this timer. What it should do is let you set it up, then take the picture by pressing the button thing on the end of this wire thing.'

'Yes, clear as mud,' she giggled. 'Far too many "things" to contend with.'

Liam placed the camera on the bridge and retreated to where Alice was still sitting on the blanket, surrounded by picnic debris. He sat just behind her to the side, both of them in the same pose with one arm outstretched. 'Now this is the tricky bit,' he said. 'I have to press this button on the top and it should take a picture.'

'And you're sure you don't have to be holding the camera?' Alice asked.

'Well, that's the theory, let's see if it works.'

They sat for a few minutes.

'Well?' she asked, through a fixed smile.

'I heard a click,' he said. 'I definitely heard a click. We'll just have to wait and see, I suppose, though that's one exposure wasted.'

'What do you mean?' Alice laughed.

'It's not about people,' he replied seriously, examining the camera again, 'it's about boats, I told you that.'

'Like life itself, Liam McCann,' she laughed. 'Like life itself!'

In the late 1890s, when the McCann and McInally summer visitors had been running wild with the net fishermen on the Lough, traditional ways were changing there, too. Pollan, a kind of freshwater herring, had almost died out, and perch was only valued as pig feed or caught as fry, 'babes', as they were called in the warm summer weather in June, as bait for catching eels. There were still some pike, bream, gudgeon, lampreys and roach to be found, along with the higher-valued trout and salmon, but it was the eels, all the way from the Sargasso Sea and fattened by years of rich Lough-living on worms, water insects, beetles and fish fry, that were the most important. For Brendon, the younger McCann, and Harry, the eldest McInally, it was the fishing that mattered, but it wasn't the fish or the eels that made Liam a constant companion to the fishermen. Liam was fascinated by the way their boats were built, from the early flat-bottomed cots that could be rowed or poled, to the clinker-built boats, with their overlapping planks and ribs for strength, a skill that had come from the Vikings when they arrived in their longboats to pillage Ireland centuries before, some said. He watched the boat-builders selecting the right kind of light timbers so that they would bend easily to shape without steaming, Russian spruce for the hull, Oregon pine or Douglas fir for the gunwales, oak for the stem and stern. From an early age he learned to use the tools, the 'foot edge' for 'scarfing', notching the wooden boards to get the right shape, the 'caulking chisel' that drove flax or oakum into the joints to waterproof them. He could judge the right amount of tar to close the seams, hoping it wouldn't melt too badly when the weather was hot. The boats, usually between eighteen and twenty-four feet in length, had to cope with waves on the Lough six feet high, so the heavy oars had a broad, flat wedge of wood, a 'clog', held in place on the gunwale with a thole-pin, to give the rowers purchase against the pressure. When Liam was a boy, the nails produced by local blacksmiths had given way to Canadian 'rosehead clincher nails', but the Lough blacksmiths still provided irons for the building process, the bolsters, keel, rudder irons and the rings that held the jib masts on the sailing boats.

Sailing boats on the Lough was a fine and acceptable pastime for well-to-do youngsters from sophisticated Belfast, being, as it was, a demonstration of how far they had come from their peasant roots, but that didn't interest Liam either. He took his excitement from the classic curve of the wood and the skill it took to produce a boat. He had no time for hobbies.

At first it was because he was who he was that he was

tolerated during the construction process, when childish curiosity was not normally encouraged, but as years passed and he learned more he was respected for his genuine love of boats and his willingness to get his hands dirty. And wherever Liam was, Alice was to be found. Difficult to believe that she had ever been a follower, but where Liam was concerned she had been. He was always tall for his age, long limbs tanned by the sun, deep blue eyes and blond hair with a tinge of red that Lough Neagh summers bleached almost white. He wasn't a joker, but he wasn't solemn so much as a boy built for concentration. All his energy went into focusing on whatever he was doing, a clever boy who didn't have to be told anything twice, nodding his head at every explanation. 'I'll say this for you, young Liam,' Jimmy Devlin used to say, laying an affectionate hand on his shoulder, 'you come up with some questions for a lad of your age. If only I could come up with the answers,' and Liam would briefly tear his eyes away from the bending of the planks as the latest boat formed, politely acknowledging the remark with a quick smile, before returning his full attention once more to the creation taking place in front of him. And when work was finished for the day, he would make his way home, Alice by his side, talking of the glorious craft he would build when he was grown up, describing each one as affectionately and proudly as his great-grandfather had his pigs all that time ago, his eyes shining with joy and enthusiasm in his glowing, tanned face.

If the sight of Liam dreaming entranced Alice, it hurt his father to his very core. Bridie saw that clearly, though Seamus himself could never admit it, not that she expected him to, nor did she need him to. The years and passions of his youth were all so long ago, but he remembered how it felt. Seamus hadn't wanted to be a businessman, Seamus had wanted to be an artist. Seamus was an artist. Put a pencil in his young hands from the time he could hold one and he didn't count up a column of numbers, he instinctively drew whatever was around him. He produced portraits of his family, scenes from Lough Neagh, or the Minnow Burn beeches keeping watch majestically, as they had for as long as anyone could remember, over Shaw's Bridge, with its little arches bestriding the burn below, reproduced perfectly in scale and detail. It was what Seamus did, what he was for and who he was, and all his life everyone had encouraged him and taken pride in what he did, so that he never expected to have to do anything else. In his mind, he would grow up and be an artist, earn a living doing what he did best and loved; one day he would go off to the West Bank in Paris and learn by living among his own kind, artists. He was an only son, yet for no reason that he could understand later, he simply had no idea that his dreams wouldn't happen, until his father, Dermot, arranged for him to officially join the family firm at the age of fifteen, where he would learn about imports, exports and accounts. He suddenly understood that all those visits to the various McCann enterprises throughout his childhood had been to gradually introduce him to his life's work, in terms of being the boss's son: they hadn't been visits, they were a kind of apprenticeship.

The shock of it never left him. And his father wasn't being cruel as he crushed Seamus's dreams, it was as though everyone had always known he would join and eventually own and run all that was and would be McCann and Son. Everyone apart from Seamus. It had just never occurred to him, and it made him feel isolated and stupid that he hadn't realised, hadn't even suspected, what was in store for him. Somehow he had just sailed through his life expecting it would be as he wanted it to be, because no one had told him otherwise. His father didn't see any connection between his son's obvious talent for and love of art in terms of a future career, when that was all Seamus had seen in his life.

He could still remember every detail of the bizarre scene in his father's study that day. It was the main reason he had sold the family home, when the time came. Instead of taking it over he had bought a grander one for himself, Bridie and the boys, one without memories. He remembered his father's voice with other sounds running through it, the clock ticking, the noise and bustle outside, the breeze rustling through the trees, voices, footsteps, other lives going on around him as though nothing had changed, completely ignorant of his own crashing to oblivion. He had been unable to utter a word, his voice stunned into silence at the turn of events, the muscles of his face frozen in a kind of paralysis. Every other noise in the universe seemed heightened yet he could produce no words to express his anguish. In front of him his father beamed with pride as he launched his son into McCann and Son and what he regarded as manhood, while inside Seamus's head, above and through the other sounds, all he could hear was a loud scream of pain. What was wrong with him? Why hadn't he seen this coming when everyone he knew and loved could see nothing else? And he realised that the praise his family had given him for his artwork over all those years had been like patting a child on the head; that now the time had come to put away childish things and do the work of a man. Of a McCann.

So Seamus McCann did the best he could. More than that, he applied himself utterly to pushing the family's fortunes further than anyone before him. But sometimes, as he sat in his office deep in paperwork, his eyes would stray to the rain-sodden streets outside his window and his mind would take its chance to escape and wander, taking him with it. Before he could stop himself he would be thinking on how he might paint the scene before him: the horses scrabbling for purchase, the rain darkening and dulling their coats in some places, turning it shining bright with wetness in others. A tricky one that, hard to get right and so easy to make a mess of, sometimes the more you worked at it the more it got away from you. And he'd turn his head, studying the people, collars up, heads down, scurrying for cover the way people did in the rain, the tautness of their gait as they strained forward, leaning into the very discomfort they were trying to escape from. Then suddenly he would have to pull himself back to reality. He was a businessman, he didn't think that way, he told himself sternly, but in answer he heard that inner scream again, felt the pain of it. Not as loudly or as sharply, it was true, but he still felt it. He had never drawn or painted again after taking his rightful position in the family business, he couldn't bear for it to be a spare-time activity. It was a passion, all or nothing, to have dabbled would have been to die even more than he already had. Occasionally, one of his family would ask him, 'Never think of doing one of your draw-ings, Seamus?', inadvertently twisting the knife. He would reply that he had no time for such things these days. What else was there to say?

After that he met Bridie McAlinden through church activ-ities, and a respectable courtship followed before they married. The first time he saw her, though, he didn't think of her beauty in the normal way of young men. The artist in him was drawn to the contours of her face, the proportions of her small features framed by the dark hair, the incredible hazel eyes, imagining how he would set them down on canvas. She was a calm, gentle influence on his life and she soothed the turmoil that still over-took his mind at times, the love of his life without a doubt, as far as women were concerned. But week after week, year after year, standing or kneeling in church, singing, chanting responses or praying, his thoughts would often escape and wander again. He would look back and question his entire life and wonder what might have been and, more to the point, how he had allowed himself to acquiesce in the destruction of his inner self. Why he hadn't refused to join the firm out of hand, why he hadn't explained that it wasn't for him, that he knew what he wanted, needed to do.

Because he couldn't hurt his parents, that was why; his father in particular, who was a good man and had no clue that he was hurting his son. Seamus had done what was expected of him as a McCann son, and he had taken it a step further by marrying well and producing two sons, so that Dermot McCann could see his life's work confirmed and future family fortunes assured. Before he, too, took up residence back 'home' in Derrytrasna, on the slopes of Loch Neagh, Dermot made provision for his two grandsons in his will, making Seamus feel even more that he had pleased his father, he had done the right thing. The dutiful son, that's what Seamus had been, then the dutiful husband, and now he was struggling to be the dutiful father by forcing Liam into furthering the family business and ambitions.

2

It was Brendon who stepped into the latest breach between Liam and Seamus.

'So what if he does want to take a month in Lough Neagh?' he'd asked reasonably. 'What is there going on now that has to stop him?'

'Well there's the university,' Seamus fumed.

'But not this minute, Father,' Brendon had laughed. 'They won't create a term just for Liam McCann because his father doesn't want him to go to Lough Neagh for a month!'

'But there are things he could be doing here.'

'Like what? What is there to do here that you and I aren't already doing? What could Liam do more or differently?'

Seamus looked at his son doubtfully.

'Father, let him go. If nothing else it will give me and mother a rest from being referees!'

As the McCann businesses had expanded and, by necessity, diversified, the pigs got left behind. They still cured ham and exported it, but it became of less importance to them, and perhaps the only reason Seamus kept it going was out of deference to, or sentiment for, Old Man McCann. Their loyalty to the McInallys remained as strong as ever, and the McInallys stayed true to the business they had known. Seamus trusted them as he would his own, often more than he did his own.

In Henry McInally's case he stayed with the pigs purely from sentiment. He was proud of his grandfather's and father's skills, skills he learned himself without ever having the economic need to use. Henry ran the curing business in Belfast and his son Harry took his place with the firm straight from school.

In other ways times were changing, as Bridie McCann at least had acknowledged. It was the beginning of a new century, after all, and Alice learned to type and to file and joined the firm, too. Before Alice arrived business was done in an ad hoc way: no one did any filing, and most things were simply consigned to memory by someone or other who then reminded someone else as and when necessary. The few tabs that were kept consisted of scribbled notes that ended up in a pocket or written on a cuff or hand, or, in her father Henry's case, the odd piece of knotted string that he could never remember having tied. He wasn't an organised man, Henry, he was the kind of male who needed a female to care for him. When his mother died he quickly married Victoria and happily relied on his wife for every aspect of his life. When she wasn't there he got by on a wing and a prayer, and now there was another female in the office to sort him out, and what Alice brought to the operation was order and tidiness.

Alice was a girl with a talent for organisation and a determination to have things done properly, and by the time she had been there two years the curing business was running smoothly and efficiently, probably for the first time ever. To her mother, Victoria, who was less forward-thinking than Bridie, this was slightly troubling; in her day girls had spent their early lives learning to be future wives and mothers and finding the right man in order to put those skills to good use. Victoria wasn't a complicated woman: small and plump and considered a great beauty in her youth, with naturally blonde hair and cool grey eyes, her life revolved around her family, her home and her church. That was the true role of women, as far as she could see, and the very fact that Alice wanted to work troubled her, it being her experience that men did not take to women who were too clever or too independent. Besides, her girls had no actual need to work, their father supported them well – not in the style of the McCanns to be sure, but pretty near it.

'Now, now, Victoria,' Bridie had chided her as they took afternoon tea together. 'You mustn't be old-fashioned, you must let them have their own lives.'

Victoria nodded uncertainly, stirring her tea, looking approvingly around the room. She would have given anything for a big bay window like that. If she'd had one she would have stood by it all day, so that everyone would see her and admire her, as everyone, especially Victoria, admired Bridie.

'I know, Bridie, I know,' she sighed, 'but does the speed of it all not bother you? Seems only yesterday they were running around Lough Neagh together getting as black as berries, and now look at them, working in city offices.'

'Well, if you heard Seamus talking you wouldn't say that!' Bridie laughed.

Victoria looked at her.

'Liam,' said Bridie. 'Need I say more?'

Victoria smiled. 'He's a lovely boy, your Liam,' she said. 'I won't hear a word against him.'

'That's one of Seamus's complaints, he says I won't hear a word against him either!'

'Alice was saying he's working with Jimmy Devlin in Lough

Neagh,' Victoria said brightly. 'She's quite at a loss without him.' There was that slight tone in her voice again, Bridie noted.

'For a month, yes,' she replied. 'At least, that's what he's promised Seamus. Says Jimmy's getting on and there's this big boat to build. If he leaves it any longer there's a lot he might not learn from him.'

'Well that's true,' Victoria said. 'Seems to me Jimmy has been there forever already. But Liam will be going to the university, won't he? He still means to be a lawyer?'

'That was Seamus's idea,' Bridie sighed. 'You've no idea the arguments it causes in this house.'

'It would be sad if he didn't, though, you can see Seamus's point. It would be a fine profession for the boy.'

Bridie nodded. 'He keeps putting it off,' she said quietly, 'but there's time yet, he's only twenty-one. And what about your brood, Victoria? You have those lovely girls. I always wanted a girl.'

'Well, Harry's doing well in the business, as you know, took to it like a duck to water, just like your Brendon, and Alice is doing whatever it is she does —' A shake of the head.

'And she does it very well,' Bridie chided. 'What is she now? Eighteen? I wish I'd had men obeying my every word at that age, wish I had now!' Bridie laughed. She had almost said, 'Just like you and your Henry,' but she'd managed to stop herself just in time. Everyone knew Henry didn't take a breath without Victoria's permission, but it would be impolite to say so out loud, however true it was, it would cause offence. 'She keeps them on their toes, from what I hear, and that's what the office should've been like years ago. And what about Bella?'

'Oh, Bella is me all over again,' Victoria sighed happily, reaching for another biscuit. 'She's thirteen now, growing into quite a beauty, and she's not clever but she's neat and understands how to run a house properly. I don't think you'll see her taking up a career like these modern girls.'

There was a silence.

'So Alice is lost without Liam?' Bridie said, her gentle tone covering her meaning.

'Yes, well, as everyone says,' said Victoria, 'they've been joined at the hip, those two, all their lives.'

Another silence.

'It'll give them a chance to see there are other people on the planet!' Bridie laughed, a little too brightly.

Victoria sipped her tea and nodded. 'There's a time for close friendships like theirs. Once they discover courting they'll grow out of it.'

'Exactly! That's what I say! I mean, Victoria, how many of your childhood friends are you still in close touch with?'

'Absolutely!'

'Yet there was probably a time when you lived in each other's pockets, wasn't there?'

Victoria McInally nodded again, though she couldn't recall any such friendship.

Another silence.

'Oh, I must show you this dress I found in a magazine, Victoria. I've decided I must have it, though I don't know what Seamus will say!'

So there it was, settled. The question that had been waiting in the wings as a thought had been said without being spoken because neither of them could risk putting into words what both families feared. They were of the mutual opinion that the time had come, indeed it had passed, for Liam and Alice to put aside childish things, childish closeness being the main one. Something – someone, hopefully – should come between Alice and Liam for their own good. No one wanted the friendship turning into anything more worrying. Liam was Catholic and Alice was Protestant, after all. It was important that the families be in agreement about how objectionable that would be, but it was just as important that this truth everyone acknowledged wasn't said out loud either, for fear of causing offence. And now it had been handled brilliantly, Bridie McCann thought – as she always said, things could be sorted out between women without any shouting or hurt feelings. To prove it, this 'thing' had been sorted out between the mothers over a cup of tea and a look at the latest fashions. They were of one mind, an understanding had been reached, no one need worry any longer.

In Belfast Alice had put her life on hold, biding her time till Liam came home, while at Lough Neagh, Liam, who had always felt that his life was being decided for him without any input from him, was happily unaware that it had happened again. He was enjoying his work at Jimmy Devlin's yard and was wondering how to break it to his father that he wanted to become an apprentice under the old man who had taught him so much since he was a child. He didn't want to be a lawyer, never had, just as he didn't want to go into any branch of the family business, he wanted to build boats. Quite why that should have caused so many years of aggravation with his father, he couldn't understand.

'He never listens, Mother,' Liam had protested to Bridie before he left.

'Liam, he does listen, the problem is that he doesn't like what he hears,' she had laughed back, to make him laugh, he knew. That was what his mother did, she took the sting out of situations.

'But I don't tell him what to do with his life, why must he

always tell me what to do with mine?' he asked, genuinely puzzled.

'You know his story very well, Liam,' Bridie said gently. 'Your father wanted to be an artist, he was very gifted from what I've been told, but I don't think he was given very much choice by his father. Going into the business was your grandfather's decision, not your father's. He did what he considered to be his duty, but it's not what he would've chosen.'

'Then he should understand my position,' Liam said logically.

'But don't you see, Liam, he does!' she cried. 'He went into the business and it's worked out very well. He doesn't want you to make the mistake he nearly made by following a childhood dream. I'm sure he's told you this many times when you've talked.'

'Talked?' Liam grinned wryly. 'We don't talk, Mother. I can't talk to him about anything without him erupting into this huge, arm-waving monster.'

Bridie laughed. 'Yes, he does get a bit like that, doesn't he?'

'I don't know what to do about him,' the boy continued. 'I mean, you and Brendon get on with him, you all laugh and talk together. He gets on with everyone I can think of, in fact, except me. He doesn't seem to like me very much.'

'No, no,' Bridie said, shocked, 'you mustn't say that, you mustn't think it!'

'But it's true,' he said calmly. 'The minute he lays eyes on me he gets that expression on his face, like he's gearing up for battle. At least everyone will get some peace for a while if I go away for a month. Me included.'

He was a straightforward boy, that was the problem, Bridie thought. He was his father all over again, but brought up to be honest and truthful rather than compliant, and, above all, brave, only Seamus didn't know how to handle that, especially the brave part.

She looked at her son, at the familiar tall, rangy figure. He'd always been tall for his age, people always took him for older than he was. He had filled out nicely now – at fifteen he had seemed so impossibly thin that she thought he might blow away in the wind, but now she wondered at how solidly handsome he was. Her boy was twenty-one, not a boy at all, really, but a man. That was something Seamus didn't always recognise when he was talking to him – shouting at him, more likely. Liam was the way he was, the way they had reared him, or she had: like most fathers Seamus had been too busy working to take much interest in his children, and besides, rearing children was women's work. He had missed many stages in the boys' lives, but Bridie's greatest concern these days was that he was missing the biggest change of all, the one Liam was going through, from boy to man. When she thought of the two of them it was with a sense of the situation slipping through her fingers, of the sands running out, and she could think of nothing to halt the process, except to continue to mediate.

She reassured Liam that his father loved him and had only his best interests at heart and, even if that was hard to appreciate at times, Liam would understand in time. She explained to Seamus that Liam was just Liam, that he wasn't trying to upset him, he was just being himself, and that all the shouting would drive the boy away if he wasn't careful. That was a scenario she couldn't bear, but couldn't banish from her mind either. He was her firstborn, they shared that special bond, and she remembered holding him for the first time and feeling such an intense love that it had almost made her dizzy. Much as she loved his father, the strength of what she felt for her son had surprised her, so the merest hint of losing him made her feel dizzy all over again, but with dread this time. Whatever happened, she had to keep the peace.

Something else had happened to Liam at Lough Neagh during that month. It was Alice – or it wasn't Alice, that was the point. They'd been together for as long as he could remember, they were closer than brother and sister, but that's all it had been, until now. There had been the odd week apart, and when they got together again they had talked for hours, filling in the gaps, but this was different. Jimmy Devlin would be imparting some nugget of his immense knowledge, and Liam would find his mind drifting off, wondering what she was doing, remembering her laughter and the way the long, thick braid of auburn hair swung from side to side when she ran. It was quite strange and he couldn't explain it properly to himself, but it was almost painful; the hunger to see her was like a low-grade headache he couldn't shift, and he just found himself longing to be with her again, yet nervous in a way he had never felt before. He had felt it about a boat going into the water for the first time, but not about a girl, and certainly not about Alice!

In Belfast, Alice was feeling something similar. Life was dull without Liam, that was what it was, every day lacked something. She had taken one of their favourite walks on the banks of the Laggan and stopped on Shaw's Bridge, as they always did, to throw twigs and leaves into the water and talk. Only she had felt a deep loneliness, a feeling of not being quite complete, so the next time she insisted that her younger sister Bella went with her. Bella was thirteen now, turning into the family beauty with her golden hair and cool, clear grey eyes, and a figure was emerging that promised to live up to her looks. Like Harry she took her colouring from Victoria's side of the family, and Bella was what their mother had looked like when she was a girl, as their father often remarked with a wink to his wife. Somehow Alice and Bella had never been close, but then there was five years between them, and in those five years Alice and Liam had already found each other, and neither of them had ever really needed anyone else. But Bella was pressed into service for the walk by the river to the bridge, and confirmed what Alice already felt, that she was missing Liam more and in a way she had never missed him before. Either that, she reasoned, or she was ill.

After the second week she felt better because it was halfway through his absence, then in the third she was seized with the need to go to Lough Neagh, only to stop, telling herself that one more week wouldn't make much difference. Just as she seemed reconciled to waiting she decided to go, a quick visit down and back, no need for luggage. Then she wondered how it would look – never a consideration before – and was unsure all over again. In no time at all she was at the station, waiting for the train to Lurgan, still debating with herself whether to get on or not. She was sitting down, trying to work out just what was going on in her head, when she looked up and suddenly he was standing in front of her.

Three weeks ago they had stood together on this very platform as Liam boarded the train, and there hadn't been time for everything they wanted to say. 'Don't forget . . .' 'Remember to . . .' 'Tell so and so I said . . .' Even as the train was pulling out of the station they were shouting forgotten instructions to each other. Yet here they were together again and they couldn't think of anything to say, anything sensible, that was.

'Hello.'

'Oh, Liam, yes, hello.'

'What are you doing here?' he asked, almost shyly. Why had he never noticed the shape of her nose before?

'Um, I was seeing someone off.' She waved a hand in what she hoped was a casual, dismissive manner. Was he always that tall? And his eyes, were they always so blue?

'Who?'

'Oh, a friend, no one you'd know.' As soon as she said it she winced inside; there were no friends that Liam didn't know. It made her manner even stiffer.

'Oh.' Why was she lying to him? And why was she behaving so strangely? It must be someone she didn't want him to know about.

'And you?' she said, looking around her, looking at anything but him.

She was looking really guilty and he thought her cheeks were flushed.

'Sorry, what?'

'I had no idea you were back,' she said. 'Weren't you supposed to be at Lough Neagh for another week?'

'Oh, that. Well the boat got finished earlier than expected, so I thought, no point in hanging about there.'

Liar! Wild horses couldn't drag him from Lough Neagh! He must've come back secretly. But why? To meet someone he didn't want her to know about! It was the only reason, she decided angrily. Why couldn't he just admit it? Did he think she cared?

'So, are you going home now?' he asked.

'What? Home? Yes, yes, going home,' she said absently.

'I'll take you.' He reached towards her to take her arm, out of habit, and she shrank away from him.

She laughed nervously. 'I'm not helpless, you know!' she said. 'I can stand and walk without support!'

'I know you can,' he murmured, hurt. What had happened to her? Was it connected to this friend – this man – she had been seeing off? 'Maybe you can see yourself home without any support as well, then.'

'Maybe I can.'

'Right.'

'Right.'

As she stamped off, leaving him feeling confused and angry, he watched the long braid of hair down her back bobbing about and wondered when it had become so auburn, so richly, deeply auburn. Well, damn and blast her auburn hair to hell and back! He should have stayed at Lough Neagh, he thought, livid. He had come all the way back to see her, only to find her at the station, seeing off some man she had been romancing behind his back. What a fool he'd been! Well, he had never had to learn the same lesson twice, and it would be no different this time. He was off back to Lough Neagh, and when he did go home to Belfast just see if he contacted her again!

Thoughts were flying through Alice's head as well. How dare he treat her like this! To think she had been planning to go all the way to Lough Neagh to see him, and all the time he had come back early to see some floozy! Come to think of it, he'd probably jumped off the train before it left the station three weeks ago. He'd never intended on going to Lough Neagh, he'd been cavorting with his floozy in Belfast all that time, taking little romantic train trips here and there. The floozy in question was probably refurbishing herself in the Ladies Room at that very moment, if she went there right now she'd find her, if it bothered her, that was, which it did not. It made no difference to her if he was keeping a whole harem of floozies, it was the fact that he'd kept it secret that bothered her. It was an insult to her intelligence, that was all, expecting her to care that much what he did that he felt he had to keep it secret – and she didn't care, not one jot! She could tell from his whole manner that he was up to no good. Well, at least she had found him out, and at least she had got away without telling him she'd been on her way to see him, what a fool she'd have looked then! Just goes to show, you can't trust anyone.

Liam was on his way back to Lough Neagh as Alice arrived home. Victoria and Bella were at the kitchen table together, baking.

'We didn't expect to see you,' Victoria smiled. 'We thought you were going to see Liam?'

'What? Oh, no,' Alice said calmly. 'I was thinking about it, but I couldn't be bothered. I said so last night.'

'Did you?' Victoria asked.

'Yes, I'm sure I did.' She picked up a magazine and sat down to flick through the pages in what she hoped was a nonchalant way.

'But you're late,' Bella said suspiciously.

Shut up, you nuisance, Alice thought savagely, what business is it of yours? 'Well I met someone, if you must know,' she grinned at her sister.

'A boy?' Bella demanded, giggling.

'Yes, a boy,' Alice giggled back.

'Alice has been courting!' Bella sang, laughing and clapping her floury hands. 'Alice has been courting!'

'I have not, I just happened to bump into someone, that was all.'

'Who?' her mother asked.

'What is this?' Alice demanded, trying to keep it all on a teasing footing. 'The Spanish Inquisition?'

'We're just interested, that's all,' Victoria smiled, returning to her baking, sensing that there was something different about her elder daughter this evening.

'Just someone I met at church.' She sighed heavily, turning another page of her magazine. 'We bumped into each other when I was on my way home, and I thought it might look odd if I refused to say hello because I had to run home to my mother and my nosy – my very nosy – sister!'

Bella stuck her tongue out at Alice. 'Was it that boy you were talking to the other week, the one with the red hair?'

Alice couldn't remember talking to any red-haired boy the other week, but she clutched at the lifeline. 'Yes,' she replied absently.

'Which one was he?' Victoria asked conversationally.

'Billy Guthrie,' Bella replied.

'Oh,' her mother said quietly. 'Billy Guthrie.'

Alice shook her head at them. 'Now are you both satisfied?' she asked. 'You have his name, would you like his address, too?' She rolled her eyes, laughing at them, thinking that this turn of events meant she would have to go out of her way to talk to Billy Guthrie next time their paths crossed, as long as she recognised him that was.

'No, no, that's enough,' Victoria replied primly, nudging Bella with her elbow and starting her giggling again.

'Oh, I give up!' Alice said. 'You two are impossible! I'm off to have a bath, would you like to make sure there are no strange men waiting on the stairs for me?'

So, Victoria thought. Good news, or good-ish at any rate. Her sister had already had to face the tragedy of one her daughters marrying into the other side, and Victoria remembered that time with horror. Her sister's distress; the girl, Maggie's, foolish determination in refusing to accept that she was doing wrong and her complete disregard when told she would never be welcome within the family again. It was a bad time and it had caused the entire family great upset, and upset was something

Victoria did not like. Not that she had ever had any real worries about Alice, but it was nice to see things working out. Billy Guthrie was a boy from church, too, a Protestant boy, so there was much to feel satisfied about, if not everything, though she would keep any doubts to herself for the present, till she saw how things developed, or not.

When Liam arrived back at Lough Neagh the first thing he did was write to his mother saying he intended staying there a month longer than planned. Seamus hit the roof when he heard, as usual, but Bridie calmed him down.

'This is good news,' she said, both mothers in agreement again. 'Don't you see? It means he's not missing Alice. I was speaking to Bridie the other day and she tells me Alice is seeing some boy from their church.'

Seamus stopped shouting and looked at her, eyebrows raised. 'Oh, I see,' he said surprised. 'Well, that is good, isn't it? Let him stay there to help loosen the ties, that sort of thing?'

'Yes, that sort of thing,' she smiled, hugging his arm. 'I'll just mention it to Liam when I reply to his letter, how good it is that she's found someone nice, someone from her own side.' She looked at Seamus, who nodded firmly.

'It's for their own good,' he said.

'Of course it is,' Bridie replied. 'And it's not as if it wasn't already happening, is it? I'll only be saying what's going on while he's away.'

'I shouldn't think he'll bother,' Seamus replied. 'He probably knew before we did.'

'Yes, exactly, and the fact that he didn't even mention it shows how little it matters to him.'

3

While Liam was at Lough Neagh he had plenty of time for thinking, and something happened to him and within him. It was as though the encounter with Alice at the station had made him turn a corner, or perhaps he was there already and just didn't know it till the moment arrived. Somehow he took the mental step from boy to adult and, just as his father had done before him, he came to a decision: he would go to university and become a lawyer. His father's joy was matched by his mother's, and was topped only by his further decision to study in Dublin. Dublin was so nicely, safely far from Belfast, Bridie mused with satisfaction. She had been right all along: she had always believed that all she had to do for everything to turn out well was stay in the middle and keep the peace. The boy had simply needed a couple of months away from all the arguments and fighting to clear his mind and think calmly. She knew her son, knew that he was too sensible a boy not to appreciate the logic of what his father had been saying all along. Even Seamus remarked that he should listen to his wife more often, should trust her judgement, and swore that he always would in future.

The news was conveyed to Alice by her mother after one

of Victoria's teas with Bridie. It didn't surprise her. The distance between her and her childhood best friend had gradually widened while he was away, though neither she nor Liam had any idea that the course of the gulf had, with the very best of intentions, been helped along. During his absence in Dublin, when she looked back at the time when her feelings for him had changed, she realised it hadn't been to something deeper, but to something different – she had just misunderstood. She had sensed a shift and, being a teenage girl, she had made the mistake of wondering if romance might be involved. She could even laugh about it now, though she still felt slightly embarrassed and would certainly die if Liam ever found out. Not that he would, for quite apart from his going to university and so far away, their relationship had changed: they would never be close enough again to discuss their feelings and thoughts. They were no longer children, they were adults now, with adult lives of their own, and both sets of parents would pass greetings between them in a friendly and affectionate way, together with odd snippets of information. 'Victoria tells me Alice is still seeing that nice boy from their church, Billy Guthrie,' Bridie wrote to her son. 'His people came originally from Lough Neagh, apparently, and he's going to be an engineer. He works at Harland and Wolff and he's very clever, they say, bound for better things.' And Liam replied that he was pleased life was going so well for his old friend, and to be sure to tell her he was asking after her.

He meant it, too. He had long ago worked out all his angry feelings and had transformed them to sad feelings, then consigned them to the days of his childhood, to the past. The fact that he hadn't realised Alice was changing had been his fault, not hers, and she had been quite right not to tell him about the private parts of her life. Maybe he had sensed there was something altered about her and thought he must be involved, tapping in to some heightened emotional part of Alice over the Guthrie chap and, purely and simply, he'd got it wrong. He had been silly to have taken such offence, but by the time he worked this out the situation had gone too far to go back, and everything he had heard from home had further convinced him of that. To think back now to having dashed from Lough Neagh that afternoon, like some lovesick schoolboy, expecting her to be pining away for him, well, the colour still rose to cover every part of him, so he learned not to think about it. Everyone makes mistakes when they're young. One day, when they were both much older and had children of their own, maybe then he could tell her and they would laugh together. But not now.

No one knew what liaisons Liam might or might not be having in Dublin during those years. These were things he would not have discussed with his mother, but it didn't stop Bridie from using her imagination and presenting her thoughts as fact.

'He doesn't say much, Victoria,' she said smugly, 'but I get the impression he's quite the young man about town.'

'And why wouldn't he be?' Victoria replied approvingly. She so admired Bridie's taste, and her ability to afford it. Real Brussels lace on these napkins, she was sure, and for everyday use, too. 'He's a very handsome young man, he must be irresistible to the girls in Dublin, I should think.' She took another sip of tea. 'Is there anyone in particular?' she asked, as though it hardly mattered at all, a polite, casual inquiry of no consequence.

'Well, he's being very discreet,' Bridie obliged, 'but I do think there's a change in him that only a young lady could bring about in a young man, if you see what I mean, and he certainly hasn't denied it, dear.'

He hadn't admitted it either, because the question hadn't been asked, but if Victoria had even suspected as much she wasn't going to give in to her suspicions when she passed the news to Alice.

'Bridie tells me Liam's "involved" in Dublin,' she smiled.

Alice looked up with a puzzled expression. 'Involved?' she asked, exchanging amused glances with Bella. 'In gambling, espionage? What?'

'Now you know perfectly well what I mean,' Victoria said primly. 'Bridie says Liam has a young lady.'

'Oh,' Alice chuckled, 'you mean he's turned into a ladies' man, Mother, running around after all the women in Dublin?'

'Well I wouldn't have put it in quite that way, Alice,' Victoria said reprovingly.

'Go on, say it, Mother!' Bella teased.

'I don't know what you can possibly mean, Bella.' She had moved into her kitchen, always a sign of Victoria on the run, for her kitchen was her sanctuary.

'She means,' Alice said slowly, 'tell us how things have changed too quickly, that in your day –'

'– young people wouldn't have been so brazen!' Bella chimed, and the two sisters looked at each other, laughing delightedly.

'I must confess,' Victoria protested, flustered, 'that I just cannot understand what you both find so funny.' She was reaching for her baking tins. A date and walnut loaf lay in the near future, if they were any judges, which for some reason amused her daughters even more. 'But, as you mention it,' – another burst of giggles – 'that is exactly what I do think,' and this time even Victoria joined in with the laughter.

Later, when she was on her own, Alice examined the news for her reaction. A slight twinge of something, perhaps, because it was strange to think of Liam being so close to any woman, a twinge of nostalgia more than anything. For herself, she had no intention of becoming involved with anyone, but the explanation of her late arrival home that evening months ago had set in train a series of events that she had never intended nor foreseen. At church on the Sunday following the station confrontation, as a cover for her story, she had to engage the Guthrie boy in conversation, which hadn't been difficult once she recognised him vaguely and was reminded that the odd word had passed between them once in a while. From this unlikely beginning a genuine friendship had grown, and Alice, now without male companionship for the first time in her life, had no problems with that. Billy was hardly forgettable, being very tall, thin, red-haired and with very pale blue eyes, not exactly handsome, but striking, and he grew on her by being agreeable, by not doing anything that made her dislike him.

By the time Alice's brother Harry married Mattie, two years later, Billy had become very much a member of the McInally family. Both Alice and Bella were bridesmaids at the wedding, but Mattie's sister had been chief bridesmaid and so had possession of the best man, leaving Alice in need of a partner for the evening (Bella, at just sixteen, was considered too young for such thoughts). Billy was the obvious choice. Since Alice's fictitious 'chance encounter' with him he had earned everyone's approval and the bride had personally invited him to accompany her new sister-in-law. This rankled slightly with Alice, who was twenty-one, after all, and perfectly capable of choosing whoever she wanted, but she said nothing, because Mattie, a generous soul who loved Harry very dearly, was another neat, delicate blonde who made Alice feel huge and lumpen and, if truth be told, almost intimidated. You could never imagine Mattie running wildly across Shaw's Bridge, for instance. Mattie pattered delicately wherever she stepped and had never, as far as Alice was aware, ventured onto anything as alien as grass. Mud was not even a consideration. Mattie's hair was always immaculately caught up by some means on top of her head and, though Alice had looked hard, not a strand ever seemed to work its rebellious way loose. She was the kind of female who could truly be described as exquisite and the general view was that she had all the skills that would enable Harry to advance even further up the social ladder. Trust Harry to always do things right, Alice thought, though not disapprovingly. It was just a fact: Harry seemed to have been born with some kind of inbuilt code that enabled him to know what to think, say and do. It was part of what Alice had always admired about her brother, and his choice of Mattie as his bride simply confirmed this.

Mattie, for her part, though she was Belfast born and bred, knew that the Lough Neagh connection was important to the McInallys. To her and the others, Billy was ideal for Alice. Victoria, however, though she had said nothing, was less sure, as her elder daughter would have noticed the evening she had first 'bumped into' him, had she been less on her guard over being found out. Even so, when Mattie asked for advice and consent from her future mother-in-law, Victoria had agreed to Billy attending the wedding with Alice. In the past two years he had proved himself to be agreeable, hard-working and ambitious, it was true, but Victoria knew of the Guthries, especially of Billy's mother, and she didn't like what she knew.

The women around the Lough had long talked about Jessie Guthrie. She had been an odd creature, very odd, incredibly stupid, so everyone said, never even learned to read or write and didn't seem to understand the need for either. Apart from her spectacular stupidity, or maybe even because of it, she had

62

pursued every man in the vicinity, though it was noted that she targeted those with a bit of money, so perhaps she had a kind of animal cunning, an instinct for survival. Eventually she had become pregnant and, far from feeling ashamed, she didn't seem in the least bothered about it, the child being, as everyone knew, part of her plan to snare the son of one of the richer fishermen. Knowing her reputation, however, he had no interest in marrying her: he had no means of knowing if the child was even his, for it truly could've been anyone's, after all. So she had the child, Billy, then found a simple, insignificant little man from Belfast to marry her and make her situation respectable, or so everyone thought. Now she would settle down and put her past behind her. She would probably become a moralistic pillar of the church, if others like her were anything to go by. The marriage made no difference though, and as a married woman she behaved in Belfast as she had at home, giving birth exactly nine months from her wedding night to the little man's son, whom she loathed for that very reason. The next child was fathered by someone else entirely, and she didn't much care for that one either, regularly dumping the two youngest with whoever might be prepared to give them a bed, and taking Billy on her adventures. Billy she idolised, for some reason. Billy was a god, but what, Victoria wondered darkly, could it have done to him, being exposed to that woman and her immoral, unhealthy lifestyle all through his childhood? And no normal woman would behave as Jessie Guthrie had, that's what Victoria, a good Christian who tried to see the best in people, had always thought. Jessie Guthrie had to have 'something wrong with her head', and no one wanted their daughter married into a family like that, though she shared none of this with her own family at the time. And there was Jessie Guthrie's gross stupidity, so quite where her son got his quick brain from was a mystery, though probably from the clever, red-haired fisherman who refused to marry her, come to think of it.

Still, let's not panic, Victoria told herself. He was keeping company with Alice, that was all, marriage wasn't exactly imminent – no sign, indeed, that it was even being considered. She was just more sensitive to these things because of Maggie, her wayward niece who had married out and was now lost to her family. And on that thought, Billy was at least a Protestant, and despite being slightly more outspoken than Victoria entirely approved of Alice was basically a sensible girl, so calm down. Besides, Billy was a strong church member, something his now deceased mother had never been, but after her death he had lived with his grandmother, who was a decent old lady, forever embarrassed by the ways of her errant daughter by all accounts. If the earlier part of his life had been too influenced by his mother, the later part with his grandmother must have gone some way to countering it, so everything pointed – if the worst came to the worst – to Billy having left all of that behind, to not being like his mother. So let's, as she told Bridie, wait and see, even if having him as an official member of the family at Harry and Mattie's wedding would inevitably signify something more than keeping company.

'It's always a bit of a worry, Victoria,' Bridie advised, 'who your children will become involved with, but she is twenty-one now, a woman in her own right, after all. I'm sure you're judging the situation perfectly by not interfering. And you have enough on your mind with the wedding, even if you are only the groom's mother. I'm sure I'd be out of my mind with worry, but you always take these matters in your stride.' She glanced at Victoria. 'Not that you should be worried, dear,' she said consolingly. 'It's just that everyone's nerves will be in a tangle at this time, you don't need any other distractions, so don't you even think about it. Besides, he does seem a very acceptable kind of young man now. It might be very different if the dreadful mother were still around, but she isn't. If you didn't know about his unfortunate past you probably wouldn't think anything of him seeing Alice, would you?'

In Bridie's mind there was nothing to lose in having Alice safely married and off McCann territory. Not that she disliked the girl – on the contrary, she was very fond of Alice, of all the McInally family – but a possible problem had been solved with Liam's departure for Dublin and it would be nice to have it finally filed away. Done and dusted, so to speak.

'Oh, he seems very nice from what I know of him. He behaves impeccably within the family and always takes part in church events, there's nothing I know of to be said against him. As you say, if you didn't know about his mother you'd never suspect,' Victoria agreed. 'Anyway, it is only a wedding, a single day, there's nothing to say any more will come of it.'

There was one of their silences.

'Is Liam going to manage to come to the wedding?' Victoria asked, sipping her tea. Beautiful bone china, Royal Albert, she'd always admired it. And the family crest on the teaspoon, that was new, but so nicely done. Noticeable, but not garish. How very Bridie.

'No, he's not, it's such a shame!' Bridie cried. 'He has so much studying to do if he's to make up for lost time. He's quite heartbroken about it, but it was always Brendon who was Harry's best friend, wasn't it?'

Now it was Victoria's turn to sigh inwardly with relief, though part of her thought Liam seeing Alice with Billy Guthrie might be a good, confirming thing, odd mother or not. 'Oh, that's a shame,' she smiled. 'But you're right, dear, Brendon was always Harry's friend. He would've had him for best man if it hadn't been for the churches, too. One of his cousins will stand in, but it won't be the same. It's just a pity he couldn't have had Brendon.'

'Well, there's nothing to be done about that, it's just life,' Bridie said cheerfully.

And it was. Brendon was Roman Catholic and therefore couldn't take part in a Protestant ceremony, not even for his best friend. Everyone accepted that with no offence given or taken. It was, as Bridie said, just life, in Ireland at any rate, and the two young men would go on being best friends.

'Don't they look well together?' Bridie remarked to the mother of the groom at the reception.

'Oh, Harry and Mattie? Yes, they do indeed, we'll have some handsome grandchildren one day!'

'No, dear! Alice and the young man – what's his name?'

'Billy,' Victoria replied, watching him dance with Alice, 'Billy Guthrie. And yes, they do look well together.'

'You must forget any fears you might have had, dear,' Bridie said, with the calm authority that was her trademark. 'He is quite the most acceptable and charming young man here.'

'Yes, he is,' Victoria replied, 'and they're the same age, only a month or so apart.'

They watched as Bella, now a stunningly beautiful teenager, approached the young couple, obviously demanding to be danced with. Billy smiled, bowed lavishly, then led Alice's younger sister into the middle of the floor.

'Now wasn't that charming!' Bridie cooed, looking up as Alice joined their party. 'My dear Alice,' she said, taking in the girl's rosy cheeks and bright eyes, 'we were just saying what a nice young man your Mr Guthrie is, the kind way he treated your little sister there.'

'I'm just glad of the chance of a breather!' Alice said, sitting down and fanning herself with her hand. 'But yes, he is very nice, Mrs McCann, though I don't exactly own him!'

'Just a matter of time, Alice,' Bridie teased, 'from what I've seen tonight that's just a matter of time.'

Alice indulged her with a smile. It was common knowledge that at weddings the younger generation danced while the older generation anticipated the next one by pairing off every single person in sight. She got up and moved to another table, where her Aunt Bessie and her family were sitting. Aunt Bessie was Victoria's sister, but the families weren't close, they had only been invited to Harry's wedding to impress upon them how well the McInallys had done in life. Besides, even though they carried a social scar, they were family, just as long as they knew their place, and that place wasn't right beside Victoria.

'Hello, Aunt Bessie,' said Alice brightly, and Bessie responded by covering her nose and mouth with her handkerchief and weeping quietly. Alice looked to her cousin, Louise, who indicated with her head and got up. Louise was few years older than Alice, a tall, pretty young woman, her features very much in the mould of Bessie and Victoria's family, but with black hair piled on top of her head, pale skin and hazel eyes, and with what Victoria hinted was a mischievous streak in place of the tightly controlled family behaviour. On the few family occasions when their paths had crossed over the years, Alice had always regarded Louise as slightly eccentric. She dressed differently, for one thing, she obviously wasn't wearing a corset, and apart from that you could spot Louise anywhere in a crowd, given the kind of thing she was wearing now. As she walked to join her cousin, Alice looked at the long, sleek black dress under a full-length silk coat made of different coloured diamond shapes, emerald, bright blue, purple and scarlet, while every other female wore dresses in the demure pastel hues deemed suitable for wedding attire.

'I love what you're wearing,' Alice smiled. 'Where do you find such wonderful colours and materials?'

'Oh, I find the materials first,' Louise said, 'then I make the outfits myself.'

'You make them yourself?'

'Of course! How else could I get such class?' Louise laughed. 'No one sells this kind of thing,' she looked her cousin up and down, and grimaced, 'as you know only too well, Alice, you poor dear!' and she threw her head back and laughed out loud. 'I had to get away from the histrionics at the table,' she said eventually. 'I mean, wouldn't it drive you mad!' She glared at her mother from a safe distance.

'What's wrong with her?'

'Oh, she's indulging herself in what we have come to know as an attack of the vapours. Nobody does it better, but then she gets in plenty of practice,' Louise sighed.

'But why?'

'The old, old story,' Louise said wryly. 'The wedding that got away, what else?'

'What?'

'Come along, Alice! Do keep up!' Louise chided, laughing. 'My sister, Maggie? The one who ran off with the Catholic?'

'But that must be, what, ten years ago?' Alice laughed.

'And we've had to put up with ten years of this. Poor old Maggie had no choice but to get married in Glasgow, so my mother was cheated of a wedding, you see, so she commemorates that non-event at every wedding she goes to. My wedding was a real riot, as I recall: no one could dance, it wasn't safe, the floor was awash with old Bessie's tears.'

Alice chuckled. 'I do remember that, but I just thought she was indulging in a few normal mother-of-the bride tears.'

'No, old Bessie only does the abnormal variety,' Louise laughed wryly. 'I was sure my dear old Georgie would do a runner even before he had defiled the bride.'

Alice glanced at Louise to see what kind of reaction she was expecting to this, and saw that she wasn't expecting any.

'Where is he?' she asked, for something to say.

'I gave him the day off,' Louise laughed. 'Can't remember now whether it's business or a very bad cold, but he's put up with more than enough of this kind of performance with incredible good humour,' she said. 'I'm sure that one of these days he's bound to run off screaming into the night, so at least I've managed to hold that back for another time.'

'So does anyone know how Maggie is these days?'

'Yes, George and I do. We're the only ones who acknowledge that she exists, though we have to do it in secret, of course. She's fine, she and Tony have a guest house in Glasgow and are doing very well. I visit every now and again, and sometimes George comes too, if he can spare the time, but, of course, Maggie can't come back here. Thrown out of the family, blue-pencilled forever, banished, you know the kind of thing.'

'You'd think your folks would've come round by now,' Alice said quietly.

'Huh! I think that's all that keep them going, the terrible tragedy of it all. And it isn't Maggie my mother misses, if you'll notice, it's Maggie's wedding she lost out on, it's what was done to her. Tell me, Alice, do you like your parents?'

Alice was shocked. 'Of course I do, Louise! What a question!'

'No, I didn't say "love", I said "like". I love mine, but to be honest with you they've let the family be torn apart over Maggie and Tony, and I do sometimes wonder if I like them.'

Alice looked at where her mother sat with Bridie. 'Look at them,' she said, watching Victoria exulting in wedding present and her companion arranging weddings future. Then she looked at Aunt Bessie, weeping silently into her handkerchief, grieving over wedding past, and it all seemed so absurd that she and her cousin laughed out loud.

Later, to her husband, Bridie McCann remarked that she couldn't believe they had let their earlier fears over Alice and Liam get so out of hand. It looked like the situation had sorted itself out beautifully. 'Just as well we didn't go in heavy-handed, Seamus, don't you think so?' she mused, divesting herself of her wedding finery in the dressing room attached to their bedroom. 'If we'd done anything we could've brought out their stubborn streak and forced them together.' She shivered at the thought. 'Just think of the trouble we could've been in then?'

'Yes, Bridie,' Seamus smiled indulgently and a little drunkenly from the bedroom, 'you were right all along, you are always right about everything.'

'And don't you think Alice and that young Guthrie chap make a very handsome couple?' she called a few moments later, but Seamus was fast asleep.

4

In the months after Harry's wedding, Billy Guthrie became even more welcome among the McInallys as all of Victoria's concerns about his background disappeared. Even the striking resemblance to his late mother, especially the very pale blue eyes, had ceased to remind her of Jessie Guthrie. He was kind and courteous and polite. There was nothing he would not do for the family, from carrying the tea things for Victoria and discussing politics with Henry, to helping Bella with her homework, and, as everyone knew, Bella needed help with anything that required thinking. 'Harry's the good one,' Henry McInally used to say, 'Alice is the smart one, and Bella knows how to keep a tidy house,' which always prompted his wife to respond defensively, 'Well, there's plenty of call for that, there's nothing wrong with a good housewife.'

Victoria liked having a young man about the place now that Harry had gone, and her slight concern was receding the more she saw of Billy Guthrie. He and Alice took walks together to Shaw's Bridge, saw films together, danced together at church socials and looked well-suited; even Henry was so won over that he declared he had no worries about his daughter when she was out with Billy, and, he said repeatedly with a wink, no one knew better than he did what young men were like. 'Henry!' Victoria would whisper, nodding her head towards their younger daughter. 'Please, dear!' And that was enough for Henry, who knew when he sailed too close the edge.

The next wedding, a year later in 1914, was Brendon McCann's to the rather dark, lovely and splendidly Catholic Bernadette McMahon. He was an all-round good man, Brendon, one of nature's gentlemen, as the businessmen in Belfast would tell each other, a chap's chap, no one had ever been known to dislike him. He worked diligently in the family business and it was obvious that it was safe in his hands, and he was a born diplomat and peacemaker, whether by instinct or the necessity of growing up with Liam as his brother and Seamus as his father no one could tell. He was even of temper and pleasant of nature, the kind of son any parent or parent-in-law would welcome, and, happily for all, he had found a perfect wife in Bernadette.

Nothing had ever rocked Brendon's boat and it was impossible to imagine that anything ever would, though, once again, he couldn't have his best friend as his best man, Harry McInally being Protestant. Instead he had his older brother Liam, now twenty-five years old and newly graduated from university, who wouldn't need to bring a partner or have one provided for him, the chief of six bridesmaids was all his, or so she indicated in every way possible. Liam, an exceedingly handsome and well set-up young man, discouraged her without actually running away. He had his duties to perform and, as had been said in similar circumstances at Harry's wedding, it was only for one day. Still, she stuck to him like glue, insinuating her arm through his at every opportunity, till he gave up and settled for his lot for however long it took. In the distance he saw Alice and the two waved and smiled as they passed each other in the huge crowd of guests, as the McCanns put on a grand show of their status and wealth.

Alice had brought Billy Guthrie along as her partner, which would prove to be unfortunate. The trouble was that Billy partook a little too much of the McCann hospitality, which was as overdone as Bridie's good taste would allow. They were rich, they were celebrating the union of their younger son with the daughter of another prominent Catholic family, and their eldest son was making his Belfast society debut as a man with a university degree who had a fine future in front of him. With the usual matchmaking taking place at the reception, hopes were high that in this mainly Catholic gathering Liam might even line up a suitable bride of his own; that was to say, the good Catholic girl of his father's dreams, who would fill his mind and time with lots of babies. So there was much to eat, much to drink and even more satisfaction, for the occasion demanded it, McCann standing and pride were on show. And that was the problem, because a side of Billy Guthrie asserted itself that Alice had never suspected existed. He drank too much, which she had never seen him do before, and then he became surly.

'What are we doing here?' he slurred.

'Let's go out into the garden,' Alice said sweetly, leading him by the arm.

He pulled his arm away but followed her anyway.

'What's wrong with you, Billy?' she asked, genuinely puzzled.

'What's wrong with you?' he demanded, swaying in front of her. 'Why are you here with all these Fenians? I don't want to be here with them, so why did you drag me here?'

'These whats?' she asked.

He waved an unsteady arm about with such force that he almost fell over. 'Fenians!' he shouted. 'Fenians!'

'Ssh!'

'I will not ssh, I bloody will not ssh!' he yelled, proving the point.

'I don't know what you mean!' she whispered.

'He means Catholics,' Liam said quietly behind her.

Alice looked from one to the other. 'Do you?' she asked. 'Is that what you mean, Billy?'

'Yes, I bloody do!' he yelled back. 'No surrender, that's what I say, no bloody surrender, and you should be saying it too! You're a Protestant, you shouldn't be mixing with these people, and you shouldn't be making me mix with them either!' The effort of looking from Liam to Alice had caused him, in the exaggerated manner of drunk men, to spin on his toes rather than turn his head, and then to fall on the ground. Alice was deeply embarrassed, but the sight of Billy lying there shouting incoherent insults also made her laugh out loud.

'I'll help you take him home,' Liam smiled, trying to lift him.

'You bloody will not, keep your Fenian hands off me!' Billy responded, throwing a fist at Liam.

Liam didn't hesitate, he hit Billy with a punch to the jaw so hard that it silenced him instantly.

'You've killed him!' Alice said aghast.

'No such luck,' Liam laughed. 'He's more dead drunk than unconscious even. We'll take him round the back way and have him home before he wakes up. No one need see him.'

'What about your lady friend?' Alice asked, nodding behind him to where his would be companion of the evening was searching for him.

'Well, I've taken care of your pest,' he grinned, 'the least you can do is take care of mine!'

'You want me to lay out the chief bridesmaid with a right hook?' she asked.

'Oh, yes please,' he said with feeling, 'even a left one would do!'

And so they delivered Billy Guthrie to his home and left him singing and shouting 'No surrender!' to no one in particular.

'I've never seen him like that before,' Alice said quietly. 'Maybe he just felt out of his depth with all those rich people.'

Liam laughed. 'I don't think it was the richness of the people as much as the fact that there were so many Catholics about!'

'But I had no idea he was like that,' Alice said guiltily as they walked along.

'It's not your fault,' Liam replied. 'Believe me, there's a lot of it about, on both sides. This country is getting more dangerous by the day.'

'Do you really think so?' she asked.

He nodded. 'It's not just uneasy now, there are political moves going on that are polarising the differences, especially in Dublin.'

'It never mattered to me, and I don't feel any different,' she said quietly.

'Neither do I, but we were lucky enough to grow up in families where our different religions didn't matter. We're in the minority. I don't think people like us can stop what's going to happen.'

'You really think it's that bad?'

'It is,' he stated calmly. 'Your friend there isn't alone in how he feels. To his kind we're the enemy.'

'But we're all Irish!' Alice said.

Liam nodded. 'But they don't see any difference between Catholics and Fenians, and the Catholic side have nothing to feel superior about, they're just as bigoted.'

'Now there's talk of war in Europe. Do you think that will happen?'

'I'm sure of it,' Liam replied shortly. 'In Dublin the Republicans are already lining up to take part in England's war in return for independence later and the Unionists will join in to prove their loyalty to the crown. It'll be one more thing to divide the Irish,' he laughed wryly, 'as though we have any need of one more.'

It was a late afternoon on a bright May day, and her dress, a delicate turquoise silk, was pretty but flimsy, so he took his jacket off and put it about her shoulders, thinking how well the colour of the dress suited her.

'Yes, but it's not just about religion, is it, it shows a nasty streak to behave like that, calling people names, don't you think?'

He shrugged. 'I don't really know,' he said. 'Maybe the drink just brought out a nasty streak in him.'

'But there had to be one there to be brought out, surely?'

'I suppose so.'

Without realising it they were walking towards the banks of the Laggan, their old meeting place once upon a time. The last time they had met, on the station platform, they couldn't think of anything to say or how to say it, but now it was as though it had never happened. It seemed that they were chatting happily to each other, as they always had done, once. And yet there was a difference, an added dimension that puzzled them both. Though their conversation implied that they were at ease with each other, beyond the words there was a distance that they were both aware of. It was as though they were using the words to keep a physical gap between them. If Liam put his hand out towards her, gesturing as he spoke, Alice moved ever so slightly out of reach. When they moved together as they walked and it looked like their arms would brush against each other, both quickly moved apart again. Once they had been close enough to have relaxed silences, but now when there was a lull in the conversation both tried to say something, to fill in they didn't know what.

'Why are we being like this?' Liam sighed. 'We never used to be, did we?'

She smiled quietly. He was the most honest person she had ever known. 'I don't know what you mean,' she said.

'Stop lying, Alice,' he replied, looking away.

As they reached Shaw's Bridge he turned towards her and opened his mouth to say something, but for no reason she could understand she stopped him. 'Look!' she said, pointing. 'Bluebells!'

Liam looked down at her. 'Yes,' he said softly, 'bluebells.'

'I've always loved bluebells, the scent of them, the colour!'

'Yes, I know you have, Alice, I've been here with you before,' he said. 'It's me, remember?'

She had the feeling that he was laughing at her, which made her cheeks burn for some reason and she lowered her head so that he couldn't see it. The evening was chasing what was left of the afternoon sunshine away, and the descending darkness was bathing everything in a soft lavender glow.

'Twilight makes everything beautiful,' he smiled down at her, 'not that you need any help, Alice.'

She laughed and turned to the side.

'What is it? Too corny?' he asked shyly.

'Well, yes, but it wasn't that,' she said. 'I was just thinking how long it's been since I heard you say my name.'

'Me, too,' he said.

She turned and looked up at him. 'Liam,' she said, reaching out to touch his cheek lightly with her fingertips.

He caught her hand, kissed her fingers then drew her to him and held her close, both of them shaking.

'It's getting colder,' she said, though she knew it wasn't that.

'Yes, better get you home.'

But they continued to stand there in silence, in the shadow of the Minnow Burn beeches, for what seemed like a very long time.

'I've missed you,' he said, very quietly, into her hair, her incredible auburn hair.

'Me, too,' she murmured into his shoulder.

5

Years later, when she thought back on that time, she sometimes regretted the years they had wasted, but at other moments she would think they had needed those years apart to grow and get stronger, to meet other people and face situations without each other in order to be sure. At first they kept it to themselves, not out of fear, but because it was theirs and they didn't want to share it. Liam was now back at home working with a Belfast law firm, while Alice continued with the ham-curing arm of McCann and Son, so they were able to meet at different times through the day without anyone knowing. And Billy Guthrie helped: though he wasn't aware he was doing so, he became an unwilling decoy.

After Brendon McCann's wedding he had sobered up and seen the error of his ways, though he and Alice meant different things by that. To Billy, it meant he should not have shown his dislike and suspicion of Catholics so openly, that it had been a tactical error, while to Alice the change in him meant he really did feel badly about behaving as he had, about even saying such things. The thought that he said them because he believed them simply didn't occur to her because it was unthinkable. Not that it mattered, for if Billy had ever entertained plans to marry

Alice that notion was now over on both sides. Alice had Liam, though she told no one, and Billy's convictions led him to turn away from thoughts of Alice. He was a loyal member of the Orange Order, a Freemason, he couldn't think of any kind of alliance with someone who didn't share his prejudices. Not that Alice sensed any of this, and neither did Billy tell her. As far as she was aware he was an orphan who loved being part of the McInally family as much as the rest of the family loved having him, and there was no reason to deprive either of that. When he had apologised she had told him she wouldn't tell her parents what had happened at the wedding, as her parents were fond of him and she knew they would be shocked, but afterwards a slight but amicable distance grew between Billy and Alice, and it happened so gradually that no one else noticed. He was still in the McInally home when Alice wasn't there, but he always had been, and when both were elsewhere it was assumed they were together, so little had changed, little that was disclosed at any rate.

When Alice wasn't at home she was with Liam, much as she had been in years past, though everything was different now. They were no longer children and best friends, they were now a couple, their future together was set, but they were, as they always had been, a self-contained unit of two private people. There was no proposal, it wasn't necessary – they both knew marriage would happen and assumed everyone else realised this too, it was too normal and natural a progression for them not to. The only concession to romance was Liam's insistence that Alice have a ring, and he wanted to buy one with money he had earned himself rather than family money, not that there was any shortage of the latter, as his grand-father had left much of his fortune in trust to Liam and Brendon on their marriages. Alice, who had never put much store in gestures, protested that she didn't need a ring, but she saw that it meant more to Liam so she gave in with a smile. Liam wanted a stone as near to the colour of bluebells as possible and chose a sapphire surrounded by diamonds, but it would only be placed on Alice's finger once the usual courtesies had been satisfied. Liam wasn't entirely sure what those courtesies were and how they should be performed, so he and Alice consulted Brendon and Bernadette, who had already travelled this road.

'Well, for a start,' Brendon advised, 'not a word to anyone till the parents have been informed and Henry's been asked for his daughter's hand. I know what you're like, Liam, but please take my word for it, you do not wander up to Father and Mother together with the ring on Alice's hand.'

'Well, that wasn't the plan,' Liam said mildly, 'but why not?'

Brendon and Bernadette exchanged looks. 'Because you don't!' Brendon said. 'They're part of Belfast society, there are procedures for these things and Mother and Father like procedures.'

'I can't see why we have to jump through these hoops,' his older brother protested. 'It's really nobody's business but our own, after all.'

Brendon shook his head and looked at Alice for help, but she laughed and put her head down. 'And that is the sum total of all the trouble you've had with Father since the day you were born, Liam,' Brendon chided. 'You have never given him his place, never paid him due respect.'

'Respect?' Liam asked. 'For what? For having been born his son?'

'Exactly!'

'Oh, poppycock!' Liam replied dismissively. 'What choice did I have in that? Why make a big thing out of something everyone's known would happen all our lives? It's downright silly.'

Brendon looked again to Alice for support. 'Do you understand any of this?' he asked her.

'I suppose I understand both sides,' Alice said quietly. 'I can see that the families will want the social niceties, but I agree with Liam. I don't want any and I can't see why we should have to put up with them. It's simple, we just want to get married.'

Bernadette, sitting beside Brendon, laughed out loud. 'My dear Alice, a wedding in the family can never be simple, believe me! There will be times in months to come when it's all taken out of your hands and you'll wonder who this is happening to. Many's the time we felt like eloping, didn't we, Brendon?'

Brendon nodded. 'Being paraded about at parties and dinners where we didn't know anyone, then who was and was not to be invited, mostly those same people neither of us knew, as it turned out. Endless earnest discussions on who should sit beside who and where, which church, which priests, and the day itself was a nightmare.' He shook his head and Bernadette giggled.

'You didn't enjoy it?' Alice asked.

'Not one second!' Bernadette laughed. 'But we weren't supposed to enjoy it, the families enjoyed it, for us it was something to get over and done with. Accepting that fact is the key to getting through it.'

'Well we're not doing any of that,' Liam said firmly. 'We'll tell the parents and then plan the thing ourselves.'

'Don't you want a wedding, though?' Bernadette asked, looking at Alice.

'I just want to be married,' Alice replied calmly. 'I'm with Liam on this. Why should anyone else take it over, it's just us, as it's always been.'

'Look, Liam,' Brendon said firmly, 'I'll tell you how to handle this. First you have to tell Mother and Father that you intend asking Henry's permission to marry Alice, then you trot over to her house and talk to Henry. Then you can produce the ring, when you've got his permission, not before. After that you can do what the rest of us do, sit back and let it happen, because happen it will, whether you like it or not. Just content yourselves with the knowledge that one day it will all be over and you'll be on your own again, only with both sides breathing down your necks demanding grandchildren.'

Bernadette laughed, patting her stomach. 'Take my advice, give them one as quickly as possible, it's the only way you'll get peace.'

'Until it arrives, anyway,' Brendon commented wryly. 'It won't be long after that before they start demanding the next one.'

After Alice and Liam had gone, Brendon sat by the fire looking grim.

'A penny for them,' Bernadette smiled, squeezing his arm.

'I'm worried about them, that's all.'

'Me too,' she sighed. 'The religion thing.'

He nodded. 'There's something odd about the two of them, always has been. They've been so wrapped up in their own little world all their lives, protecting each other from reality, that they don't see life as other people do. I don't think my parents will be exactly ecstatic on the religion front, and I don't think the McInallys will be either.'

'Why didn't you say something to them?'

'They wouldn't believe it, would never understand it . . . they're innocents, the two of them, honest innocents. Liam's my older brother, but I've always felt he was younger.' Then he gave himself a shake and laughed. 'But I'm probably wrong, everything will be fine, my family love Alice and her family love Liam.'

'What about having a quiet word with your parents before Liam does?' Bernadette suggested. 'They listen to you. It might smooth the path, or at least give them time to get used to the idea.'

'I thought of that,' Brendon sighed, 'but it might have the opposite effect: give them time to think out their objections and plan their resistance. There's a chance that when he tells them it will catch them off guard and they might just have to capitulate.'

'You make it sound like a battle!'

'I'm rather afraid it could be,' Brendon said quietly. 'But if I'd even hinted at that to Liam he'd barge in there, all guns blazing, and there wouldn't be a shadow of doubt about their reaction, my father's particularly. Let's just see what happens.'

Liam took Brendon's advice and decided to tell his parents first then visit Henry McInally to ask for his daughter's hand in marriage, however silly the whole charade seemed. When he arrived to see Henry, at a time Alice had pre-arranged so that Bella would be out of the house, his face was taut. Nerves, Alice assumed. Complying with the social niceties had taken its toll on him.

'Why are you so nervous?' she chided him in the hallway.

'Oh, you know,' he replied.

She showed him into the study where Henry was doing his paperwork, and shut the door behind him. When they emerged, moments later, Henry looked stunned and, asking Liam to sit in the parlour, instructed Victoria in a very stiff manner to accompany him back to his study. Alice looked at Liam.

'Whatever happens, meet me at Shaw's Bridge as soon as you can,' he whispered.

'Why? What's —'

Just then her parents came out of Henry's study. The first thing that registered was the severity of Victoria's ashen expression; her lips were so taut and thin that they had disappeared completely, yet her eyes blazed, while Henry looked red-faced, embarrassed and confused.

'We cannot agree to this,' Henry said. 'I think you both know that.'

Alice stared at Liam, wondering if he had somehow asked the wrong question, while Liam kept his eyes on the floor.

'Mrs McInally and I are both stunned, Liam,' Henry continued. 'We had no idea anything like this had been going on.' The way he said it made it sound as though he had discovered something dirty and scandalous, as though he'd caught Liam in bed with both his daughters at once. He looked at Alice. 'We are shocked that you could've been so deceitful, Alice,' he said angrily. 'Your poor mother is distraught.'

Behind him, to confirm his observation, Victoria alternately sniffed into her handkerchief and looked at various points on the walls, anything but look at Alice and Liam. Somewhere in her mind Alice remembered Aunt Bessie in a similarly tragic pose and thought, An attack of the vapours, it must run in the family! She jumped to her feet. 'Deceitful?' she said, amazed and shocked. 'What do you mean, Father? This is Liam, not some stranger. What do you mean?' she repeated, genuinely bewildered.

'Alice, you know very well that there was never any intention of your marrying outside your own faith,' Henry said, trying to control his voice.

'Intention?' Alice demanded. 'What on earth are you talking about?'

'Don't speak to your father in that tone of voice!' Victoria cried, subsiding into tears.

85

'I just want to know what he means!' Alice said, confused. 'What intention?'

'It was always understood,' Victoria said angrily. 'You know what your cousin Maggie did to your Aunt Bessie and how the whole family has suffered because of her wilfulness and selfishness! And do you think for one moment that the McCanns would agree to this?'

Alice looked at Liam, who returned a slight, pained shake of his head to buy her silence.

'We only want what's best for you,' Henry said, 'for both of you. That's all any parent wants, and the best thing for you – and for Liam – is to marry within your own kind.'

Alice sat down, putting both hands over her ears to block the sound of their voices. 'Our own kind?' she cried. 'We're both people, one of us isn't a lion or a tiger!'

'Liam, would you please leave us now?' Henry McInally asked very formally, and Liam got up to go, with Alice following.

'Why are you talking to him like that?' she demanded.

'Alice, kindly join your mother in the parlour!'

Alice and Liam exchanged a glance, and then he was gone.

'I don't know what you could've been thinking,' Henry said as he returned to the parlour.

'And I don't know what you're thinking!'

'Alice!' Victoria cried.

'Well, I don't,' she replied. 'This is Liam,' she stressed.

'Liam is a Catholic –' Henry said tersely.

'He's Liam!'

'– and you are a Protestant.'

'And? That's how we've always been, what's changed?'

'What's changed, my girl,' Henry shouted, 'is that both of you aren't a couple of children running barefoot about Lough Neagh any longer, you are contemplating inter-marriage here!'

Victoria's sobs sounded out even louder than before as she headed for her kitchen.

'See what you've done to your poor mother!'

'Oh, don't worry, Father,' Alice shouted at him, 'she'll just whip up a dozen fairy cakes and that'll put the world to rights!'

With that she stormed out of the house, grabbing her coat and bag from the hallstand as she went, and headed for Shaw's Bridge.

Liam was waiting for her, head down, staring into the water.

'Well, was that what you expected?' he asked, smiling tightly, his face pale.

'No. You?' she asked.

He shook his head, putting an arm about her shoulders and drawing her close. 'You should've heard my parents!' he told her.

'I had no idea they hated me so much,' she said, hurt and bemused.

'Oh, don't think that,' he replied, 'it's not you, they're very fond of you, they just came up with the same objections as your parents.'

'And you had no idea they would?'

He shook his head. 'No more idea than you had.' He laughed bitterly. 'What was it I once said? "We were lucky enough to grow up in families where our different religions didn't matter." What an idiot!'

'I thought they would be happy,' she laughed quietly, on the verge of tears, 'I thought the worst we'd have to put up with was what Brendon and Bernadette described, I really did. I pictured the two families celebrating together.'

'Well,' Liam said quietly, 'they'll be together, no doubt about that – I think we've united them as never before – but they won't be celebrating. Puts Billy Guthrie in an altogether more respectable light, don't you think?'

'So what happens now?' she asked forlornly.

He shrugged. 'We have to accept that they are totally against it.'

'Totally.'

'And I don't think they'll be talked round, how about you?'

She shook her head. 'The cousin my mother mentioned, Maggie, she married a Catholic years ago. Aunt Bessie still regards it as on a level with mass murder.'

'And, knowing that, you still didn't think we'd get the same reaction?' he asked.

'No, I didn't, it never even occurred to me,' she laughed uneasily. 'That was years ago, and Maggie married someone the family didn't know anything about. We're different, our families have been connected for years, been best friends for generations. We've been closer to each other's families than to our own. I thought they'd be delighted, funnily enough.' She shrugged helplessly. 'Besides, I, well, I suppose I expected better of my parents.'

They stood silently, in shock almost, trying to make sense of where they were.

'So,' Liam said eventually, 'as I understand it, if we want to stay together it would seem that we have to leave Belfast.'

She didn't know what to say, her mind torn between responding first to 'if' or 'leave Belfast'.

'There is no "if" as far as I'm concerned,' she said at last. 'And if we have to leave Belfast, then we'll leave Belfast.'

Beside her he sighed deeply.

'You don't agree?' she asked, her voice tight with fear.

'If I hadn't already decided that after my parents' reaction I wouldn't have gone to your house, would I? No, it's not that,' he said, hugging her tightly. 'I'm just relieved that you feel like that too.'

'Did you doubt it?' she demanded.

'It's a big step,' he said, 'especially for a girl. We may not ever come back, we may not ever be able to, and they may never see us again. It could mean losing your family forever.'

'Like Maggie,' she smiled sadly. 'So let's take the big step.'

'Where will we go?' he mused. 'Dublin?'

'I think we'll have to go further than that,' she said. 'You keep telling me that Ireland is becoming more dangerous these days, and if that's a sample of how people will react to us, I don't want to stay here.' She shook her head. 'Dear God,' she said hopelessly. '1915 and we're at war with Germany, boys we know are disappearing to France every day, and all they have to worry them is that you're Catholic and I'm Protestant.'

'So where can we go?' he asked.

'Well, Maggie, the family criminal, lives in Glasgow,' she said, 'she and her husband run a boarding house there, or so I understand from the grapevine. No one talks openly about her, the older ones have always whispered about her between themselves so that we younger ones didn't hear, but whispers make you determined to hear, don't they? I'm sure her sister Louise would get in touch with her for us. Maggie would at least understand.'

'OK then,' he said, 'Glasgow it is.' Then he reached into his inside pocket, withdrew the ring, dropped to one knee and said, 'Alice McInally, Protestant spinster of this parish, will you marry Liam McCann, Catholic bachelor of this different parish?'

'Fool!' she said, as he slipped the ring on her finger.

'I couldn't get one the exact colour of bluebells, but this is pretty near,' he said.

'It's perfect,' she told him gently. 'I love it.'

★   ★   ★

Back at the McCann house Bridie and Seamus had been hurriedly joined by Victoria and Henry McInally. It was significant that the McInallys had gone to the McCann home and not the other way round. Old friends they might be, but the McInallys had never been equals and each knew the other's place in the pecking order, knew also that it would always be preserved without a word being spoken. They would have a war council, thrash out the best way to deal with this crisis, omitting the two people it would affect most, Alice and Liam. Victoria was still in the grip of her fit of the vapours, too overcome to utter more than a few sniffles and sobs without disappearing once again behind her handkerchief, while Henry blustered up and down making noises but not saying very much that was helpful, apart from supplying clichés when others spoke. Henry was doing the best he could given his personality. He needed his wife to provide him with the right words for this situation, as she did all situations, and she was out of reach, having withdrawn behind a veil of angry but silent tears.

Seamus, too, was behaving entirely true to character, by yelling and acting, as his son had aptly described, like some giant, arm-waving monster. Only Bridie could think straight enough to actually communicate, even if that did take the form of being so shocked she couldn't complete a sentence, and she had to keep stopping to rediscover her train of thought. All her poise had been submerged in her horror, all her tactics had deserted her.

'It's quite out of the . . . the thing . . . and for another . . . I mean to say!'

'You've never said a truer word!' Henry chipped in.

'And behind our backs, without a thought for our . . . and to think I believed he was an honest boy . . . who would've thought . . .?'

'Biting the hands that fed them!'

'That they should break the, um, hearts . . . it just can't happen, that's all, I mean, it won't be . . . um . . .!'

'Many a slip between cup and lip for them!'

'Seamus, stop dancing about there and do something!'

'Like what, woman?' Seamus demanded. 'He's your son and you've always indulged him, I always said it would end in tears!'

'You said I'd happily wave him off on a boat to Paraguay –'

'– and I wish you had, it would've been better than this!'

'– but not once did you say he would marry a Protestant!'

'I didn't think I had to,' Seamus yelled back, 'you said you and Victoria had sorted all that nonsense out long ago.'

'We did, we had!' Bridie protested. 'Hadn't we, Victoria?'

Victoria raised her face from her handkerchief and nodded solemnly. She took no offence at the McCanns' horror over their son wanting to marry a Protestant, regardless of which Protestant. She felt just as shocked that her daughter proposed to marry a Catholic, even Liam. The McCanns spoke the simple truth for both families: the thing was unthinkable, it was distasteful, such treachery from one of your own was impossible to bear.

'I'm so sorry this has been done to you, Bridie,' Victoria sniffed. 'She's my daughter, and I apologise to you and to Seamus.'

Bridie got up and crossed to where her friend was sitting and threw her arms around her. 'No, no, my dear,' she cried, 'you have nothing to reproach yourself for. I feel just as badly for you and Henry, I am so sorry that our son has violated your trust as well as our own!'

'This communal wailing is all very well,' Seamus said, exasperated, 'but what are we to do now?'

'We must make it very plain to them that we do not and will not approve,' Victoria stated.

'Yes, indeed!' Henry said staunchly, grateful that his wife had renewed a supply of thoughts and words to him once again. 'Make it very plain, that's what we must do!' and he thumped the arm of the chair.

'We must point out the error of their ways, the grave error, and demand that they give up these notions immediately and forever,' Victoria continued.

'Forever!' Henry repeated with another thump. 'That's the ticket!'

'It's most likely just a phase anyway,' Bridie said almost cheerfully.

'That son of yours is a bit old for a phase, Bridie,' Seamus muttered.

'They'll grow out of it,' Bridie continued soothingly, ignoring the interruption. 'Why, a year from now they'll wonder what it was all about, and so shall we. We must keep calm, that's all.'

'Calm,' Victoria said, now back on an even keel, 'but firm. Very firm.' She looked at Bridie and Seamus, she didn't need Henry's agreement, and the three nodded in unison.

'Yes, indeed,' said Henry. 'Indeed, that's what we need, firmness!'

When tempers had been slightly restored the two sets of old friends sat down and contemplated the tragedy that had befallen them, that these two children, whom they all loved dearly, could have treated them thus. Had they wanted to marry different people the news would have been greeted with great joy by both families; had they been the same people but brought up in the same religion, that too would have caused huge celebration. So there they were in the grand McCann parlour with its enviable bay windows, gulping hot, sweet tea from Royal

Albert china, napkins with real Belgian lace on their knees, weeping, muttering and declaring, their emotions spinning incoherently, but of one mind in their stern, immovable opposition. Despite generations of genuine friendship they had been divided by the belief that the other's religion was neither as pure nor as good as their own: the very belief that now united them.

In the following weeks Alice and Liam stuck to the plan they had made. Louise would write to her sister telling her of their situation and ask for help, and, meanwhile, Alice and Liam would go along with whatever their families said without uttering a word of disagreement. What this amounted to was that they must not see each other, nor contact each other, understandable sanctions but ones that, had the McInallys and McCanns thought them through, would be impossible to enforce. The two errant offspring, now adults in their twenties, could hardly be followed during their working days, nor could they be locked up after work, so they said nothing, but met when possible, ignoring the turmoil and upset in both families as best they could. Over the weeks Alice took bits and pieces of her clothing, placed them in her bag, and handed them to her cousin Louise at lunchtimes for safe-keeping, then met her on Sundays after church to discuss progress. From Victoria's point of view, this was a good thing: her niece would be explaining to Alice the horrors the family had gone through as a result of Maggie's betrayal. It was called family unity, she thought, shrugging off a slight feeling of guilt that when the terrible event had taken place, she herself had opened up a slight distance from her sister. At the time she had told herself she was giving Bessie and her family space to deal with their grief, but the truth was that the two young people had marked all their connections with a stigma, a deep shame, and so Victoria had acted to ensure that her own family's contact was minimal.

'I hate to involve you in this, Louise,' Alice told her as they sat having coffee together.

'Don't be silly!' Louise responded, clearly in high spirits despite her cousin's worried expression. 'Now, my contact at the other end' she continued, looking about furtively 'has written back saying come when you're ready.'

'Maggie?' Alice asked, though it could be no one else.

'Ssh!' Louise whispered, looking around again. 'You are not allowed to say that name, don't you know that? Either my mother will drop dead, pierced to the heart, or the ground will open up and swallow you!'

Alice giggled, though she felt far from happy.

'And don't worry about me, Alice,' Louise said reassuringly. 'I think it's wonderful!' Her hands had been clasped in front of her on the table, but when she said 'wonderful' she unclasped them, threw them wide, then clapped them back together again, her eyes shooting open as far as they could go. 'Dear God, when I think back, I've always wanted to be a rebel, but I've done what was expected of me all my life. I can't tell you how I'm enjoying this!'

'Well,' said Alice miserably, 'I'm glad at least one of us is.'

'Oh, come on, Alice! You'll tell your grandchildren about this one day, of your romantic elopement with both sides snapping at your heels. It's wonderful!' 'Wonderful' was again given the hand treatment, making Alice laugh. 'What else would they have in their miserable, comfortable little lives if someone didn't spice things up a little now and then?' Louise demanded, hazel eyes narrowing. 'You're doing something worthwhile here, just keep thinking that. You aren't creating this problem, they're creating it by their attitude, just as happened with Maggie and

Tony. And he's utterly gorgeous, your Liam, he's worth it, isn't he?'

Alice nodded, smiling as she thought of Liam.

'And you're worth it for him?'

She nodded again, shyly this time.

Louise put her very mobile hands over Alice's. 'This time will pass, Alice,' she said with gentle conviction, 'once you settle into your new life it will be like some half-remembered bad dream.'

'You think so?'

'Yes, I do!' Louise said firmly, her hands repeating their familiar clapping routine. 'And I'll do whatever I can to help. If sin-by-proxy is all I'll ever have, then sin-by-proxy it shall be!'

'Well,' Alice said in a relieved tone, 'if you're sure, there is one thing . . .'

'Oh goody, more subterfuge for Louise!' her cousin shrieked, nearly jumping out of her chair.

Alice laughed. She hadn't been close to this cousin, and now she wished she had known Louise better.

'There aren't too many boats now across to Scotland with the war and everything, but Liam's arranged for some chap with his own boat to take us across to Glasgow. We're leaving first thing on Tuesday morning. If I write a letter to my parents and Liam writes one to his, could you, would you, deliver them to Harry and Brendon at their offices?'

'But you work with Harry, don't you? Won't he be suspicious if you don't turn up in the office?'

'That's why we've chosen Tuesday. Liam will say he's arranged to meet a client and Harry's out of town on business every Tuesday, comes back about four thirty. I'll go in as usual in the morning, tell the others that I'm feeling off-colour and that

I'm going home, so there's no reason for anyone to be suspicious.'

'Thought of everything I see!'

'Fingers crossed,' said Alice. 'So if you deliver the letters by hand late in the afternoon . . .?'

'By which time the birds won't just have flown, they will have landed in Glasgow, eh?' Louise asked with a conspiratorial wink.

'Yes, that's it exactly,' Alice laughed. 'You really have a talent for this, don't you?'

'I'm just one of those people for whom the chance to do something really bad and outrageous never really turned up,' Louise said sadly, then she looked across at Alice, her eyes bright again. 'I just hope that one day I can stand up and confess my part in this crime to the families, but in the meantime I'll know, and that'll be enough.'

And so that's how it was. Alice and Liam left for work at the same time, meekly and quietly, having given every sign in the weeks before that their sins were behind them, and boarded a boat for the Ayrshire coast. From there they travelled by train to Glasgow and made the last part of their journey by tram along Great Western Road, a sight that had to impress anyone, from its wide thoroughfare fringed with trees to the beauty of the red sandstone and pale Giffnock Stone buildings nestling discreetly behind the leaf-laden branches. It was at the time that would later be known as Great Western Road's 'Golden Years', when the best and the richest lived in the villas and terraces along its expanding length. It was the only place to live if you were stylish and had class, though the citizens of Glasgow's South Side would always dispute this. Past the elegant Grosvenor Terrace they travelled, and just beyond to the twenty houses that made up Kew Terrace and Maggie's large and beautiful terraced house opposite the Botanic Gardens.

Alice's cousin waited for them in her parlour while her maid greeted them at the door. From the little she had heard of Maggie's circumstances Alice had been expecting a small guest house, somewhere cosy and easily managed, but this house was bigger than the McCann house in North Belfast and several times as grand. Had Victoria McInally been aware of its opulent existence she would have been in tears of frustration, that a relative of hers could own such a place, yet she could have no dealings with her, no possibility of dropping in for tea, of boasting of it to the members of her church.

Alice's memories of her cousin were from childhood. She had been barely into her teens when Maggie had left Belfast, and the stately matron that held out her arms to her was only vaguely familiar because of her likeness to Louise. Same height, same colouring, but Maggie was more refined, had more decorum, thanks to the gravitas of age and experience.

'My dear Alice,' Maggie smiled politely. 'How nice to see you. And Liam – I have such fond memories of you both as children. Please, sit by the fire and I'll arrange tea.' She glided effortlessly across the room and rang the bell. 'So. How are your families?'

Alice and Liam exchanged glances. 'I think you can imagine that, Maggie,' Alice said, with a tight smile.

'Well, it was to be expected after all, Alice,' Maggie said calmly. 'You must have known that.'

'I didn't,' Alice replied. 'I truly didn't.' She shrugged. 'Our families have been closer to each other than to their own relatives. I didn't expect such fury.'

'Yes, well, dear, you must remember that to them there is such a thing as a step too far, and you two have taken it.' She smiled at their worried expressions. 'You are both young, and the trouble is that the young always expect so much of their parents. We expect them to act in accordance with what they say, to only speak the truth and never let us down, but no one can ever live up to that, can they? Everyone lies and cheats to some degree in whatever circumstances they find themselves in. They bend the rules, see things as they wish them to be, that sort of thing. What you will understand in time is that parents are people, too, and when their children find them out, they tend to be deeply disappointed that they've been living with flawed human beings, and the parents feel exactly the same about the children.'

'You sound as though you approve!' said Alice, trying to laugh but not quite succeeding, so that it sounded like a cry in disguise.

Maggie put a hand out to her young cousin. 'My dear,' she said quietly, 'I've had a long time to think this over. I understand why it happened to me and now to you, but please don't think it means I agree with it. If you two have even half the feelings Tony and I had, then nothing will stop you and nothing should. Just don't hate your parents, that's all I'm saying: they are as they are, not as you'd like them to be.'

Across the hearth, Liam nodded.

The tea things arrived and conversation stopped while the maid laid the tray out and left.

'Now,' Maggie said in a businesslike tone. 'Let's be practical. What will you do for money?'

'I have contacts in Dublin,' Liam said. 'I went to university there, and a friend has lined up a job with a law firm here in the city.'

Maggie nodded approvingly, handing out tea and biscuits.

'I also have money my grandfather left in trust for when I

marry,' Liam continued. 'My family can't do anything about that, there was nothing in his will about not marrying a Protestant.' He looked at Alice and smiled, in a gentle attempt to stop her from crying.

'And you, Alice?' Maggie asked.

'Liam's friend has got me a job with the same firm. I'll be working in the office,' she replied.

'You have experience of office work?'

'Oh, yes!' Liam said proudly. 'Alice has been running McCann and Son for years now. My mother always says Alice took it over by the scruff of the neck and made it run efficiently for the first time in its life.'

'Very good. So when do you plan to marry?'

'We don't really know,' Alice replied, glancing at Liam. 'The thing is, I'd rather give the families time to come round, you know? I'd rather have them there, than . . .'

'Than risk my fate?' Maggie laughed wryly.

'I'm sorry, I didn't mean –'

'My dear Alice, don't apologise, I know just what you mean,' Maggie said reassuringly. 'This isn't how I would've wanted it to be either. I've often wondered if our families would've come round if we'd waited, but their reactions were so violent that we couldn't see any possibility of that at the time.'

Alice didn't want to think too deeply on that. 'In the meantime, we will be able to pay our way, if you have room for us here,' she said, trying to cover her embarrassment, 'until we sort things out.'

Maggie looked deeply hurt. 'That isn't what I meant,' she said archly, 'and I'm surprised you even thought it.'

'I just –'

Maggie held a hand up without looking at her. 'Let me explain the situation,' she said, carefully laying down her cup and saucer and placing her hands neatly in her lap. 'Tony and I have worked very hard over the last years. This is a good house, and in the early days, while Tony was making his way, we couldn't have afforded it without the income from well-chosen guests. Happily, that time has passed now.' She allowed herself a proud but still tasteful smile. 'Tony works with James Blackie, the publishing firm, you know. He worked his way up and is now a director, and he's also in partnership in various business ventures with a few friends. They have four shops so far at St George's Cross, you'll have passed them on your way here.' This time she smiled widely. 'As I was saying, we only ever took people who were recommended to us, professional people, you know, as a favour, because we had so much room. Decent people, but not often, and now we no longer have to.' She sighed. 'We had planned to fill this big house with children, but it wasn't to be, so far at any rate, so I've made the upkeep and decoration of it my own little venture and I'm involved in various committees, charitable bodies, you understand. Sometimes we have friends to stay, or business contacts of Tony's from out of town, but that's all, so I have already selected rooms for both of you. But I have to be sure we are very clear.' She looked first at Alice and then at Liam. 'I'm sorry if you'll think me old-fashioned, but you must both understand that there will be two rooms. We'll be delighted to have you with us for as long as you wish, but while you remain under our roof and unmarried, you will remain in single rooms, is that clear?'

Maggie was a woman whose character had been unfairly sullied, and thereafter she had deliberately become not just respectable, but openly, transparently respectable, to show them all, presumably. Even if they were in Belfast and would never see what she had achieved, apart from Louise, of course, Maggie knew. The rest of the family who had turned their backs on her would be impressed if they could see her now, though they never would; she knew that, too. Alice nodded and looked down as her cheeks flamed, but Liam returned Maggie's frank look.

'We never expected, never intended anything else,' he replied.

'Good,' Maggie smiled. 'And as for you, madam,' she said mock-seriously to her young cousin, 'we are family and I am hurt that you would think I'd take a penny from you, especially as you know that I was and am in the same position as you now find yourself.'

Alice tried to protest, but Maggie laughed. 'My dear girl, it's quite all right,' she said gently. 'I know how confused you are at the moment, who would know better than I? Lord knows, since I heard about the two of you I've found myself weeping at odd moments – it seems like only yesterday I was going through the same thing.'

'Did you have any doubts?' Alice asked.

Maggie shook her head. 'Not then, not now,' she said. 'I don't think we really understood what a big step we were taking at the time, and I don't suppose you do either, but no; no regrets. Tony's religion meant, means, more to him than mine ever did to me, so we married in a Catholic church here. I would have happily done so in Belfast, but that wasn't the issue for either family, was it? I agreed to any children being raised as Catholics, so a priest was prepared to marry us, though he would've been happier if I'd converted, of course. I couldn't do that, it would've been so false, don't you think? To say you've changed your beliefs just to please a priest? Tony didn't mind, so I didn't see that the priest should. Not that it mattered about the children in the long run. For you it will be the same, marriage in a church or a declaration before a lawyer. Either way, and I have to be honest with you, my dears, I don't think your parents will ever accept what you've done. By all means wait and hope, but do be careful not to harbour false hope in that direction.'

Alice swallowed quickly. Until that moment she had no idea that the hope she was harbouring could prove false, and the thought of being cut off from her family for the rest of her life was like a physical blow. 'But you still have Louise?' she said quietly.

'Oh,' Maggie laughed out loud, 'my sister, the secret agent! Yes, I have Louise, but she wasn't at my wedding, nor I at hers, and we haven't been allowed a family occasion together in all these years, not a birthday, Christmas or even a funeral, come to that. We are in contact and she has come over a few times since her marriage, but only because her husband is a good fellow and indulges her. If the family ever found out both he and she would be ostracised, have no illusions about that. Time is not always a good healer.' She stared silently into the fire for a few moments. 'It's a strange thing, I often think, to deliberately divest yourself of your own, withdraw your love and reject theirs after all those years, just because they don't believe as you do. I mean, where does it go, all this unused, unwanted love? If we'd had children I'd hope we wouldn't think of such a thing. It's as though I became unclean in the eyes of my parents, became something putrid and terrible. It makes you feel ashamed even though you've done nothing shameful, and that's an awful feeling to have. Yet I hadn't harmed anyone: all I did was meet someone, fall in love and want to marry him.'

'Only he was Catholic,' Liam smiled.

'Only he was Catholic,' Maggie sighed, then smiled at Alice. 'These thoughts will occupy your mind for years to come, Alice, I give you fair warning! Now, go to your rooms, rest, have a bath, take time to settle in and come down when you feel like it.'

★   ★   ★

Later they met Tony, a tall, imposing man in his middle years, with red hair turning sandy with age and a great many whiskers. He greeted the two young people graciously and repeated Maggie's invitation to stay as long as they wished. It was hard to imagine him as a dashing lover who had whisked his lady from under the noses of her family: he looked every inch the respectable businessman that he was.

'Don't worry about all the fuss,' he told them grandly, 'it will pass, everything passes eventually, you know,' then he retired behind his newspaper where he fell asleep.

'I'm so sorry,' Maggie said, embarrassed. 'He works very hard, you know, and very long hours, too.'

'It's his house, Maggie,' Liam smiled. 'He can do what he wants and we're grateful for his kindness, and yours.'

6

When Alice and Liam's flight from Belfast was uncovered, there was such an outburst of hysterical sobbing that the River Laggan threatened to burst its banks, or so Louise reported in due course. Those first attacks of the vapours that had accompanied the discovery that Alice and Liam wished to marry bore no relation to the heights of emotion that erupted when they left for Glasgow. Victoria and Bridie had abandoned their respective parlours and taken to darkened bedrooms, unable to communicate for days, except in bursts of noisy tears, while Henry, once again without Victoria's wisdom to guide him, strutted about uttering whatever stray words came to mind, and Seamus whirled around waving his arms and shouting a lot. But once again the families were united: they would cast their children out, never see them again, rather than agree to any marriage.

'"*I didn't deliver the letters myself,*" Alice read from Louise's letter. '"*I paid a boy in the street sixpence to do it, and before you accuse me of cowardice I only did so to add to my own enjoyment. Besides, I'm a lady in a certain condition these days, so I'm sure my pieces of excitement will have to be restricted for a while. Anyway, what's that thing people say? 'Light the blue touch paper and stand well back'? Well that's what I did, and the fireworks were all that I could have hoped for, I have to say. What fine performances they have put on for my benefit! And my own dear mother is so grateful to you both.'"* Alice stopped reading the letter out and looked from Liam to Maggie. *'"Your own dear mother, my Aunt Victoria,"'* Louise continued, *'"made sure her sister never got too near her family after Maggie and Tony behaved so disgracefully, made her feel like a social inferior."'*

'She did,' Alice said sadly, then went back to the letter. *'"And now my mother is taking the greatest pleasure in being Aunt Victoria's supporter and adviser. She's never at home these days, she's taken on an entirely new lease of life, forever by her sister's side, sympathising with her (in a pig's ear!) and telling her what to do, and in such a wonderfully bitchy way I can hardly believe Aunt Victoria doesn't throw her out into the street. It's so rewarding to see my mother so enthusiastic about life again: one banned relationship felled her, now another has brought her back to full vigour – how strange, don't you think?"'*

'Well,' Liam grinned. 'What's that other thing people say? "It's an ill wind that blows nobody any good." Is that right?'

'And Billy Guthrie has got himself in on the act,' Alice said, reading on. 'He's become indispensable, apparently, even offered to track us down and drag me home.'

'You must be joking!' Liam said in amazement.

'No, that's what Louise says,' Alice laughed. 'I'd imagine he has a pretty fair idea it wouldn't happen, but he's got the credit for being prepared to do it.'

'"The wonderful thing is,"' Alice read out, *'"that because we attend the same church and I'm related to you and to Maggie, Billy regards us as being on the same side and seeks me out as often as possible to tell me his thoughts and plans. You've no idea how he's grown in stature, at least in his own eyes. He wanders about like some high, thin tree being blown about by the wind but determined to stay*

upright and do his moral best for the family. I have to say, I find him quite repulsive, but, and I do hate to even suggest this, I do feel that he has Bella quite in thrall."'

'Oh, surely not!' Liam whispered.

'Well,' Alice shrugged. 'She's not exactly bright, as you must've noticed.'

'But she can't be stupid, surely?'

'I think she can,' Alice replied. 'He certainly wouldn't have any trouble making her think as he does. Bella has never had any thoughts of her own as far as I'm aware.'

'Alice, your own sister!' Maggie said.

'But it's true! And when I think back on it, she knew who Billy was long before I did, she told me his name, come to think of it.' She went back to Louise's letter. '"*And furthermore,*"' she read out, '"*I don't like his eyes. Not only are they too close together, but they're far too pale a shade of blue. Blue should be blue, in my book, I hate insipid.*"'

'Logic was never my sister's strong point,' Maggie said, shaking her head.

'And she could never be accused of admiring anything insipid,' Alice smiled.

'Those things she wears!' Maggie closed her eyes and shuddered.

'She makes them all herself, you know,' Alice said.

'Quite,' Maggie said tersely. 'No one else would dare!'

'But she has a good heart,' Liam protested.

'Yes,' Maggie replied contentedly. 'She has.'

Later that evening, walking in the Botanic Gardens, Alice said to Liam, 'Do you know what has surprised me most?'

'Tell me.'

'Not a word from Harry or Brendon, nothing. Harry didn't

even try to talk to me about my parents' reaction before we left. What about Brendon?'

'The same,' Liam said quietly. 'He looked at me sympathetically and seemed on the verge of speaking a couple of times, but he never did.'

'Aren't you surprised?'

'Oh, I don't know, Alice,' he sighed, squeezing her hand in the crook of his elbow. 'Maybe they were both too shocked, or didn't want to interfere or take sides. Whatever we did, they had to stay there, they were settled: if they'd rocked the boat they could've made the situation worse, or been thrown out of the family as well.'

'I'm still surprised,' she said. 'I didn't expect anything of Bella, Bella wouldn't know what to say or think until someone told her, she's always been the same, but Harry and I . . .' Her voice trailed off. 'I suppose I'm disappointed. I expected more of him, too.'

'But what could he do? Or Brendon, for that matter?'

'I thought they'd find out where we are and make some kind of contact, if they were interested. After all, Louise keeps in touch.'

'Louise is different,' Liam laughed. 'There's no one like Louise, she's fearless! Can you imagine her trying to melt into the background as the boy delivered our letters, trying not to be noticed and dressed like some exotic Bird of Paradise?'

'Yes, I can,' Alice joined in with his laughter, 'but still . . .' When they returned to Kew Terrace, Maggie was sitting quietly in the parlour re-reading Louise's letter. Alice looked at her and noticed that her eyes were bright. Louise's baby, she thought. Poor Maggie, she really must mind. Then she concentrated on folding the letter. 'Nice news about Louise, isn't it, Maggie?' she said pleasantly.

'Yes, it's quite lovely!' Maggie smiled. 'That will cut down Louise and George's visits, I suppose. But still, I'm to be an aunt, so that is nice, as you say, dear.' She was silent for a moment. 'Maybe I should knit a few little things in pastel colours,' she said thoughtfully. 'Lord knows, if it's left to my sister the poor mite will be wearing black and maroon from birth!'

And so life began to settle down, at least that was the plan, with the war in France rumbling on beyond the Christmas that was supposed to, but didn't, see all the boys back home again, adding to the concerns of everyone. There was no conscription for Irish citizens, but every day, as they set out for work together, Liam and Alice would sit on the tram watching the citizens of Glasgow anxiously scanning the lists of casualties in their newspapers for names they didn't want to see. Sometimes you would see a businessman with arms outstretched, holding the newspaper wide, then it would collapse in a sudden, awful movement into the reader's lap and stay there with a stunned, silent stillness, revealing a shocked, disbelieving face, and everyone would look away. That was as near as the war came to them, near enough as it was, and they began to put down the roots of their new life and make new friends.

In due course Louise gave birth to a daughter that she called Emma, though she told her sister the child was called Tallulah Esmeralda, so that Maggie's pangs of jealousy were submerged in exasperation. '"*She looks like me*,"' the new mother wrote, '"*except for her feet. She has big feet like you, Maggie*."'

Tony laughed out loud as Maggie read the letter out at breakfast.

'I don't think that's funny,' Maggie scolded.

'Not to you, but to everyone else,' he smiled at his wife, 'which is precisely why Louise wrote it.'

'Honestly, I cannot understand why you all think my very rude sister is so amusing! I've a jolly good mind not to send her a present!'

'But you will,' he grinned. 'How about a big pair of wellington boots?' and he swept out of the room to start the journey to his office before Maggie could reply.

Maggie and Tony were kind and gracious hosts who made the young couple feel that it was their home, too, though it had to be said that Maggie was slightly disappointed. She was twelve years older than Alice, which meant that she had been in her young cousin's position at roughly the same age. She expected to be able to play, if not a maternal role, at least an older sister role, to guide Alice through the phases and feelings that lay ahead, to be her confidante. But Alice wasn't that kind of young woman. Alice was what some people called self-contained, or private: she neither invited confidences nor bestowed them. At first Maggie had thought it was the shock of it all: the girl needed time to calm down and think, and then she would lower her defences and learn to rely on her older cousin more. And so Maggie tried to involve Alice in her life, inviting her to various charity functions and tea parties with the other ladies of means in her circle.

'There's just so much poverty and need in this city, another pair of hands is always useful, Alice,' she wheedled, 'if you can be bothered, my dear?'

'Yes, yes, of course,' Alice replied, wondering where this poverty must lurk, because all she had seen was an affluent, elegant city with people to match. In fact it had quite surprised her: she had expected Glasgow to be a large, grim, dark industrial wasteland, but it was full of greenery and grace. 'Are there many poor people here?'

Maggie and her ladies looked at each other and laughed genteelly. 'Oh, Alice, you have no idea!' Maggie sighed, shaking her head. 'If you only knew the squalor some of them have to live in, and the number of children who die in infancy. TB is rife, you know. It sometimes seems that every second person dies of it, it's quite heartbreaking.'

'I had no idea,' Alice murmured.

'Well how could you, my dear?' a bejewelled matron asked at her side. 'You've only just arrived and you're obviously a well brought-up young lady. How could you imagine such things?'

Alice shrugged. There must have been similar conditions in Belfast, but her life was far-removed from the areas where they occurred. They were Catholic areas, because people there found it almost impossible to get work, but the only Catholics she knew were the few rich ones she had known all her life.

'Now look what we've done!' the matron said. 'We've upset the poor girl!'

'No, no,' Alice protested, blushing. 'I was just thinking, that's all.'

'This is a poor city in places, but we mustn't make you think any less of Glasgow. I mean, look around you in this part of the city, it's quite beautiful, don't you think?'

Alice nodded and tried to reply, but the question was clearly rhetorical, because the matron rushed on.

'Not what it was when I was a girl, of course,' she sighed. 'Even ten years or so ago, before there were so many beastly cars on the road, you could've joined the Sunday church promenades from Byres Road to Bingham's Pond, everyone dressed in their finest clothes. The richest and "best" people occupied the middle of the road, of course, while lesser mortals, knowing their place, confined themselves to the sidewalk.' She gave a girlish giggle. 'But everything's changing with the war, all the old traditions are going. It makes me feel quite sad to think they won't ever come back again.' She sipped her tea. 'Do you know, Maggie, I saw a tram being driven by a young woman the other day? I swear, it was a woman!'

'Yes, I know,' Maggie replied, 'and I think it's quite splendid!'

'Maggie!'

'I was talking to her on my way back from town the other day,' Maggie said smugly. 'Her name's Mary Campbell. She says she loves the work, but she's struggling to think of a ladylike way of dealing with the carters.'

'It's the war again,' sighed her friend. 'I suppose the more men who disappear to the Front the less there will be to drive trams and women will have to fill in for them. Let's hope it will be over soon and ladies can go back to being ladies before standards fall too far.'

Maggie looked at Alice and the two of them put their heads down, smiling, and just then Tony arrived home from the office, striding in, newspaper in hand as ever. Maggie had her back to the parlour door but Alice was looking straight at him, so he put a finger to his lips and, with surprising grace for a man of his size, tiptoed backwards from whence he had come before anyone but Alice knew he had ever been there.

It was true, though: the war was bringing changes everywhere and both Alice and Liam had a great deal to learn in a new life that wasn't standing still. However, in 1915 the area around Great Western Road was still a place to be proud of, a civilised and cultured area of the city. Liam and Alice spent their free time seeing the latest films at the Hillhead Salon cinema in Vinicombe Street, attending open-air concerts together, and walking in the nearby Botanic Gardens and

Kelvingrove Park, without looking over their shoulders in case anyone saw them and reported back to their families. Strange, really, to remember that they had spent so much time together when they were younger and no one thought it was evil, or bad, or put an unhealthy slant on it. The world of grown-ups was an odd one. But, if they thought they were coming to a new land for a fresh start, a land free of the prejudices and bigotry that had forced them to leave their families and homes, they were mistaken. Scotland, particularly the west of Scotland, was a popular place with Irish immigrants, the poorest of them anyway. The richer ones could afford the boat fare taking them further afield to Canada, America and Australia, whereas the poorer ones had only the wherewithal to take them the short sea journeys to the cities of mainland Britain, those bound for Scotland usually travelling to Ayrshire and then to Glasgow. Given that they were poor, they were prepared to do any work for less than the native Scots, as immigrants the world over always are, and the predominantly Protestant Scots resented their jobs being taken from them. In Glasgow, having an Irish name came to mean being Catholic, regardless of whether or not this was true, and the Irish immigrants added to this by bringing their sectarian rivalries with them, importing a difficulty that fitted in with Scottish resentment.

Job vacancy notices routinely stated that no Catholics should apply, and Catholics, or the Irish, were not allowed to be tradesmen, consigning them to lower wages, so that they could only afford the worst standards of living and housing. By order of Rome, so it was said, they had far too many children, many more than their Protestant hosts, a myth that was clutched to the bosom of Glasgow bitterness and nourished until it became established as fact. That Rome, or more likely its local repre-sentatives, did indeed order it was true: numbers meant power, so the Catholic Church wanted as many adherents as possible. But in an era when there was no family planning, partly because it didn't exist and partly because infant mortality was so high that it was unusual for a full brood to survive to adulthood, the truth was that one 'side' reproduced as often as the other. And so the average Irish immigrant, unwanted, frequently vilified, denied decent wages, living in Glasgow in an extreme of poverty at least equal to what they had left behind in Ireland, must have wondered why they had gone there. Some only stayed long enough to scrape together the money to leave again, to go back home or maybe to those far distant lands the rich people went to, while others stayed and made their way, helped by their own kind and then helping others that came after them.

Liam worked in Pat Murphy's practice, a wealthy firm of solicitors in St Vincent Street that was regarded, rightly, as Catholic. He would not have been employed by a Protestant firm, and Alice was employed because of Liam, though she would probably not have got work anywhere else either, given that her surname was Irish and therefore 'Catholic'. But at least they had new friends through work, and if anyone disapproved of their relationship it was not made obvious and was devoid of family hysteria. Besides, Pat Murphy might have been made for the situation the two young people were in. He was a kindly if loud middle-aged man, a first-generation Scot, and as soon as he had been contacted on Liam's behalf by mutual legal friends in Dublin, he had literally jumped at the chance to help. Even before he set eyes on them he had a very soft spot for Liam and Alice. He had made his fortune from Catholics, a fact that irked him slightly because it implied his religion was the only reason they came to him, so he constantly justified it by stating that if a Protestant client came to him he would make no distinction and would do his best for them. In Pat's case this was undoubtedly true, as true as the undeniable fact that no Protestant would have consulted him. They stuck to their own because the other side forced them to – that's what both sides said, thereby confirming each other's views.

That clannishness extended to everyone, educated lawyers or clients, the feeling of not quite being at home in their own country – as Scotland was to the generations born there after the first wave of immigration.

The year after Alice and Liam arrived in Glasgow the Easter Uprising had taken place in Dublin. It was an armed uprising in Dublin, though the weapons on the Irish side were weak and ineffectual; mainly it consisted of rebels fighting for Irish Independence taking over buildings in the city. They were armed with rifles, but the British government ordered the military to crush them by any means, so artillery was used and a gunship. With no distinction made between civilians and rebels, who were outnumbered by 20–1, many died whether they had been involved or not, and when Dublin had been flattened the surrendered leaders were marched through the streets to secret military trials, followed by secret executions. One, James Connolly, so badly wounded in the Easter Uprising that he couldn't stand, was tied to a chair and shot dead, and 3,000 people were rounded up and held in British mainland prisons until the fear of a backlash and further unrest brought about their release.

'This is just what you said would happen,' Alice said to Liam as they read the newspapers in the office.

'It didn't take a genius to work out it was heading this way,' he replied grimly. 'I didn't think the British would react like this, though.'

'Why not?' Pat Murphy asked angrily. 'Don't they always?'

'But it says there are more than a thousand dead in Dublin,' Alice whispered, horrified. 'Why would they just shoot anybody they saw?'

'Because Ireland is a British colony, that's why. To them the Irish are no more human beings than the Indians in Delhi or Calcutta, they're not really citizens of a United Kingdom, they're rebellious natives who have to be taught who's master, that's how these people think,' Pat said bitterly, old resentments surfacing from past generations, resentments he carried in his blood and his heart.

'But it makes no sense, it can only lead to more unrest,' Liam said. 'The rebels hadn't a lot of support at the start, but I can see that they will have now.'

'Exactly,' Pat replied. 'You can never believe that our masters will do what they do, and yet they always do, history tells us that over and over again. No wonder the news from France is getting worse by the day while they go on about victory by next week. You can't help feeling that the world is slipping out of control, and all those tinpot Neros are fiddling away as it burns. Where the hell will it end?'

'I've never seen Pat that angry,' Alice said on the way home on the tram that evening. 'I mean, he's not even Irish, is he?'

Liam laughed. 'I wouldn't say that to him. At this moment he was born and bred there.'

The other side of Pat, though, was his love of company, and he and his wife had made their home the sumptuous Great Western Terrace, further along the road from Kew Terrace. It had been one of the last large designs by the renowned Glasgow architect Alexander Thomson, nicknamed 'Greek' for his love of the classical form, and it was probably the most prestigious address in the West End, an outward sign that the Murphys were people who had made it. There Pat delighted in throwing dinners and parties where he regaled everyone with wit, good humour and, as his wife wryly commented, far too much drink, and Liam and Alice were always welcome. He was a big man with steel grey eyes and a huge amount of completely white hair, while Molly, his long-suffering, adored and adoring wife, was tiny and dark. They had four children aged from ten years old to fourteen, the two boys being exactly like their father, and the two girls like their mother, but all of them had a freedom that Alice envied. In a good-natured way they asked forthright questions, said what they thought and formed their own opinions, and they had been brought up to regard this as completely normal. Unlike other children of the day, they were seen and heard, taking their place at the dinner table and in conversation with whatever adults Pat had brought home with him. There was nothing kept from the young Murphys, they discussed the events and people around them with confidence. When it had been explained to them that the reaction of the McInallys and McCanns had forced Alice and Liam to flee to Glasgow, it struck them as so peculiar that they laughed, and they did exactly the same when confronted with Glasgow prejudice, which Alice admired.

'They're so open,' she said to Molly.

'If that's a euphemism for far too full of themselves,' Molly muttered, 'I can see your point.'

'No, no,' Alice protested, 'I think they're wonderful, I really do.'

'It's Pat's fault,' Molly sighed. 'He insists they should know everything and speak up.'

'But don't you think he's right?'

'Well, yes and no.'

Alice laughed at her glum expression and Molly looked up and joined in.

'It's fine when they're at home or in the company of the kind of people Pat brings into our circle —' She looked at Alice and put a hand on her arm. 'Oh, I don't mean you, my dear,' she said, 'I mean he does attract such outspoken companions, doesn't he?'

'Even eccentric,' Alice suggested.

'Yes, exactly! But I worry that the children will grow up thinking everyone is like that, like them, if you see what I mean. It's all very well being opinionated, but they're like Pat, they don't see why their opinions shouldn't be aired, even among people who hold other opinions.'

Alice looked at her quizzically.

'Pat's brought them up to accept that other people will not always agree with them and that they shouldn't take any offence; in fact they find it as stimulating as he does to argue and debate, but they don't understand that other people will take offence at their opinions, that people outside their own circle aren't like them.'

'Ah.'

'Pat doesn't accept that there's any place for diplomacy, he just comes out with it.'

'I think he's wonderful, too,' Alice said staunchly.

'That's all he needs,' Molly replied mournfully, 'another admirer when he already admires himself far too much!'

And right on cue, Pat proved her point.

'You two,' he told Liam and Alice, glass in hand, 'are the future. The more who marry out of whatever faith they might be in, the better, as far as I'm concerned.'

'Pat, will you keep your voice down!' Molly complained, looking around their parlour for a spy in their midst. Unlike Pat, Molly had been brought up in Glasgow, and she instinctively understood undercurrents that passed Pat by completely.

'But it's true!' he said. 'It's the only way to sort this ridiculous situation out, to put everyone into the same melting pot so that one day no one will know or care what anyone else is.'

'We'll know when someone's drunk, though!' Molly said pointedly.

'I'm only saying –'

'Yes, we all know you're only saying, you're always only saying, Pat, and am I not always only saying back again that there are people who find your opinions offensive and perhaps even a bit scandalous?'

'In my own home? Who?' Pat demanded, spinning about. 'Where? I'll fight them all here and now!'

'You see?' Molly demanded of Alice.

Alice laughed, remembering Billy Guthrie at Brendon's wedding, wanting to fight purely from mindless prejudice, and here was this nice man wanting to fight anyone with prejudice.

A generation before, Pat Murphy's father had arrived in Dundee as manager of a Jute Mill, not as an impoverished immigrant but as a skilled worker recruited from Ireland, although the prejudices of the day made no distinction. It had always been Old Man Murphy's intention to return home, but he married the daughter of another comfortably off Irish immigrant and, again like immigrants the world over, they wanted their son Pat to have a good education. While studying Law at Glasgow University, Pat had met and married the Glaswegian Molly and moved to the city, though he found the bigotry deeper in Glasgow than in Dundee, and tiresome, so he retreated to the family's holiday home in Rothesay, the capital of the Isle of Bute, at the slightest opportunity, where, he said, religion didn't matter. Bute was a mere fifteen miles long and less than five miles wide, and only five hundred yards from mainland Scotland at its northern tip, but the fifty mile journey by sea from Glasgow made it feel like a world away. As was the tradition for well-off families, Molly and the Murphy children spent the summer months in Rothesay with as many relatives, usually the women of Molly's family, as wanted to accompany them. The entire household and servants decamped on the various steamers on the River Clyde, taking with them everything they might need, from cutlery and pots and pans to linen, being joined by Pat at the weekends. Being a sociable man, he usually brought a collection of friends with him, including, inevitably, Liam and Alice.

The large red sandstone house sat on a hill above the harbour, almost but not quite high or far enough away to be out of earshot of the comings and goings of the huge herring fishing fleet and the steamer on its regular visits. On one perfect Friday evening, Liam and Alice had joined Pat on the journey from Glasgow for the weekend. The July sun was dazzling but with a slight cooling breeze. A German band played on deck as the giant paddles rhythmically slapped the water, a sound that could be heard from miles away as the steamer approached Rothesay, bringing children running in welcome.

In the large garden of the Murphy house, facing the front, the sound of the accordions on board the steamer wafted gently up as the women and barefoot children sipped tea and lemonade, fighting drowsiness induced by a long day in the sun, the quietness and the buzzing of the bees among the flowers. The arrival of Pat always brought such reveries to an end, and the garden was suddenly empty of children as they ran to him, to be grilled on what they had been doing, why, when, and what they thought of the latest news from the Front, and did they believe anything the newspapers said, and if so, why, and if not, why not?

'Pat!' Molly said helplessly and hopelessly. 'Will you at least get in the door before you start on them? They are children, they are not lawyers. You're just this minute off the boat and they just want to hug you, you great oaf. Why do you insist on debating with them?'

'Because it is a useful skill. They are part of the world, after all, and the world is ruled by eejits!' Pat replied, grey eyes wide with innocence.

'But they are children, Pat, that is my point. Can't you just be their father and do fatherly things with them?'

'Like what?' he asked, confused.

'I don't know!' Molly shouted. 'Go for a walk, catch fish, feed the ducks? There will be time enough for them to be adults when it's their turn.'

'Explain that,' he said in his debating voice.

Molly turned to Alice. 'You see?' she demanded of her young guest. 'I urge you most earnestly, Alice, give up this mad idea, do not marry a lawyer!'

'Speaking of which,' Pat said brightly, 'when are you two planning to tie the knot?'

Alice and Liam looked at each other, and Molly slapped her husband on the arm. 'That is none of your business!' she said severely.

'Nonsense, of course it is! So when is it to be? If you don't want a church affair I'd be happy to have you declare yourselves married before me and the regulation two witnesses, won't even charge you the going rate! Trot off to the sheriff for a warrant, then see the registrar for the certificate, and you're all set. What the hell's stopping you?' He laughed loudly.

'Well, it's not really up to me,' Liam said gently. 'Alice is the one who has to name the day.'

'So what's up, Alice?' Pat beamed. 'Got cold feet?'

Molly put her hands over her face and shook her head. 'I give up! The man has no sense of civilised behaviour,' she said limply.

Alice felt the heat on her cheeks spreading all over her face and neck. She didn't welcome straight questions and so rarely got them. 'I'm probably being silly,' she whispered, 'but I'm hoping the families will come around.' She looked up. 'If we give them time, I mean.'

'No, you're not being silly,' Pat said reasonably, as though he had given the matter a great deal of careful consideration, 'you're being downright stupid. You can't keep this fine, healthy young man waiting for connubial bliss forever, it will rot his constitution, don't you know that?'

Molly sat down in her chair and closed her eyes.

'I mean, my dear girl,' Pat continued, 'you have to consider the war. It's coming closer and closer to everyone, every day. What if Liam has to go away?'

'Yes, that's what I was thinking,' Alice explained. 'Don't you see? The families will know this too. It's more likely that they'll think it through and come to the conclusion that the war has changed everything.' She looked from one face to another, desperately seeking agreement.

Molly leapt to her feet. 'Right, you've heard that, Pat Murphy, haven't you? You've intruded on the girl's privacy and instead of telling you off she's been courteous enough to give you an explanation. Let that be an end to it.'

Pat opened his mouth.

'Pat!' Molly shouted, and he closed it again.

Alice didn't know what she was thinking, not entirely, that was the truth of it, and it was partly the fault of the Murphy family. She had watched them, listened to the children, such young children, too, speaking their minds freely to their parents, heard them argue their corner as equals, all to Pat's delight. It felt so good be part of a family again, a different one from the one she had known, but it was a family, exactly the kind she wanted for herself and Liam. But she already had a family, and though she was hurt by their attitudes she still loved them, still felt part of them. Her cousin Maggie had been right: all that love, that history of belonging together, it couldn't just vanish as though it had never been, it must still exist, somewhere, all she had to do was find it again. Sometimes she convinced herself that she had fled from Belfast to give them time and space to reflect, with the hope that they would come to understand what was really important. Inside she still felt that their situation, with the shared history and closeness of their families, was different from Maggie and Tony's, that one day she and Liam would be welcomed by them again, if they only waited a little longer. She wanted them at their wedding, wanted them in their lives, in time to delight in the grandchildren she and Liam would give them, and she really believed that was what they would want, too. In time. She imagined Liam's parents sitting in Belfast, reading and hearing of the progress of the war in France and wondering if their eldest son would be sent there, then deciding that what divided them was nothing compared to the thought of him going off to fight without them having seen him again, touched him, wished him well. Any day now they could hear from their families, any day now.

At other times she felt just as strongly that they would never come round, that she and Liam would have to start a completely new family of their own, and so there was no reason not to marry whenever they felt like it. At those times, though, it was Liam who told her to wait, because that was what he knew she wanted to do, and he wanted her to be sure, because tying the knot with him meant severing another forever.

Liam sat in the garden in the late evening with Pat, watching the sun dip slightly as it does at the height of summer in that part of the world, darkness never quite taking over.

'I'm going to move here one day soon,' Pat smiled, a glass in his hand.

Liam laughed. 'You always say that.'

'Yes, but I mean it. I've been thinking it through so that I can counter Molly's objections.'

'You think she'll object?'

'Bound to, laddie,' Pat grinned. 'She's a woman, she does it on principle if nothing else, always has. She says she wants to wait till the children have finished school and are at university at least, but I can't see that they would suffer from going to school here, with all this freedom and good air.'

'But the house in Glasgow, would you give that up?' Liam asked dubiously. 'Would Molly?'

'Oh, I would,' he smiled gently. 'For me it's just a symbol of what I've achieved, but Molly? I don't know. It is beautiful and all that, but more and more I feel constrained by that existence. Do you know what I mean?'

Liam nodded.

'I can do the odd day in the office if I have to, without actually having to stay in Glasgow, semi-retire, that sort of thing, and I have a few investments, we won't starve. Why spend your life in the city doing what you don't want, when you could have this all year round?'

'But you like the law.'

'Yes, I do, I enjoy it, but less than I did in the early days, Liam. I've done it, if you see what I mean.'

Liam nodded but said nothing. Once again he did see what Pat meant, for he'd been thinking similar thoughts himself recently. His visits here had awakened thoughts of Lough Neagh in him. The feeling wasn't quite the same, but near enough. The pace of life, the way of life, with the fishing and the boats – though unlike the Lough Neagh Fly, the dreaded West Coast midge bit and was a constant nuisance, but he could get used to that, he decided. He almost felt he knew the fishermen as he walked along the harbour, the boats in such numbers that he could've walked across them from deck to deck. Watching boats being built on the island Liam had ached to get his hands on the tools and the wood. It was almost like coming home. And Alice had said it would be nice to have a place of their own on Bute, a tiny place, of course, where they could bring their family one day on holiday. And that thought branched off into other ideas in his mind. When they married he would have his grandfather's money and he was already earning well at Pat's office, so why couldn't he set up his own boat-building yard on the island? He wouldn't be building huge craft or in great numbers, that wasn't what he wanted to do, he wanted to build a few boats really well, to be a craftsman working with his hands. In time, of course, not right away, there was the war first, and he couldn't see any way out of joining up. As an Irishman he wouldn't be called up, but he had left Ireland and had no intention, no prospect of ever returning, and he had come to Scotland, so in his mind it wasn't right that he should play the Irish card to keep out of the fighting. He knew he couldn't stand by and watch more and more men he had come to know in his adopted country disappear in uniform, it made him feel a fraud, if not a coward. After that he could do what he had always wanted to do, build boats. He knew how to do it, old Jimmy Devlin had taught him the skills, skills Pat Murphy didn't have, so he could earn his living here without even spending another day in the city. He had tried the law and he didn't hate it or anything, he explained to Alice, just as he didn't hate Glasgow, but like Pat he found the religious thing irritating and, as Pat said, the island was free of that.

So they found a cottage in Port Bannatyne, a sheltered part of the island that would be ideal for his boat-building business. The water was shallow and there might be a struggle launching a new boat in a north-easterly, but the predominant wind direction was westerly, so that wouldn't be much of a worry. The cottage needed some work, but that was fine, they could do that, and it faced the sea, so that you could hear the waves lapping the shore. Alice looked at him, his eyes shining, his voice full of a boyish enthusiasm she hadn't heard in a long time, and now that he had a second chance she knew she couldn't deny him the dream his father had stolen from him all those years ago. Besides, there was another factor that she understood probably better than Liam did: he was setting up his return route from the war, his insurance of a life ready and waiting for him. They both knew he would have to go to France: the politicians had lied to everyone once again, the 'home by Christmas' promise was either a lie or the product of deluded minds, either way ordinary people were caught in the middle.

They had been in Glasgow for over a year, and now she gave up hope of the families changing their attitudes. Time was running out with the war coming closer, so she decided that she would marry Liam anywhere, anyhow. If he had something to come back for, his life with Alice and the dream he thought was lost forever, well then, he had to come back, didn't he? It made sense, didn't it?

Then a letter arrived from Louise with disquieting news. She had written to tell Alice that Bella and Billy Guthrie had been married.

'"*It was a quiet ceremony,*"' Alice read out in the Kew Terrace parlour. '"*I suspect the family didn't want to celebrate too much, given what you two criminals had done, but on the other hand I think they felt family honour had been upheld. Billy Guthrie to the rescue once again, odious creature, he gave them an entirely Protestant union, proving they could get it right after all. My mother enjoyed herself hugely, making sure that you and Liam were the spectres at the feast, never missing a chance, especially when things were looking happier, to voice heartfelt regrets that 'others' hadn't behaved as impeccably as dear Bella and Billy. It's true what they say, you know, revenge is a dish better eaten cold. My mother has waited years for her opportunity and she's gorging on it. Bella is now a great favourite, you must understand, as I was for a time after Maggie's betrayal.*

'"*Aunt Victoria bore it with great restraint, I must say: if I'd been her I'd have punched my dear mother squarely on the nose, but she was probably struggling to maintain some dignity, given that the McCanns had declined their invitation to attend. I don't think there's a rift, in fact they sent a very nice gift and Aunt Victoria seemed relieved they hadn't come. I'd imagine they just thought it would have been too difficult. After all, they would've had to indulge in the usual 'who's next' marriage game, and in the circumstances who could they possibly have lined up?*"'

'Still,' Liam said comfortingly, 'who knows? Maybe they'll suit each other. I mean, we're in no position to say anything, are we, even if we disapprove.'

'Do we disapprove?' Maggie asked quietly.

'Oh, I don't disapprove so much as have reservations,' Alice sighed. 'But even if I had disapproved, I wouldn't have thrown them out of my life.'

'Yes, that is the point, Alice, I do agree,' Maggie smiled. 'Let's just hope that they've found true love.'

'But she is so stupid, and he's so clever.'

'Alice!' Maggie said, laughing. 'You really must stop saying that!'

'I'm sorry, but it's true! He really is very clever, and she really is very stupid. I remember being amazed at how long it took her to read and write. She was still asking me to tell her words in magazines when she was in her teens, and she's never had a thought of her own, she just said the same as the last person she talked to. My mother used to say Bella's role in life would be as a housewife – at least she taught her to cook and clean, but that was all Bella learned.'

'So what is the attraction, do you think?'

'Well, I've given that a lot of thought,' Alice replied. 'Billy Guthrie has no family of his own and he desperately wanted to be part of the McInallys, and there was no one left except Bella. Plus, Bella is very beautiful, she truly is, like a porcelain doll, and she is a blank canvas.'

'So he won't face much opposition in their household,' Maggie agreed. 'I can see how that might work out. But if he's as bright as you say, might he not find her boring after a while? After all, beauty doesn't last forever.'

'Yes, well, that's the worry,' Alice said thoughtfully.

Maggie watched the two young people. She did a lot of that. Part of never having the houseful of children she and Tony had planned meant having a great deal of time on her hands, time not taken up by family. There were no nieces and nephews, no cousins, no one except Louise, George and their daughter at a distance, and now her young cousin Alice. Maggie filled her life up with good works, with being seen to be dependable and respectable as well as a model wife, and, perhaps because she knew from experience that even the most normal, perfect life could hide a great deal, she watched people. She didn't know what to make of Alice and Liam; that was the truth of it.

'What do you make of them?' she asked her husband later.

Tony glanced up from the business section of his newspaper. 'Maggie, I don't make anything of them,' he replied.

'But they seem so, I don't know,' she said in an exasperated voice.

'Not quite what love's young dream should be like?' he laughed.

'Well, yes!'

'Maggie, leave them alone and give yourself peace,' Tony sighed. 'You have no idea what they feel, what they're like when they're alone, and you have no right to know either.'

'That's a bit unfair,' she replied, hurt. 'I worry about them, that's all. What if they've made a mistake, what if they've cut themselves off from their families on a whim?'

Tony put his newspaper down and looked at her. 'Is that what you think you did, Maggie?' he asked softly. 'Are you afraid they've made the same mistake as you did?'

Maggie stared at him. 'I wasn't aware of having made a mistake,' she said coldly, 'until now, perhaps.'

Tony laughed. 'You see? You accuse Louise of playing every scene for dramatic value, but you do it yourself! You want the heaving bosom, the sobbing and the agony of it all, and if it isn't paraded for you, you have to introduce a bit of drama. Hasn't it occurred to you that Alice and Liam are keeping a tight rein on themselves because they know they have to?'

Her severe expression changed instantly. 'Is that what you think they're doing?' she said brightly.

'I don't know, Maggie,' Tony said, 'maybe. On the other hand perhaps they don't have your family's dramatic bent, or it could be that they just keep their emotions to themselves. There's no law against it, you know.' He picked up his newspaper again and Maggie sat in silence at the other side of the fireside.

'You may be right,' she said eventually, 'but don't think I'll ever quite get over the fact that you accused me of being like Louise!'

Tony smiled but made no reply. It was his fault, he knew that. If he had given Maggie children she wouldn't go about the world trying to save waifs and strays and determinedly mothering Alice and Liam. They had a fine lifestyle, a grand house, respectability and financial security, and he had worked hard to give her those. As part of the bargain she had lost her family and he hadn't been able to give her another, the one thing she wanted, needed, most.

The truth was, as others had noticed before, that there were no high emotions in the two young people, no emotional displays of any kind. Despite what Tony had said, to Maggie they didn't seem like a couple deeply in love, and she knew what that felt like, so it made her wonder sometimes if the families' extreme opposition had created a problem that would have solved itself in time. They were quiet and companionable and kept themselves to themselves, though they were perfectly sociable and friendly. Alice was a difficult one to work out. She didn't say much, never discussed her feelings or her plans, and when asked outright parried the question to the point of almost clamming up. And now they were talking about living on Bute, in a tiny cottage by all accounts, and in a perfectly ordinary manner, as though it were the most normal thing in the world – just dropped it into the conversation in passing and moved on to something else. Liam would give up his profession as a lawyer, guaranteed to provide well for them, provide very well, and together they would go off to some tiny island and he would build boats for a living. The thing made no sense, in fact it was quite ludicrous. Still. Say nothing and it might never come about; for all she knew they were simply daydreaming aloud. Nothing to be gained from trying to talk sense to them both, especially when she didn't know what to make of them. She wouldn't make the same mistake as the families had.

The house at Port Bannatyne was a traditional whitewashed cottage and it reminded them both of the Lough.

'Nancy O'Neill's,' Liam smiled, looking at Alice to see if she remembered.

'Yes,' she said softly.

Nancy O'Neill's was the name given to the whitewashed gable of a cottage at Anneetermore on the Lough by local fishermen. No matter how bad the weather or how rough the water, when they saw it they knew exactly where they were, it made them feel safe. And that was what the cottage on Bute did, it made Liam and Alice feel safe, as though they had come home. Sitting high over the sea and the bay in its own six acres of land, it hadn't been lived in for some time and would need a lot of work, but it could be a very comfortable home one day. There was a space at the side, part of the house, but intended for a cart to be kept; upstairs were three bedrooms, plenty of room for their future children, and a walled and gated garden for them to play in. They would raise an island family of bright, noisy, happy and free children there, they decided, and Liam would build boats, as he had always dreamed of doing. Their future was opening up in front of them.

They worked on it together at weekends, but returned to Pat Murphy's home in Rothesay each evening for the sake of decency. For the first time in many years the cottage was given a fresh coat of whitewash, applied with a floor brush and speckling both of them all over, and the roof tiles and guttering were repaired and renewed, so that it would be weatherproof, the inside being of less importance in the short term. The windows and doors were painted around in bright red paint.

And that's when it struck, as fate has a habit of doing: the war finally intervened. Like other young couples with their futures spreading out before them, they had hoped the war would soon be over, so Liam had delayed joining up, thinking that with any luck he wouldn't have to. But in early 1917 he enlisted as a captain in the Cameronians. Alice had known he was planning to enlist, but it still came as a shock when he did. It brought the fighting from the front pages of the papers to right there between them.

'So we'll get married before you go,' she said quietly.

'No, of course we won't,' Liam replied.

She was shocked. 'Why not?' she asked, twisting the blue-stoned ring on her finger. 'Don't you want to?'

'Now that's a silly question,' he said, 'and you know better. We'll get married when the war is over, Alice. Thinking about you will be bad enough, but if there were anyone else to worry about . . .'

'You don't have to worry about me,' she protested.

'But you and someone else . . .?' he asked gently.

'Ah,' she said.

They had never needed many words, it was their way, and she understood. He would have enough to think about without worrying about leaving a child behind. He could have joined an Irish regiment, but this was a commitment to his new country, to where he planned to put down roots and raise his children, and so it was a Scottish regiment with links to the West End of Glasgow. Their cottage would have to wait, but it would wait, it would be there when he came home, with Alice continuing the gradual, albeit slower transformation while he was gone.

To Alice and Liam being separated was a tragedy, but it was the same tragedy other young couples were enduring at the time; it was a way of life they had to become used to. And it would soon be over. They had been hearing that since 1915 but they had to keep believing that it couldn't last forever, it would end sometime. Sometime soon.

Strange, ironic, cruel even, that they should already have gone through so much, left behind so much to start a new life together, and suddenly they were apart. Worse, Liam's brother Brendon and her own brother Harry were exempt from the call-up because they were Irish, but as they were involved in food production they were doubly excused from going to war. If Liam had joined the family business, he too would have remained safely at home. Instead he was being sent overseas to fight.

7

When Liam arrived in France he found men who had lived in the carnage for three years before him. Winning the war and going home as triumphant heroes was no longer in their minds; their entire existence had become distilled into staying alive for one more hour or one more day, few could see beyond that. Liam was quickly diverted to the Third Battle of Ypres, which had started on the last day of July 1917, thrown in the deep end in the battle that would be seared into history as the horror called Passchendaele. He had no idea what he was doing, yet he was supposed to lead men who had been fighting longer than him. They crept forward, from Boesinghe in the north to Le Ghee in the south, and, quickly advancing, the greener among them, those like Liam, were lulled into thinking they were winning by the Germans, who put a weaker defence first then backed it up with a heavier one further on, which pushed them back about a mile. Then their real enemy descended, the worst weather in seventy-five years, turning the whole area into liquid mud and stalling the attack until the tenth of August. Men died in the mud, not from bullets but from drowning, and it was estimated that the battle cost the Germans 260,000 casualties and the Allies lost thirty men for every yard gained,

300,000 in all. Many of them died in the mud and were never found, but their comrades would come across them sometimes, their limbs sticking out the ground like grim signposts of what awaited them.

By the time the battle was over in November, Liam felt like a veteran, permanently scared like all the rest. He was sent to life in the trenches, which consisted of long periods of inactivity punctuated by shorter periods of frantic action, making no sense to anyone on either side. Sometimes they were replaced at the front line by other regiments so that they could go back to safer areas to rest, bathe and train, but it didn't matter how far away they were, they knew they had to return to the trenches. One of Liam's first actions began one morning at 8.15, with a raid on nearby enemy trenches. His heart was beating so fast and loud that he could barely hear any other sound and, strangely, he felt more alive as he waited to be killed than he had ever felt in his entire twenty-seven years. His company bombed several German dugouts, set one on fire and captured one machine gun, but there were no prisoners to round up because no one was there. This was followed up by another raid, backed up with artillery and mortar fire, where they captured a Lewis Gun and some rifles and thought there would at least be German bodies lying in No Man's Land afterwards, but there were none.

As was the pattern, more cold, uncomfortable days in the trenches followed, with no one on either side doing anything very much, and you soon learned to keep your head below the parapet of the trench or you would be easily picked off by a bored German with nothing better to do than take pot-shots. Then they were given something to do, another attack that advanced them three hundred yards. They logged up the usual meagre list of equipment and enemy captured, but it lost them five men and wounded thirteen more. No one advanced huge amounts: yards were considered victories, by the military hierarchy at any rate, from their positions well behind the fighting. On one attack the soldiers were required to advance for thirty-five minutes without any supporting artillery and mortar fire, walking undefended straight into heavy German artillery and machine-gun fire. The raid was judged a failure and casualties were high, but they ended up one hundred and fifty yards from their original line.

Part of the problem, one that would last till the very end, was the poor training of new arrivals who didn't know who their officers were; and new officers, like Liam, who didn't know their men. At one point the Cameronians and the Black Watch were ordered to advance on German lines in poor light in the early hours of the morning, with visibility of about fifteen yards. At two hundred yards Liam's company lost direction, heading south-east instead of east, and to add to the difficulties the equally handicapped Black Watch moved off course to the north-east, so that the two companies became hopelessly intermingled and their commanders had no hope of controlling them. They were then annihilated – that was the only description Liam could think of, because it was the truth. And for what? If he had been able to see any sense in this war when he first joined up, it quickly evaporated in the reality, as it did for all the men. They were there to die.

He kept all of this from Alice, as was the way of the men of World War One. The last thing they needed was for the wonderfully mundane news of home and messages of enduring love that kept their souls alive to be replaced with as much anxiety and fear as they felt themselves. The norm, if anyone asked, was to simply reply that the war was composed of a lot of drilling, a lot of boredom and a lot of fighting.

For Alice, waiting became a way of life. Before Liam left she would have married him – had desperately wanted to in any way that it could be accomplished – but this time he had been the one against it. She was right, he told her, the families would come round, especially now. When he came home from the war they would be so relieved and happy that they would not only agree to the marriage, they would attend it, and their mothers would sit together, matchmaking as usual. That's what he told her, but in reality he was saving her from being a young war widow, should the worst come to the worst, and from perhaps having to rear a child on her own. If he didn't come back, he didn't want Alice to live for the rest of her life with the image of her first true love so freshly and deeply etched in her mind that she might never consider another man. He wanted Alice to have a life without him, if it came to that.

When he had gone, Alice wrote to Louise in Belfast, asking her to visit Liam's brother Brendon and pass on a letter from her. In it she told Brendon that Liam had gone overseas and she included the address Liam had left with her. And as Liam didn't know she was doing this, she wrote, if Brendon wanted no contact with his brother then all he had to do was ignore her letter. Liam would never find out from her. Not that she expected anything to happen to Liam, of course, she didn't, she simply couldn't have countenanced such a thing; rather it was an attempt to reach out to his family. For later, when Liam came home. She had been making compromises with herself, making the best of what she had, and hoped they would do the same. Given a choice, it would be better if the attitude of the McCanns softened, she decided, because the truth was that her family, being slightly in awe of their friends, would follow their lead. There was no way, she thought, of the McInallys remaining hostile to them if the McCanns welcomed them, and there was more chance of that happening if they knew their son was in danger.

However, even if her family never did accept them, she would settle for what Maggie had done, marrying Liam in a Catholic church and agreeing to their children being raised as Catholics. Peace with both sides of the family would be ideal, but if peace with one was all that was on offer then so be it: they had to work with the cards they were dealt, after all.

Louise wrote back that she had maintained her secrecy by paying another boy sixpence for delivering Alice's letter. '"*It may have been the same boy, for all I know,*"' she wrote, '"*you know that age when they all look the same? Ten? Eleven? No matter, I may well be providing some boy with a living delivering letters, so I'm being a benefactor rather than a coward. I just feel the longer I can stay incognito the better; the moment they all know we are in touch I'll be frozen out of all the news, and that would be a great hardship, I do so enjoy their nonsense.*"'

There was no good news from Ireland: the religious and political tensions were increasing by the day. '"*This is not a nice place to live nowadays,*"' Louise wrote. '"*There is a feeling of doom everywhere.*"' And the families were as they had been, except for one thing. '"*I don't know how you'll take this,*"' Louise said, '"*I have my own suspicions, but Bella and Billy Guthrie have moved in with your mother and father. Yes, yes, I can see the sense in it, a young, newly married couple trying to make their way, and Uncle Henry and Aunt Victoria all alone in that big house, that very fine big house — but I don't like him, that's the bottom line, Alice. Getting his feet firmly under the table, that's what I think Mr Guthrie is about.*"'

Alice put the letter down and thought. Louise was probably right. Until he found the McInallys Billy had been alone. He had told her his mother had died years earlier and he had been raised by his widowed grandmother, who was also dead. She

137

had always thought he had been attracted to her family because he didn't have one, and, in time, the house would have to go to someone. Harry had his own home with Mattie, and Alice was no longer part of the family, so why shouldn't Bella have it, she thought? She knew where everything was, she had learned to run it from her earliest years, so it was as well going to Bella as anyone else. And if Billy Guthrie got it too, well, that would annoy no one but Louise. Then Alice put it out of her mind. She was tired of thinking about it, she other things to worry about now.

Two weeks later she had a letter from Brendon McCann in reply to hers. He was glad she had written, he said, and of course he would write to his brother, he was grateful that she had given him this opportunity. He hadn't known where they were, he said. After asking him to forward the very first letter from Liam to his parents when they had left Belfast, there had been no further word, so he had assumed that was how they wanted it. He hadn't told her brother Harry that he now knew where she was, and unless she wrote to him asking him to do so, he wouldn't. The position the families had taken, he reported, was unchanged. He apologised for dashing any hopes she might have had, but he hoped she was well and that in time they could meet again.

Alice decided against asking him to tell her brother where she was. Brendon McCann had no reason to suspect she and Liam were with Maggie and Tony, but as far as she was concerned Harry could have worked it out for himself. The fact that he had not was a matter of choice. She could imagine him not wanting to rock his own boat, and she was content to leave it at that. If there was one thing you could be sure about with Harry, it was that he always did what was expected of him.

8

For Alice, Liam's departure had brought a sudden rush of loneliness, coldness, and constant waiting that she knew she had to
get used to, but never did. Even though there were other people
around and with her, she existed in some other world. When
Liam left she went to work every day and came home to Maggie
and her grand house every evening. Her cousin, being especially kind and sensitive, tried to include her in her social whirl
even more – dinners for Tony's business partners, drinks with
clients, soirees for all sorts of occasions – and though she dressed
up and attended and made polite conversation, she was never
really there. It was as though she had two parallel existences,
the one where she worked in an office and lived with her
wealthy cousin in a pleasant world full of pleasant people engaged
in pleasant social chit-chit, and the other one, the real one, where
there was just waiting for Liam. Everything was secondary to
when the next letter might arrive, the worry when none did,
then, when three arrived at once, the reply written and posted
immediately, and the awful, aching void between. Thinking about
how long it might take to actually see him again was so hard,
so painful, that it had to be resisted. All she could think about
while going through the motions of supposedly normal everyday

life was that the day of his homecoming was one day nearer. And the house at Port Bannatyne kept her busy, even if every second she was there she missed him more than ever. The refurbishment continued, furniture was bought, a home was created for Liam's return. It felt slightly haunted, a home without life, without a family, as perfect as she could make it, but empty. Waiting for life to begin, just like her.

She tried to keep it in perspective – after all, she was hardly alone in this situation, but there was something about your menfolk marching off to war that tore your heart out. It was more than fear – that was perfectly understandable – it was something to do with the lack of control, the inability to state your case and register your disapproval, she thought. You wanted to say, 'Wait a minute, you can't do that!' but you couldn't, of course, who was there to listen? Pat Murphy used to call those who ruled and governed them 'eejits', and he had been right, and now the man she loved, who was part of the fabric of her being, had been sent to fight at their behest.

In April 1918 Captain Liam McCann was granted a week's leave before yet another big push. He didn't know for sure till the last minute, so he hadn't told Alice in case it didn't happen after all. He had changed in his year as a soldier, which was hardly surprising – none of them came back the same men who had left home so hopefully. In the long, boring days between acts of horrendous and pointless horror in the trenches he had had a lot of time to think. Before he'd left Glasgow he had done the honourable thing by refusing to marry Alice, but all that had changed. There was no honour left anywhere. At the best of times, when there was no war, men inhabited a brutal world compared to women. He had always known that. Women softened life, made it sociable and civilised, but now, in this mud-soaked, never-ending, bloody existence, with the constant stench of fear and death, he yearned for the company of females. Not the prostitutes who operated behind the lines when the men were resting, but a normal woman, someone soft, someone who smiled and talked kindly to him. He longed to feel gentle arms around him, to relax in a tender embrace. He longed for Alice. Arriving at Kew Terrace in early morning, he hadn't wanted to waken the household so he had come through the servant's entrance at the back and lain down on the couch in the front parlour. One of the maids found him there and crept into Maggie's bedroom to tell her there was a soldier, young Mr McCann, she thought, asleep downstairs, and after a quick look Maggie decided to let Alice discover him for herself.

Alice was on her way down to breakfast, a full day at the office in front of her, hoping a letter from Liam might be waiting for her, when she saw him. She stood still for a long time, watching him, sure she must be dreaming, and, if she was, afraid to awaken and touch him in case he disappeared in a puff of smoke. He looked older, she thought, tears running down her cheeks, older than the year since she had last seen him, but he was alive, he was home. Then he opened his eyes and she ran to the couch, pinning him there, her arms around his neck. If this was a dream she would hold on to it forever, no waking consciousness would take it away from her, and Liam lay there, basking in the softness that had been occupying his mind for months, home at last.

By the time Maggie joined the scene all emotions had been contained, indeed it didn't look to her as though there had been any. They would be leaving almost immediately for Bute, they informed Maggie. Alice had already been on the phone to Pat Murphy, who had told her to take whatever time off work she wanted. There was no discussion, it was simply what they intended doing, once Liam had had a bath, something to eat, and changed into civilian clothes. Maggie decided to say nothing until Liam had left them, then she tried to talk to Alice.

'But you don't want to miss Louise, dear,' she suggested with a smile. 'She and George will be here with the baby later today.'

Alice shrugged. 'They'll still be here at the weekend,' she replied, puzzled.

'Yes, but we haven't seen them in such a long time, I was hoping for a real family get-together.'

Alice looked blankly at her. 'Maggie, I haven't seen Liam for a very long time,' she stated simply.

Maggie glanced about, desperately searching for a way of putting her concerns into words.

'The thing is, Alice,' she said quietly, 'the Murphys won't be in Rothesay until the weekend, am I correct?'

Alice nodded, her mind straying from the conversation that, for some reason, seemed seriously important to Maggie.

'Well, what I mean is, dear, that you and Liam will be at the cottage in Port Bannatyne during the day, but you won't have the Murphys to return to in the evenings.'

Alice stared at her.

'I mean,' Maggie said pointedly, 'overnight.'

'We'll be staying at our cottage overnight,' Alice said simply. 'For a week?'

'Well, for five days. Liam has to go back on Friday.'

'But, dear,' Maggie said sweetly, 'do you think that's wise?'

'Going back on Friday? He hasn't any choice!'

'No, dear,' Maggie said carefully. 'I wonder if it's wise for you both to stay at the cottage.'

'In what sense?' Alice asked.

'Well, you must understand what I'm trying to say.' Maggie gave a little embarrassed laugh to cover her annoyance; it was obvious that Alice understood exactly what she was saying. 'Alice, I'm only trying to look after you.'

'Oh, Maggie, that's very kind of you, but honestly, you don't have to, I'm a big girl now,' Alice smiled back at her. She got up to leave the room and Maggie rose and caught her by both forearms and looked her in the eye.

'Alice, you do know that you have to be very careful of your reputation, don't you?' she asked softly but firmly.

There was a slight but definite shrugging movement as Alice freed herself, so slight that it was almost more of an atmosphere than a movement, and Maggie felt a shutter come down. It was for all the world as though Alice had actually said 'This far and no further.'

'Maggie,' she smiled, 'please don't worry about me, about us. I know you only do so out of kindness, but you don't have to, you know, you really don't.'

There it was again, that strange something about the girl, that part of her you couldn't reach because she stopped you, so that you never knew for sure what she was thinking or what she might do.

Maggie decided to persist. 'Perhaps Tony and I should come with you,' she suggested, 'just in case.'

Alice stopped at the door for a second, then turned round to face her. 'That' she said coldly 'is out of the question, Maggie. We wouldn't put you to that trouble, but thank you anyway.' She stared at Maggie, almost daring her to reply, until Maggie dropped her eyes. Then Alice turned and left the room.

Maggie had never known anyone like her. Her younger cousin could be incredibly sweet but there was a containment about her that Maggie had never met before. Louise had a very independent mind, but Louise gave you an argument when you disagreed with her. Alice, though, drew a line in the sand and ever so politely refused to let you step over it. There was never any discussion, calm or heated, about anything: when the girl made up her mind she did so once and for all, and, what was more, she seemed to see no point in explaining her decisions or her thoughts.

'I do worry about her,' Maggie told Louise later at dinner.

'Well don't,' Louise replied blandly.

'That's what I say,' Tony murmured.

'Do you think the families in Belfast know how things stand?' she asked Louise.

'Well, I speak to Brendon occasionally, and the grapevine has worked well. They know Alice and Liam aren't married, though they pretend not to care. Brendon says they all expected they would be by now, but they have their reasons, I suppose.'

'Alice was hoping they'd come round,' Tony said sadly.

'And you didn't tell them that wouldn't happen?'

'You know Alice.' Maggie returned to her theme again. 'No one tells her anything. That's why I worry about her, as I said.'

Louise, who didn't believe in nannies and nurseries and was struggling with her daughter on her knee, thrust the child at Maggie. 'Here, worry about Tallulah for a while instead,' she said. 'I'm pretty sure she's well on the way to being a reprobate.'

'Louise! How can you say such things about your own child?' Maggie's eyes softened looking at the baby. 'And she's so beautiful!' she cooed. 'How could you possibly be her mother?' she shot at her sister.

'That's what I ask every day,' George said. 'Emma-Tallulah is the sweetest thing I've ever seen.'

144

'You may just be biased,' Louise replied. 'Anyway, I'll soon knock the sweetness out of her, sweetness doesn't get you anywhere in life.'

'Now how would you know that?' Maggie demanded, and the others laughed. She looked at her sister's latest creation, a long, flowing gown in dark green crushed velvet and of no discernable shape. 'And I see your abysmal dress-sense hasn't made any concessions to motherhood. What it must do to this poor babe's mind to be surrounded by such garish colours, well, I just don't know!'

'No, you don't,' Louise said lazily, 'but then you never did, Maggie.' She sat up in her chair and glared at Maggie's waist. 'Do my eyes deceive me, or are you still wearing corsets?' she demanded loudly.

'Louise, really!'

'Yes, really! You are, aren't you?' She turned to Tony. 'Is this your doing?' she asked severely. 'Do you believe any woman should have that shape?'

Tony, who had been used as a pawn in similar sisterly discussions many times, continued with his meal without replying.

'My God, man, tell her to let her body go free, she'll never do it of her own accord, she hasn't the intelligence!'

'Louise, I don't know why you insist on being so unpleasant!' Maggie exclaimed, turning the child away from her mother as though to protect her. 'How this child will grow up properly with you as her mother, I just can't imagine!'

'She'll grow up a savage, Maggie,' Louise smiled. 'Her mind won't be restricted by your manners and conventions, that's for sure.' She leaned forward and poked Maggie sharply in the ribs. 'And her body won't be restricted by torture garments like yours either!'

'Seems to me, Louise, dear,' Maggie complained, 'that a bit of restriction at some point in your life might well have done you the world of good!'

The ploy had worked. Maggie was no longer fretting over Alice and Liam.

It was bright and clear on the crossing over to Bute, and they journeyed from Rothesay to Port Bannatyne on 'the toast rack', a local single-decker tram with no sides and no roof, only rows of seats on a platform with wheels. Then they were at their cottage, transformed since Liam had last seen it. It was now a home, she thought, because he was there.

He looked above the front door to the nameplate she had put there: 'Anneetermore'. She hadn't told him about it, wanting it to be a surprise, and he smiled and hugged her. She took his camera to take a picture of him under the sign and watched him as he stood just inside the door, taking in the place where their future lay, knowing how often he must have pictured it in his mind during the fighting of the last year. There was a vulnerability about him that almost made her cry out, as he walked about the cottage, touching the fireplace, the stairs, looking through the rooms.

'We have furniture,' he laughed. 'It's really a house.'

She smiled.

He looked out of the window. 'A bit too soon for your bluebells,' he smiled.

'Yes, but we know they're there.'

She let him walk about, reacquainting himself with the place, with their life together, then he pulled off his coat and lit the fire, and they sat down on the couch, watching the flames.

'I have things to tell you,' she said.

He looked at her, waiting.

'First of all, I have decided I want us to get married as soon as possible, before you go back if we can. I know why you said we should wait, but none of that matters any longer, not your reasons, not mine. I'd happily get married in a Catholic church if it would appease your family, but if it won't we can do as Pat is always saying we should, marry before him.'

She had expected an argument, but either he agreed or he was too weary. He took her hand. 'We can't get married in a Catholic church before I go back,' he said, 'there just isn't time. Besides, I wouldn't want to get married in a Catholic church.'

She opened her mouth to explain to him that this was part of her plan to at least get his family on their side but, mis-understanding, he stopped her. 'I've had a lot of time to think about this, Alice,' he said. 'I haven't had anything to do with the church since we left Belfast. Tony asked me once if I'd like to go with him to Mass and I said no thanks.'

'I didn't know that,' she said quietly, though she did know he had never gone in Glasgow.

'It wasn't because of you, truly. I was raised as a Catholic because that was what my parents believed, but I'm an adult now, I can make up my own mind. The way I see it, I had no choice about carrying my father's name, but I do have a choice over whether I carry his religion, and who I marry. Besides,' he said sadly, 'some of the things I've seen . . . as far as I'm concerned religion isn't something I care for.'

'I see.' She was relieved. It wasn't about her, then. She had lost him his family, she didn't want to lose him his religion, too, but Liam's feelings went deeper than that.

'I watch them blessing the men before they go into battle to commit bloody murder on people they don't know and have no grudge against, and I know that on the other side there is another holy man doing exactly the same for the Germans.'

He stopped for a moment. 'Anyway,' he said brightly, 'this is Monday, I leave again on Friday, so if you're sure we'll call in at the office on Friday afternoon and Pat can do those "honours" he keeps nagging us about. He'll see it as winning a long campaign, won't he?'

'Which means,' she said, taking a deep breath, 'that this is our honeymoon.'

'You mean . . .?'

'Here we are, Liam, in our own home. What does it matter if we have our honeymoon five days early?'

It was a magical time, that's how she would look back on those five days, a time when every thought and feeling seemed to be intensified, almost as though she was storing them up. But there was something about his eyes that bothered her. If someone had asked her to describe the new expression that lay there, she couldn't have done so. She couldn't describe it even to herself because it changed so rapidly. It was like standing on Shaw's Bridge in spring, with the sun out again after a heavy cloudburst. You would look down on the Minnow Burn as it raced towards the river, trying to keep track of the dancing rivulets of water, first bright, then dark, then bright again, changing so quickly that you couldn't keep up, no matter how hard you tried. That's how his eyes were, a mixture of expressions, of weariness, hurt, fear, bewilderment, anger, and a preoccupation that you couldn't quite get through. And in the night she would waken to find him struggling and calling out as he lay beside her, and when she woke him he would stare at her in terror for a few seconds, like a trapped animal, before remembering where he was and smiling again, becoming Liam again, though not quite. She understood, of course: a few days before he was fighting in a war, and in a few days more he would be back there again, but even as she tried to rationalise the change in him it chilled her to the bone.

Later she would wonder if Maggie's well-intentioned interference and concern for her reputation had put the idea of them sleeping together into her head out of sheer defiance, but she knew that wasn't fair. She had never been like that, never would be; she made her own decisions. The idea had been there and Maggie had simply given it a push. What her cousin hadn't realised was that Alice was no longer the blushing girl who had arrived on her doorstep three years before – the war had changed everyone it touched, and not only those who fired a gun. What there was between her and Liam was deeper and more urgent than before, as other young people were finding the world over at that time. The imminence of death put the niceties of polite society and the accepted morals of the day firmly in perspective and showed them to be of less importance than living for the moment. So they spent their few precious days in each other's arms, wondering how they could ever be apart again but knowing that they must be, and the inevitability of it added to the intensity of the experience, made it more complete.

They walked along the shore and he pointed out the spot where he planned to build his boatyard, and they chose names for the children they would one day have and take for walks in the very footsteps they were creating at that moment. One day, they said, laughing, they would tell their sons and daughters of another day in the past, long before they were born, when they had decided to bring them on this very walk, on this very shore, and their sons and daughters would shake their heads in despair, as children do at such tales, at how boring their parents were.

Then it was time to go. They arrived back in Glasgow in the early afternoon, stopped to buy a gold ring on the way to Pat's office, then presented themselves without warning, to surprise him. Only he wasn't there. They hadn't thought of what else was happening in the world, there was only themselves and their world and the five days they had together; they hadn't thought of the calendar beyond Liam's leaving again. But in Glasgow they discovered it wasn't just any Friday, it was Good Friday. It was Easter weekend, and Pat had already left on the boat for Rothesay at midday, half a day earlier than usual, but there were still a few of the lower minions around. One of the younger lawyers was still in the office, so he had them make their declaration before a secretary and a clerk, then they dashed to the Sheriff Court for the necessary warrant to take to the registrar. The Sheriff Court was still open, but the Registry Office had closed, and in two hours Liam would have to leave in the other direction, southwards, for the journey back to the war. They stared at each other in total horror, then Alice pulled herself together and made light of it.

'Look, it doesn't matter, does it?' she said brightly. 'We'll do it as soon as you arrive next time!'

'But . . .'

She knew what he meant. 'We were careful, weren't we?'

'Yes, but I wanted you to be Mrs McCann before I left, in case.'

'But I am Mrs McCann, and there won't be an "in case", so stop being a pessimist. You'll be home again in no time, everyone says so,' she said, both of them deciding to ignore the fact that everyone had been saying very similar things since 1914.

He took the gold band from his pocket and slipped it on her finger, under the sapphire ring he had given her at Shaw's

Bridge three years before. 'We are married,' he smiled.

'Yes, we are, that's all that matters.'

And so she had waved him off, smiling happily and seemingly without a care in the world, and then she had returned
to Kew Terrace where Louise and her family waited with
Maggie and Tony, and told them she and Liam were a married
couple.

''Bout bloody time, too!' Louise remarked.

'Louise!' Maggie exclaimed. 'The child is listening!'

'She's heard worse,' Louise retorted. 'It's not me she thinks
is the odd one, it's you.'

Alice, for once in exuberant mood, laughed at the expressions on the faces of her cousins, one accepting and calm, the
other shocked and almost hurt. George sat beside Louise, as
gloriously different from the 'exotic Bird of Paradise' as could
be, from his polished shoes to his neatly pressed suit, high
starched collar and perfectly knotted tie. He was tall and slim,
his fair hair slightly receding at the front, and always every inch
the conservative, well-mannered businessman. They seemed an
odd couple, as Maggie often remarked: it was hard to understand how he put up with his unconventional wife's unconventional way of dressing and of speaking her mind, but
whatever their secret was, it worked. For all Alice knew they
could wonder about her and Liam when they weren't around,
she thought, though she couldn't imagine why, and the thought
made her laugh. Then she looked at Maggie and, realising that
she must be anxious for details, she made a great story out of
the mix-up over the holiday and Pat having already left the
office. 'He was probably on the boat over that passed our boat
when we were coming back!' she giggled.

'It just all seems so sudden,' Maggie murmured. 'If we'd
known, dear, we would've made it more of an occasion for

you, especially having more of the family here this week.'

'Oh, no,' Louise said suspiciously, 'you're not involving me in this, Maggie, you're the one who wanted a fuss, not me. God, how glad I am that you were a fugitive and couldn't be at my wedding, as if the whole silly nonsense wasn't bad enough as it was! What on earth convinces you that everything has to be "an occasion" anyway?' She turned to Alice. 'You did exactly the right thing, Alice,' she said warmly, 'eventually. Everyone should elope, that's my opinion.'

'And you'd be happy if Ta— I mean Emma, were to do that?' Maggie demanded.

'She may not get married,' Louise retorted.

'Louise!'

'Why should you assume that she would want to?' Louise asked calmly. 'With any luck the whole archaic habit will be outlawed by the time she grows up.'

'I don't understand you!' Maggie replied, close to tears.

'I know,' Louise said quietly, 'and I don't understand you either, but I have enough manners not to make a great song and dance about it.'

As neither George nor Tony looked likely to say anything, Alice decided to cut in. 'Anyway,' she beamed, 'one of the other lawyers wasn't going to Rothesay this weekend, so he did the necessary, and great relief all round!' She made no mention of the closed Registry Office and the missing, all-important marriage certificate.

'But it's so impersonal, dear,' Maggie persisted. 'Don't you think?'

'Well, Liam was there and I was there,' Alice replied, a slight note in her voice betraying that she was growing tired of explaining. 'I don't see how it could've been more personal.'

'Exactly!' Louise said, trying to bring the discussion to a close before Alice turned on her heels and left the room.

'It's such a shame Pat missed doing what he called "the honours", if that's what you mean,' Alice smiled, though she knew it wasn't what Maggie meant at all. 'He'll be so annoyed, and he missed seeing Liam. But never mind, next time he's home.'

Little did she know – how could she? – that next time would come sooner than anyone expected.

9

When Pat Murphy heard about the mix-up he was so angry that no one could speak to him for the rest of the day, and for more days after that he would come out of his office, glare at Alice and demand, 'How could you?' in a hurt voice.

'But you kept nagging us to get married!' Alice laughed.

'No I didn't! I nagged you to let me marry you! There's a great deal of difference, my girl!'

'But you weren't here, how were we to know that?'

'How was I to know you two were here?'

'Does it matter, Pat?' she sighed. 'I mean, someone was here, the honours were done.'

'But not by me!' Pat headed for his office and, before he shut the door, he turned again. 'How could you?' he demanded once more.

It seemed they had upset everyone but themselves – and Louise, of course – but that couldn't be helped. Maybe when Liam came home she would relent and allow Maggie to host a small celebration to soothe all the hurt feelings – one of her elegant teas, she thought. Maybe. She'd think about it.

★ ★ ★

Two weeks after Liam had gone back he had written his first letter, addressing her as 'Mrs McCann', with the news that he'd been injured. He was safe, he wrote, he was recovering well from gunshot wounds to the left knee and shoulder, that was 'all', nothing to write home about, even though he was, and he was coming home. In the spring of 1918 influenza was sweeping the trenches, killing more men than the fighting and the mud. They called it Spanish flu, and in those first months of the year the field hospitals were full of young men suffering from it – and there was Captain McCann taking up a bed just to recover from gunshot wounds, and of no good to anyone, given that he couldn't hold a gun, so the decision had been taken to send him home forthwith. From the shock and fear of finding out he had been injured came the great prize of his homecoming, and for good this time. Alice had never allowed herself to think about the danger he was in until she had seen the change in him when he had come home on leave. It was a measure of how important he was to her that she couldn't envisage being without him, but the sudden realisation that she could lose him to a bullet or a shell coincided with the news that he was coming home and wouldn't have to face either again. And Liam was ecstatic, despite the feeling that he was letting down men who had been at the Front longer than he had. He was leaving the hard, callous world he had inhabited and was going home to Alice. He could easily have been killed; and he would never consider the number thirteen unlucky again.

It had happened in one of those meaningless skirmishes that the generals seemed to think up to keep them busy. He had been part of a raiding party of twenty officers and three hundred and twenty other ranks. They had taken forty-three German prisoners, destroyed dugouts and a machine-gun emplacement, captured two machine guns, a trench mortar, some rifles and three hundred yards. The price was five dead and thirteen wounded, the last of them Captain McCann, who had turned to his right on the retreat and felt two sudden hard thumps to his shoulder and knee. If he hadn't been turning and thereby deflected the course of the bullets, the one that hit his shoulder could have continued through his back and into his chest. It just hadn't been his time, that was all, but he knew his time was waiting for him if he stayed there, fighting for a few yards that the Germans would take back next week. Now he wouldn't have to; now he was going home.

A week after she had received Liam's letter, Alice arrived home in Kew Terrace to find Brendon McCann waiting for her in the parlour, and she knew. One look at his face and she sat down slowly, covering her ears. She didn't want to hear, refused to hear, even though she knew she had to. Liam had died on the boat home, of Spanish flu.

He was being taken home to Belfast, where his next-of-kin, Seamus McCann, was waiting for him with the rest of the family who had turned their backs on him, and he would be buried in the family plot at Derrytrasna on the south shores of Lough Neagh. Brendon had taken it on himself to contact Alice, and to convey to her that her presence there would be not just unwelcome but would not be tolerated.

She couldn't see properly. The faces of Brendon, Maggie and Tony were swimming before her, and she could only hear the odd word here and there, but she got the gist of it. Poor Brendon, poor Brendon, she thought, desperately, having to tell her this; poor Maggie, desperate to be of help to her, even though she didn't understand.

'This may not be the time to discuss this,' Maggie said quietly, 'but Liam and Alice were married on the day he went back. As his wife, his widow, she has the say on what happens from this moment.'

Brendon looked at Alice. She was aware that she was supposed to contribute to the discussion, but it seemed irrelevant. Liam was dead, that was all that mattered.

'Alice?' Maggie said. 'Isn't that so?'

'No,' Alice said eventually. 'I'm sorry, Maggie, it isn't. Not quite. We bought the ring and went to Pat's office, but he'd gone, as I said. It was Good Friday, if you recall, and we hadn't thought of that. There was one lawyer still at the office and he did his part, then we got the warrant to take to the Registry Office, but it was closed. So we were half-married, I suppose, not that it mattered − as far as we were concerned we were married already. It wasn't a lie − the next time Liam came home we would just get the Registrar to issue the certificate. It was just a piece of paper. '

If she had been able to pay attention she would have noticed an extra edge to the silence in the room, her words adding to the atmosphere of shock and horror. She would have looked at Maggie as her cousin worked out in her mind why the need to appear married had been so strong, and seen the under-standing register in her expression and her eyes. The two young people had just spent five days − and nights − alone together, they had to be married, or seem to be. Oh, dear god, what if . . .? And Brendon, his face already creased with grief, didn't know what to say, and Alice couldn't help him.

In Belfast, Bridie and Seamus McCann were in deep mourning for their eldest son, but they were slightly further forward in the process than Alice was at that moment.

'I can't think why Brendon took it upon himself to find that girl and tell her himself,' Bridie said bitterly. 'It wasn't as though they were married. I'm sure Liam was coming to his senses. I am so disappointed in Brendon, he should be here at home with his family, helping us.'

For once Seamus was silent. He had no words and no arm gestures to use.

'She is the last person who merits consideration – it was all her fault, after all,' Bridie continued. 'If she hadn't taken Liam away from home he would still be here with us.' She subsided into tears. 'And to think how fond we were of her, how we trusted her! My poor, poor boy, falling under her spell!'

Still Seamus didn't speak. Their reactions were the reverse of normal, but this wasn't normal. Bridie's need was for talk, but it grated on his brain, all he craved was peace and silence, so he got up and went out to the garden.

'Seamus, dear, it's raining,' she called.

He didn't reply. He had to get away from her noise to the place where she often got away from his. She was right, though, he reasoned, his boy wouldn't have behaved as he had without the McInally girl's influence. If only he had realised it at the time he would have put a stop to it. He never wanted to see her again. He would, he decided, making a fist with his hand and staring into the leaden sky to stop his tears, refuse to acknowledge her very existence. To the end of his days he would not hear her name mentioned, would banish every vestige of her from his mind, this evil woman who had taken his dear, beloved son from him. So both bereaved parents thought their thoughts in North Belfast, one sobbing and ranting indoors, one raging silently outdoors in a steady drizzle, conniving to turn their grief and their guilt into anger, turning it away from themselves, because it would have been unbearable otherwise. There was only one person they could attack, so they turned their raw emotions in the direction of Alice McInally, who had cruelly deprived them of their eldest son, and of his last three years of life, come to that. They had known her all her life, loved her all her life, but now she was their mortal enemy, having lured their trusting, generous son to a premature death. And Liam himself, the boy they had brought up to be honest and brave, whose intentions, hopes and dreams had caused his father to be intermittently incandescent with rage, became in death a courteous, kind and easily led chap who hadn't been able to handle the wiles of that devious McInally female.

In Glasgow Alice knew nothing of this, only that they didn't want her at Liam's funeral, but she had always had a talent for organisation and in this crisis that skill rose to the fore. There were things to do, priorities, and the disapproval of the McCanns was of no consequence, so she took no notice of it, had no time for it.

'Brendon,' she smiled weakly, 'I'm so sorry I'm keeping you from your family, but if you could bear with me for a little while, please?'

Brendon's pale features had taken on a greyish tinge. After passing on the merest hint of his parents' feelings to her, he felt mortified and didn't know what to say to Alice. Of course he would do whatever she asked of him.

'I won't attend the family funeral. I won't be with them, but I want to be there. Will you help me?'

'Of course.'

'When you know, can you tell me when it is to be? Somehow I'll get over to Lough Neagh in time. I won't cause a scene, I'll stay out of sight, but I have to be there. Do you see?'

Brendon was amazed at her self-control and her courage. He would have granted any wish she might dream up. He thought quickly. 'You don't have to make any arrangements,' he said. 'You'll presumably be able to stay with your cousin, Louise?'

She hadn't thought of that, but she nodded, sure that Louise wouldn't let her down.

'I'll arrange for a taxicab to take you from Belfast to Lough Neagh then back again afterwards.'

'But the expense . . .'

'I don't give a damn about the expense!' he whispered furiously, enraged at how she was being treated. 'I'll call on Louise as soon as I get back home and tell her, if that's all right with you?'

Alice nodded. Then she retreated to her room and lay down, feeling suddenly and desperately exhausted, but, though she slept for a time, she was aware of the doors in the large house opening and shutting, of voices murmuring in the rooms below. The strange thing was that she felt totally calm; all she could think about was making arrangements. She got up and sat at her dressing table, looking at her reflection. She would need something black, she decided, then the thought threatened her so she cut it off and decided to go downstairs again. Louise had arrived and Pat Murphy was with the family. Her hand went to her heart. She hadn't thought of telling him and started to apologise.

'His brother caught me at the office,' he said, hugging her tightly. 'Is there anything I can do?'

'Not that I can think of,' she said, smiling wanly. 'I've been trying to think if there's anything I should do.'

'Brendon told me about the mix-up at the Registry Office,' he said. 'We'll talk about that later.'

Alice nodded, though she couldn't understand what there was to talk about. 'Where is Brendon?' she asked.

'He's gone back to Belfast, dear,' Maggie said tearfully. 'He has things to arrange, you understand.'

'And Bernadette's due any moment,' Louise said, trying to stave off Maggie's emotion. 'How many's that now?'

'Only the second, Louise,' Alice smiled, understanding what Louise was doing.

'What kind is the first one?'

'A girl,' Alice replied, 'called Bridie.'

'Dear God!' Louise retorted. 'I expected better of him than appeasement to his harpy mother!'

'Louise!' Maggie said sharply. 'This is hardly the time! The McCanns are in mourning; Bridie has lost a son!'

Louise rolled her eyes. 'She lost him three years ago, and it was of her own doing, Maggie!' she shouted angrily. 'Let's not lose sight of the facts just because Liam's dead!' She turned to look at Alice. 'I'm sorry,' she said, 'I didn't mean it to sound like that.'

Alice rose and put her arms around Louise. 'You never do, Louise, you never do,' she said softly. 'I think I'll go upstairs to Liam's room,' she murmured. 'There are things that will have to be sorted out.'

Maggie opened her mouth only to be silenced by a sharp look from Louise.

'Do you need any help?' Louise asked.

'Yes, that would be nice,' Alice smiled, knowing that Louise could be counted on to stay in command of her feelings. The last thing she needed was anyone collapsing with grief, and Louise could be trusted on that score more than Maggie. From her seat across the room, though, Maggie looked at them and felt a stab at her heart. She had always wanted some show of emotion from Alice, something that indicated she was close to her, and the only time she did allow feelings to surface it was in the direction of Louise of all people, who removed emotion from every situation. She couldn't help feeling a little let down.

Together they packed Liam's clothes in suitcases and collected his few bits and pieces: a pair of binoculars Alice had given him and the camera he had bought some years before to take pictures of boats. In an envelope Louise found a few snapshots and held them out to Alice, who smiled and shook her head. 'Boats?' Alice asked, and Louise nodded, but there was one she slipped in her pocket without showing to her cousin, of a young Alice and Liam sitting together, taken at Shaw's Bridge, by the look of it. She understood that Alice was trying very hard to deal with this terrible situation as her character dictated, it was all she knew to do, and the picture might be the undoing of her. It would keep, she decided, for another time, a less raw time.

When Louise went downstairs the mood was sombre. Everyone in the household was held in thrall by a kind of collective shock and horror, even the maids were in tears. Maggie was becoming more distraught by the hour, it seemed to Louise, and a becalmed Tony was no use to her whatsoever. It struck Louise that these two might well love each other, but they were so different and the years of hard work had added to the distance between them, and she felt sorry for her sister. The differences between herself and George were superficial, but underneath they were alike; and where they weren't they granted each other licence to be unalike. They were united in a way that Maggie and Tony weren't.

'Does she need anything?' Maggie asked.

'No,' Louise said wearily. 'Just leave her alone, Maggie.'

'But what about tonight?'

'What about tonight?'

'Will she able to sleep?'

'Oh, I don't really know, Maggie. That's anybody's guess, isn't it? I'm not sure I'll sleep tonight, never mind Alice.'

'Should we call the doctor?'

'For me?'

'No,' Maggie said irritably. 'Why must everything be a joke to you?'

'Because that same everything has to be hugely complicated to you, Maggie.'

'I mean for Alice,' Maggie said. 'He might be able to give her something to help her sleep.' As she spoke Maggie was already reaching for the bell-pull.

'Yes, call the doctor,' Louise said gently, 'but not for me, not even for Alice, Maggie, but for you.'

'Me?'

'Yes, you.' Louise looked at Tony for his consent, but Tony, realising his own uselessness, simply put his head down, his cheeks flushed, so Louise decided to take that as his agreement.

'You're exhausted, you poor old thing,' Louise said. 'You need some sleep yourself.'

'But Alice needs help!' Maggie protested.

Louise took her sister by the shoulders. 'Maggie, dear, listen to me. She needs to be left alone, trust me. This is a strong young woman who will have a lot to bear over the coming days and weeks and long after that. You must not undermine her, let her deal with this in her own way.'

'Oh, I don't know . . .' Maggie sank into a chair and cried softly.

'But I do. Tony, call the doctor for your wife.' Louise wanted to shout 'You great useless lump!' but she didn't, even Louise could see that he knew he was.

★   ★   ★

Alice travelled to Belfast with Louise the following day. There was no need to go so quickly, but Louise wanted Alice out of Maggie's way, and wanted Maggie to have time and space to recover herself. She also wanted to consult Brendon on the chances of some conciliation between Alice and the McInallys, so leaving Alice to rest she went to Brendon and Bernadette's house, and discovered that while Brendon had been in Glasgow he had become the father of a baby boy, to be named Liam.

'I went to see the McInallys this morning,' he told Louise, shaking his head. 'I wouldn't have believed anyone could be so hard. They don't see that the situation has changed, they felt more for my family than their own daughter.'

'Both of them?' Louise asked.

'Her more than him,' Brendon replied. 'You know what Henry's like, couldn't tell you his own name without hearing it first from Victoria. He kept trying to change the subject, wanted to talk about the business and how things aren't going too well at the moment.'

'Because he didn't have the guts to face his wife and address the situation,' Louise said bitterly.

'Yes, that's what I think. How is Alice?'

'She's Alice,' Louise said with a shrug. 'It hasn't really sunk in yet. One moment you can see a lost look in her eyes, the next it's as if she doesn't believe any of it and expects him to come home.'

'I'm a bit like that myself,' Brendon replied.

Later, Louise looked out the least outrageous of her black dresses for Alice to wear and insisted on going with her to Lough Neagh for Liam's funeral. For Alice it made no difference, other people only registered slightly, they, too, were of little importance, even those she was fond of, like Louise. Alice remembered Lough Neagh well, knew every shortcut, every field and tussock of grass, and told the taxicab where to stop so that she could observe what was happening in Derrytrasna without being there. It was one of those spring days when the weather can't make up its mind and, as Liam's coffin was carried to where past generations of McCanns lay, a sudden flurry of snow broke out from the sunshine and quickly smothered the landscape. As the men in the family presided over the rites, cows and bullocks grazed unconcerned on the grass around the little cemetery against the backdrop of the Lough, bathed in sunlight, the water sparkling. It was so peaceful, such a beautiful scene, but even though she recognised the black-clad men in the distance, she couldn't link them or the event to Liam, it was too unreal. There was Seamus and her father, her brother Harry beside them, and Brendon, scanning the area to find where she was. All the people she knew from the Lough Neagh communities had turned out. Jimmy Devlin, who had taught Liam all his boat-building skills, was there with his sons; she must write to him and tell him how much it had meant to Liam. As the priest went through the usual ritual she remembered how offended Liam had been about the blessing of the soldiers before they went into battle, and knew this scene would have angered him. Dotted about, listening, praying and crossing themselves, were all the cousins the McCann and McInally children from Belfast couldn't quite relate to on their visits 'home'. It was a fitting place for Liam, though, not because of ideas of family history or 'home', but because he really loved the Lough Neagh area.

When those who had a legitimate reason for being there had left the graveside she waited a little longer and, when she was sure that they had gone, she asked the driver to take her closer. Then she asked Louise to leave her alone and, standing by his grave, still not quite believing any of it, she looked around and saw the freak covering of snow had melted almost as quickly as it had blanketed the ground, so that the greenery and wild-flowers emerged once again into the sunshine. She hadn't thought of bringing flowers and now wished she had, then she looked around in the early May sunshine.

'Look,' she said softly, 'bluebells.' She picked a handful and laid them on Liam's grave, then stood there silently for a long time, until Louise came for her.

'I don't know what to do,' she said in a small voice.

'It's over, Alice,' Louise said softly, 'we have to go.'

'But I don't want to!' she said helplessly. 'I want to stay here with him!'

Louise put her arms about Alice's shoulders and firmly guided her back to the taxicab. As it moved off she watched her young cousin looking out at the grave till it was out of sight and wished she could help her. But she couldn't. No one could.

IO

In the weeks after Liam had been buried in Derrytrasna, everyone involved in the tragedy had their own thoughts and feelings to cope with. In the grand red-brick home of the McCanns, Brendon was pleading Alice's case.

'She is his wife, to all intents,' he said to his father.

'It's the intents that matter in this case,' Seamus replied dismissively. 'As I understand it she has no marriage certificate, therefore she is not and never was married to my son.'

Brendon had noticed that these days Seamus always called Liam 'my son', and, recalling how differently he had talked about him in the past, had to bite his tongue to stop himself pointing this out. 'But that was clearly what Liam intended, Father,' he persisted, trying to keep his voice friendly. 'He left here with Alice because he wanted to be with her, he stayed with her, he bought a house for them to live in and he went through every part of the marriage with the full intention of being married to her.'

'Every part but the important part, the legal part,' Bridie chimed in tartly.

'Precisely. And as for the rest of it, it's my firm belief that my son wasn't thinking straight,' Seamus said shortly. 'Anyway, the church wouldn't recognise such a marriage, even if she did have a certificate, and he knew this. I don't believe my son would've entered into anything like that, it was because she influenced him, but in the end he did not go through with it.'

'My son.' There it was again. Brendon stood up. 'Father, if you had one criticism to make of Liam all through his life it was that he knew what he thought and he said what he thought. Even when you disagreed and shouted at him, he stood his ground. I simply do not recognise the Liam you now see.'

'Brendon, I'm deeply upset that you can talk to your father in that tone of voice!' Bridie said from her armchair, one hand clutching theatrically at her chest. 'He is in mourning, have some consideration.'

'But who is he in mourning for, Mother?' Brendon demanded. 'It certainly isn't the Liam I know. Knew.' He had to bite his lip as he corrected himself and cursed himself for risking losing control. 'I've been in touch with Liam since he joined up and –'

'You've what?' Bridie gasped, exchanging a shocked look with Seamus.

'Alice wrote to me giving me the address she had for him. I thanked her and immediately got in touch with him. We corresponded all the time he was fighting.'

'You didn't say a word about this!' Seamus yelled, the Seamus of old again.

'How could I?' Brendon shouted back angrily, quite unlike himself of old. 'How would you have reacted? Look how you're reacting now.'

There was a charged silence in the parlour. Even the clock ticking in the background seemed to be doing so more quietly than usual.

'I had this hope that one day you might see sense and understand the hurt you had both caused him —'

'We caused him hurt?' Seamus demanded, arms waving.

'Yes, Father, you did. I hoped in time you'd see that and
think better of it, but now he's gone and you can never do
that, it's too late. It isn't too late to make amends with his wife,
though.'

'She is not his wife!'

Brendon tried desperately to think of something to say. He
had lost his case by getting angry, he knew that, but in the
circumstances he had done well to hold on to his temper for
as long as he did. He would have preferred to strike Seamus,
to feel his hand crunch against his father's skull, his thick, stupid
skull, but despite his present anger he was a dutiful son, so he
left as quickly as he could without saying another word.

Brendon was too close to the situation: he was blinded by
emotion, all he could see was the injustice. He felt so disgusted
by the bile and hatred his parents were directing at Alice that
he couldn't understand that the sum total was in direct propor-
tion to their own guilt. They had driven Liam away, and that
had led, indirectly, to his death. If they had ever had any hopes
of reconciliation one day, those hopes were now gone.
Somewhere in their souls, Bridie and Seamus knew they had
brought about their own misery, but that was too hard to face,
so tacitly they had reached a mutual agreement to bury that
knowledge in a deep, dark place where it could never be found.
To finally cover it over they needed a scapegoat, something or
someone evil to shoulder the blame, and they decided to nomin-
ate Alice, the person who meant more to Liam, their dear son,
than anyone on earth.

Brendon was too emotional to work any of this out at the
time, but as he left his parents' home that day he felt a gulf

open between him and them, and was horrified they couldn't see that they were in danger of losing their only remaining son. Another child had been disappointed in his parents.

It wasn't just his parents Brendon was in the process of separating from. He was finding it difficult to understand his lifelong friend and Alice's brother, Harry McInally. He had expected some support from Harry, but Harry had simply looked back at him blankly as he recounted the conversations and the indignities being heaped on the grieving Alice.

'Harry, isn't there something you can do?' he demanded.

'I don't see that there is,' Harry replied.

'But she's your sister, you must have some feeling about what has happened to her?' Brendon persisted.

'Well, when you think about it,' Harry said reasonably, 'if she had wanted anything from me she would've come to me before she ran off to Glasgow, but she didn't. She knew what she was doing when she left with Liam.'

'For God's sake, man!'

'You don't understand Alice,' Harry smiled, and Brendon couldn't understand why he was smiling. 'Alice has always been able to take care of herself, there's no need to worry about her.'

Brendon thought he might be going mad. Once the calmer, more reasonable of the McCann boys, now he felt there was no one in his life that he understood any longer. 'But you must be able to do something!' he persisted. 'Surely you could talk to your parents?'

Now Harry laughed. 'I don't think that would be advisable,' he said, seeming to be as perplexed by his friend's reactions as Brendon was by his. 'Look, Brendon, if either one of us interferes we'll be treated in exactly the same way. As I see it, we have nothing to gain and everything to lose from trying to get your parents or mine to take Alice back. They wouldn't listen anyway, and we'd be caused a great deal of trouble. We haven't done anything wrong and there's nothing to gain from rocking the boat, is there? Far better that we leave things as they are. You have a family of your own to consider. My Mattie has miscarried twice, I know, but we are still hopeful. We can't risk causing trouble over something we can't do anything about, can we? We have to consider the future of our own families. Besides, as I said, there's no need to worry, Alice can look after herself.'

And though Brendon could follow Harry's logic, twisted though he felt it was, for the second time he felt like hitting someone he thought he knew and had once loved and respected. He wondered why it was that losing his brother had transformed him into a violent man. And if he found it hard – no, that was wrong – if he found it *impossible* to understand Harry, he had no idea what to make of Henry and Victoria McInally. What was that old saying? 'Your son's your son till he finds a wife, but your daughter's your daughter for the rest of her life.' It was an accepted fact that daughters were always closer to their parents, everyone knew that, yet these parents seemed to have cast their daughter out of their lives for good. How could that be?

When Alice had gone back to Glasgow without seeing any of her immediate family, Louise thought it over for a few days and then decided to visit Uncle Henry and Aunt Victoria. Despite Brendon's failed attempt to enlist Harry's support for his sister, she would try one last time to locate the love Harry and Victoria must once have had for her. Bella wasn't there, so Louise was doubly annoyed to see that Billy Guthrie had included himself in the meeting. He sat silently beside Victoria as she told them Alice was with her sister, Maggie, in Glasgow, though she was fully aware that they knew this. Brendon had told his parents and they would, without a doubt, have passed it on.

Victoria made a great show of being shocked, then said bitterly, 'I should've known. Two sinners and traitors together!' Louise, never normally one to hold back, was doing so today, albeit with a great deal of trouble, afraid of losing any sympathy she might be able to stir in them by being too frank. Looking at them, though, she wondered if that was the right strategy, but she tried again. Ignoring the insult to her own sister as well as to her cousin, she urged them to consider sending a few words of affection to Alice. Their response was a bemused silence from Henry and a stony, tight-lipped one from Victoria that spread from her lips to her entire body, so that Louise wondered if she might fall off her chair and crash to pieces on the floor, like shattered glass. 'Whatever has happened in the past, surely you must see that Alice needs her family now,' she said quietly.

'She gave up the right to call herself our daughter when she did what she did,' Victoria said icily.

'But Aunt Victoria, what did she actually do? She wanted to marry someone you both knew and loved, and when you tried to stop them even seeing each other, they went somewhere they could. What was so bad about that?'

Another stony silence. Louise was struggling with her own anger. 'After all, if the families had been more understanding Alice and Liam wouldn't have been put in the position of leaving home, would they?' she said, regretting it immediately. It was their fault, but there was nothing to be gained from telling them so.

'Louise,' Victoria almost hissed, 'this is really none of your business, but your family has suffered as we have and I accept that gives you some insight into the situation. We do not believe in nor accept mixed marriages and we have no wish to see her again, none whatever. Isn't that so, Henry?'

Beside her, Henry McInally, looking at the floor, nodded but said nothing.

'Good day, Louise,' Victoria said haughtily, then got up and left the room, followed by Billy Guthrie, leaving her sitting with Henry.

Probably heading for her kitchen, Louise thought, and a furious batch of sponge cake-making. She seized the chance of having her uncle on his own. 'Uncle Henry,' she whispered, but he silenced her.

'What can I do, Louise?' he said miserably. 'You can see how it is.'

'Uncle Henry, it doesn't have to be, does it? Think of Alice's position. She's lost Liam; she has no one close.'

'But your Aunt Victoria has made her decision and nothing will alter that,' he said plaintively.

'Do you agree with her decision?' she demanded.

'I have to go along with what she says,' he replied pathetically.

'No you don't! You can be a bloody man for once in your life!' Louise said savagely.

'Louise! I'm in a very difficult position, can't you see that?' he whined. 'How can I go against my wife?'

'For God's sake, she's only some woman you married, and I choose to believe you didn't know what you were doing, but your daughter!' She threw up her hands in despair. 'Well, I'm sick of your lily-livered weakness, Uncle Henry, I really am! Of course you can do something about it. Alice is your daughter and I'm telling you how devastated she is at this moment. You can tell that harridan you were ill-advised enough

173

to marry that you've made your own decision, and you can help Alice!'

'It's not that simple,' he said, wringing his hands. 'The McCanns are really angry, you know, and business isn't good at the moment. If we took Alice back, who knows what they might do? The whole family could suffer, you see.'

'So you just abandon your daughter, do you? Leave her to her grief? I'll never forgive you for this, Uncle Henry, you're a disgrace as a man and as a father,' Louise spat at him. 'As far as I'm concerned, if Alice is no longer family, neither am I! Here,' she thrust a piece of paper into his hand. 'This is Maggie's address in Glasgow. Now don't ever say you didn't know where your daughter was.'

Henry, looking utterly miserable, opened his mouth, but nothing came out, then Billy Guthrie suddenly appeared to escort her to the door, obviously sent by Victoria to see her off the premises.

'We appreciate that you are trying to help,' he said, hand on her elbow to propel her on her way, 'and it's very kind of you, Louise.' He smiled the coldest smile she had ever seen. 'But this is family business, after all.'

She wanted to slap him, but she was so shocked by the cheek, the callous nerve of the man, that she couldn't summon up the energy to raise her hand till he had shut the door on her.

The mindset in the McInally household was complicated by various things. They had never been equal with the McCanns: the McCanns were the bosses and the McInallys the workers. Though it was never stated as crudely as that, the feeling was there, and part of Victoria McInally's hardness towards her errant daughter came from an anxiety to protect the rest of her family and their standard of living. She did object to Alice's relationship with Liam on religious grounds, to be sure. She truly disliked Catholics as a species, a dislike heightened by the awful things that were happening in Ireland, all down, in her mind, to Catholic influence. All the trouble was coming from the predominantly Catholic south, where they were hell-bent on splitting the country and allying it to Rome instead of the British Crown. She had been called after the dear Queen, for heaven's sake. Not that she was prejudiced, it was just that Catholics were fine in their place and, kept in their place, she had nothing against them, but their place wasn't in her family, regardless of how she felt about them as individuals. It just wasn't right, no discussion, no question, and the thought of any grandchild of hers being raised to show allegiance to Rome gave her feelings of anger and distaste that often culminated in an attack of the vapours.

She liked the McCanns as people, admired them, their bay windows, Royal Albert china and napkins edged with real Brussels Lace. It was a measure of how tolerant she was that she could mix with them even though she found their religion abhorrent, just as they found her religion, and that knowledge did not offend her, or them, in the least. What Alice had done was to put the McInallys in jeopardy, and that did offend her. Liam and Alice had blurred the line between the two families, so that neither could be sure where the other was. If this union succeeded then the McCanns would no longer be sure that they were superior and, more to the point, they would no longer be sure that the McInallys recognised that they were inferior. The young couple had threatened not only the stability of the pecking order, they had ignored it as though it didn't exist. When 'the offer' had first been made, what united the two families, a shared background, money and business, was stronger than the religion that divided them, but Liam and Alice had ensured that would no longer be true, which in turn questioned that they had ever been unified, or, if they had, how strong it had ever been.

The McCanns had as many legitimate objections to the union between Alice and Liam as the McInallys did, and they shared Victoria's disquiet in particular at the prospect of their future grandchildren being raised with a parent from the other 'side'. These arrangements always brought about a weakening of the faith, therefore the priests and ministers didn't approve of them. On this the McCanns and the McInallys were of one mind, and the last thing Victoria wanted was for Bridie and Seamus to think she and Henry were soft on the issue. Besides, the business was going through a bad patch, so they had to stay on good terms with the McCanns to carry them through it. She and Henry had to be seen to disapprove as much as the McCanns did, and when the McCanns settled on blaming Alice especially, they had to go along with that, too, had to believe it, and Victoria did. Perhaps that was why she took an even harder line than Bridie did, to make it utterly plain that she could not be blamed, thereby safeguarding her family's prospects in this odd friendship. Besides, women had their own ways of getting what they wanted from men, Victoria knew that. If a woman set her cap at a man he had no chance. Women made all the running and always had, though they contrived, out of decency and femininity, to make it look the other way round. So Alice had the power to stop whatever had been developing with Liam, who was only a man, after all, but out of selfishness she had not done so, preferring instead to put her family in an awkward position with the superior McCanns.

There were times when Victoria thought back on Alice's childhood and wondered if there had been any sign of how wilfully she was developing, some warning she could have acted on sooner. Alice had always been her own person, she knew that, everyone commented on it – there were no daughter–mother confidences between them as there had been between Bella and herself. And there was a tendency in Alice to say what she thought that Victoria had occasionally found irksome: speaking your mind was no way to get a man. But there was nothing she could think of that could have alerted her to how her own daughter would one day betray her, and she felt more comforted by this every time she thought about it. She had already mentally divorced herself from Alice, there was no way back from where she had taken herself. Thank heavens for Billy, she thought. He understood and always backed her up, because the religious question was beyond dispute. In that Victoria could not give way, though she suspected Henry could be persuaded otherwise if she didn't keep a close eye on him.

Who knew where it could lead, business-wise, with both her own remaining family and Harry's now dependent on McCann and Son? No, Victoria could not back down, it simply wasn't in her.

11

In the Murphy house in Great Western Terrace, Pat was distraught. The boy's death had hit him as hard as any he could think of, including his parents. He was desperately trying to think of ways to help Alice. If she wasn't legally married to Liam then she had no claim on his estate, and he knew there would be an estate.

'Look, there has to be a way round this. You have the warrant from the Sheriff Court, all that's missing is the marriage certificate, so we'll go round to the Registry Office and present them with the warrant anyhow,' he said, 'and say Liam's still away.'

'You can't do that,' Alice said simply. 'They'll just say to come back with the warrant when he's next home, and he won't be coming home, will he?'

'Pat,' Molly said, 'Alice is right. It's a terrible situation, but the girl is right.' She took Alice's hand and patted it sympathetically.

Pat paced about. 'Well we'll get someone from the office to go with you, say he's Liam.'

'Pat, you can't do that either!' Alice smiled at him weakly.

'But they'll never know, will they? They don't care, they just work there.'

'You can't involve someone like that, ask them to obtain a marriage certificate for a groom who has been dead for weeks; you'd be asking someone to perjure themselves, or whatever.'

'But anyone would do it.'

'No, Pat. Think what would happen if it was found out, how many of us would be blamed. You have a good name, I can't see you risk that.'

'I'd be doing it on my own,' he replied. He was silent for a few moments. 'You know, the more I think about it, I'm sure we could approach the court and ask for Liam's presumed consent in this case.'

'And have his family oppose it? Even if the court agreed, think of having to fight his parents. Even if we won, at what cost?'

'They wouldn't fight you, would they?'

'I think they would.'

'But that would be outrageous! Liam went through the whole thing of his own free will! Maybe I could talk to the McCanns, explain it to them?'

'Then you'd become their enemy, too.' She looked at him, grateful for his kindness and willingness to ruin himself. 'Look, Pat,' she smiled, 'none of this matters. Liam and I were married, I don't need a piece of paper to know that.'

'What will you do now, Alice?' Molly asked gently.

'I don't have too many choices,' Alice replied. 'I can't go home, I have no one in Belfast to go back to or for, except Louise, of course, and she has her own life. I'm here in Glasgow because this is where Liam and I came to start a new life together, but Liam's gone now and there won't be any new life together, so I keep asking myself what reason I have to be here now. I have no idea what I want to do or where I want to be, nothing makes sense any longer.'

'Give yourself a little time, my dear girl,' Molly said comfortingly, 'it's very early days. And remember, there's still your little house in Port Bannatyne.'

'Yes, there is that,' Alice smiled softly, remembering the last time she had been there with Liam.

Pat paced about as the women talked. 'It's all my fault,' he said miserably. 'I should've been here.'

Shortly, though, Alice would understand part of what had been worrying Pat Murphy. The terms of their grandfather's will stated that if Liam or Brendon died before marrying, the money should revert to the other, and if both died as single men, the money would revert to the family. Liam's inheritance, therefore, would go to his brother, Brendon. Alice didn't mind this, it was old McCann money and meant nothing to her, but the house in Port Bannatyne was in Liam's name, and as he was unmarried it went back to his family, to his parents who promptly sold it.

Brendon let Alice know he was coming over to Glasgow. He wanted to see her face-to-face to explain what was going on, but Pat Murphy was already so angry at how Alice was being treated that he insisted Brendon came to his office. He knew how Brendon felt about Alice, that he was a good friend, but all McCanns had become his enemies now and he resolved on a show of strength, to let the younger McCann and, beyond him, the older McCanns see that Alice had powerful legal friends.

'I don't want the money,' Brendon said painfully. 'I have all I need or want, and as far as I'm concerned it's Alice's money.'

She shook her head. She didn't need it either and, given the circumstances, she didn't want it. If Brendon didn't want it then let the McCanns keep it, she thought, and much good may it do them. The house was a different matter. It was their house, hers and Liam's, it was where they had intended raising their family of happy, free children, where Liam could be a boat-builder, where their future had been planned. While he had been away she had spent all her free time there, she had decorated it, furnished it, and put up the nameplate that had made Liam smile when they had spent their first and only five days as man and wife, regardless of the paperwork. To lose the house was to finally lose all connection with Liam.

Pat Murphy was incensed. 'You simply cannot do this!' he exploded at Brendon.

Alice sat silently by the window, looking down at the people and traffic on St Vincent's Street below.

'Believe me, I'm not doing it,' Brendon replied, his face etched with misery. 'If I had any control over what's happening I'd have stopped it. They moved very quickly about selling the house, they even sold it at a loss so that the deed was done and there was nothing I could say or do. They knew I'd have bought it myself to give it to Alice, so they didn't tell me. I've tried talking to them –' He stopped, emotion overcoming him. 'The reason I came was to say that I intend transferring Liam's money to Alice. It's mine now, though it shouldn't be. I can do what I want with it, and this is what I want.'

'Right, we'll arrange that now!' Pat said aggressively.

'No. Stop it, Pat,' Alice said wearily. 'Brendon isn't your enemy or mine, he's been terribly kind to me. It's not his fault, any more than it was Liam's, how his parents think or feel.'

The two men stared at her helplessly.

'Brendon, thank you for the offer, but I really don't want the money. The house, though . . .' She put her head down. Taking a deep breath, she said, 'They've taken the house out of revenge, to break my heart, so tell them they've succeeded and I hope they're happy. Tell them I feel sorry for them, because

I know Liam would despise them for this. They'll have to live with that, not me.'

It would be another three months before Alice discovered she was expecting Liam's child. She had been feeling tired and ill, but in the circumstances that was to be expected, she supposed. It had never occurred to her that it could be for any other reason than grief and shock. She only went to the doctor because Maggie insisted she needed a tonic, though, looking back, she realised that Maggie must have had her suspicions. 'You need plenty of rest, Mrs McCann,' the doctor intoned. 'My condolences over your loss, but you have another life to think about now.'

They had tried to be careful, but they were too inexperienced to know what careful was, and, in this case, it wasn't.

12

They covered it up well. The only people in Glasgow who knew there was no marriage certificate were the Murphys and Maggie and Tony, and they were the only ones who knew about the coming child as well, apart from Louise in Belfast, of course.

'What about Brendon?' Louise asked. 'He's been a good and honourable friend, after all.'

Alice shook her head. 'Why burden him with this?' she asked. 'There's no need for him to know, is there? There's nothing he can do.'

'But what harm can it do?' Louise persisted. 'He's already estranged from his parents.'

'Exactly, but they may make it up in time. He didn't marry a Protestant, after all, and he's their only chance of good, Catholic grandchildren, so they may relent.'

'He may not want them to!' Louise shrugged defiantly.

'But he may,' Alice replied. 'Let him have that choice.'

'I don't see how you can keep it from him, though,' Louise said, mainly because she didn't want it kept from him. She was thinking about Liam's money, which should go to Liam's child, and Brendon was the route to that end.

'I think we have to regard Brendon as part of my past,' Alice said sadly. 'He's the brother of the man I almost married, and Liam's dead now, so why should there be an ongoing connection?'

Louise nodded. 'Yes, I can see the logic, but it's sad, Alice.'

'It's all sad, Louise,' Alice replied quietly. 'But he has his own family and his business, his own life, hasn't he?'

Before she left for Belfast, Louise handed Alice the photograph she had found of Liam and Alice together.

'Where did you find this?' Alice asked.

'With the snaps of boats in his room. Remember? Wonder why he never gave it to you?'

'You've just explained that,' Alice laughed gently. 'He took it at Shaw's Bridge to see if the timer thing was working. He'd just bought the camera, you see. It was before he went to the Lough to work with Jimmy Devlin.'

Louise raised a quizzical eyebrow.

'The camera was to take photos of boats, Louise, not people,' Alice explained. 'He'd have forgotten about it.'

As far as everyone outside was concerned, the young woman wearing the wedding band under the sapphire and diamond engagement ring was a war widow – worse, she was expecting a child whose father had tragically died before it was born. If the real situation had ever leaked out the society of the day would have been scandalised. Not that Alice would have been alone: there were many young women in the same position, her real or accorded one, as there always are in wartime. Most of them, like Alice, were neither sluts nor even 'right cows'. During those months, though, she thought more than once of Jessie Guthrie, mother of Billy, now her brother-in-law, and the stories she had heard about how the loose wench with no

184

morals had been castigated for having him out of wedlock. If the truth were known, she would have received the same judgement and treatment as Jessie Guthrie had, but as it was she would be accorded the sympathy of all she met.

As far as Pat Murphy was concerned she would continue to work in the office, where she was already known as Mrs McCann, and Maggie, who had longed for a child for so many years, would have one to care for.

The child arrived a month early, at the end of December 1918, a month after the end of the war. It was a girl, which disappointed Alice at first – she had so wanted a boy to call Liam – but when she saw the baby, with her blue eyes and golden wisps of hair tinged with red, she was happy enough. As happy as she could be, at any rate, without Liam. Maggie, who had tried to warn her against what had happened and who had been subtly rebuffed by Alice for doing so, was besotted with the child from the first glance.

'What are you calling her?' she asked, gazing adoringly at the baby.

'Oh, I don't know,' Alice smiled quietly. 'I only had one name in mind, but that won't do now.' She looked at Maggie, who had been so kind to her. Maggie, who had hardly known her, yet had supported her all the way through, given her and Liam a home, and now was prepared to welcome his child into her home and into her heart, even though her own social position would be compromised if the truth ever came out. 'I was thinking about calling her Margaret,' she said.

Maggie tore her eyes away from the baby. 'You mean . . .?'

'Yes, after you,' Alice said.

Maggie blew her nose and protested, but not too much. 'Actually,' she sniffed, 'my first name is Elizabeth, after my mother. Margaret is my middle name. I was always called Margaret at home to avoid confusion, but I'd have preferred Elizabeth, had I been asked.'

'I didn't know your mother's name was Elizabeth, I never thought of her as anything but Aunt Bessie.'

Alice laughed at the thought of Victoria McInally's reaction if she knew that her granddaughter was to be named in honour of her own cast-out sister. But her mother would never know, and Elizabeth – Beth – was a good enough name.

Regardless of Beth's Christian name, there would be a pang of pain to come over her surname when her birth had to be registered. Alice walked into the Registry Office where, less than a year before, she and Liam had stood outside, locked out by the Easter holiday. She explained that the child's father had died in the war, but despite the rings on her finger she didn't have a marriage certificate, so the baby would always be Beth McInally, and under her name, in brackets, it would be recorded for all time 'Illegitimate'. One day she would have to explain to the child why she had been labelled a bastard, but that day was far away, she had time.

Back at Kew Terrace, the plan to convert one of the rooms into a nursery more than a decade before had finally been realised, and no one was happier than Maggie. Fate had been unkind to Maggie. Some women need a man, any man, to be content, but Maggie was the kind of woman who needed children to complete her. Once Beth arrived, though, Maggie withdrew from much of her charitable work to be with the child, and when she did attend meetings she did little but talk about the baby. She could no longer devote herself quite so selflessly to good works, she explained, as Beth took up so much of her time, and she was sure the other ladies on the various committees understood. The ladies, mothers of several children each, nodded and smiled sweetly over their teacups, then expressed their doubts to each other behind Maggie's back. They didn't understand what had happened to Maggie Doyle, it was only a child, one child, after all.

In the meantime, Alice continued with her work at Pat Murphy's office. Financially she was well-off. Maggie had refused to take a single penny from her and Liam since the day they had arrived in Kew Terrace and, though some of her savings had gone on the Port Bannatyne cottage, she now had no real expenditure to talk of. Beth's every need wasn't just catered for by Maggie, but anticipated well in advance. The child wanted for nothing, and neither did Alice. But leaving the child behind when she started work again was a wrench, and the strength of the feeling surprised her. She found that she rarely saw Beth, leaving early in the morning and, as her responsibilities at Murphy's increased, often arriving back at Kew Terrace when her child was already asleep. Not that Beth was neglected: Maggie and Tony danced attendance on her and took every opportunity to show her off. For the first time in many years they even took to walking regularly in the Botanic Gardens with Beth in the grandest pram available, or along to Bingham's Pond to picnic and feed the ducks, becoming the kind of people those without children avoid. For Alice, the moment of truth came when she arrived home early one afternoon, looking forward to spending time with her daughter, only to discover that Beth didn't know who she was. As Alice picked her up the child screamed to Maggie, holding out her arms and kicking against her mother until she was placed in the safety of Maggie's arms, where she glowered at Alice.

The episode horrified Alice and made her think. She had lost Liam, and now she had lost his child. She had been drifting, which was understandable, given the changes in her life in such a short time, but the first anniversary of Liam's death had come and gone and Beth was now six months old and didn't know her, so the drifting, she decided, had to stop. She had to get her life together, for the sake of Liam's daughter more than anything, and the next thing that happened was like a push from fate to make sure she did it.

A frantic phone call had come to the office one day to tell her Brendon had arrived at Kew Terrace. There had been no hiding the child from him, so Maggie had told him Beth was her daughter and, given the child's attachment to her, there was no reason for him to doubt that. He had been over on business, he told Alice when she arrived home, and just wondered how she was doing, if she needed anything. There was nothing, she told him, and she didn't ask about anyone in Belfast, nor did he offer any news. When he had gone Maggie contacted Louise, the only member of the family across the Irish Sea who knew of Beth's birth, and told her about the visit. If any word of the child should leak back, though there was little chance of that, Louise was instructed to present the same story.

It had been too close for comfort though, and it brought Alice to a decision. Every penny she had saved would be used to begin a new life with Beth. She looked at various houses to rent before finding one in Inchcraig, in the East End of Glasgow, that she could afford to take without working. It wasn't what she had ever been used to – the East End had never been the most affluent area of Glasgow – but it was respectable enough. She could start afresh there where no one knew her and she would no longer be called 'Mrs McCann' but 'Mrs McInally', the same name as her child. All connection with Belfast, apart from Louise, would finally be severed to protect Beth's identity. As was her way, she had it all worked out before she told anyone. Maggie, understandably, was horrified.

'You can't have thought this through,' she protested. 'I mean, my dear, what about Beth? You can't take her from the life she has here with people who love her, and put her in a place like that.'

'She's six months old, Maggie, she's too young to know one place from another,' Alice said. 'As long as she's looked after and cared for, she'll be happy.'

'But she barely knows you,' Maggie cried, too distressed to realise that she was adding fuel to the fire.

'I know that, Maggie,' Alice replied quietly. 'That's why I'm doing this. I'm her mother, she should know me.'

'But must you go so far away?' Maggie persisted, willing to consider any compromise that would continue her relationship with Beth. 'I'm sure you could find somewhere in the West End, somewhere we could be of use to you both.'

'Not for the money I have, Maggie.'

'Well, if that's all you're thinking about, Tony and I will help out.'

'Don't you see, Maggie?' Alice smiled gently. 'That's the whole point. I'm nearly twenty-seven, I have a child – it's time I stood on my own two feet. You've helped enough, more than enough, you've been so kind – to me, Liam and to Beth – but I have to make an independent life for the two of us now.'

'But what if you use up all your savings? What good will that do Beth?'

'I've spoken to Pat about it. He can still provide me with work to do at home if I should need it, but I'm hoping not to.'

Maggie ran from the room in tears. Alice had set the whole thing up with Pat Murphy before breathing a word to her. It was so like the girl, she thought furiously, it was part of that bit of her you couldn't reach: she just did as she wanted and broke your heart. Then she calmed down. Maggie was a good person, and the truth was she was thinking of herself and Tony. They had become so attached to Beth that their lives revolved around her, and the thought of going back to a childless household was too awful.

Alice came after her. 'I'm sorry, Maggie, I know you'll miss Beth,' she said, 'but you can see her whenever you like, you'll always be part of her life, you know, and mine.'

'But the East End!' Maggie wailed.

'Maggie, it's not the far end of the moon!' Alice laughed.

To Maggie it was, though – to Maggie and to any inhabitant of the West End.

However, Maggie soon had other things on her mind, or another thing, at any rate. Like many unwillingly childless couples, Maggie and Tony had needed something to think about beyond their childlessness. Having had Beth to focus their attention on, a miracle of a kind had occurred, and Maggie Doyle was expecting her first child.

13

Inchcraig was a hangover from a farming village that had long since given up farming. Once it had huddled around Inchcraig House and its estate, but the house had long since crumbled and the estate was no longer there either. They had decayed to nothing in a surprisingly short time, leaving little clue of the grandeur that had existed, apart from the name. Even so, in mid-1919 it could still have been described as a country area, though it was in imminent danger of being swallowed up by the expanding city of Glasgow. All that was left of the original village was a collection of small, oddly spaced, former farm-workers' cottages, with a later development of flats, the kind of tenements that would have been regarded as above average for Glasgow. The slum-dwellers of the city would have thought they had landed in paradise if they had seen them, though they were markedly downmarket if you were used to Great Western Road's prestigious abodes. Though Inchcraig was in the process of being taken over by Glasgow, the place still had its own identity that it guarded fiercely, if hopelessly, when Alice moved there with Beth. There were green fields nearby, and a grassy area at the back of the three-storey tenement for washing to be hung out and where children could be left safely asleep in their prams to take in the fresh air and sunshine – if older brothers and sisters were prepared to leave them to their slumbers, that was, and if they didn't it was the kind of community where anyone could tell off another's child without umbrage being taken. People there knew each other but were equally content to accord each other privacy, if that was what was wanted, as in Alice's case. She hadn't told them anything of herself and her circumstances, so the neighbours picked up what signals they could and settled on her story. She was a war widow with a child to raise, a pleasant young woman who would say a friendly hello in passing, they said, but kept herself to herself and wasn't interested in joining gossip sessions. Each to his, or her, own.

And so it continued for the next six months, the mother getting to know her child, who had just turned a year old, the child getting to know her mother, and both sharing a contented existence, until one cold, wintry afternoon in the week between Christmas and New Year. They had been driven back to Inchcraig by Maggie's driver the day before, after spending Christmas at Kew Terrace admiring Anthony Junior, the longed-for child. It had been a good Christmas, marred slightly by the absence of Louise, who had gone with her family to her in-laws in Bangor, promising to travel to Glasgow in a fortnight. Beth had been put down for her afternoon nap when Alice answered a knock at the door and found Maggie's driver standing there again, bearing a hastily written letter from Mrs Doyle, which Alice was urged to read immediately. It seemed that Maggie had had an unexpected visitor on the doorstep of Kew Terrace, in the form of Henry McInally, Alice's father. Maggie, now with Anthony Junior to lavish time and affection on, had been knocked off any remaining balance she possessed by finding her Uncle Henry calling on her. He was looking for Alice, he said, and when she explained that Alice now had her own home, he had been intent on going straight there, but, mindful of what he didn't know, Maggie had insisted on sending the car to bring Alice back to Kew Terrace instead.

And so Alice had wakened her daughter and made the journey back to Kew Terrace with a feeling of doom, arriving in the early evening, though it was already very dark. She handed Beth to the maid and walked into the parlour, where Henry sat with a very agitated Maggie. When Alice saw him she was even more astounded and confused than Maggie had been. The last time she had seen him was from afar, at Liam's funeral. Now, close-up, he looked much the same, very well turned out, but he had always been a bit of a dandy, hair as black and slicked down as she remembered, as though not one strand had moved in years. His expression was anguished, and she wondered how, or even if, she should break the news of his granddaughter, but above all she wondered just what he could be doing there. And Henry, for his part, didn't know where to start explaining, so that the words spilled out of him in a disjointed rush, as she and Maggie tried to concentrate.

When World War One ended in November 1918, and the surviving soldiers went home, it soon became clear that they had taken with them the flu that had swept the trenches the year before, and the infection that killed Liam had gone on to cause havoc all over the world, hitting civilians this time, in their millions. It killed the young rather than the old, and it went from nothing to death very quickly, rapidly filling lungs with so much red-tinged fluid that they couldn't breathe. First, he informed her, it had killed Mattie, Harry's wife, just days after she had produced her first live child, then, the following day, Harry had also died.

'It all happened so fast,' he wept. 'Mattie seemed fine after

Matthew was born, but half a day later she was desperately ill. Same with Harry. One minute he was happy to have a son, then he was turning his mind to burying his wife, and next morning he was gone too. That was a week ago. Your mother and I brought Matthew home and we cared for him, but I came back earlier than usual four days ago and he was screaming and there was no one about. Your mother was dead in her chair in the kitchen where I'd left her in the morning. The poor child had been alone and untended all day.' He took out a handkerchief, blew his nose, then wept uncontrollably again. 'I keep thinking of her dying all alone, sitting in her chair all that time and no one in the world knowing she'd gone. What a terrible way to die!'

Alice felt as though she had been physically assaulted. It was too much tragic news to take in at once, but there it was. 'Did mother have the flu, too?' she asked, suddenly afraid for Beth.

'No, the doctor thinks it was her heart. She hadn't moved an inch from when I'd left, so it was very sudden.' He looked at her. 'I didn't know where else to turn, then I thought of you,' he said plaintively.

'But what about Bella and Billy? Can't they help?'

'Oh, they've gone,' he replied matter-of-factly.

'Gone? You mean –?'

He looked at her blankly before the penny dropped. 'No, no, not that,' he said absently. 'They're on a boat that's just sailed for Canada, they left immediately after we'd buried your mother. One of the neighbours helped me look after the child, at first, then I didn't know what to do.'

'Canada?' Alice asked.

'Yes, Billy has been offered a very good job there, although I didn't think he'd take it,' Henry said in a detached voice. 'But he changed his mind, and there was a boat about to sail, and luckily he managed to get them berths. So you see, there's no one but you.'

Had Alice been thinking straight she might have asked him what he was thinking, after all that the family had heaped on her, to come to her door years later expecting help, but there was too much to absorb to indulge in vengeance. 'Where is the child now?' she asked, trying to rearrange her thoughts.

'He's upstairs in the nursery,' Maggie said, 'with Anthony Junior.' She didn't add 'and Beth', but it was hanging there between them.

Alice couldn't understand why she hadn't heard anything of this, then remembered that Louise had left Belfast for her holiday. 'So what do you want of me?' she asked, confused.

'I thought you could help me raise your brother's child,' he said, as though it were the most normal thing in the world.

Alice stared at Maggie, who stared back. There were so many different responses whirling about in her head that she didn't know which one to actually say out loud.

'You're asking me to go back to Belfast with you?' she said incredulously.

'No, no,' Henry replied, 'I meant here, in Glasgow. There's nothing left in Belfast, and the whole country has become very dangerous.'

'But what about McCann and Son?'

'Oh, I should've explained about that,' he said absently. 'The reason I came home early the other day was because McCann and Son had closed down.'

'What?' she said, losing track of how many times she had been shocked in the last half hour. Her father didn't seem particularly perturbed, but with all that had happened to him in the last week – burying his son, his daughter-in-law and then his wife, losing his lifetime's work and having to decide what to do with a tiny baby – perhaps it wasn't surprising that he was thinking rather oddly. He must have been in some kind of shock.

'Business hadn't been too wonderful for a while, tastes change, you know, and the organisation of the place went downhill after you left. And now Harry wouldn't be there in future to sort things out, of course, so I wasn't surprised really. A bit shocked at how quickly it was done, though. Arrived as usual in the morning, a lot to catch up with, and Seamus McCann walked in after lunch and told me that was it, goodbye. Just like that. After all those years together, too.' He sighed. 'I went home, wondering how I could break the news to your mother, and then found I didn't have to. In a way I'm glad she never had to face it.' He covered his face with his handkerchief and sobbed noisily again.

Alice was casting around, trying to make sense of everything. 'What about Mattie's family?' she asked. 'How do they feel about you taking her baby away from Belfast?'

'There's only her sister. You remember her? She was chief bridesmaid at Mattie and Harry's wedding? Well, she has seven of her own, she couldn't take Matthew on as well.'

'So you've just up and left?' she asked, dazed. 'What about the house?'

'What about it?' he asked, perplexed.

'Well, presumably you'll have to arrange to sell it?'

'Sell it?' He looked at her blankly. 'I never owned the house, it was rented.'

Alice sat in stunned silence for a moment.

'Did mother know that?' she asked, amazed.

'Oh, no,' he almost smiled. 'She would've been very disappointed if she'd known, so I didn't tell her, I couldn't bear to hurt her. We couldn't have afforded the lifestyle we had if

'I'd had to buy the house as well, and your mother liked our lifestyle. I suppose that's another thing she won't have to face, finding out that all these years we've been tenants.'

In the four years since she had left Belfast with Liam, many things had happened in Alice's life that she would never have believed could happen, but what she had heard in the last thirty minutes topped everything. Her mother dead, her brother and sister-in-law, too, Bella and Billy emigrated, McCann and Son gone, and now here was her father telling her that the life she had left behind had been a sham – even the close connection between the McInallys and the McCanns had been non-existent. She didn't even feel emotional, though she felt she should, only dazed, as her father sat crying noisily again. Alice looked at Maggie and shrugged, seeking advice, and eventually Maggie took charge, getting up and ringing the bell for the maid.

'Uncle Henry,' she said pleasantly, 'until we have this sorted out I think you and the child should stay here. Now, you must be exhausted, so the maid will show you to your room. We'll decide what's to be done when you're rested.'

When he had gone the two women looked at each other again.

'What are we like?' Maggie said with a little forced laugh. 'We've done nothing but stare at each other since –' she waved a hand in the air, trying to find the right words, then gave up, '– since this thing happened.'

'I know,' Alice said in a little voice. 'I wish I could think of something to do or say, but I can't. There's just too much to take in.'

They sat in silence, deep in thought.

'I mean, can you believe it?' Maggie whispered.

'To just turn up like that,' Alice replied.

'After all that's happened . . .'

'. . . and after all these years . . .'

'. . . and just expect you to . . .'

'Yes,' Alice said, 'I know.'

'So what's to be done?' Maggie asked.

'I wish I knew.'

'But, my dear girl,' Maggie said, trying to get to grips with the situation. 'Shall I ring for tea? You've had such a shock. Your mother, your brother, just awful.'

'I keep thinking I should feel something,' Alice smiled weakly, 'but I don't.' She looked up at Maggie. 'Isn't that terrible?'

'It's the shock, dear,' Maggie said gently. 'Why don't you have a lie down?'

'Yes, I think that might be a good idea. I have a lot to think about.'

Alice thought she might rest for an hour or so to get her mind straight, but she instantly fell asleep and dreamed of things past. Her mother in her kitchen, and the very chair she had died sitting on – she could even smell the baking. Then she was running wild at Lough Neagh as a child with Liam, both of them barefoot; meeting on Shaw's Bridge on the banks of the Laggan, with the Minnow Burn beeches overhead and bluebells on the ground, and lying in his arms in the bedroom of 'Anneetermore', the whitewashed cottage on the Isle of Bute, then standing by his grave in Derrytrasna, where bluebells also flourished in spring.

When she awoke she was shocked to find that it was early morning, and weak sunshine was shining through gaps in the curtains at the bedroom window. Maggie must have crept in and closed them while she slept. Her mind was clear, though, as though her dreams had been cards she had to file in her head till some sort of order emerged. She stopped at the nursery to pick up her daughter then made her way downstairs, where Henry, Maggie and Tony were having breakfast.

'Father,' she said clearly, 'you and Matthew will be most welcome to stay with me once I have a bigger house, but first I have some news for you, too.' She looked at him and took a deep breath. 'I have a child, Father. Liam's child. Her name is Beth.'

He looked at her, then at Beth. 'But you and Liam were never married,' he said in a bemused tone.

'Well, we were. There was a mix-up with the paperwork and he died before it could be straightened out,' she said. That would have to do for now. 'And she is Liam's child, but I don't want the McCanns to know about her. I need your assurance that you will do nothing that could lead to them finding out about her.'

It seemed to Alice that, given the catalogue of disasters and tragedies he had just thrown at her, finding out that she had a child should have had little impact on him, but Henry looked utterly amazed. He got up and looked closely at the sleepy, cross child, who rubbed her eyes and stared at him as he stared at her. Then he smiled. 'Well, no doubt about that,' he said quietly, 'she is Liam's child. Did he know?'

She shook her head.

'That's very sad,' he said.

14

A few days later and held up by the holiday, a letter arrived at Kew Terrace addressed to 'Mrs Alice McCann'. It was from Brendon. He was writing to tell her how distressed he had been over his father's treatment of Henry. 'Once again I had no idea he intended doing this till it was over,' he said. 'I went to the house but a neighbour told me he'd gone to his niece's house in Glasgow. I hope you can find it in your heart to believe me. I can hardly express how disgusted I am and I have resolved to resign from the family businesses and have nothing more to do with my mother and father.'

Alice handed the letter to Louise, who had arrived at Maggie's house from spending Christmas and New Year with her in-laws.

'I know about this,' she said quietly. 'He left a message at home for me while we were away. I called on him before we set off to come here.'

'So what does he intend on doing?' Maggie asked.

'As far as I can make out,' Louise replied, 'he's going into business by himself.'

'It's a huge step, though,' Alice remarked.

'I'm sure he can afford it,' Louise commented wryly. 'None of the McCanns are short of a few coppers, are they?'

'No, they're not, but that's not what I meant,' Alice said sadly. 'He's cutting himself off from his family and that's his choice, but he's cutting his children off from them, too.'

'From what I can gather, he's thought of that,' Louise said. 'Things have been pretty fraught within the family since Liam died. What Seamus did to Uncle Henry was kind of the last straw.'

'I feel so sorry for him,' Alice said. 'He's tried to do the decent thing for so long. I suppose he just couldn't win.'

In Belfast, Molly and Seamus McCann were busy laying their latest loss at Alice's doorstep, blaming 'that McInally girl'. In their eyes the family's woes had started when she had wickedly seduced Liam. Their decision to sever links with Henry had come as a relief to them, for things could never be the same between the two families after Liam's death. All the reasons for closing down McCann and Son that Henry had presented to Alice were true, only more so in the minds of the McCanns. The ham-curing business was an increasingly less important part of the family's interests. It had been kept in existence through sentiment more than anything for many years. As one generation had succeeded another that sentiment had gradually weakened, as was bound to happen, and with everything else that had come about it was inevitable that it would become irrelevant. The plain truth was that Alice and Liam's situation had opened up a rift between the two families, though they were of one mind at the time, so they probably weren't completely aware of it. Liam's death meant there could never be a reconciliation, and the further vilification of Alice that came afterwards ensured the gulf would never be bridged. Molly found it difficult to see Victoria because it reminded her of what she had lost forever, and so contact between the two old friends was cut back. There were always very good reasons: a forgotten appointment elsewhere, a slight cold, anything that could stretch the gaps between meetings, so that the routine afternoon teas became less of a habit, and in no time at all they hardly saw each other, though, of course, they intended on 'getting back to normal' very soon. So, though it may have seemed callous to others, the terrible run of tragedies that had befallen Henry came as an opportunity to finally break with the McInallys. Business was poor in the weakest part of the McCann empire, Harry wouldn't be there to run it any longer, and for the first time in living memory, given that Henry had no more sons and was extremely unlikely to produce any in future, there would be no male McInally to revive the fortunes of the ham-curing business. Best to end it now, quickly – it would even help Henry to do it this way, when he had so much more to think about. As Seamus had said to Brendon after the deed had been done, Henry wasn't family, he had merely been an employee all these years and had been paid handsomely for his labours. There was no question of compensating him in any way. Where would the McInallys be now if it hadn't been for the McCanns? Back in Derryhirk, probably, curing pigs for a living, so Henry had nothing to complain about when you thought it through on a business level. Above all, they were now free of the McInally connection that had brought so much grief into their lives, and Brendon would come round, he was just being emotional, as he had been since Liam's death. It was all down to that McInally girl, one day he would realise this.

'And what,' Maggie asked, 'are we to make of the flight from Belfast of the Guthrie creature?'

'Yes, creature indeed,' Louise seethed. 'Are you asking for my opinion?'

Alice and Maggie nodded.

'The rat left the sinking ship, that's all.'

'What can you mean?' Maggie asked, shocked.

'Well, everything had crumbled around him, hadn't it? There was no family any longer, and he's sly enough to have worked out that the business would probably fold – the two families hadn't exactly been close for some time now. Billy Guthrie looks after Billy Guthrie. It was case of much slimmer pickings for him than he had expected, so he was off.'

'Oh, Louise, that sounds very harsh!' Maggie whispered. 'And what of Bella? She must've had some input, surely? She wouldn't have left her father and the baby in those circumstances.'

'Oh, Bella,' Louise waved her hand dismissively. 'She's too stupid to work any of this out.'

'Louise!' Maggie looked at Alice, who smiled back at her.

'She is,' she said sadly. 'Louise is right, haven't I told you that many times?'

Louise's summing up of 'the Guthrie creature' was more accurate than she imagined. At that moment he and Bella were on a boat to Canada, and on the high seas, en route for a new life and a fresh start, he was attending a meeting of the Freemasons. On the outside he looked as he always did, a very tall, very thin, red-headed man with an air of confidence about him, slightly smug even, but inside he was in turmoil, so perhaps it was understandable that he should be clinging to what he knew, to what was stable. As the meeting went on and the secret rituals were enacted, he turned it over in his mind yet again in case he had missed something. He had planned everything to perfection, yet his life had come apart in his hands and he couldn't understand why.

Long ago he had made the decision that he was worth more than his background, and in plotting a way out he had abandoned his younger brother and sister to ensure his own survival. Reasoning that he had a better chance of making something of himself, he had taken the money from selling off their grandmother's possessions and bought himself a decent set of clothes as a passport into his new existence. It left his brother and sister with nothing, but they were both little people, ordinary people, and, as children of Jessie Guthrie, he was sure they would know how to survive. The plain facts were that he would be better able to make use of the money than they would. He owed them nothing, and, besides, they would be of no use to him and he would never need to see them again.

Then he had identified the McInallys, who were well-known in his church and highly regarded in business circles. Even if he did disapprove of their connections with the Catholic McCanns, they had money and standing, and Billy needed all they had to offer. More to the point, they had two daughters, and if he didn't manage to capture the eldest, there was always the younger one as a reserve. The mother was a complete pushover, he quickly realised, and the son and the father didn't matter, they did as the mother told them. So he had made himself indispensable to the family through her, by quietly ensuring he was around to be noticed, then the eldest daughter, Alice, had spoken to him at church, and from there on he was in. Pity nothing had blossomed with her, but it proved to be a blessing in the long run. She was too close to the McCanns, and she was a bit too independent-minded for Billy, so he decided on the younger girl, Bella, who was besotted with him anyway and, it had to be admitted, was the prettier by far.

Thus far all had gone well: he had progressed through the helpful-friend stage to become a family intimate, then, after the slight hiccup over Alice had forced a change of direction, he had successfully married Bella and become a full member of the family. Victoria relied on him for everything, which wasn't surprising given that her religious leanings were closer to his own than to any of her family's – all he'd had to do was re-inforce them, keep assuring her she was right, and they'd hard-ened up nicely. The absence of Alice had helped enormously there, he had to admit. Once she'd gone there was really no opposition. And yet somehow it had all gone wrong, first with the deaths of the son and his wife, then of the mother – and the final tragedy came when Henry McInally's job had folded, leaving him alone, with no money or influence and a newborn to provide for. When it came down to it he hadn't even owned the house, it had been rented all along.

Where had he gone wrong, that was what was endlessly worrying Billy. He had planned it meticulously, but was there something he could have, should have, done differently? Chosen a different family, perhaps? Well, he couldn't be faulted on that, he was sure; no one could've suspected what would befall the McInallys. Still, he had this opportunity, and Bella, though she wasn't bright – and that was no bad thing – was beautiful; that was bound to help him. But even so, he couldn't help feeling a bit low, a bit jinxed in a way.

Over tea at Kew Terrace, the cousins moved on to the sudden changes in Alice's family.

'I must say, Alice,' Louise said tartly, 'I think you're quite mad. Terribly good, dutiful daughter and all that, of course, but if Uncle Henry had been my father I'd have kicked him off my doorstep, kicked him right up the backside.'

Maggie almost dropped her cup and saucer but Louise ignored her reaction.

'He had a real cheek coming to you looking for help,' she continued, 'and as for expecting you to look after Harry's son, when Harry hadn't done a thing to help you all this time, well, I just think you're quite mad!'

Alice laughed quietly at Louise. 'I couldn't think of what else to do,' she explained. 'It wasn't the poor child's fault, was it? What would become of him otherwise?'

'Yes, yes, but still,' Louise said moodily, stirring her tea hard enough to break either the cup or the spoon. 'Although I have to admit that I always had the feeling the real opposition came from your mother, backed up by the Guthrie creature. She called you and Maggie "two sinners and traitors" once, you know – sounded like a snake hissing, as I recall.' She sighed. 'I'm told she died of a heart problem. I said at the time, and I'm sure it's true: the problem was that Aunt Victoria didn't have one.'

Maggie's face flushed with embarrassment. 'You are talking of Alice's mother, Louise,' she said severely. 'Regardless of how she behaved, she was her mother.'

'Yes, that's what I thought,' Louise replied calmly. 'It was just a pity she didn't realise that herself, don't you think? I tried to reason with Uncle Henry once, and all he said was "What can I do?" I told him, "You can behave like a man for once and stand up to your wife!" And I gave him your address so that he could never say he didn't know where Alice was.'

'You didn't tell him to be a man!' Maggie said in a hushed voice.

'I did, Maggie, do you really doubt it? He was supposedly the head of his house, though he didn't say a word, let his wife and her cohort, the odious Guthrie creature, do their worst all this time – and now here he comes crawling to the "two sinners and traitors" for help.' She stirred her tea again with renewed vigour. 'I'd have kicked him up the backside, I tell you straight! But what happens? The two of you take him in, welcome him with open arms! There is no justice, that's all I can say! I told him then that I would never forgive him, and I shan't. You may, Alice, but I shan't, so don't ever expect it.'

'I've been waiting for you to arrive,' Alice smiled, trying to change the subject. 'I need both of you to listen.'

She explained that the doubling of her household and the move to a bigger house presented her with an opportunity and a dilemma at once. Looking ahead, she wondered how their different circumstances would affect the children. 'We are all called McInally, yet Beth is my child and I'm supposed to be a war widow,' she explained. 'What I'm afraid of is people guessing that Beth is illegitimate, and people can be very unforgiving.'

'But what can you do about it?' Maggie asked.

'Well, it would be so much easier if Beth and Matthew were brother and sister, the orphaned children of parents who had died in the flu epidemic, being raised by their spinster aunt and their grandfather.' She looked from one to the other.

'You mean, bring the two children up as your niece and nephew?' Maggie gasped.

'But why would it matter, Maggie?' Alice persisted. 'I'll be the only mother either of them will ever know, and it would make life easier for Beth, wouldn't it?'

Louise looked thoughtful. 'You're right, Alice,' she said slowly.

Maggie couldn't believe what she was hearing and protested.

'Oh, sit down,' Louise said. 'Listen to her, my sister the scarlet woman, and she comes over like Mistress Purity.'

'Louise, really!' Maggie turned to Alice, wringing her hands.

'Couldn't you do it the other way round? I mean, what's wrong with you being a war widow and the mother of both children?'

'Well, my father, mainly,' Alice explained. 'I need him to go along with this, but it's partly the name problem, too – all of us being called McInally, I mean. I'd have to change my name to something else to become a widow, wouldn't I? That would mean changing Beth's and Matthew's names as well, and I don't think he could go along with his grandson taking the name McCann, do you? This way he'll be able to tell Matthew stories of his mother and father that he wouldn't be able to do if we made Liam Matthew's father. Both children will be the same, both will benefit this way.'

'This is all getting terribly complicated,' Maggie said uncertainly.

'Yes, exactly,' Alice said. 'Don't you see? If we make them brother and sister it will be less complicated.'

'I don't know why you're making such a fuss. Just think about it, Maggie,' Louise said calmly, 'Alice is talking sense.' She sipped her tea. 'And she'll be referred to as "Mrs McInally" anyway, the way all women who've missed the marriage boat are, as a kind of consolation prize for no man wanting them.'

'Louise!' Maggie said angrily, standing up and walking to the window. 'I really don't like the way you talk at times, I find it quite offensive!'

'I know you do.' Louise smiled across the room to Alice. 'That's partly why I do it.' As Maggie opened her mouth to protest again, she said, 'Oh, hush. Alice is being purely practical, think about it and you'll see that. You go ahead, Alice, you're doing the right thing.'

'It's just, well, Liam, you know?' Maggie said quietly. 'It's like pretending he never existed, for Beth, I mean. It seems so sad.'

'I'll tell her one day,' Alice replied. 'When she's grown up and can understand. But this is better for her as she's growing up. She won't have to face the stigma of being illegitimate, of her mother being unmarried.'

'A whore and a slut!' Louise said merrily.

Maggie glared at her. 'Louise, that is quite enough!' she said angrily. 'Another word and I'll have to ask you to leave!'

'Oh, please,' Louise replied, shaking her head, 'you sound just like your old mother, and that's no compliment. You'll be getting an attack of the vapours any minute.'

Maggie calmed herself and sat down. 'And Uncle Henry, will he go along with this?'

'I shouldn't think he has much choice,' Louise said bitterly, 'if he wants a roof over his and his grandson's head. I still think he's getting off far too lightly. If I had my way he'd still have a kick up the backside.'

When Alice had gone the two sisters sat in the parlour sipping tea. Maggie was still thoughtful.

'You get the feeling that,' she said uncertainly, 'that she's already made up her mind when she tells you things, don't you?'

'Of course she has!' Louise laughed. 'Honestly, Maggie, these bolts of lightning of yours!'

'But that's what I mean,' Maggie persisted. 'When she does mention something you think she wants to discuss it, that she's looking for advice maybe, or even your thoughts, but she isn't, is she?'

'I can't believe you ever thought otherwise,' Louise shrugged. 'She thinks things through for herself, Maggie, she's not a weakling in any way, I've told you that before. You'd save yourself a great deal of needless heartache if you chose to believe it. Alice doesn't mean to hurt your feelings, she just thinks things through from every angle and comes to a decision long before she ever mentions it, then you jump to the conclusion that she's some flibbertigibbet who does things at a whim. No wonder she gets short with you at times. Anyway, you have a child of your own, don't you think you should restrict your mothering to him?'

'That's a bit harsh, Louise. I've always had Alice's best interests at heart, you know. She was in my care, after all.'

'Oh don't be so pompous, of course she wasn't!' Louise retorted. 'She was living here, but she was always in her own care.'

The McInallys moved into the new house within weeks, along with an influx of other tenants. It wasn't within the original Inchcraig, that and its dwindling inhabitants were another world away and the two didn't mix. It simply took the name without sharing the history and had been swiftly built to house the enormous number of slum-dwellers swamping the city centre. There were many families as oddly comprised as Alice's, World War One and the flu pandemic had seen to that, as had TB, the disease of the poor that was still decimating the slums. So there were other families like hers with several generations and no male head. As Glasgow grew outwards the village of Inchcraig lost the battle for survival and identity, as it was always bound to, and as many others were doing.

The tenement had three storeys, and Alice had been allocated the middle flat on the right, with three bedrooms, one each for Alice and Henry and one for the children to share. They had an inside toilet, but there were no grassy areas to play in and there were many more people to contend with. Henry quickly got himself a job in a nearby grocery store, Galbraith's, cutting bacon on a slicer this time instead of running a business supplying it, and he was so good at it that the customers asked for Henry by name. Alice watched him behind the counter, white apron tied around his waist, chatting knowledgeably to the customers on matters bacon, still a dandy, master of all he surveyed, and marvelled at how he had adapted to the abrupt change in his circumstances. He was settled again, he was being looked after by a woman, and for Henry any woman would do, so he knew how to function again. From Inchcraig he wrote to Bella and Billy, but there was no contact with Belfast and it was rarely mentioned.

Liam had been pessimistic about Ireland, but he hadn't seen it become a divided country in 1920, with the predominately Protestant six counties in the north remaining as part of Britain and loyal to the Crown, while the south, Eire, became a mainly Catholic Republic. Had he lived he would no longer have been an Irishman but a Northern Irishman, and if he had wanted to keep his faith he would've been regarded as part of an inferior and deeply suspicious minority or been forced to move south.

For Alice's part, her former life and all it had encompassed were in the past. Not only did the generations of the McInally–McCann alliance cease to exist in her mind, but she kept to her decision of not keeping in touch with Brendon. In her reconstituted family she didn't want to include anything or anyone with a link to the McCanns. And it was the same with the friends she and Liam had made in Glasgow, though less deliberately so. She lived a different life in a very different area, so she gradually lost touch with them, especially with Molly and Pat Murphy, who were linked too closely to the Isle of Bute for comfort. Memories of the island, of Port Bannatyne and the whitewashed cottage they had called 'Anneetermore', of the life she and Liam would have lived there with their happy, free children, would always be too painful, and the Murphys were part of that pain. Besides, she had enough to do raising two small children without dwelling on the past, on what might have been, though she kept in close touch with her cousins, Louise and Maggie, who had supported her through all her troubles. Matthew thrived with his 'sister', a happy child who proved to have a pleasant personality, and he gave Alice a great deal of joy, though she blushed occasionally at the admiration she received from her neighbours for 'taking on two orphaned children'.

Just as life settled into a new routine, Maggie raised questions about Beth. They were having tea in the parlour at Kew Terrace, Maggie pregnant for the second time, the three children playing on what had once been a prized, pristine rug that not a speck of dust was allowed to threaten.

'I've been meaning to talk to you for some time, dear. I don't think Beth is hearing properly,' she told Alice gently.

'She just ignores what she doesn't want to hear,' Alice replied. 'You can't distract her if she's doing something and doesn't want to be disturbed.'

Maggie coughed quietly. 'Alice, I think it might be more than that. She doesn't react to sound at all. I've been thinking about it for a while now.'

Alice stared at her, thinking that Maggie had always had a tendency to become too absorbed. Maggie got up and positioned the three children away from them, then clapped her hands behind them. Anthony Junior and Matthew turned round, but Beth kept playing with her toys.

'Maybe she just isn't interested in hands clapping,' Alice smiled, though fear was clutching at her heart.

'All right, dear, we'll try something else.' Maggie smiled

tightly as she took a music box from the mantelpiece, wound it up and removed the key. Once again, the two boys turned to look in the direction of the tinkling tune, while Beth ignored it. Then Maggie knelt behind her and said her name, and Beth didn't move. Maggie looked up at Alice, tears in her eyes.

'No, don't!' Alice said, desperately trying to banish any possibility of something being wrong with her daughter. 'It's because she's more used to my voice now. Beth. Beth!'

But once again, Beth continued playing, giving no indication that she had heard a sound.

Maggie was wiping her eyes, but Alice was too shocked to even cry. How had she missed this? She had been looking after both children for six months now, how could she have missed that one could hear and one couldn't? It was impossible, it couldn't be true. Beth was a happy, healthy, perfect child, there couldn't be anything wrong with her.

'I've been thinking about it for some time, Alice,' Maggie said quietly. 'I've been trying to find a way of talking to you about it. She hasn't said a word, that's what first made me wonder. She's eighteen months old and she hasn't said a word, you see. Then one of the maids dropped a tray of tea things in the nursery last time you were here and it scared Anthony and Matthew out of their wits, but Beth didn't even look round.' She was rushing on, her long-held fears suddenly released.

'She makes noises, though,' Alice said miserably, staring at her daughter, 'and she cries. I thought she was just taking her time in talking.'

'Yes, and I suppose you're used to the noises she makes, and you react to them as though they were speech. All mothers do that,' Maggie said. 'Look, dear, we have a friend who is a doctor, Doctor MacDonald, he lives just along Great Western Road, on Redlands Road. All I've told him is that you're raising your brother's orphaned children and we're a little worried about one of them. He would be very happy to see you and Beth.'

And so they had embarked on what she would look back on later as a time in her life as dark as any before. Dr MacDonald performed various tests on Beth and pronounced her fit and healthy, but deaf, and Alice, who rarely showed what she was feeling, sobbed till she thought she would never stop. Her beautiful, perfect child, Liam's perfect child, what would her future be now? Dr MacDonald sat quietly in his office and waited for the tears to subside.

'How did I miss it?' she asked. 'How could I miss something like that?'

'You mustn't feel guilty,' he chided her. 'Have you ever had charge of a child of her age before?'

Alice shook her head.

'Has anyone ever explained to you in any detail the milestones in a child's early development?'

Again she shook her head.

'Well then, that's why. What you have to concentrate on now,' he suggested, 'is how you can help Beth.'

Alice nodded.

'Naturally you're sad, the poor child has already lost so much and you've already taken on more than enough with her and her brother, but time is important in these cases, help has to be given sooner rather than later. I know of someone, a teacher, who would welcome the money. You see, once deaf children used sign language, with their fingers, you know, but it was decided by those who make these decisions that they should be taught to talk and lip-read instead, that signing was a bad thing. Now I don't know how you feel about this, you've hardly had time to think anything, I know, but it seems to me that the deaf should use whatever means they want to communicate.'

Alice nodded again, but she wasn't taking any of it in. Beth was on her knee, blissfully unaware of the discussion around her, reaching out determinedly to a large dog sitting by the doctor's side.

'The young woman I'm referring to found herself out of a job when signing became outlawed. I'm sure she would be a great help to Beth.'

But Alice didn't want her daughter to learn to sign or to lip-read, she didn't want Beth to be deaf, for her precious child to grow up without hearing or speech. She couldn't bear for Beth to be cut off from normal life. Beth wriggled free and tottered to the dog, immediately putting him in a headlock hug. 'Don't, Beth,' Alice said instinctively, but Beth didn't hear her and she subsided in tears once more.

'Don't worry,' Dr MacDonald smiled, 'he's quite accustomed to robust affection, that's why I keep him here.' Then he rang the bell and asked for the car to take Mrs McInally and Beth back to Kew Terrace. There was no point in trying to push the young woman on faster than she could go at the moment, he decided. He had mentioned someone he knew of who could help the child and, once she had time to get used to the situation, she would remember and come back to that thought.

Alice sat stunned in Maggie's parlour, unable to talk, her hands cradling her cup as the tea in it grew cold. It was her fault, had to be. It must have been something she had done, she decided, or not done. She remembered that day more than two years ago when she had arrived home early to find Brendon waiting for her in this very parlour. Somehow she had known what he was about to tell her, so she had covered her ears with her hands so that she wouldn't hear him say that Liam was dead. Was that what had caused it, she wondered? In blocking out words she didn't want to hear, had she blocked out the ability to hear in the child she hadn't known she was carrying at the time? Liam's child. She had let him down, and the child, too. She felt weak, as though all her strength had suddenly vanished. So many things had happened in a short time and she had managed to struggle on, but this was too much, she couldn't bear it.

15

Maureen Murray, small, plump, with dark hair and blue eyes, came into their lives a week later, her presence at Kew Terrace arranged by Maggie and through Dr MacDonald. Maureen was a lively woman in her early thirties, a few years older than Alice, and she instantly lifted Alice out of her depression.

'You're already communicating with Beth by signing, aren't you?' she smiled.

Alice shook her head.

'Of course you are!' she grinned. 'What do you say when you ask her if she wants a drink?'

Alice thought, then slowly smiled. She motioned with her hand as though drinking from a cup and nodded. If Beth wanted it, she nodded back, if not, she shook her head.

'You see? I told you so! All mothers use a form of signing before their children can talk,' Maureen said brightly. 'And when it's time for bed?'

Alice joined her hands together and rested her left cheek against them.

'Didn't I tell you?' Maureen chuckled. 'Now, it's important that when you do sign to her like that, you also keep saying the words. "Drink,"' she said, with exaggerated clarity. '"Sleep."'

"Bed." You see? Just because you know she can't hear you, don't assume you shouldn't talk to her. That's how she'll learn to lip-read and eventually to read, by associating the signs with the lip movements and the written word.'

'Will she be able to talk?'

'Well, she may,' Maureen explained. 'You see, deaf people have some hearing, but it isn't what the rest of us hear. The simple rule is that whatever sound they make to you, a high sound or a low sound, that's what they're hearing, but the range isn't very good and can be difficult for the hearing to understand, so mostly they choose not to use whatever voice they have. That's why people call them dumb, but that's very rare. They choose to be dumb because it's easier and less embarrassing.'

'They call them "dummies",' Alice said miserably.

'People can be very cruel, it's true,' Maureen conceded, 'but we can't do anything about ignorance and stupidity, can we? We certainly can't bow down to it.'

'It's just that it all seems so hard. I mean, how can she learn to read?'

'Well, everyone has to learn language, don't they?' Maureen said efficiently. 'We weren't born with language, and Beth is the same, though to her our spoken word will always be a second language, her first will be signing, because that's what she's already learning from you. I have to explain to you, though, what provision there is for the deaf at the moment.' She glanced uncertainly at Maggie. 'The usual advice is that you send your child to a special deaf school where she would stay during the week. Now it may be that's what you think would be appropriate for Beth.'

'No!'

'I'm glad about that,' Maureen continued. 'She would be

banned from signing at a deaf school. She would be taught to speak if possible, and to lip-read, and the current belief in some places is that signing hinders both. In fact, in order to stop her signing she might well have her hands tied behind her back.'

'I don't believe it!' Alice cried.

'Well, it's true. It's part of the "cruel to be kind" philosophy, and if the children are caught signing to each other, they are punished.'

The three women sat silently, digesting the information.

'None of that will happen to Beth,' Alice said firmly. 'I will not send her away from home. How would I explain that to her? The idea is ridiculous!'

Maureen Murray smiled smugly to herself. She so admired this young woman taking on her brother's two children, and she was reacting as any courageous natural mother would, which was even more to her credit. She had seen it so many times before. When she had first sat down Alice had been subdued, her eyes dulled by the pain of the child's handicap – now they were glowing with indignation. It was a start.

Maureen had long been at odds with the way deaf children were treated, which meant she had little work. Shocked parents rarely had the confidence to argue against the 'expert' view, neither could they afford private tuition for their children. But Alice could, so it was settled that Maureen would teach Beth at home to sign, to lip-read, to communicate any and every way she was capable of, and teach Alice, too, to communicate with Beth.

'I still don't know how I missed it,' Alice said sadly. 'It was Maggie who noticed it.'

'That's often the case,' Maureen replied. 'You're with her all the time and, as you now know, all mothers have ways of communicating with their children that don't always involve speech. When they're very small you don't need them to talk clearly, do you? What Maggie did was look at Beth in comparison with other children, that's how she became suspicious. She had time to do that, she has people to help her care for her child, but you look after these two on your own, don't you? It must be a great deal of hard work, one eighteen months and the other only six, and you were landed with them both out of the blue, plus your widowed father.'

Alice and Maggie exchanged a glance.

'I must say,' Maureen continued, 'I think you're doing a splendid job, and you mustn't blame yourself for not picking it up.'

When the McInally family had moved into the newer part of Inchcraig, building was taking place around them as houses went up for the, mostly but not exclusively, Catholic slum-dwellers throughout the 1920s. Inevitably, they brought the gang culture of the inner city with them, though they were in the process of stepping up from sectarian vendettas to criminal activity that was conducted outside Inchcraig – it was where they lived, after all, they weren't going to cause trouble on their own doorsteps. Even in those early days it wasn't the kind of neighbourhood Alice had been used to, but she was happy enough, or would have been if money wasn't proving such a problem. Henry loved his work at Galbraiths, but spent a great deal of his wages buying little knick-knacks he chanced upon, pieces of glass and porcelain mostly, and, later, silver that he stored in his bedroom. It had always been an interest of his, one that Victoria hadn't shared and very firmly disapproved of, but Henry's enthusiasm, once curbed, was now free. And that would have been all right, if it hadn't been for the way Beth's tuition ate through the money Alice had saved over the years; and there was Matthew to care for, too, to feed and clothe.

After a few years it was obvious to Maggie that Alice was struggling. From her days as a helper of Glasgow's poor, she had learned how to spot such things, though Alice was never on a level with those desperate souls, of course. The same dress worn many times, showing signs of being repaired just as many, the hems of the children's clothes let down, little things really, but the kind Maggie was built to recognise. And, being Maggie, she couldn't leave it alone, of course.

'You must be finding that money doesn't quite go as far as it once did, dear,' she suggested over their weekly tea at Kew Terrace.

Alice, instantly on the alert, smiled sweetly. 'Well, that's to be expected, isn't it?' she countered. 'It has much further to go these days.'

'Yes, yes, I know, dear,' Maggie sighed, 'even we find this. What a difference two children can make to one's finances.'

Alice laughed, deciding not to understand. 'No wonder,' she said, 'for Tony must hit the roof every time you come home with yet more things for the children! How many suits and dresses can one little boy and one little girl wear? They must run out of time to wear them all.'

'Well, that's the thing, Alice, you know me so well, and just because something is too big doesn't mean I can't buy it. I was thinking –' Maggie said, but Alice wasn't walking into that trap. She did know Maggie so well, she had seen it a mile ago.

'Just as well you still do a bit of your charity work for the poor, Maggie, at least those clothes won't go to waste, will they?'

Later, Maggie approached Tony about her fears.

'Well, what about her father?' Tony asked reasonably. 'He works, doesn't he?'

'I don't think Uncle Henry will earn very much cutting bacon in a shop, Tony,' Maggie replied. 'And I'm not entirely sure Alice would broach the subject with him if she needed money.'

'I'm sure she'd ask for help if she really needed it,' he replied.

'That's just what I'm telling you, dear,' Maggie insisted a little impatiently. 'She wouldn't and she won't.'

'But maybe you're imagining things,' he protested. 'What if she does wear the same dress more often than you would? After all, it would be pretty odd if she dressed in Inchcraig the way you do in Kew Terrace, wouldn't it?'

'Are you suggesting that I am extravagant?' she demanded.

'No, Maggie, of course not,' he lied. 'But Alice doesn't have to change two or three times a day, now, does she?'

'I am your wife!' Maggie said, close to tears. 'I dress well for your standing in the community. I'd be perfectly happy in rags!'

Tony retreated behind his paper just in time to hide his laughter. He knew he was fighting a losing battle anyway, and that the next step would be to bring in the heavy artillery: Louise would be consulted.

At the next afternoon tea there was a surprise guest, though Alice couldn't understand the fuss. Louise and Tallullah-Emma were frequent visitors these days.

'Let's get to the point,' Louise said. 'Maggie thinks you're short of money.'

Maggie wanted the floor to open up and swallow her. 'I didn't say that exactly, dear,' she smiled weakly.

'Oh, drop the act, Maggie,' Louise said dismissively. 'And you' she said to Alice, 'know perfectly well that Mother Hen here won't give up, so let's not waste time on being insulted.'

'Well, Maggie's not wrong, but she's not right either,' Alice replied quietly. 'We have had to cut back on certain things,' she looked pointedly at Maggie, 'but I resent the suggestion that we are destitute and in need of charity. Not everyone has to live such an opulent life, you know. We manage and we are perfectly happy, thank you.'

'Told you she'd blow up,' Louise remarked amiably. 'You have no idea how to handle her, Maggie.'

'But dear,' Maggie said contritely, 'I was only concerned for you and the children, that's all. I didn't mean to interfere.'

'Huh!' Louise muttered.

There was a long silence.

'Look,' Louise sighed, 'it's quite simple. Do you need money?'

'No,' Alice replied firmly.

'Right, end of discussion,' Louise replied. 'Now, this signing thing, Alice, are there any really rude things you could teach me?'

Two weeks later Alice opened her door and found Louise standing there, and beside her was Brendon McCann. Her heart sank. She had wanted the McCann connection severed, and now Brendon knew where she was, brought here by her own trusted cousin.

'You may as well know now,' Louise said bluntly, 'that I've told Brendon everything.' She sat down in Alice's sitting room, planted Beth on her knee and glared at her cousin. 'He knows Beth is Liam's daughter.'

Alice gasped, appalled and shocked at her cousin's betrayal.

'And you can save the accusations,' Louise said blandly. 'You need money, but you made it clear you wouldn't accept help from me or Maggie, so I decided to tell Brendon, because he has Liam's money and by rights it's yours and Beth's.' She looked at Alice. 'All right, I've said my piece, you can start with the accusations now, I'm ready.'

Instead, Alice looked at Brendon, who was watching Beth playing, and saw he was even more shocked.

'She's his double!' he whispered, tears in his eyes. 'How old is she?'

'She's four, nearly five.'

'My God, Alice, how could you keep this from me?' he whispered.

She tried to find the words to explain the position she had been in but Louise interrupted.

'I've told you, he knows everything, Alice, he knows why. The poor man's just upset.'

The poor man hadn't taken his eyes off Beth, who was busily pulling at the necklace round Louise's neck, so Louise took it off and gave it to her.

'Don't,' Alice said, 'she'll put it in her mouth. She does it with everything, I don't really know why, maybe it's a way of finding out about things when she hasn't got any sound clues.' She took the necklace from Beth, held her face to get eye contact with her and said 'No!', then gave her a biscuit instead. 'Besides, she can't get everything she wants just because she's deaf, you know.' She looked at Brendon. 'I'm sorry, Brendon, it just seemed the best thing to do. I didn't want to burden you with the knowledge, and the McCanns wouldn't play any part in her life anyway, would they? Your mother and father wouldn't believe she was Liam's, even though she is his image, as you say. They'd just have said I was after McCann money for some other man's child.'

Brendon looked down, knowing she was right.

'Besides,' Louise said savagely, 'the miserable pair didn't, don't, deserve to know about her, they'd only poison her life.'

'Louise!'

'Why does everyone say "Louise!" to me in that tone of voice?' she demanded. 'I only tell the truth, why is that so wrong, Alice?'

'She's right,' Brendon sighed, 'you're both right. But I could've helped, Alice, I'd have wanted to help.'

'I didn't want help, Brendon, I wanted to stand on my own two feet and be in control of my own life, and my daughter's.'

'But the cards have always been stacked against you, Alice,' he persisted, 'and she is Liam's child. I'd have given anything to know there was something of him still alive.'

Alice suddenly felt ashamed. She had regarded Liam as hers alone, but Brendon had loved him, too. Brendon missed him as much as she did.

'I wanted to give you the money our grandfather had left Liam, and you refused to touch it, but wasn't that selfish? I mean, it was Beth's money, wasn't it? It should've come to her from her father.'

'Brendon, I'm sorry, I didn't mean to hurt you. I suppose I just didn't want to risk your parents finding out about her.'

'Well, there's no chance of that. I haven't laid eyes on either of them since McCann and Son folded the way it did.'

'I've always wished you hadn't done that,' she said quietly. 'I know what it's like to be adrift from your family. I wouldn't have wished that for you on our behalf.'

'Oh, it was only partly that,' he explained. 'Mostly it was on my own behalf. I was disgusted by their behaviour and by the fact that they couldn't see it. I felt as though I didn't know them.'

'What are you doing now?'

'I have my own supply business, still in the grocery trade, doing well, you know. I have no idea how my parents are doing. Our paths never cross and I don't ask anyone who might know.'

Beth had wriggled free of Louise and had edged across to where Brendon was sitting. She was now holding on to his right knee, staring intently at him.

'But look at this one,' he smiled. 'Who does that look remind you of? Liam watching Jimmy Devlin building a boat on the Lough.' His voice cracked. He picked the child up and hugged her till he could speak again. Beth didn't pull away, but continued to examine him closely.

'Man sad,' she signed to Alice.

'Yes, man sad.'

'Why? Does he want a biscuit?'

Before Alice could reply, Beth crammed the half-chewed biscuit into his mouth, and they all laughed.

'Man not sad now,' Beth signed, nodding solemnly.

'Since Louise told me –' he started, and Alice shot an angry look at her cousin.

'Oh, stop it!' Louise said. 'We've dealt with that.'

'Louise, you should have asked me first,' Alice said severely.

'No, I shouldn't,' Louise replied, 'you'd only have said no, and before you tell me I had no right – I had. I've been involved in this story for a very long time. I'm part of it, that gives me the right, so there!'

Brendon laughed quietly. 'As I was saying, since Louise told me I've been thinking of how we deal with this situation. I know a little bit about deafness, you see. My mother's eldest sister was deaf.'

'I didn't know that,' Alice said, surprised. 'Liam never mentioned it.'

'Well, he probably didn't know. It was kept very quiet within the McAlinden family, they saw it as an imperfection, something to be ashamed of. I was closer to my mother's family than Liam was. He spent all his time at the Lough and fighting with my father – he was very much a McCann, as you know.'

'In the best possible way, of course,' Louise muttered.

'And Liam tended to concentrate on what he was doing at that moment. He didn't have much time for things other than boats. I heard two of my aunts talking once and put two and two together, so my mother told me about her sister and swore me to secrecy. They sent her to live with the nuns when she was only three years old, she very rarely came home, and when she did she became very distressed. Hardly surprising she lashed out occasionally, given that she didn't know her family and they hadn't bothered learning ways to communicate with her, but it frightened them, convinced them she was mentally unstable. The nuns taught her to sign and kept her at the convent till she died a few years ago. Did you know that there's a Catholic sign language?' he laughed.

'Oh, come on!' Alice said, looking at Louise.

'No, seriously, there is,' he said. 'They have their own schools to educate children their way, so I suppose it would follow that they'd do the same in their deaf schools. Why they still persist in having their own version of signing, though, well, they'd have to explain that one. Anyway, what I want to suggest is that I do what I wanted to do in 1918 and transfer Liam's money to you to care for Beth.'

'No!'

'Oh, do grow up, Alice,' Louise said wearily. 'You'll need it to go on paying for Beth's tuition. Where's the money to come from?'

'I was thinking of asking Pat Murphy for some work to do at home,' Alice said stubbornly.

'You haven't seen him in years! And who'd look after the

children while you do work for Pat? Look, it isn't charity, it's really simple. The money was Liam's. Apart from the paperwork you are his widow, this is Liam's child, therefore the money is yours, yours and Beth's.'

'I couldn't have put it any better,' Brendon agreed.

And so the matter was settled, if not happily, at least amicably, and Alice wouldn't have to worry about how she would pay for Maureen's lessons, she would be able to give Beth every chance that was available. Before he and Louise left, Brendon turned to her.

'Where's the little boy?' he asked. 'Can I see him?'

'He's asleep. He's much livelier than Beth – she's a great thinker, Matt runs around all the time and tires himself out.' Alice smiled, opening the bedroom door.

Brendon looked at the sleeping child. 'He's fair, like both his parents.'

'Yes, it helps that he and Beth are both fair – in different ways, of course, but people don't examine what they see, they just accept it.'

'She's reddish-fair, though,' he murmured, 'like Liam. Alice, would you mind if I came to see her sometimes?' he asked. 'To see both of them?'

'I don't want her to know anything, Brendon,' she said sadly. 'Not till she's older and can understand.'

'Well, that's all right,' he smiled. 'I can just be Uncle Brendon to both of them, an old friend from Lough Neagh,' and he hugged her.

Beth looked up as the strange man hugged Alice, not something she was used to seeing.

'Either that,' Louise said saucily, 'or you can just tell them Uncle Brendon is Aunt Louise's fancy man, they'll believe that.'

'Yes,' Alice replied, 'I'm sure they would.'

Beside them Beth signed to Alice, 'What's a fancy man?'

'She's asking what a fancy man is,' Alice explained, glaring at Louise, then she signed back and said the words as she did so. 'It's just one of Aunt Louise's little jokes.'

Beth looked from one face to another. 'No one's laughing,' she signed.

'People rarely do at Aunt Louise's jokes,' Alice replied, giving Louise a wry look.

'She's too smart for her own good, that one,' Louise said sniffily, turning to go. 'A bit like her mother in that respect.'

16

Over the next few years Alice settled into the character who would be remembered in Inchcraig. It wasn't the character or the life she had wished for, but no one could've suspected that Alice McInally would've ended up where she had, least of all herself. She did what all women of her time did: she became a housewife, caring for her elderly father and two children. It was also an era with few domestic appliances, so housework took much longer to do, and if sometimes she was aware of a slight restlessness, she imagined most women left at home to look after children must feel the same from time to time. Besides, there was nothing she could do about it. Summed her life up, really: it was full of aspects she was stuck with and could do nothing about, again like most females in the 1920s. There was a sameness about her existence, but she had arranged that herself, an orderliness. She knew the routines and familiar noises of Inchcraig life and felt safe in them: footsteps in the morning as the leerie came to turn off the flickering light of the gas mantle outside, and the sudden silence where the hissing of the gas had been; the yells of the coalman that you could hear streets away. Judging how close he was to you was like listening to the radio as it was gradually turned up. He would arrive on his horse and cart, shouting 'Co-ell!' and when you'd signed from the front window he would lift a bag off the cart, throw it onto his back and climb the stairs, to deposit it in the coal bunker in the kitchen. If you were fast enough you could have newspaper on the floor for him to stand on, to protect the lino – those who had lino – from his dusty boots and overall dustiness. After he'd emptied the sack into the bunker, the trick was to smartly snap the lid and the side door tightly shut and fasten them to stop the dust escaping and covering everything in the kitchen. And depending on what day it was, the butcher came round the streets, and the baker and the fishmonger, boards of produce on their heads.

Occasionally there were more exotic merchants. A little man with a beret who claimed to be French, though Alice didn't really believe him, cycled around, strings of onions hanging dangerously around his wheels; and another chap, with dark skin this time, an exotic accent and a turban, lugged a suitcase bursting at the seams with clothes, trying to sell his wares to the women. Then there was the noise of children playing in the street after school – kick the can, blind man's buff, peever – the girls skipping with a rope till the boys jumped in and spoiled it, which was their idea of fun. The leerie appeared again to light the mantle as night approached, this time with a crowd of local boys anxious to watch the ritual at the end of his shift as he emptied the powdered carbide out of his stick and down a drain. It was the fact that he instructed them with such severity never to touch the carbide that made the whole thing so fascinating, and from behind her curtains Alice would watch the boys staring into the drain as the cast-off powder foamed and bubbled, just so that they could fall about the ground at the acrid smell, each one trying to outdo the other in theatrical retchings. Matt was always among them, he was popular with everyone, but never a part of any particular group. Matt came and went wherever there was excitement to be had.

It was accepted that Beth stayed indoors. Her deafness made her as difficult a playmate to the girls as their lack of communications skills made them to her. That always made Alice sad, but once again there was no choice, the situation was as it was. As far as she knew, though, they didn't make fun of her, laugh at her and call her names, the usual treatment meted out to anyone who was 'different', but it was a fear that would stay with Alice. Beth proved to be clever, though, and, like her father, picked things up quickly and never had to be told the same thing twice, but she was taught at home by Maureen, which cut her off from other children even more.

Matt, meanwhile, went to the local state school, regarded in Scotland as a Protestant school. He was a bright boy, but he was easily bored and had a tendency to want to do things immediately, as he saw no merit in patience. He and Alice picked up signing from Maureen's lessons, but Matt picked it up far faster, then got fed-up and turned to other things. There was in Matt's nature, Alice would brood, the capacity for trouble. It would have been easier if she'd had someone to share her concerns with, a partner, a husband, but that thought never once entered her head. There had been Liam, only Liam; there would always be only Liam. And there was no point in talking to her father, for Henry lived in his own little world, happily with them but not really part of them. He was, anyway, of a generation that believed children are best left to women, and he had his new life as the life and soul of Galbraiths, and his collecting. For Henry that was enough. He never once explained why he hadn't taken a stand against his wife all those years ago, in support of the daughter who was now caring for him, and despite Louise's mutterings it never occurred to Alice to ask him to do so.

Brendon came to see them regularly, bearing presents and photos of Bernadette and the children, though it was quickly noted that Bernadette was pregnant in every one.

'How many's that now?' Alice asked.

'Six,' Brendon winced. 'We'll have to stop one day.'

'In my mind's eye I can see a horse running away and the stable door being bolted behind it!' Alice laughed.

'You've no idea how calm and biddable only two can be,' he sighed. 'Would it be all right to take Beth and Matt to the zoo, do you think?'

'Be it on your own head!' Alice laughed. 'I'll head for Maggie's, I hear Louise and George are in residence with Tallullah.'

'I'll deliver them back there, then?' he asked.

'I'm sure Maggie will be only too pleased to organise tea for everyone. But not too much candy floss, Brendon, more than six makes them impossible to control.'

'That's a deal,' he smiled.

At Kew Terrace, Louise was in full flow.

'Did you know Mother Hen is with child again?' she demanded of Alice. 'I mean, dear God, woman, have you no decorum?'

'Louise, will you please stop being so vulgar!' Maggie complained.

'But when do you intend stopping?' Louise demanded. 'When Mother Nature stops you? I mean, it's so animalistic, dear!'

A flustered Maggie was handing out cakes and tea while attempting to control her embarrassment.

'And I don't know why you're blushing,' Louise taunted her. 'You can't be that shy, giving in to carnal desires at your age!'

'Louise, really!'

'"Louise Really", that's me,' her sister said, exchanging a smile with Alice.

'It is, as you have pointed out, nature, and nature can't be stopped,' Maggie protested.

'But Tony can! For God's sake, woman, once in a while tell him you've got a headache!'

Maggie was too shocked to reply, so Alice said, 'Ease up, it's only her third,' to get her out of her predicament.

'In almost as many years!' Louise scoffed.

'Bernadette McCann's expecting her sixth, you know.'

'I don't understand women who have no respect for themselves,' Louise murmured.

'Whatever do you mean?' Maggie demanded.

'Women who see themselves as brood mares, Maggie, that's what I mean! Women who'll go on pushing them out every nine months till their bodies give up. It's so undignified!'

'I can't believe you're saying such things in my house!' Maggie protested. 'And when I'm in this condition, too!'

'That's the point,' Louise giggled, 'you're always in that condition these days!'

When Brendon brought Beth and Matt back that evening, they were both tired, but Beth was excited whereas Matt was merely happy. On their day out, Beth had taught Brendon some sign language and they went into a huddle while he practised till she was satisfied, before he faced Alice and made a series of gestures with his hands and fingers. Beth was in a corner of the room, laughing so hard she couldn't catch her breath.

'Yes,' Alice said, 'thank you for that, Uncle Brendon, it's terribly nice of you to tell me I've got a big red nose!'

Brendon gasped and ran after Beth, who had taken off at speed a second before. He returned with her in his arms and tickled her till she begged him to stop, her cheeks bright red and her eyes shining.

'I don't know why I bothered telling you to be careful with the candy floss,' Alice chided Brendon. 'Look at the state you've got her in! She'll never sleep tonight.'

From a chair by the fireside Matt looked on. He was smiling, he was happy enough, but he wasn't really involved. Alice, watching him, thought it summed the boy up, but she had no idea what to do about it, or if, indeed, there was anything that could be done about it. It had nothing to do with Brendon treating Beth differently from Matt, as he never made any difference between them and they were both glad to see him. It was something about Matt.

Only the week before, Alice had had a visit from a teacher at his school, an unusual event in itself at a time when school and home were very strictly separated and teachers did not call on parents, nor vice versa. She was a small, nervous woman in her thirties, with the kind of dull, fairish hair that hinted she had bloomed a long time ago. No ring either, so she was single, Alice thought, then twisted her own rings on her finger and smiled. She was no judge of that.

'I'm sorry to bother you, Mrs McInally,' the little woman said, 'but I wonder if we could talk about your nephew, Matthew?'

'What's he done? Is he in trouble?' Alice asked, any parent's natural response.

'Well, he's not done anything. That's why I'm here, in a manner of speaking.'

Beth was out with Maureen, so Alice led the way to the sitting room and indicated the chair at the other side of the range. The little woman sat down. Simpson, was it? Yes, Miss Simpson, that's what she had said.

'I'm a little worried about Matt, Mrs McInally,' she said anxiously. 'You see, he's a very bright boy – I don't think I've ever come across a brighter one, in fact – but I can't get him to do anything.'

'I know what you mean,' Alice smiled grimly.

'I mean, he really is clever,' the little woman insisted. 'Let me explain. We did some IQ tests and his score was so high that we wondered if we'd done it wrong, but we hadn't. So we tried him with some long division, gave it to all the class, a little early, to be sure, and I wasn't surprised when they all had difficulty. All except Matthew, he got the idea instantly. The problem was that once he'd got it, he refused to do any more, you see – said he'd done that once, why should he have to do it again?'

Alice laughed despite herself; it was a Matt she recognised.

'He does the same with everything, actually. As soon as he understands he refuses to do it. Not in an aggressive way or anything like that, he's perfectly amiable about it, but he won't budge. And he's very good at art, too, for a boy of seven,' the teacher explained, 'but he has no interest in developing it, or improving. He produces amazing charcoal drawings, but he gets fed-up with it very quickly.' She looked exasperated. 'He's a gifted athlete for such a little boy, he can beat all the others at running, but after he's done it once he just refuses to do it again. Same with jumping and climbing ropes.' She shook her head slightly.

'So the problem is that he excels at everything?' Alice laughed.

'No, it's not really that, it's that he loses interest, do you see? My experience of very clever children is that they are eager to learn, to do more, but Matt isn't, not at all.'

'He's probably bored,' Alice remarked.

'Yes, that may be so, but part of the discipline of growing up is accepting that things have to be done over again.'

Alice wasn't sure where she stood on that one, but she promised to speak to Matt. When Matt came home that day he was met with his favourite rock cakes and milk and was instantly suspicious.

'You haven't done anything,' she reassured him, 'you're not in trouble, but I've had a teacher to see me, a Miss Simpson.'

Matt bit into his rock cake and nodded.

'She says you get fed-up and don't try.'

Matt nodded again, concentrating on eating the chocolate base without disturbing the little tower of coconut meringue above.

'Well? Is she right?'

Another nod. As he sank his tongue into the softer interior of the meringue a dab of the creamy stuff stuck to the tip of his nose.

'Matt, will you say something? You can't just nod all the time!'

He sighed deeply. 'What's the point?' he asked, looking at her calmly.

'What do you mean, what's the point?'

'Well, I know how to do sums, then they want me to do them every day and every next day. I can do them,' he said simply, 'I get them all right, so what's the point of going on doing them?'

It was a logic she found hard to argue with. 'She says you're good at sports, too, but you won't do them.'

He nodded again – that was one thing he firmly believed in repeating, obviously. 'I can beat everyone at running. Do pretty long jumps and things, too,' he said thoughtfully.

'But that's good, isn't it?' she asked. 'Don't you like winning?'

This time he shrugged. 'Once you've beaten them, you've beaten them,' he replied. 'Why do they want me to go on beating them all the time when everybody knows I can anyway?'

There it was again, that inescapable logic. 'Yes, but the thing is, Matt, it could lead to bigger things if you stick at it. Maybe you could be a footballer when you grow up, if you keep training.'

'Football's daft,' he stated. 'I can do that, too.'

But wouldn't you like to be famous for doing it? Like the men in the newspapers?' she suggested.

'No,' he replied. 'I got fed-up with football before I got fed-up beating them all at running.'

'And you're good at drawing, too, I hear.'

'I know,' he said, reaching for another rock cake to demolish.

'Well you could be an artist one day. If you wanted to, you could go to a special college to learn more about it.'

'No,' he replied, 'that would take a long time. Besides, I'd get fed-up drawing all the time.'

'So what do you want to do?' she asked.

'I was thinking I could leave school,' he suggested solemnly, staring at her from behind a heavy fringe of blond hair. 'I know everything they want me to know and now they want me to keep doing it and they just get upset when I won't. So I was thinking it might be a good idea to leave school and get a job somewhere, then the teachers could get on with teaching the others who don't know how to do things. See?'

Alice nodded. She did 'see', even if she didn't agree. But how to explain this to Matt, that was always the problem, one she never solved. Over the years she spent time talking to him, making jokes with him, but she never felt that he took in anything he had set his mind against, all he did was laugh at her jokes.

From forty to forty-five years old Maggie Doyle had produced five children, two boys and three girls, and, as her sister had foretold, had nature not intervened she would undoubtedly have produced enough to fill the Kew Terrace house, as she and Tony had once planned. Both Maggie and Alice's children thrived, even if there was something about Matt that unsettled Alice, partly because she couldn't put her finger on her concern. Henry continued working at Galbraiths and his appearance never changed; Alice strongly suspected hair dye might have been involved, but that was his business. He had fitted into his Glasgow life as though he had been born into it, and though his circumstances were quite altered, it was hard to remember who and what he had been in Belfast. His collecting continued, his great vice and his great joy, and he would slip past Alice with a gleam in his eye and a parcel under his arm, as though waiting to be chastised, before heading towards his bedroom with his latest purchase. Away from his bacon-slicer he developed a great love of silver and would take himself off to the local library to read about some piece he had spotted before committing his money to it. He kept in touch with Bella in Toronto, where she had produced two children, a daughter, Sheila, who was small and blonde like herself and Victoria, and a tall, red-haired boy called Gary, who looked exactly like Billy. Apart from the fact that Billy was doing well at work, her letters didn't contain much information, which Alice put down to the fact that Bella didn't have the imagination to think of more, nor the ability to write it. Not that she knew directly, as Henry received the letters and Henry replied to them. She herself was never invited to enter into correspondence with her sister,

which Alice took as a sign of Billy's influence and his continuing disapproval of her, not that it worried her.

Financially, the McInally family was worry-free, thanks to the
decency of Brendon. They didn't have a lot to spare, but they
had enough to live happily. Beth and Matt lived among poorer
children in Inchcraig and so weren't used to seeing displays of
wealth. Alice supposed it just never occurred to them to ask for
what they didn't see around them, even if they saw it at Maggie's
house. Maureen would take Beth on trips and, on Wednesday
afternoons, to a club for the deaf, to meet what Alice was told
was 'her own kind', and though she had reservations about that,
Beth certainly seemed to be more relaxed when she came home
– due, she supposed, to being included by 'her own kind'.

Alice was wrong about Matt, though. He was sharp-witted
and he did notice the differences between the lives of his cousins
in Kew Terrace and his own. He wanted for nothing, he was
well fed and clothed, but it wasn't on the same level as Maggie's
children, and he resented it, though he never said so out loud.
He put it down to his cousins having a father, while he had a
man in a photograph.

'Don't you wonder why we can't live in a house like Kew
Terrace?' he asked Beth.

Beth, now nine years old, thought for a moment then shook
her head. 'Do you?' she signed.

Matt nodded. 'It's not fair,' he said. 'It's because they have a
father.'

'We have a father,' Beth smiled back.

'Not really,' Matt replied, 'he's dead. Can you remember him?'

'No, but Grandpa tells us stories about our parents and so
does Uncle Brendon.'

'I hate those stories,' Matt complained. 'They're stupid. I
think they make them up.'

'But why would they do that?'

'To make us feel better,' he sighed. 'But I don't. Do you?'

Beth didn't know what to reply. She didn't understand what her brother meant, but then she missed a lot in what other people thought and said. What was normal conversation to them was pretty black and white to her, because she couldn't hear voice tones or nuances. She could feel changing atmospheres in the house, though, and she saw the way Aunt Alice's eyes lingered on Matt, with concern rather than affection, she thought, though she was never sure, and she was always aware of Matt's separateness, that distance between him and everyone else, even if she couldn't understand it.

And while Beth watched Alice with Matt, Alice watched Beth and worried about how and when she would tell her about her father, hoping desperately that no one else would do so first. There were times when she planned to tell her, but something always got in the way. She was doing so well with Maureen – unlike Matt she applied herself diligently to learning – and it seemed wrong to burden her with a situation she would find hard to handle. No matter when she was told it would be difficult, but surely she would find it easier when she was older and could understand a bit better, and didn't have other distractions? Yet there she was, all that was left of Liam, and she didn't know. And Alice couldn't tell her, this beautiful child who personified all they had meant to each other, whose existence justified their flight from home and family all those years ago. Alice would look at Beth, head bent over a book as she mastered the difficult skill of reading, and she would see Liam in her so strongly that it hurt, making the deception seem not only unnecessary but cruel. Cruel not just to Beth, but to Liam. None of it was simple, there were strands within strands, and she had the feeling that if she cut one all the others might unravel.

Just as Alice thought she could see things clearly, other considerations took over, mainly to do with Matt. She was afraid of the character she was seeing emerging; there was a sense of foreboding about the boy that she couldn't shake off. She had a semi-plan in her mind that he might care for Beth later, that he would look out for his deaf sister, but Alice was more and more aware that he wasn't who or what she wanted him to be. With Beth she could predict what she might think, what attitude she might take, but not with Matt, never with Matt, and she wondered what he would do if he knew Beth wasn't his sister. If he found out that he wasn't tied to her by a shared past, that they weren't two orphaned children against the world together, he might well abandon her when she needed him most. That was her main fear, that one day, when she was no longer there, Matt might walk away from his cousin Beth in a way that he might not from his sister. And she hated thinking this, she was fond of the boy and wanted only what was best for him, but the thought wouldn't go away. So each time she felt she might tell Beth she left it, deciding to wait a while to see how both children developed. Her fears might come to nothing, after all. Perhaps it was just an understandably heightened feeling of protection towards her daughter's future, but she would wait, just in case.

And then life changed again.

It was the money that brought it about. Not that she made a show of having a bit extra, but people noticed things. They knew that a well-dressed man and a strangely dressed woman visited from time to time, and no one could miss Maggie's car calling every week to take Alice and the children for tea at Kew Terrace, but Alice had done no one any harm and there was an understanding among the women of Inchcraig that she had fallen on harder times and was making the best of it. They admired that, and they liked that she had no airs and graces – the fact that she didn't mix as much as the others was put down to shyness. Besides, even if she didn't stand in the close gossiping, she was friendly and approachable, if quiet. She just kept her own counsel.

Not that it stopped those closest to her, like Isa downstairs and Marie upstairs, from bringing her the latest tales from the streets. It was from them she learned who was involved in crime and who just wanted other people to think they were; they were streetwise in a way Alice could never be. Therefore, she knew to give people like Bernard Pollock a wide bodyswerve, though, on reflection, she thought instinct would've told her that before Isa and Marie did.

'Did ye hear that racket last night?' Marie asked Alice.

It was Monday morning and Alice was collecting the bottle of bleach left weekly from the doorstep, so Marie must have been listening for her door opening so that she could ambush her into conversation. She smiled at the tiny, birdlike woman. 'There was something, Marie. I remember waking up but I didn't know why.'

'Big Pollock,' Marie said, nodding her head. 'Some daft sod gave him cheek in the middle o' the street.' She was halfway through the weekly wash, her arms with their rolled-up sleeves crossed over her apron. 'Would ye credit it?' she asked, pursing her lips. 'Somebody frae here bein' that stupid?'

'What happened?' Alice asked calmly, taking one step backwards inside the house to indicate this would not be a long conversation.

'So ye didnae hear it, didnae see it?' Marie asked, delightedly prolonging the moment.

Alice shook her head.

'Carved him up, so he did,' Marie said triumphantly. 'Left him tae run hame tae his mammy wi' a face like raw meat. Helluva sight it was. Blood everywhere.' She pointed out from the tenement. 'Ye can still see it oan the street if ye want to look,' she suggested.

Alice decided she didn't want to.

'Did it hissel' as well, so Ah hear,' Marie continued. 'Big Pollock, like. No' often he bothers these days, usually gets somebody else tae dae that kinda thing for him, so he really wanted him tae know he meant business.' She gave a thoughtful shake of the head. 'Well, that's me then, the washin' won't dae itsel', will it?' she said cheerfully, and disappeared back upstairs.

Marie was the neighbour Alice had most to do with, because Marie made sure she was, and when her husband was killed at work in an iron foundry, like everyone else, Alice gave a donation to cover the funeral costs. She hadn't intended to go any further, but the woman's grief brought out a fellow feeling. Alice knew what it was to have your man dead and to have to bring up children alone, something that would stay with her for the rest of her life, and later she gave the widow a little more. The women of the area had their own loan company in operation, they called it the '*menodge*', as banks weren't interested in people of their class. Each week they would pay in what they could, sixpence or a shilling, and in time it would be their turn to be given a lump sum to spend as they liked. In reality the money bought children's shoes or an extra bit of food, a whole chicken in a tin perhaps, that great Christmas treat. At all costs it was kept from their menfolk, who would just drink it. But emergencies like Marie Duffy's weren't covered by the *menodge*, and that, unwittingly, was how Alice became a businesswoman.

She had thrust some money into Marie's hands and been

embarrassed by her neighbour's honest gratitude, but a few months later the widow was at her door to return 'the loan', which it hadn't been, with added interest. Alice hadn't known what to do, it wasn't what she had intended, but when she protested the woman had insisted and she hadn't wanted to insult her. Before long there was another neighbour at the door, Johnny Hall, a bricklayer who had fallen at work and hurt his back. He had a young family to support and no compensation, but he had an idea.

'Ah was thinkin', Mrs McInally,' he said quietly, 'that there has tae be somethin' I can dae for my family. The doctors say Ah need tae keep movin', ye see, so Ah asked around and the thing is, women need bleach.'

Alice stared at him blankly.

'Tae wash wi', clean things, ye know?'

So far she was with him.

'If Ah could lay hands oan a wee bitta money, I could set myself up, ye see, buy the bleach in drums frae the chemical works, put it in bottles, then sell it round the doors.' He was twisting his cap in his hand with nerves, but his eyes were bright with the idea. 'Ah've made this wee wheelbarrow contraption ye know, a bogey, an' Ah was thinkin' that runnin' about the streets, up and down the stairs, that would keep me movin', an' Ah could stop when Ah felt Ah needed tae. The women would get their bleach cheaper as well, ye see, so everybody would benefit.'

So Alice gave Johnny the huge sum of thirty shillings to start up his business and told him he could pay it back when he had made enough from it. She didn't think she'd ever hear from him again, but a week later he was back on the doorstep with two shillings in his hand.

'Are you sure you've made enough to keep your family, Johnny?' she asked anxiously.

'Ah have, Mrs McInally,' he replied gleefully. 'Everybody's takin' the bleach, it's a wonder naebody thought of it afore me!'

Every week after that he was back with what he could afford from his week's takings – it was only a shilling on the week he had to replace a wheel on his wheelbarrow – until Alice told him to stop, that he'd paid back every penny. He insisted on paying her interest as well, though, an extra four shillings. From that day she never had to buy a bottle of bleach either, one appeared on her doorstep as if by magic every Monday morning. The word spread, of course, and soon Alice McInally was a moneylender. Any woman in dire need of a very small amount of money and Alice had handed it over, only to be repaid with interest once again and without a murmur, at first making her feel that she was the only one who didn't understand the rules. It was her own fault, she knew that, she should never have started it, and, once started, she should have stopped it, but she didn't because she felt she couldn't: there was no case less deserving than another. Not that she advertised for customers – in a place like Inchcraig she didn't need to – but she tried to restrict what was fast becoming a business. She gave money to women, small amounts only; she had no intention of financing large-scale projects, just helping people out.

Then, one Wednesday afternoon, when Henry was at work, Beth was out with Maureen and Matt was at school, Bernard Pollock arrived at her door, though she could never work out how or why it had happened.

It sounded such an unthreatening name, she had always thought. Bernard Pollock. It made you think of a little pot-bellied grandfather, well-worn slippers on his feet, heavy braces holding up his trousers, and a pipe maybe, hanging from his mouth beneath a walrus moustache. But the reality of Bernard Pollock couldn't have been more different. She knew him, or of him, of course, no one could live in Inchcraig and not know him, but he inhabited an existence light years from hers. He was part of that dark side of the place that everyone knew about but tried to steer clear of, operated by men who looked ordinary in many ways, but you knew weren't. There was an alertness about them, an easy friendliness among them that you just knew could turn sour at any minute, and it often did. She had heard the stories about Pollock from the other women, from Marie upstairs mainly, and knew that he financed crime to build his empire – factory break-in and the like, for a cut of the proceeds – and, as she also already knew, he wasn't averse to using violence to protect his empire. Anyone who encroached on his territory was swiftly and brutally dealt with, everyone in Inchcraig knew this, but it didn't affect the ordinary people, just those involved in the same business as himself.

When Alice passed Pollock on the street he always had a dog with him, for protection she supposed, averting her eyes and crossing to the other kerb. She didn't know the man and didn't want to. He had moved to Inchcraig in the same circumstances as most of the other inhabitants, but the stories she had heard convinced her she would never seek a closer acquaintance. He was a gang leader, or he had been in the mainly Irish-populated slums he had come from, where the street battles had been bloody and based on religion, Catholic against Protestant. He had moved on from that, though: now he was more of an overlord, the head man, the one in charge of all crime, the one everyone had to fear. And here he was, on her doorstep, with his dog.

Alice didn't know what to do, and, even if she had known, she was instantly paralysed with fear. She couldn't think what he wanted, but whatever it might be, he certainly wasn't welcome in her home. The sight of him on her doorstep that afternoon chilled her to the bone. He smiled at her, a man of about thirty, tall, dark and, yes, handsome, very strikingly handsome, but threatening in a way she couldn't understand. It wasn't anything he said or did, he was charming and friendly, but she still felt herself shrink back from him and wished he would disappear. She suddenly realised that if this man meant her harm there was no one she could call to help her. Even the neighbours she had helped out would be no match for him: he feared no one. But, above all, she didn't want her neighbours to see him there, so, as he made no move to leave, inviting him in seemed the best course of action.

'You don't mind Buster?' he asked, nodding to the dog by his side.

Now that she saw it up close she wondered why she had ever imagined it was a guard dog.

'No, no,' she said uncertainly, watching the little round ball of hair sitting panting at his master's feet.

Pollock nodded graciously and walked past her into the sitting room, where he waited to be asked to sit down before engaging her in small talk. She didn't know what to think and waited like a coiled spring, unsure of what he could possibly want or what he might do, reluctant to sit down in her own chair because the one he sat in was nearest to the door and he could block her escape, if she had to try. She was trapped, she realised, so there was nothing to do but carry the moment off with as much dignity as she could muster.

'Can I ask you for a bowl of water for Buster, please?' he said. 'He gets hot, it's all that hair, you see.'

As she went to the kitchen to find a bowl to put the dog's water in, she had the sensation of every passing minute confusing her more. Returning to the sitting room she handed Pollock the bowl and he placed it in front of the little dog, who had settled happily at his feet, then he patted the animal and from somewhere at the back of 'all that hair' there was a movement she assumed was his tail wagging.

'I understand you come from Belfast?' he asked politely, finally turning his attention to her, now that Buster's needs had been attended to.

'Yes, a long time ago,' she replied. She tried to smile, but her mouth was so dry that her top lip stuck to her teeth, so she put her head down to hide it.

'My people, too, as you say, a long time ago. Still, these things matter.' There was a silence, then he said, 'I notice the boy doesn't go to the Catholic school?' he said.

'My nephew, no, he doesn't.' Her head was whirling, she couldn't begin to imagine where this was going.

'So you'll be the same as myself, then,' he smiled kindly, 'not a Catholic. I don't always find it easy being surrounded by so many Catholics.'

'It doesn't bother me.' She smiled back at him. 'People are just people.'

'No, nor me, but it's natural to prefer your own kind. The girl –'

'Beth?'

'She doesn't go to school?'

'She's deaf, Mr Pollock, she gets taught at home.'

He stroked Buster as he nodded, and she realised that he knew all of this and felt slightly queasy at the thought of him checking up on her, which was just as he intended. Suddenly it struck her that his arrival on a Wednesday afternoon had been deliberate. He knew the movements and habits of her family, and her throat tightened with panic as she wondered just how much this man did know about her. She had kept a great deal hidden, she was a woman who 'kept herself to herself' by instinct, but she had taken control of her own story, her contrived story, and had a great deal to lose if this man found out and chose to make the truth public or, worse still, chose to let the children know.

'You have to be careful of your children in this day and age,' he said sagely. 'There's danger all around.'

She nodded.

'You wouldn't have a cup of tea in the house?' he asked, like someone's favourite uncle. 'My throat's parched as well as Buster's.'

She wondered if he had read her mind. In the kitchen she found it hard to organise the simple act of making tea and could barely hold the cups and saucers for shaking, sure he must be sitting in the next room, listening to the rattling of china and laughing at her. The thought annoyed her into calming down.

They sat in silence, sipping at their cups, listening to the clock ticking, the fire crackling.

'I'll get to the point,' he said at last, and she felt like jumping up and cheering. 'It's this business of yours.'

She looked at him blankly.

'I know your situation and I admire that you're bringing up these two wee children, but I'm a bit worried that you're turning into a competitor.' He smiled pleasantly.

A competitor? What was the man on about? 'I'm sorry,' she said, 'I don't understand.'

'You must know that I have certain business interests, Mrs McInally, and what you're doing could threaten the success of those interests.'

Another silent, blank stare.

'Your money-lending, Mrs McInally,' he said finally.

She saw from his expression that he was serious, but she still had a struggle not to laugh out loud. 'Mr Pollock,' she said quietly, 'I don't know what you've heard, but all I've done is help out a few neighbours, mainly women who were desperate. I'm not running a business.'

'But it could go that way, Mrs McInally, if you're not careful. Now I have no objection, unless it becomes too big. That's my concern, you see, that it could spiral out of anything you could possibly control. You have to earn a crust, we all do, but I wouldn't want you bothered, that's all I'm saying, and these kind of things can lead to bother.'

'They can?'

'Oh, they can, this is something I know about,' he smiled. 'What I'm proposing is that you decide now how big you want it to get, and when that's firmly fixed in your mind you won't let it get out of hand. That way you won't be running any risks, you see. Of bother, I mean. You don't want bother, now, do you?'

'No, no, of course not.' It struck her that it wouldn't be a matter of her deciding how big it should get, but of Bernard Pollock doing so.

'And in return for your co-operation, I'll make sure that you're OK, if you see what I mean. I'll make sure no one crosses you.'

Alice said nothing. No one here had ever crossed her. Why should they when she hadn't bothered them? But this was different, she was on the brink of bothering Bernard Pollock; or he thought she was, and that was just as bad.

When he had gone she watched him from behind the curtains as he walked away, Buster at his heels, as peculiar a twosome as she could imagine, and she went over the conversation in her mind. He had been threatening her, she was pretty sure of that, but she couldn't recall any specific threat. He had been assessing her and warning her off all at once, trying to find out how much of a competitor she might be, how big a player in his kind of business, when she wasn't a competitor or a player at all. When he had reassured himself on that, he had offered her his protection. But why? What did he want? She thought of the obvious and felt sick: he was charming and had a certain presence, but he was a dangerous, violent man. She would have to go very carefully until she found out exactly what he wanted from her.

Then there was a knock at the door and she found Isa O'Rourke from downstairs standing there. At first Alice thought her neighbour had seen her visitor and must be checking up to make sure she was all right, but it was a business call.

'The thing is, Mrs McInally,' Isa said, 'Ah've been tryin' tae thinka a way Ah could earn some money. Hughie's been laid off frae the yard, and the weans need things, ye know. Ah was thinkin' that if Ah had a few bob Ah could start makin' things, candy apples, candy balls, that kinda thing, an' sell them frae the hoose.' She looked anxiously at Alice.

Alice's mind was so full of her previous visitor that she could hardly think straight. Had Pollock sent Isa to test her, to find out if she was telling the truth about her 'business', she wondered. And what if she gave Isa a few shillings to help her out – would Pollock burst through the door and, well, what might he do?

'Everybody likes a wee sweetie, an' if Ah had the money, Ah know where I could get some sugar cheap,' Isa continued.

From some racket run by Bernard Pollock, Alice thought, and then wondered if Isa had noted his visit and was trying a bit of mild blackmail. But no, she decided, Isa wasn't like that, she was a straightforward type. She just needed the money and she knew, as everyone did, that Alice had helped Marie and given the bleach man a loan to set up his business.

So Alice gave her the money she needed, then crept about her own house on tiptoe, aware of every creak, every distant noise, afraid of what might happen next. When the family safely returned later, one by one, she was relieved, but still on edge, and had to tell them she thought she had a bit of a temperature. A few days later Isa's sweetie shop was in full swing. Local children would knock on her front window, which would fly open, day or night, and in exchange for a penny they received a piece of newspaper formed into a cone shape and twisted at both ends, with a few candy balls inside. Another satisfied customer.

The following week, just as Alice was settling down, Bernard Pollock and Buster called again at the same time, bringing photos of his wife and his two sons to show her, giving her the message that he had no sexual motive in mind, a message that brought her great relief. She still didn't know what he wanted, though, or why he called every Wednesday afternoon after that.

When she could finally sum up the courage to look at him she saw that his eyes were brown, the kindest, softest brown eyes she had ever seen. She noticed that he didn't speak in Glasgow dialect to her and she realised this was a man who didn't miss a trick; he tailored his approach to the situation in hand. He treated her with respect and deference, because she behaved that way to other people, but she knew he didn't treat everyone he met in a similar way. The stories she had heard were undoubtedly true, which meant that the pleasant, friendly man who took tea with her every Wednesday thought nothing of human life, but she found it hard to tie the conflicting images together. Then she remembered his ability to adapt to the situation in hand and whoever he was dealing with, so he wasn't just one man, he was many.

The most recent story going round Inchcraig was about a lesser villain than Pollock himself, who had apparently presumed to sit on his seat in the local pub, so Pollock had calmly taken a blade from his inside pocket, slashed the intruder across the throat from ear to ear, and, just as calmly, sat down to read his newspaper, leaving his victim gurgling on the floor. The following day he was sitting across from her, politely talking about the weather, asking after the children, commenting on the fine piece of bacon Mr McInally had recommended and expertly cut for his wife at Galbraiths. It was hard to imagine him committing the crimes he was accused of, but she knew he did.

Alice didn't know what the neighbours thought of the alliance, if that was what it was, but they knew Bernard Pollock called on her weekly, though they never commented on it. Alice McInally had never been one to encourage the giving or receiving of confidences – as anyone in Inchcraig would say, and frequently did, she was the type who kept herself to herself. For all she knew they might believe there was a torrid affair taking place between them, but she could do nothing about what they thought, beyond hoping they could see she wasn't that kind of woman, and he wasn't that kind of man. If Bernard Pollock had wanted extramarital female attention he would have looked further afield, common sense should tell them that; just as he didn't defile his home with his 'business interests', it wasn't plausible that he would engage in adultery so close to his home. Besides, he surely had his pick of willing women, had he wanted it, and, just as surely, his appetites would run to someone other than the decidedly matronly Mrs McInally. And what was she to do about the neighbours anyway? She could hardly make a public announcement in answer to a question that hadn't been asked, stand up and tell the world that there was nothing going on between her and Bernard Pollock, however odd his weekly visits might look. No, there was nothing she could do but, well, nothing, so silence was the best weapon she had against any gossip that might be going round. That way she would preserve her authority.

So her 'business' continued as it had started, never growing beyond what she could handle and what Bernard Pollock approved of. She only had one rule: she didn't sanction a second loan to the same person until the first had been repaid. If it wasn't repaid she did nothing, said nothing, there was never any retribution. This rarely happened, though, and she knew the uninvited presence of Bernard Pollock in her life must have contributed to that; that was what his protection did. Alice often felt very uneasy about it, but she could think of no way out. Had she told him he was unwelcome he could have caused problems for her, and she had the children to think about, he was protection for them too. Life in a place like Inchcraig wasn't easy for a woman alone with children to bring up, and even with Henry there it was like having an extra child rather than having a man about the place. There was Beth's deafness to think about as well, and the constant fear of what would be said or done to her by ignorant people. It was one of the reasons for deaf clubs, Maureen had told her, places where they could relax and not be stared at and laughed at.

Alice didn't know what they would have done without Maureen, she was part of the family now, but she didn't know what they would have done without having Bernard Pollock around either. His weekly presence meant Beth was safe from the kind of ridicule other deaf people knew in everyday life, as everyone in Inchcraig was aware that he would deal with

255

anyone who caused her grief. The truth was that Alice had used Pollock's influence to protect her children. She was an independent woman, but there was no man in her household to fend for them.

It was Marie Duffy who took it upon herself to remind her neighbour just who she was consorting with, though she didn't put it in those terms. It was one of her Monday morning briefings, traditionally the busiest housework day for women, and a time she knew Alice would be around.

'Did ye hear what he's been up tae?' she asked, glancing about her.

'Who?' Alice asked.

'Big Pollock, of course!' Marie replied. 'Who else?'

Alice shook her head.

'This is a bad tale, this one,' said Marie, who had an untapped theatrical bent. 'Lent this guy in Parkheid money for a break-in, seemingly for expenses, hirin' a second man an' things like tha', ye know? Only the guy didnae dae the job, fell sick or somethin', or so he said, but his big mistake was in no' giein' Big Pollock his money back. So he paid him a visit, didn't he? In the middle o' the night, nailed him tae the floor!'

Alice pulled back, her face frozen with horror, a sight that greatly gratified Marie's need for an attentive and appreciative audience.

'Aye,' she said, to emphasise the point, 'nailed him tae the floor and left him there, so he did. No' that the money meant a lot tae him, ye understaun', but it sent a message tae anybody thinkin' o' crossin' him in future, see?'

Alice did see. She saw the purpose of Marie's tale, also, was to warn her, to make sure she understood the nature of the beast she was dealing with.

It made her think, of course, how could it not? For all she

knew, if she told him to go and never darken her doorstep again, he might bow politely, smile and depart for ever. But maybe he wouldn't, and it was a risk she couldn't take. For some reason he seemed to respect her – she was always 'Mrs McInally', just as he was 'Mr Pollock' – maybe because she was raising two orphaned children and caring for her widowed father; maybe because, like him, she came from Northern Irish Protestant stock – but did such things really matter to a man like him?

And what exactly was a man like him? He had so many sides to him that she wondered if there was anything in the middle, if the real Bernard Pollock existed, or was that the man she was seeing? If it was, why her?

Then it would bother her that she was spending time thinking about him at all, and she decided the best way to deal with the enigma was to put up with the Wednesday afternoon visits and leave it at that, to consign him and Buster to a fenced-off area of her life for a few hours a week. This was easy; he never once out-stayed his tentative welcome, arriving and departing when she was alone, so that her father and the children never saw him, showing a consideration she came to regard as oddly gracious. Likewise, she would have the tea things washed and put away before her family came home, and no mention of her visitor every passed her lips or theirs, though she suspected they, like the neighbours, knew about him.

Two days after her conversation with Marie, Pollock was on her doorstep, together with Buster and a genial smile. He had two books with him, one by his latest discovery to share with her, and he had found out information about it that had tickled him.

'It's called *Of Mice and Men*,' he smiled. 'Now, do you know where that title comes from?' He looked as excited as a schoolboy.

Alice didn't even want to think about it. In her mind's eye she saw him nailing a non-payer to the floor simply to warn others to be careful of him.

'It's from Rabbie Burns,' he said triumphantly, 'from his poem "To a Mouse". You know the line? "The best laid schemes o' mice an' men, Gang aft a-gley." This man, Steinbeck, has taken that from Burns, isn't that something? He's a brilliant writer, and here he is paying homage to Burns. Amazing, isn't it?'

It was just as well he couldn't stop talking; it prevented him from noticing that Alice couldn't start.

'Makes you proud, doesn't it?' he asked, eyes gleaming. 'Mind you, he should have been impressed by Burns, now there was a man for you! I can never make up my mind which of his poems I love best. "My Love is like a Red, Red Rose"', he said softly, 'now no one could help being stirred by that. A bit high if you try to sing it, of course, but would Burns have intended it to be sung the way people sing it these days? A country laddie like him? I don't think so. For me, though, it's got to be "Ae Fond Kiss". I can't even read that without being moved, can you?'

He thrust the second book he'd brought – of Burns's poetry – into her hands and apologised for having to go early this week. He had somewhere he had to be. 'I have some business to do, you understand,' he smiled. 'We'll pick up where we left off next week.'

Alice wondered what, or who, he had to do. All through hearing of his delight at discovering John Steinbeck had loved Burns, all she could visualise were the nails going through some smaller villain's hands and feet, hammered there by the man who had sat in her house, not three feet from her, reciting love poetry.

Later she read through 'Ae Fond Kiss' and understood what Pollock meant:

> Had we never loved sae kindly,
> Had we never loved sae blindly,
> Never met and never parted,
> We would ne'er be brokenhearted.

The exquisitely sad beauty of the words and feelings could have been written for her and Liam, only they had been brought to her by a brutal, vicious but curiously gentle man. Their friendship made no sense, though it wasn't the first time she had thought that. By Bernard Pollock touching on what she had felt, what she had known with Liam, she couldn't help but feel it was tainting his memory in some subtle way. Yet somehow she couldn't think of a way of ending his visits.

And so they rubbed along together, the three of them, Alice, Bernard Pollock and Buster, in a strangely friendly, if uneasy, way. Pollock had moved his family to a cottage-style house on the outskirts of the new Inchcraig that had once been part of the original estate, and his boys went to the fee-paying Glasgow Academy in the city, he told her. They were doing well, he explained with pride, and he had ambitions for them, wanting them to go to university. The message was clear: they would not join the family business. He mentioned his wife, whom Alice had only ever seen from a distance, with affection, talked of films he had seen or a book he had read, and often when he next came he would bring the book for her to read, so that they could discuss it together the following week. Again there was that attention to detail: he missed nothing and had obviously noticed the books she had in the house.

He revealed a love of poetry that stunned her – how could this man appreciate poetry? Then she felt ashamed of herself. As though reading her thoughts once again, an unnerving feeling she often had about him, he arrived one afternoon with a book of poetry by another American she had never heard of, Robert Frost, and proceeded to read aloud a verse that had touched him.

'I know we were supposed to go back to Steinbeck,' he smiled, but listen to this. It's called "The Road Not Taken", about someone coming to a fork in the road and taking one, but always wondering what would have happened if he'd taken the other. '"Two roads diverged in a wood, and I – I took the one less travelled by, And that has made all the difference." Doesn't that sum it all up?' he smiled wistfully. 'I mean, did any of us have any idea we would be where we are now? Can't we all look back and see a fork in the road in our lives and wonder if we took the right one?'

When he had gone she thought back on her own life and how it had turned out. Who was to say he had somehow taken the road he had without him wishing it that way? And yet . . . and yet, he was a gangster, no doubt about that. Bernard never discussed what he did. He would refer to his 'business interests', but she knew they included extortion, violence, grand-scale theft and protection rackets. Everyone in Inchcraig and beyond knew that. She never saw any of it, though, looking and listening to the man who took tea with her every Wednesday, who sat in her sitting room discussing the affairs of the day in an intelligent, informed way. It made her doubt all of the stories she knew were true. However, looked at simply, he had no job, yet it was obvious he was gradually growing in wealth and a status accorded out of fear, and his family wanted for nothing. He could easily have afforded to live in a more salubrious area, but Inchcraig was the hub of his 'business interests'; it was his seat of power, from where he directed the money-making criminal activities that took place outside the area. The Pollock family lived increasingly well among poor people, they wore good clothes and took holidays, without Bernard, naturally, who had to keep an eye on business.

One Tuesday Alice was taking tea at Kew Terrace when Maggie produced an evening newspaper and showed it to her. Maggie had never accepted Alice's perverse decision to live in Inchcraig, and had been waging a campaign to get Alice to move out. No opportunity was missed.

'Have you seen this?' she asked, thrusting the paper at Alice.

On the front page was an account of a court appearance by one Bernard Pollock, where he had been charged with convincing a businessman to sell his business to him by removing two of his fingers. He had been found not guilty, because no one would testify against him, not even the man who had been separated from both his livelihood and his fingers. To Pollock the press coverage was undoubtedly good for business: the next individual who thought of standing in his way would think twice and decide against it.

Alice handed the newspaper back to Maggie.

'Do you know this man?' Maggie asked.

'Maggie, Inchcraig is a big place these days, I can't be expected to know everyone!' she laughed, evading the question.

'I really think you should move out. You must surely be worried for yourself and the children, living near a man like this?'

'Not really,' she smiled back, 'it's not part of my life, if you see what I mean. These people live in Inchcraig, so they don't bring violence to their own doorsteps.' She decided against adding, 'unless some unfortunate sits on their seat in the local pub', just as she had decided against ever telling Maggie about her business, knowing she would disapprove. No point in telling her what would only hurt and worry her.

'But how long will that last? How long before it comes to your doorstep?'

Alice simply smiled back once more. How could you say to Maggie that 'a man like this', indeed this very man, sat in her sitting room every Wednesday afternoon, that they held literary discussions and read poetry over cups of tea? And she suspected that it would make little difference to Maggie's opinion of Pollock if she were to tell her how fond he was of Buster.

Besides, she was now in a similar position to Pollock: in one way she could afford to move elsewhere, but in another she couldn't. The money Brendon had given her for Beth's education had long gone, and what she now made from money-lending was more than welcome.

Beth decided she had to earn a living, but the news from Maureen was hardly encouraging.

'There isn't a great deal of choice,' she told Alice and Beth. 'Some clerical work, filing and the like.'

Beth shook her head.

'Or bookbinding.'

'Bookbinding?' Alice asked. 'Why bookbinding?'

Maureen laughed. 'I have no idea, it's just one of those jobs that has traditionally been done by deaf people.'

'Doesn't matter,' Beth signed, 'I'm not doing it. I want to teach.'

Maureen looked at Alice. 'There's a problem,' she said. 'I've already explained this to Beth. Everything now is about oralism, about making deaf children talk and lip-read, and Beth hasn't been brought up like that, as you know.'

'And her education has worked out perfectly,' Alice said.

'Yes and no,' Maureen laughed. 'The establishment view is still that signing is not just wrong, but harmful. There's a belief that it stops people from learning to speak or lip-read.'

'But it doesn't,' Alice replied.

'Yes, we know that, but the trouble with challenging the establishment is that it makes them dig in their heels. The way Beth has been taught is still regarded by many as disgraceful.'

'But we weren't deliberately challenging anyone, and we weren't trying to be disgraceful either,' Alice said. 'It seemed, and still does, perfectly natural for Beth to learn in any way she could. The hearing world is difficult enough for the deaf, surely?'

'And that's part of the problem,' Maureen explained. 'A great many deaf people feel the deaf should stick to their own world and leave the hearing to their own. There's always been a danger that Beth would be accepted by neither world.'

'Nonsense!' Alice replied, slapping the table in front of her with her hand. 'All I ever wanted was for her to be part of the world.' She thought for a moment of the divided world that had led her to where her life now was. 'There are enough little worlds as it is, the last thing we need is more.' She sat quietly for a moment, thinking. 'So are you saying she has all this knowledge, she is a success, yet she won't be allowed to train as a teacher for other deaf children?'

'That's what I'm saying,' Maureen said quietly.

Beth watched Alice fuming and laid a hand on her arm. 'Why are you getting so upset?' she signed. 'It's not as bad as you think.'

'It seems bad enough to me!'

Beth shook her head and smiled. 'Tell her,' she mouthed to Maureen.

'What I propose Beth should do,' Maureen said, 'is what I do. She won't be able to train as a teacher, but she can be a tutor, just like me. There are always people who won't take the official line and can pay for private tuition. I can train her and recommend her to them.'

'And she'll make a living?'

'Well, I do, and she has more knowledge than I have of her subject. I think it would suit her very well, actually. She has her own strong views and she thinks nothing of airing them, even in the enemy's camp. I think she'd cause havoc on a conventional training course!'

Alice's mind went instantly back to Liam. One of these days she must sit his daughter down and tell her about her father. But best wait till she was established in her new career. There were bound to be obstacles, let her settle into that first before introducing what was certain to be turmoil into the equation.

Henry died in 1935, at the age of seventy-three. That morning he had been behind the counter at Galbraith's, holding forth on the details of the Wiltshire Cure and how it had transformed the bacon industry. Then he slipped on a piece of fat that had fallen from the cutting machine and the back of his head hit the counter. He was more angry at the stray piece of bacon fat than the bump his head had taken. It was these young lads, he told everyone, they had no standards these days: Henry McInally would never have allowed a stray piece of fat on his pristine slicer, or on his bleach-scrubbed floor.

Then, as it was his afternoon off, he had set off for the library as planned. He was found sitting at a table in the reading room, a book on Georgian silver open in front of him. No one had thought anything of the fact that he had been sitting there in silence for hours, it was his usual position, after all, but eventually someone sat down opposite him and by then Henry had been dead for some time. The cause of death was a bleed in his brain, caused by the thump on the head earlier in the day at Galbraith's.

Henry McInally had been killed by a piece of bacon. When his wife had died alone he'd wept and said, 'What a terrible way to die,' and it had happened to him, too. Thinking about it later, Alice supposed he'd rather have died peacefully in his bed, surrounded by his treasures, but few have the choice.

The community of Inchcraig was devastated. Henry had become a popular character there and would be genuinely missed. There wouldn't be anyone who could cut bacon like Henry McInally, while giving a seminar on its origins and how it differed from the bacons of the past. His hair was still black as he lay in his coffin, as was his clipped moustache, and his appearance immaculate, right down to the gold chain across his waistcoat holding the gold pocket watch, as though he was still a well-to-do Belfast businessman.

As Alice soon discovered, that was the least of his little deceptions. She was surprised to discover that her father had left a will, and even more surprised to find what was in it. He had been sitting on a nest egg, a vast fortune of over £50,000 pounds that he had left to her. He had saved it during his working life in Belfast, 'for a rainy day', he said in his will. Alice wondered how her mother would've reacted to that, though she knew, smiling as she pictured Victoria's rage. Then she thought of Billy Guthrie, 'the Guthrie creature', who had 'abandoned the sinking ship', without having the slightest inkling that it was pretty well afloat after all. She cast her mind back to harder times in Inchcraig, and remembered that there had been days when the rain poured down, as Henry waited for his mythical rainy day. Just how wet did it have to be for him, she wondered?

She was torn between anger and laughter – that he had all that money salted away when he arrived from Belfast and he hadn't said a word, rather, he'd pleaded poverty and thrown himself and Matt on her mercy. More than that, his collection of odd bits and pieces turned out to be worth another fortune: he had, as the antique collectors told her, 'a good eye'. For the first time Alice could afford to move out of Inchcraig to somewhere Maggie would have approved of, had she told Maggie, which she didn't.

Maybe Alice had inherited some of Henry's secrecy. For a moment she considered moving, but something stopped her. Instead she left Henry's money in the bank for Beth and Matt, for their future, she told herself, but she was aware it was more than that, though she didn't know exactly what. So not only did she not tell Maggie, she didn't tell anyone. She just bided her time – there was no reason for rocking the boat.

One thing she did, though, was to contact her sister Bella in Canada, to tell her that Henry had died, and a tentative contact was opened between them. Billy had gone from strength to strength in Toronto, and had risen to become Chief Test Engineer with an aircraft manufacturer. This took him all over the world, on trips that Bella didn't share, apparently, though she got the impression Bella had either not noticed this or didn't mind.

When Louise was next in Glasgow the cousins discussed events.

'Yes, well,' Louise said smugly, 'I have a feeling everything isn't all sweetness and light in Toronto, regardless of what Bella tells you.'

'Why? What have you heard?' Alice asked.

'Well, the Guthrie creature wasn't the only one who emigrated to Canada, and quite a few went from Harland and Wolff at the same time as him, church members who went to the same church in Toronto. They don't exactly spread about – clannish, the lot of them – and from what I hear on the grapevine he's been having real problems, drink problems,' Louise smiled.

'You mean he's hitting the bottle?' Maggie said.

'Well, obviously, Maggie, that's what I mean!' Louise answered. 'Having all these children is making you dense. Anyway, he's held his job down, so far, but who knows how long he'll manage that? Seems he's turned into a bitter, twisted creature, too; thinks the entire world has conspired against him, for some reason.'

'Seems a bit odd, when he's done so well,' Alice mused. 'I mean, what does he have to be bitter about?'

'Who knows?' Louise said. 'And Bella hasn't hinted?'

'Not a word,' Alice replied, 'but it isn't a very deep correspondence, if you see what I mean.'

'Well, it wouldn't be, would it?' Louise replied. 'She was never capable of anything deep, now, was she?' She looked teasingly at Maggie, who was frowning at her, and then at Alice, and the two of them laughed.

'Really, you two,' Maggie chided. 'I can't think what you find so funny!'

'You!' Louise said.

17

One Wednesday, Bernard Pollock appeared on her doorstep as usual, Buster by his side and a newspaper in his hand containing a story about the build-up of arms in Germany that everyone was so worried about.

'Mark my words,' he said seriously, 'this will end in war again, and my sons and your Matt will be caught up in it.'

It had been a long time since a visit from Bernard Pollock had frightened her, but this one did. Matt had gone to work in the fruit market in the Candleriggs straight from school at the age of fourteen. Bernard had told Alice that a friend of his was looking for someone and Matt was interviewed and given the job. Alice was determined to believe it was on his own merits, but these days she couldn't be sure. Matt was a good-looking boy, very clever with a sharp wit, but he still couldn't settle at anything and didn't seem to have any real ambitions, probably because ambitions required consistent application. He talked well and had an easy charm, and it came naturally to him to handle various thoughts at once. Indeed, it was part of his problem, but it made him an asset to the business, able to deal effortlessly with different orders and consignments from all over the world. Even if Pollock had made the suggestion to his friend, she thought, Matt had earned his job by doing it so well. If she and Liam hadn't taken flight, she mused, and the McInally–McCann alliance had continued, he would have been in Belfast instead, being groomed to take over McCann and Son from Harry, doing pretty much the same job he was doing in the fruit market, and he would be just as restless, he was that kind of boy.

Matt was nineteen, going on for twenty, when World War Two was finally declared, and without a word to anyone he enlisted the day after Chamberlain's radio broadcast informing the nation. Working in the food industry once again qualified as a reserved occupation, as it had with Harry and Brendon in World War One, so Matt told the recruiting officers he was no more than an office boy, and no one checked up.

Alice was horrified when he told her, but not shocked – his easy boredom had always worried her. She had put her faith in him maturing with age, setting herself milestones, getting him through his school days, getting him through his teens, but once again a war had intervened to spoil her hopes, though they were pretty small, reasonable hopes. She had only asked that the men in her life should live their lives, after all. All too soon he had left with the Argyll and Sutherland Highlanders, eyes shining, full of excitement and relief at getting away from boredom, and Alice was pitched back into that life of waiting again. For this war, though, there were things for civilians to do. Railings were removed and pots and pans donated to make guns, a ruse to make the people feel they were making a contribution, spare land was dug over to grow vegetables, and, in the back courts of the tenements, air raid shelters were built, huge rectangular constructions, dark and forbidding, that made no one think of safety. And they were made of red brick, which made Alice dream of Belfast for the first time in many years.

It was so quiet without Matt. Alice hadn't realised till then how much noise he contributed to the home, but it was more than that: he had been a good, if slightly worrying, companion. On a normal day there was no one to talk to, not in the sense of using her voice or of hearing someone else's. Beth's world was a silent one, which didn't matter to Beth as she had no real appreciation of sound, but now that there was no other voice in the house it gave Alice an insight into how isolated Beth's deafness made her.

Maureen still arrived and had become a trusted friend over the years, but she was there for Beth and there was no reason why that should suddenly change because Alice felt lonely. Maureen had become closer to Beth than her mother or her aunt, and, though it niggled a bit, Alice supposed it was inevitable. Maureen understood Beth and her situation better than anyone else could.

So, a solitary person by nature, Alice fell into her own thoughts even more than usual, and her memories, which led her to wonder why she had never found the right time to tell Beth about Liam, her real father. There was no answer to that, she had covered her tracks so well that it just hadn't happened, and the longer it didn't happen the harder it became to broach the subject. One day, though, she would: one day.

Alice supposed the lack of company and conversation was what made her actually look forward to Bernard Pollock's weekly visits rather than tolerate them. Bernard had learned the lesson of his first court appearance, valuable as it had been as a demonstration to those who might wish to challenge him, and he had never been arrested again. These days Bernard got other people to do his dirty work for him, and the trail never led back to him. He was known all over Glasgow in the 1930s, the acknowledged king of all he surveyed, but Alice noticed no change in him apart from perfectly understandable anxiety about his two sons, who had also enlisted in the Argylls when war was declared, which gave him and Alice something else to share. It upset him deeply, the fate of his boys caused him great fear, and she would look across at his worried face, at the pained eyes, and feel utter confusion, wondering if he ever thought that the families of people he had harmed had felt as he was feeling now.

When news came that one of Bernard's sons had been killed in action he was inconsolable, and sat in her sitting room crying for an hour. He read no poetry that day, or for many afterwards. Mostly he sat in silence, stroking the little dog who was his constant companion, only speaking to thank her for the tea she had prepared and to bid her goodbye. And throughout, she shared his silence with him, not even offering a comforting hand, but just leaving him to his tears and sorrow, because she couldn't make sense of him.

Alice still had no idea why Bernard came to her home every Wednesday. Perhaps it was a place – the one place for all she knew – where he could be himself, where he wasn't judged, and he knew she neither needed nor wanted anything from him. But why he should seek that or find it with her, she couldn't begin to fathom. Just as plausibly, or implausibly for all she knew, he could be putting on an act, though she had no idea what his motive for that could be: he had nothing to gain from impressing her and never attempted to do so. However, they were locked into this peculiar relationship, had been for years, and there it was.

Next came news that Bernard's younger son was a prisoner of war, and Alice watched him first crumble, then raise himself and harden before her eyes, as a kind of rage took over that pulled him from the grief he had slipped into for his dead eldest son. It was as if he had been told he had to pull himself together, and he did it, determined to get through this. He would ask after Matt and seemed genuinely pleased that he was at least still alive, and then he returned to whoever he had been before, the vicious, violent man everyone feared. Outside Alice's four walls, and buoyed by the black-market trade that ran through the war, Bernard presided over an ever more lucrative crime empire, using, or sanctioning, more and more extreme callousness, from what she heard. But once he arrived on Alice's doorstep he dropped the overlord's persona, like a snake shedding its skin, she often thought. He petted Buster and became a human being concerned about human things, the way the war was going, the utterings of politicians, what kind of world would exist afterwards, if afterwards ever came to pass.

Long ago she had made up her mind that if he had offered her some contraband, or if he were to ask her to store some items for him, stolen items, of course, as she knew he had 'asked' of other people (which meant giving them no choice), she would refuse. He never did, though. Alice simply bore witness, trying not to dwell on why he had chosen her, but sharing her waiting with him, and with millions of others all over the world.

When the end of the war came in May 1945, Alice got news that Matt was safe, but Bernard Pollock had to wait a bit longer, until after VJ Day a few months later, to find out that his only remaining son, John, had survived, and she saw that the waiting became somehow even harder, even more painful for him. John and his brother had also joined the Argyll and Sutherland Highlanders, a regiment of choice for East End men, but while his brother had died fairly early on, John had gone to fight in the Far East, and been captured by the Japanese after the fall of Singapore. But the fact that he was alive was the best present of his father's life.

18

With Matt safely back home, life in Inchcraig returned to normal, for Alice at any rate. For others, though, the end of the war brought fresh heartache, and one day when she looked through the spyhole, one such unfortunate was standing at Alice's door. It was Annie Feeney, an anxious look on her face, and Alice quickly padded her way in to the sitting room and signed to Beth to open the door. When Annie was ushered in, Alice glanced towards the fire, glad not to have to look at the woman's face, though her grief and agitation seemed to inhabit the whole room.

Alice already knew Annie's story, everyone in Inchcraig did. Her husband had been posted as missing in 1944, then had been confirmed as a POW before a telegram had arrived in the closing days of the war to say he had died in the camp. It struck her that as she had waited impatiently for Matt to come home, Annie Feeney and her children were no longer waiting for anyone. Annie had been left with no army wages and three children to raise on her own, not that she was alone in those circumstances.

Annie had been raised in Inchcraig and there had been talk of arranging some kind of collection for the Feeneys, as there often was on such an occasion. She had family close by and they were well-liked, but in the poor city of Glasgow this was one of the poorest areas, and, though they would help as best they could, none of her family would have much to help her with. Eventually some money would trickle through to her from the state, but not enough and not quickly enough, and the last thing Annie needed now was to be worried out of her mind.

Annie was a decent woman, Alice knew that. After an inevitable spell of despair she would pick herself up and sort herself out, if only for the sake of her children. One day, though she couldn't envisage it now, some nice man might – should – marry her, someone with enough heart to take on another man's three children; but for now Annie and her brood needed help.

'Mrs McInally,' she said, a little too loudly, and Alice could picture her practising her speech before plucking up the courage to climb the stairs and knock on Alice's door to deliver it.

'Sit down, Annie,' she said quietly, then, turning to Beth, she said, 'and get Annie a cup of tea, Beth.'

Beth had never known her aunt to entertain a client before, but she did as she was bid. Annie Feeney sat down by the fire, grateful for the heat; it was true what they said then, Auld Nally's house was always warm. The cup and saucer shook against each other in her left hand and she placed her right hand on the top, holding them together to steady the tremor.

'How are things, Annie?' Alice asked quietly.

Annie Feeney looked down and blinked furiously before she replied, 'Well, ye know, Mrs McInally.'

Alice nodded. She did know, but Annie wasn't aware of that, it was just a figure of speech. It was what you said when you didn't want to appear pathetic, when you wanted to maintain a shred of self-respect because it was all you had left, and if that went you might spiral downwards to some fearsome bottomless pit and never come back up again, even though you knew you had to. As Annie Feeney knew she had to.

'I've been thinking of you since I heard, Annie,' Alice said. 'I've been meaning to get in touch with you to see if I could help.'

'Well, that's why Ah'm here, Mrs McInally –' The practised voice again.

Alice held her hand up; she wouldn't threaten the dignity this nice, respectable young woman was desperately trying to keep hold of by making her ask. 'I was wondering if you might let me help you and the children,' she said, 'but I'd appreciate it if you kept it between ourselves, if you see what I mean.'

Annie Feeney stared at her, confused. Clearly, whatever she had heard about Auld Nally, it wasn't this.

Alice rummaged around her waist and handed the press key to Beth with a nod, then, when the box had been removed and carried to the kitchen, she looked back at Annie Feeney. 'I'd be grateful if you'd let me give the children five pounds,' she said calmly, feeling rather than seeing Annie's eyes opening wide and the slight gasp at the other side of the range, then her cup hitting her saucer a little too hard.

'Mrs McInally,' she said breathlessly, 'that's awfy good o' ye, but Ah canny take that much, Ah couldnae pay that much back if Ah lived tae be a hundred!'

'You misunderstand, Annie,' Alice said. 'This is a gift, and it's not for you, it's for the children. I don't want you to pay it back, just use it to look after the children. They've lost their father, the least anyone can do for them is to see they're fed and clothed and have a roof over their heads.'

Annie sat in silence for a moment. Before she started crying, which Alice knew was inevitable, she left her in the warmth of the hearthside and made her way to the kitchen. There, as though this was a normal transaction, she counted out the money and placed it on the coal bunker, but this time there would be no entry in the book, no debt recorded before she relocked the box. Returning to the sitting room she nodded to Beth and said to Annie Feeney, 'Beth will see you out, Annie, and I hope you'll remember our agreement.'

'Not a word, Mrs McInally,' she said, and pausing at the sitting-room door she turned. 'And if there's ever anythin' Ah can dae for ye, Mrs McInally, you only have tae ask.'

'I know that, Annie,' she replied with a quiet smile, 'and I'm grateful.'

When Beth had put the box back in the press she handed the key to her aunt and looked at her quizzically.

'She's a decent sort,' Alice mouthed, her hands translating the words. 'Comes from a good, hard-working family.'

'But still . . .' Beth signed back.

'She won't say a word,' Alice explained, 'and even if she did, who'd believe her?'

Beth laughed. 'But five pounds? That's a fortune!'

'Only if you don't have it,' Alice signed back.

Alice knew that there would a settling-in period for Matt. He had been away for six years in all, and those years had inevitably changed him, the nightmares proved that. Still, she hoped he would now be grounded in a way he hadn't been as a child or a teenager, and that his need for constant changes of direction and fresh excitement might have abated. He was now twenty-six; he had gone away a boy and returned a man, at least that was the theory.

What Alice had no way of knowing was that Matt's state of

mind was worse than it had ever been. He had spent his life waiting for something to happen, something that would take him away from the mundane and catapult him into the life he should be leading. The trouble was that he had no idea what that life was, only that there was a life somewhere that was better than the one he had, had to be, or else what was the point of it all? As a child he had been aware of the differences between his life and the lives of his Doyle cousins, Maggie's children, at Kew Terrace, though he had mainly kept it to himself. The two Doyle boys had even come back from the war unscathed and hardly changed, they had just carried on with their lives where they had left off years before. And Matt had looked around Inchcraig and felt that he didn't belong in a world where the only ambition people had was to survive, to get by happily and worry-free. It had never been enough, and after six years away that conviction had hardened. He had to get out: any way he could, he had to get out. He toyed with emigration, but decided that would have to wait till he had some cash behind him. He had no intention of moving some-where and starting from the bottom. Working in the normal manner would take too long, too – what Matt wanted was more money and status, and he wanted it now. He'd spent six years fighting; he had earned it; he was due it.

Alice knew nothing of this. As time went on she put his deeper moods down to the problems of returning to civilian life, and to the nightmares that she hoped would go away now that he was home. All Matt needed was home and family. He was having better times than others, that must be good sign, she thought, clutching at any straw, but Christmas of 1948 was a bad time. He had hardly slept and looked like death – that was exactly what she thought when she saw him, his eyes sunken, his face haunted – but he refused to admit anything other than an upset stomach. She didn't believe him, of course, but he was a grown man in his late twenties, she couldn't demand entry into his deepest thoughts.

What Matt was doing was reliving a Christmas Eve at the end of the war. He had been a marksman, though he hadn't told anyone this, and he had been in Berlin, mopping up, as they called it. A young German girl with a baby clutched in her arms had been found riddled with bullets, and they were to find the man responsible. Everyone knew who had done it, he was a Pole who had caused trouble in the area before, so Matt and his partner had set off to find him, and when they did, he ran. It took them hours to corner him, and then he had started firing again, killing the other marksman, so Matt had taken careful aim and brought him down, fatally injured. He didn't mind, it was his job, and he'd seen a lot worse; besides, the Pole was a truly evil man, there was nothing to feel guilty about, and Matt didn't. The sight of his partner lying dead didn't affect him unduly either, he wasn't the first partner, the first friend he had seen killed at his side. No, it was sight of the girl he couldn't get out of his head, not at the time, not since. He had never seen anyone with so many bullets in them, and the child, months old and dead, the look on one side of its face as though it was sleeping peacefully, but in a kind of ghastly repose with the other side, where most of its head was blown away.

Afterwards the other soldiers talked of the incident, of what the Germans had done to the Poles, so who knew where right lay, but to Matt it wasn't a question of right. She had only been a girl, about fourteen, he guessed. Maybe the child was hers or maybe it wasn't, but she hadn't harmed anyone in Poland, and certainly the mutilated child hadn't either. He'd calmly cleaned his rifle, listening to the talk around him as the soldiers opened presents from home, Christmas carols playing in the background;

and he could still see the girl and the child, see every bullet hole, and wondered if he was the only one sane or the only one mad.

The girl and the baby haunted his waking hours and crept into his sleeping ones, but Christmas Eve was worse than all the other times. It would never be the same – Christmas had been brutally murdered, too, and he couldn't tell anyone, not Beth, not Aunt Alice. All he could do was pretend he hadn't noticed their puzzled, anxious looks.

Bernard Pollock was finding the same with his son, who had returned, emaciated and desperately ill, from years in a Japanese POW camp. He didn't venture outside his home, but he looked, according to his father, like an old man, with eyes that were dead apart from moments of fear.

'The dreams are terrible,' he told Alice. 'He wakes in the night screaming, and when you try to waken him it takes a long time, then he curls up and turns away without a word. We find him lying on the floor some mornings; he says it's because he isn't used to a proper bed, it's too soft. He barely eats, but he steals food, we find it hoarded all over the place.'

'Does he talk to you?' Alice asked, mentally comparing notes.

Bernard shook his head and stroked the little dog. 'I've asked him what he dreams about, but he denies having any dreams.'

It was the same with Matt. Alice didn't ask him about his dreams, just if he'd slept well, and he always replied that he had.

'I don't know,' Bernard said sadly, 'having lost one son I thought I'd be grateful just to get John back alive, but I look at him sometimes and I wonder if I have, and I don't know what to do to help him. I've bought a house on the Clyde coast,' he said, laying a newspaper on the table. 'I thought if he could get away somewhere quiet it might help him.'

Alice nodded at the newspaper without seeing it, her mind on the problems they both faced. 'I think everyone with a man coming back is in the same position,' she said reassuringly. 'I suppose it will take time.'

Even as she said it, she wondered just how long it would take. She had always been concerned about Matt. That was partly why she spent more time with him and on him, she felt he needed it. Beth was capable, Beth could cope and Beth had Maureen, but in some ways Matt was more isolated than Beth's deafness had ever made her. He was still Matt, but there was an edge, a darkness about him now that worried her even more.

'It's not really a house,' Pollock continued, breaking into her thoughts, 'it's a tenement, I suppose, though it doesn't seem like one – better than we're used to in Inchcraig. But what's the use of money if it isn't for your family?'

She nodded absent-mindedly again.

'It's on the Isle of Bute,' he said. 'I saw it in the newspaper there a while back, thought you might like to see it.'

'The Isle of Bute?' she asked. Her voice sounded to her as though it had an echo, and every nerve in her body tingled.

'Yes, in Rothesay,' he explained. 'I don't suppose you know it, coming from Belfast.'

'Oh, I think I've been there a couple of times,' she smiled, playing for time, trying to keep herself calm, trying to stop her hands fidgeting and her legs jumping.

'It's above Gary's Tea Room, opposite the Winter Gardens. Anyway,' he said, his mind still on his son, 'I was hoping he'd spend some time there, but he doesn't seem interested.' He shrugged, too wrapped up in his own concerns to notice Alice's reaction. 'I suppose you're right, it will just take time.'

When Bernard had gone she picked up the newspaper and looked at the advertisement for the house he'd bought, and then her eyes travelled down further and there it was. Another for sale, this time a charming whitewashed cottage property in Port Bannatyne.

There was a name painted on a sign above the door of the cottage. It said 'Anneetermore'.

19

Beth couldn't understand why her aunt had bought the cottage on Bute, and, more than that, why she had bought it without even seeing it. She had never been impulsive, Aunt Alice was more the quiet and careful sort. She hadn't breathed a word about Grandpa's money till she bought the cottage.

'It was a bargain,' Alice signed to her. 'And the advert was a month old. If I hadn't moved quickly I could've lost it.'

'But what is it for?'

'I don't really know,' she shrugged. 'I thought we could let it out in the summer. There are always people looking for holiday homes on the islands in the Clyde, it'll make the money back in no time.'

Beth nodded. That she could understand, that was better, more the Aunt Alice she knew.

'But have you seen it?' she asked. 'Do you know what condition it's in?'

Alice decided to answer the second question. 'The newspaper only had a picture of the outside, but it looks nice enough.'

'Shouldn't we go across there, then?' Beth asked, shaking her head at her. 'Have a look at the place maybe?'

'Oh, I suppose so,' Alice replied. 'There's no rush.'

'What's wrong with you? I'm dying to see it!'

'It's not important,' Alice lied, 'it's just an investment. It's not like I've bought back the family home.' Why had she said that? As soon as it came out of her mouth, sooner, in fact – as she was saying it – she couldn't understand why.

'But it's a cottage!' Beth insisted. 'And it's not joined onto anything – even Aunt Maggie's pile is joined onto something – and it's beside the sea! I've always wanted to live beside the sea!' She danced around the room, staring at the newspaper photograph.

'You never told me!' Alice replied.

'Well, I have, so there. When can we go over?'

'Soon,' Alice said weakly.

'Not good enough!' Beth mouthed back to her. 'You're getting old and lazy,' she chided. 'We're going now.'

'Don't be silly, we can't just go now! There are boats and trains and timetables to find out about.'

'Tomorrow then!' Beth insisted, coming close to Alice and looking into her eyes determinedly.

For some reason she hadn't been expecting this reaction from Beth. She had wanted to build herself up for her first visit to the cottage in all these years, but how could she possibly refuse?

They left Glasgow by train, arriving at Wemyss Bay on the Ayrshire Coast, where the Caledonia, one of the railway steamers, waited to ferry passengers across eight miles of sea to Rothesay. Alice felt confused and afraid as she watched the island come closer; it was so familiar yet it scared her. As the boat approached Rothesay she could see Pat and Molly Murphy's big house high above the pier and wondered if they might still be there, her head full of happy ghosts from the years she had consigned to history.

At Port Bannatyne she was so full of dread that the very thought of walking into the cottage was almost too difficult. It contained her happiest memories, but it was so much Liam's house that she wouldn't have been surprised to hear his voice or catch a glimpse of him. This is where their daughter had been conceived. In front of that fire he had lain in her arms, happy but for the weary expression in his eyes. She was glad it was the wrong time of year for bluebells.

Beth had seen the cottage from a distance and ran on, pausing only to tell her, 'It's beautiful, I didn't realise it was so beautiful!' The cottage was empty, not a stick of furniture in it, whereas the last time she had been there it had been decorated and furnished, by herself. The paraffin lamps had been replaced by electric lights now, she noted. It had been well maintained and the name still hung above the door: 'Anneetermore'. She remembered how happy Liam had been when he saw the name and mentally she thanked someone for leaving it there and for looking after their home. With her attention on the past and all her senses heightened she had lost sight of Beth, who now came bounding downstairs, her face flushed with excitement.

'It's wonderful!' she signed excitedly with rapid movements. 'Wonderful and beautiful! What do you think the name means? Isn't that a lovely fireplace? I love it!'

'Calm down,' Alice signed back, smiling as she watched Beth spin circles on her toes, her hands clasped under her chin.

'You should see the view of the sea from the windows upstairs, and the garden at the back,' her fingers rushed, trying to keep up with her thoughts. 'Can we stay here?'

'There's nothing to stay with, it's empty!'

Beth looked crestfallen, then her face lit up again. 'I don't care, I'll sleep on the floor!'

'Well I won't! I'm not your age, you know, my bones ache enough as it is.'

Alice was glad it was empty; she couldn't bear to stay here and then leave again. When she came back the next time it would be with the intention of staying for the rest of her life.

'Let's make a plan of how we'll do it up,' Beth mouthed. 'That bit on the side, what's that for?'

'I think it's where the cart would've been kept in the old days,' Alice told her.

'We'll extend that, make it part of the house, we'll get another room out of it at least,' Beth announced, searching feverishly in her bag for a piece of paper, everything else spilling out onto the floor. 'Why can't you ever find what you want?' she demanded impatiently. 'Have you got a pencil, Aunt Alice? I can't find a thing I want!'

But Alice had found what she wanted, here, in this little house, many years ago, and then she had lost it. Still, it was her house again, and she was happy that Beth liked it so much. But the truth was that she had no clear idea herself why she had bought the house, except that it was and always had been her house, hers and Liam's, and it was right that she should have it. It was like those stories of people who lose precious wedding rings and then find them, years and years later, when they're digging in the garden. 'Anneetermore' had been returned to her; beyond that she hadn't thought at the time, but the idea took root in her mind then that somehow she would go back to Port Bannatyne to live in their little cottage. There was an order about it, a rightness.

'Can I do it up?' Beth asked, rushing through the house without waiting for a reply. 'I've got lots of time to do it, haven't

I?' she signed, returning for a fleeting moment before dashing off again, then coming back and informing Alice, 'Your taste is a bit old-fashioned anyway, isn't it?'

'Thank you,' Alice replied.

'Well, if we want people to rent it for their holidays we only want the best people for this house, don't we? And look at you, the way you dress, it's hardly stylish, is it?'

'Whatever do you mean?' Alice laughed.

'Well, you're as bad as Aunt Maggie in your way. She wears all those pastel colours and frills and lace and things, like something out of the 1900s, while you've only got as far as 1920. Why do you like those dark suits with those long skirts, and those black straw hats! I said to Louise once that you should go for the full look and stick a basket of fruit on top.' She screwed up her face at the thought.

'And what did Louise say?'

'She said I shouldn't encourage you, that Carmen Miranda just about pulled that look off but she couldn't quite see you flashing your thighs and singing.'

Alice tried to look offended but laughed instead.

'Anyhow, this is such a special house, I don't want it rented to the kind of people who won't look after it,' Beth protested.

'*You* don't want?'

'Oh, stop being silly,' Beth signed back, giggling, 'you know what I mean. If we want the kind of people who won't make a mess of it, I – we – must do it up really well. And don't argue, we both know I'll do that better than you!'

So Beth had a project; though Alice had visions of her vetting everyone who expressed an interest in renting the place and discarding most of them. She never told Bernard Pollock that she, too, had bought a house on Bute. It was nothing to do with him, and when she told Maggie she almost laughed at her cousin's shocked expression. She was so easy to shock, though, it was little wonder that Louise constantly teased her.

'But how can you possibly afford it?' Maggie asked, before she could stop herself, then she recovered and said, 'I am sorry, Alice, that's none of my business, of course,' even if she did still want to know.

'My father left fifty thousand pounds in cash and his collection of odds and ends was worth a fortune,' Alice smiled.

'And you didn't say a word!' Maggie gasped.

Alice mistook her hurt for simple surprise. 'I knew you'd go on at me to move out of Inchcraig,' she said, 'and I wanted to think things through before I did anything.'

So there it was again, Maggie thought, sipping her tea and trying to control herself – the secrecy, the closed part of Alice. No matter how long you had known her and how well you thought you did, she still kept you out when it suited her and thought nothing of it. Maggie was upset every time something of the sort happened, though she always tried to hide it.

'So,' she said brightly, 'what are you planning to do with it, dear?'

'I was thinking of letting it out,' Alice replied, stirring her tea and waiting for Maggie to completely recover the power of speech. 'Do you think one of Tony's friends might help with that? You know, a solicitor who might deal with the business end.'

'Well, there's Pat Murphy,' Maggie suggested.

Alice looked at her, surprised. 'But surely Pat's retired now?'

'Oh, yes, he has,' Maggie smiled quietly, pleased to have some information Alice didn't have, 'Pat Senior at any rate. He went to live in Rothesay years ago, but his son took over the firm.'

Alice thought for a moment. She had built a new life, a

different life. She didn't want to go back to a time that made her feel sad again. 'I'd rather have someone I don't know,' she replied.

'I'll see what I can do,' Maggie replied, although inside she was still hurt at being left out of parts of Alice's life after all these years – after all they had been through together.

Louise, who was visiting with George, had been completely silent throughout the conversation.

'Where's George?' Alice asked.

'Out,' Louise replied.

'He's looking terribly well,' Maggie said happily. 'Got himself a nice suntan from somewhere. It suits him.'

'Will he be back soon?'

'Oh, who knows,' Louise replied in a casual tone, but Alice heard something else.

'Will I see you before you go back home?' she asked.

'We'll see.'

'Are you all right?' Alice asked quietly.

'Pretty rough crossing last night,' Louise replied with a smile. 'Everyone was sick, it was hellish. I just need some sleep.'

When Alice came back from Kew Terrace, Annie Feeney called on her. Alice had given the girl money, a gift to her fatherless children that she did not expect to see repaid, but that was what Annie wanted to do.

'The thing is, Mrs McInally,' Annie said, quickly pushing the five pounds into Alice's hands, 'that people had a whip-round for us, an' we don't need the money after all.'

Alice looked at the note in her hand. 'But I don't want it back, Annie,' she protested.

'But Mrs McInally,' the girl said pleadingly, 'Ah felt bad takin' that much frae ye, Ah said tae ye at the time it was too much.

Ah'd feel much better if ye took it back, wi' my thanks. Ye saved our lives at the time.'

Alice thought for a moment, examining the desperate look in the young widow's eyes. Then she saw it. Bernard Pollock.

'Annie,' she said quietly, 'this is my money, you understand, it has nothing to do with B—'

'No, no, Mrs McInally,' Annie protested with a speed that proved to Alice that it was, 'it's got nothin' tae dae wi' that, wi' him, honest! Ah'm tellin' ye the truth, Ah just don't need it an' Ah'd feel better no' tae be beholdin' tae anybody. See?'

When Annie Feeney had gone, Alice sat in her chair, feeling stunned that her gift had been returned. Annie was a decent young woman, but she had been desperate when she had come to Alice's door the first time, desperate enough to accept money tainted by association, by Alice's association with a gangster. That was it: Annie felt it was dirty money. Even if the money had nothing to do with him, Alice had – and being a respectable woman, that would have eaten away at Annie, so she had wanted Alice to have it back, to absolve herself, to make herself feel clean again.

Alice didn't feel angry, she understood it, but she felt ashamed in a way, and slightly sick. She had brought this on herself by letting Bernard Pollock over her doorstep the first time, and by not telling him never to come back again. As a result, she was now looked down on by decent people, and she knew she had no one to blame but herself. It was just another fact of life she would have to live with.

The next day, Louise arrived. Alice always smiled when she saw her cousin: age had made little difference to her, apart from her hair, which she had let turn entirely white because she liked the effect. The clothes were still outrageous and timeless, a cape of violet and purple swirls today, thrown majestically over a black velvet dress with a full skirt, and, as always, her signature kitten heels. Louise sat in the corner chair.

'I have something to tell you and I don't want you to blub,' she said. 'Promise me.'

'I promise,' Alice said, but she felt fear gripping her heart and her hand went there instinctively.

'It's about George.'

For a terrible moment Alice was actually relieved that it wasn't about Louise.

'He's got liver cancer and there isn't any hope,' Louise said plainly. She looked across at Alice and then away again. 'That's why we came over, for a second opinion, but it wasn't any bloody better than the first one.' She gave a little snort. 'That hellish journey over for that!' she said.

They sat in silence, then, 'You promised not to blub,' Louise said, 'so don't.'

'No, I won't,' Alice replied in a small voice.

'Maggie's in her usual state,' Louise said wearily. 'You know what she's like, poor old thing, she can't help it. We did laugh last night, though, George and I. She made such a thing about his "suntan", kept saying the Belfast climate must have changed since she was a girl, what with all that sunshine, must be like the Med there now. And all the time he was jaundiced. Poor Maggie, she never gets it right, does she?' Louise looked at Alice. 'What? We aren't allowed to laugh now? My dear Alice, if we can't laugh at our own tragedies and misfortunes in life we might as well be dead anyway!' and she gave a huge cackle.

'So what are you going to do?' Alice asked.

'Take him home tomorrow, look after him,' Louise said with a shrug. 'There's nothing else I can do.'

'Nothing at all?'

'No, dear, we've been through all that already, we've moved

on from the stage everyone else is at now. It's a one-off, the liver, you see, you don't get two like with the kidneys or the lungs so that there's a back-up. They think it will be quick, though, so the emphasis will be on keeping him as pain-free as possible for the duration.'

'What about Emma?'

'I don't know about that. She's perfectly happy in her new life in Australia with her family, so do I bring her home to dreary Belfast, and for how long? Dear old George won't die by appointment, will he? I don't want to tell her if it makes her think I want her to come home, but I don't want her to think she shouldn't, if that's what she wants to do, do you see?'

'Yes, I see.'

'Oh, God, Alice, talk to me normally, I can't bear this pre-emptive grieving! Maggie's bad enough, bursting into tears all the time, I can't take it from you, too. Poor old George was all concerned about her yesterday, wondered if there was anything we could do. I said yes, we could try a little gentle garrotting, but he wouldn't go for it, unfortunately.'

'Do you think I should go to her?'

'No, I bloody well do not! She'll only use it as an excuse for non-stop blubbing. Let her tribe take care of her, she gave birth to them, after all, they owe her something.'

They sat for a moment staring into space. 'After George shuffles off,' Louise said, 'I think I may leave Belfast.'

It was said in such a throwaway manner that Alice almost missed it, and, even when it registered, she didn't take it seriously.

After Louise had gone, Alice tried to compose herself. There had been a few knocks in the last days, but everything was fine: she had life — and death — in perspective again, there were things you just had to get through without thinking too deeply about them. However, thinking this way had been an invitation to fate to step in again and remind her she was but a tiny human being, she would think later.

It was a Friday night, or, more correctly, early Saturday morning, when there was a loud knocking at the door. Beth couldn't hear it, and Alice had no idea where Matt was, he didn't keep regular hours these days but he was a grown man, she could hardly complain. When she looked through the keyhole she saw two policemen standing there, and though she was puzzled by their presence she wasn't surprised that there were two of them, whatever they wanted. Inchcraig had become a more dangerous place recently: for the first time anyone could remember there had been street fights after dark, and these days, and nights, patrolling policemen travelled in pairs there. As a result of the increasing levels of violence the sleep of everyone was more frequently broken by police raids, with Black Mariahs arriving and dragging men off, kicking and cursing. It didn't seem to matter to the police who they grabbed, everyone in Inchcraig was a criminal in their eyes, and so there were ordinary decent people with no link to any crime taken from their beds. It didn't help community relations that there was never a word of apology; the attitude seemed to be that if those arrested weren't involved in this case, they would be in the next. What it did, of course, was to drive the allegiance of Inchcraig inhabitants further towards the gangs, who at least tried to keep a distance between their activities and innocent civilians – even if it didn't always work out that way they knew that was how it was meant to be. No one in Inchcraig went to the police about anything, and no one helped them either: what happened in Inchcraig was dealt with within Inchcraig, and visits from the police for any reason were met with silence and a steely, icy hatred.

When Alice saw the two men on her doorstep that morning she greeted them coldly, as anyone in Inchcraig would. They asked to come in and told her to sit down but she shook her head and stood her ground in the hallway. Then one of them told her she had to accompany them to the Royal Infirmary in Castle Street. It was Matt; he'd been stabbed.

Alice looked down at the pictures in the mottled lino and saw them blur together: Churchill melted into the half a woman with flicked-out hair, the bunch of grapes fell over Shaw's Bridge and surged towards her at great speed, before everything turned a deep, inky black. Then she was being helped to her chair by the range, panicky thoughts going through her mind. She had to pull herself together; she had to tell Beth and get ready to rush down to the Royal.

Pushing her way through the drunks in the casualty department, or Gate, as Royal Infirmary insiders knew it, Alice and Beth were met by another policeman. It was too late, Matt was dead. He was twenty-nine years old. He had lived through the war years and returned to his home, and in just a couple of years he had been killed in a street in a residential area of Glasgow.

It made no sense, it must be wrong, but it wasn't. Alice had been here before, thinking someone was safe only for it all to collapse around her; she couldn't go through it again. The policeman who had told them Matt was dead wanted to ask her some questions. He was small man, with fading fair hair and grey eyes: Caldwell, he said his name was, from the CID. He wanted to know about Matt's movements.

Alice stared at him, then she and Beth exchanged puzzled glances. She didn't understand the question, never mind know the answer.

'Ye know what he was doin', though?' he asked.

Alice shook her head.

The detective watched her, trying to make up his mind if she was lying or acting, and then he seemed to come to a decision. 'Mrs McInally,' he said, in a gentler tone of voice, 'ye dae know yer laddie was workin' for Big Bernie Pollock, daen't ye?'

Alice felt her eyes grow wide as she tried to think of a reply. 'Matt?' she said, more to herself than him. 'Matt?' she repeated to Beth.

Detective Caldwell caught the eye of a nurse and asked if there was an empty cubicle they could use.

'Are you kiddin'?' the nurse replied. 'On a Friday night? If yer no' kiddin' ye must be daft, Alec.'

Alice vaguely noted the first-name terms. He was doubtless a frequent visitor here. Caldwell guided Alice and Beth outside, through the Gate's normal weekend clientele of drunks and wounded, to a black police car. He put them in the back seat together, climbed into the front passenger seat and turned round.

'Mrs McInally,' he said, 'Ah'm sorry tae bother ye when yer son's lyin' dead there, but –'

'He's my nephew,' Alice replied, 'was my nephew.' She put her head down to gain control and felt Beth's arm going round her shoulders. 'He was an orphan, his father was my brother. I've had him since he was weeks old, but that's no reason to disrespect his parents.'

'Ah see, Ah'm sorry, Ah didnae know.' She didn't believe him; the police knew everything. He waited a moment, to give her time. 'So you didnae know about him workin' for Pollock, then?'

She shook her head again. 'Are you sure about that?' she asked.

'Certain,' he replied. 'An' you?' he said to Beth.

'Beth is deaf,' Alice said, sure he knew that, too. She signed to Beth. 'Did you know he'd been working for the gangs?'

Beth had already understood the gist of what was going on and vehemently shook her head. 'That's just stupid,' she replied, using her curiously muffled voice in the hope of making the policeman understand.

Caldwell looked from one to the other. 'The thing is, there's a war goin' on in Inchcraig, have you no' noticed that? The skids are under Pollock, other neds are fightin' for his territory.'

It was all alien to Alice. What the policeman and other outsiders found it hard to understand was that it was entirely possible to live peacefully in Inchcraig without ever encountering trouble – in fact, Bernard Pollock, while he was causing mayhem in someone else's backyard, kept the streets quiet. He policed the area and made sure there was no trouble in his own backyard. If you weren't actually involved in crime you only heard rumours and gossip. It was another world away, though she knew there had been more of a sense of unrest recently. She had thought it was the result of men coming back from the war, having spent years in a violent world, and finding it hard to settle down to peace again.

'The only war we notice in our streets is the one Glasgow Police bring to it,' she said stiffly, perfectly aware that it was a show of loyalty over common-sense.

'Big Bernie's losin' his grip a bit,' Alec Caldwell continued. No one ever called Pollock 'Big Bernie'; she knew he was doing it to belittle him, but she didn't reply. 'Got his mind on other things, so they say.'

Alice knew what his mind had been on: coping with the fact that one son wouldn't ever come home, while the other one, who had come home, was changed out of all recognition.

Concern for John had been occupying him to the exclusion of everything else, but the detective knew this perfectly well, he was just testing her to find out how much she really knew, how close she was to Pollock. Without a doubt he knew of Bernard Pollock's visits to her over the years. He could probably produce times and dates if asked to, but he wouldn't get any help from Alice.

'When that happens,' the detective went on in a friendly tone, 'there's a vacuum, ye see, an' it gets filled, one way or another.'

'But Matt couldn't have been involved in any of that,' she said in a small voice. One part of her thought it was impossible, but another remembered the fears she had always had for him, making her less sure but unable to say so.

'An' ye never suspected anythin'?'

Alice shrugged. 'He's been finding it hard to settle since he came back from the war,' she said, 'been having a lot of nightmares. I thought it was just a matter of time. And he was a grown man, I couldn't tell him to be in by ten every night.'

The detective nodded. 'Ah'm sorry for yer trouble,' he said gently. 'Ah'll get somebody tae take ye both home.' He got out of the car to speak to another policeman and came back.

'Just stay where ye are,' he said, 'we'll get a driver tae take ye home.' He turned to go then turned back. 'So ye don't know Big Bernie?' he asked, trying to make it sound like an afterthought, but it was so clumsy and stupid that she didn't answer for a moment. Two could play at that game, she thought.

'Detective,' she sighed, 'everybody in Inchcraig knows who Bernard Pollock is.'

The following day, on a Saturday for the first time ever, Bernard Pollock came calling, and Alice was ready for him. He followed her into the sitting room, where she turned on him.

'How could you do this to me?' she demanded angrily. 'I've given you friendship, never once cast up to you the things you get up to, never once mentioned what I knew you did. I accepted you at face value, though my every instinct told me to keep my distance.'

Bernard was stunned. No one, least of all Alice, had ever spoken to him like that, but before he could answer she launched herself at him hitting him hard across the face. He didn't stop her, didn't even try to protect himself, just stood there looking miserable.

'You wouldn't have wanted your sons to follow you into your business, would you?' she screamed at him. 'So why my Matt?'

He sat down in his usual chair. 'I didn't know,' he said wearily.

'You're the boss,' she spat at him, 'the big man. Don't tell me you didn't know!'

'Look,' Bernard said, 'that's why I'm here today. I swear I didn't know. It seems he went to one of my men, who gave him a job – thought he couldn't turn him down, given that you and I knew each other. Matt said he needed the money; he was planning to emigrate and needed some quick cash. I knew nothing about it.'

If Bernard was telling her the truth it was too much to bear. It had been her fault, then. Matt had never mentioned emigrating, but if he had needed money he could have had it for the asking. She was the one who had allowed Bernard Pollock into their home, into their lives, providing Matt with an alternative. If she had sent Pollock packing all those years ago, Matt would still be alive. Instead he was lying in the police mortuary down at the Saltmarket, not just dead, but a criminal who had been murdered by another criminal. She sank to her knees and sobbed noisily.

Bernard got up to comfort her and, without looking at him, she shouted at him to get away from her.

'I'll find whoever did this to Matt and deal with him,' he said helplessly.

'Don't you dare!' she screamed at him. 'You've done enough, don't you dare harm some other mother's son in Matt's name! Now get out, and don't ever come back here, or I swear I'll stick the kitchen knife where your heart should be! Get out!'

Matt was to be buried beside his grandfather in the local ceme-tery. Maggie had suggested taking him home to lie beside Harry and Mattie, but Alice didn't have the strength to contemplate that. Bad enough that she had to do what she had to, but adding a return to Belfast to that was too much. Besides, Matt had spent all but a few weeks or so of his life in Glasgow, that's where he belonged.

Part of Alice was consumed with grief; another part of her was bitter and a third part of her was full of anger towards Matt, and there was nowhere for it to go. She had brought him up well, provided for him, indulged him and tried to understand him – the least he could have done was not be a criminal. And there was the dreadful irony of tolerating Bernard Pollock in her home, in her life, because she thought his presence would provide her children with protection. She could have protected Matt far better if she had moved out of Inchcraig years ago, but while she was blaming herself the truth was that she felt ashamed of him, and angry that she did, so that all her emotions were in turmoil and her mood changed by the second. Everything was out of control.

'All those times when you tried to get me to move out of Inchcraig,' she wept to Maggie, 'and I wouldn't listen to you.'

'This is not your fault,' Maggie said sternly. 'You did your best for him. He's the one who let you down.'

'No, no,' Alice cried, 'don't say that!', though she knew it was the truth.

On the spring day of Matt's funeral Alice stood in the cemetery, her arms clutched around Beth, surrounded by the people of Inchcraig who stood many deep around them, most of them in tears. Their immediate neighbours were behind them, and she turned to see Sadie Duffy crying and gritted her teeth to blot out the sound. They all saw Sadie as easy, but she was a soft-hearted soul, no one seemed to see that.

She looked around and saw wreaths everywhere, everyone touched by so short a life cut down; but forcing their way through the grass she could see little clusters of bluebells, the harbingers of great happiness and sorrow throughout her life. She closed her eyes to shut them out, but their familiar scent came back and forth to her in the slight breeze, cruelly reminding her of other times, and she had to fight a strong urge to turn and run. To distract herself from the intense pain of it, she glanced to the side, to where, in the distance and separated by a low wall, the road ran. She was looking for a passing car or a bus to concentrate on, but instead her eyes settled on him standing there, Bernard Pollock, the overlord out in the open, paying his respects. Their eyes locked and he bowed his head slightly to her, and, though she instantly looked away, she felt a rush of pity for the man that she couldn't understand.

As the minister droned on, all Alice could think of was that once Bernard Pollock had been some mother's son, and somehow he had ended up where he was. Maybe his mother had been as horrified as she had been on finding out Matt had deliberately set out on the same road.

Bernard was an intelligent man, she knew that, far more

intelligent than most of the others in Inchcraig, which explained how he had reached the position he had, if not why. If he'd had more chances, an education, who knew where it would have taken him? But he hadn't had that: he was the child of Irish immigrant slum-dwellers and, as she had done herself many years ago, he had worked with the cards he had been dealt. If Matt hadn't been killed, in twenty or thirty years he could easily have ended up in the same position as Bernard Pollock was now, feared and admired, hated and loved, but ultimately tolerated only because of his reputation. Matt, she decided, had got off lightly compared to Bernard.

In the days that followed Alice felt numb, lost in a sea of blankness and nothing. Bernard came back to see her on Wednesday, but in the evening this time, prepared to walk away if the door remained closed. She signed to Beth to stay in the kitchen then she let him in, neither of them saying anything while she got Buster a bowl of water. Alice didn't know why she had let him in, there was nothing to say, but she had. He sat in his usual chair and again said how sorry he was, and she held up her hand to stop him.

They sat in silence for a long time, then, despite what Alice had said, Beth appeared with tea and biscuits on a tray, before withdrawing.

'If you'd let me,' he said, then stopped. 'I'd be happy.' Another pause. 'Not happy,' he said, sounding exasperated. 'What I mean is, I'll pay for the funeral.'

She glared at him angrily. 'You will not!'

'I'm putting it the wrong way, Alice,' he said, using her Christian name for the first time, almost appealing to her for help. 'What I mean is, will you let me pay for his funeral?'

'Never mention it,' she said coldly. 'Never even think it.'

Bernard looked close to tears, which threw her. 'I wouldn't have done this to you for anything,' he said. 'You have to believe that. You and I have been friends for a long time, you mean something to me; you can't think I'd have let him join in, not if I'd known.'

She sighed. 'I know that,' she murmured. 'I'm angry with myself – I should've noticed. I was trying to give him his privacy, but I should've asked more about what was happening in his head.'

'You can't blame yourself.'

'Why not?' she asked dully. 'I brought him up. I always knew he could be headed for trouble, and I did nothing about it. I should've got him out of here years ago.'

'It's the war as well,' Bernard said, 'it's made everything more confused. Look at my John.' He looked up quickly. 'I'm sorry. I still have him, I know, but it doesn't feel like that, it's like a living death.'

Alice decided to cut the meeting short. 'I'm sorry, I'm not up to this,' she said quietly.

He didn't argue, but as they reached the front door he produced a book from his pocket – a pathetic attempt, she thought, to re-establish the companionship of their previous meetings. 'Can I read this to you?' he asked. 'It's that book by John Steinbeck.'

'Again?' she smiled slightly. 'You and your Americans.'

His smile was almost shy. 'It started out with cowboys and Indians when I was a boy,' he explained, 'and that just kind of led on to other American things. This lad, Steinbeck, he has this character –' he opened the book and found his place, '– his name is Doc. "Doc tips his hat to dogs as he drives by and the dogs look up and smile at him." Isn't that great?' he asked gently. 'I mean, doesn't it tell you everything about his character without using too many words?'

Bernard looked raw, his eyes dark and sad. He looked like someone who knew they'd lost something precious forever but couldn't bear the thought and so had to have one last attempt at getting it back, even though they knew it could only make matters worse. It was the nearest Alice came to touching him with tenderness, even in her grief for Matt, in her rage at Bernard Pollock; she reached for a moment to close her arms around him, before stopping herself and looking away.

Later, much later, Alice suspected Bernard had been told all his life that he was different, odd, only to find someone who thought just like himself – so suddenly he wasn't the odd one after all, it was everyone else. As he turned to go, he had handed the book to her and she had taken it without thinking, out of habit, she supposed. Then she watched from behind her curtains as he walked away through the streets, Buster at his heels. As he turned the corner out of sight, she glanced at the book, saw the page he had read from, located the line with the description of Doc that he had obviously identified with. The sentence following it read, 'He can kill anything for need, but he could not even hurt a feeling for pleasure.'

20

Not long after Bernard had left there was the sound of bells ringing, but the sudden appearance of police cars in Inchcraig was hardly something to bother about, especially in recent times. Alice closed the curtains and went to bed – not to sleep, she had somehow lost the habit since Matt's death, it was just what people did at night. Maybe she couldn't sleep because Matt wasn't coming home. In the past she would lie awake till she heard his key in the lock and his footsteps crossing the mottled lino, and only then would she fall deeply asleep. Some part of her was still waiting for his safe return. Waiting was something she did well: after all, she'd had plenty of practice.

Through the night she dozed, then got up and did a crossword, went back to bed and dozed some more and had another look at the book Pollock had left with her. She smiled wryly: Steinbeck's Doc even had a habit of reading poetry to his friends.

She didn't hear till about ten o'clock in the morning. It seemed that as Bernard had walked home after leaving her, someone had kicked Buster hard in the stomach and run off through the streets. Naturally, Bernard had followed. She could imagine that, see it almost – he couldn't have tolerated anyone harming Buster, and whoever had done it had planned it well, knowing so.

They were waiting for him round a corner. No one knew how many there had been, but four would have been a fair number to take on that job. Buster, despite the kick that had acted as a lure, had tried to defend Bernard, and those who lived nearby heard him shouting, 'Buster, go home! Buster, stop!' as Bernard Pollock was battered to death in the street. Then the group had turned their full attention to Buster and clubbed him to death too.

No one had a phone, so it took time to call for an ambulance – the police were of secondary importance – and that's how they were found, together as they always were, Bernard Pollock and Buster, but both of them dead. What Alice had heard were the ambulance bells as well as the police-car bells. Later that day, Alec Caldwell, the detective she had met at the Royal, came calling.

'Ah understand he was here just before?' he asked.

Alice nodded.

'Can Ah ask what for?'

'He was offering to pay for my nephew's funeral,' she said quietly. Glancing at the book he had left that last night she decided not to mention it. Caldwell wouldn't have believed it anyway. 'I said no,' she added.

'Why would he have done that?'

'For no reason on earth that someone like you would understand,' she said coldly.

There was a silence. 'An' have ye any idea if he had any enemies?' he asked eventually.

She stared at him. 'Have you heard yourself?' she demanded. 'He was Bernard Pollock!'

'Aye, daft question,' he grinned. 'What Ah meant was, did he mention anybody in particular?'

'Now why in the world would you think he would tell me anything like that?' she asked, genuinely amazed. 'And do you really care anyway? To you he's the same as my Matt, you're just glad he's off the streets, isn't that so?'

'Aye, it is, if Ah'm bein' truthful,' he sighed, 'but Ah've got tae go through the motions, ye understand. There are reports tae write, Ah can hardly put down that it doesnae matter who did him in, Ah'm just glad tae see the back of him, can Ah?'

'Then save us both trouble and write what you want,' she said bitterly. 'There's nothing I can tell you, about him or about Matt. We both know you won't find who did it, and, as you say, it doesn't matter anyway, somebody will do the same to them in due course.'

'Ah'm sure they will, but they'll dae other damage first, it's better tae know who they are. It's a' very well lettin' them deal wi' each other, but if this thing isnae settled soon there could be blood on every street, wi' innocent people caught up in it.'

'But you don't believe anyone in Inchcraig is innocent, do you? In the eyes of the police we're all criminals here, isn't that so?' she demanded.

'Ah can see how ye'd think that,' he said, obviously less than convinced all the same.

'And I can't see why anyone wouldn't,' she replied. 'Including even a Glasgow policeman.'

'But as tae Big Bernie, as Ah said before, my opinion is that he just lost it, took his eye off the ball, if you see whit Ah mean.'

The last time Caldwell had said this he had been fishing, trying to find out just how good a friend of 'Big Bernie's' she was. She hadn't answered then, but he was gone now, it no longer mattered. 'As far as I know,' Alice replied, 'he's been very caught up with his son – anybody in Inchcraig could've told you that. The lad was a Japanese POW and came back in bad shape. From what I've heard, his father's mind was on that.'

The detective gave a short, sarcastic laugh. 'Funny tae think o' a man like him bein' so upset, no' think so?'

'Why? Because he loved his son?' Alice shot back. 'Do you love yours?'

'Aye, but a man like him, he was no angel, let me tell ye.'

'And you think you are?' she demanded furiously. 'The way you and your friends behave when you come into Inchcraig? And if he was no angel, as you put it, have you ever wondered how he got like that?'

'No' really, Mrs McInally, Ah don't have time tae think like that, Ah've enough tae dae moppin' up after him an' his kind.'

'Well I've had plenty of time these last weeks to think like that,' she told him. 'I've been turning it over and over in my mind that my Matt could've ended up like him in years to come, and I still have no idea why.'

'Don't blame yourself,' Caldwell said sympathetically, 'some people are just like that.'

'But not all of us,' she said pointedly. 'Not all of us.'

So there she was again, in the space of a few weeks, standing on the pavement, over the wall from the local cemetery this time, standing where Bernard Pollock had stood when Matt was buried. She was far enough away to be out of sight, and out of the scent of the bluebells, if they were still there, and she deliberately didn't look for them. An even bigger crowd had turned up on this occasion, some very glad to see the back of Bernard Pollock, some genuinely sad and others not sure why they were there, but curious all the same. In among them, she was pretty sure, were the men who had killed him, and killed Matt, too. It didn't seem to matter – if it hadn't been them it would have been some other murderers.

Beth was beside Alice, and on the other side Sadie Duffy, stood with her mother, crying quietly again, as she had at Matt's funeral. Maybe that was Sadie's real trouble, Alice thought fleetingly: not so much a lack of morals as too many emotions. Isa O'Rourke was there, there would be no candy balls for the children of Inchcraig today, and Johnny Hall, the bleach man, and all the others you saw in the streets every day – Bernard Pollock's subjects, regardless of how they had felt about it.

She caught the odd remark from the crowd.

'They say he was battered tae a pulp, even his wife wouldnae have been sure it was him, if it hadnae been for wee Buster.'

'Aye, well, whatever he might've done, he didnae deserve that end.'

'Canny imagine the place withoot him, can ye?'

'He wasnae a' bad, he did a lot for people here, looked efter them.'

'Aye, who'd have thought they'd have had the guts tae dae it?'

As they walked home, Alice was suddenly aware of Bernard Pollock's widow advancing on her and automatically put her hand out to show her respects. To her shock and horror, as the woman came closer she could see a look of utter hatred in her eyes.

'What are you doin' here, ya bitch?' she screamed.

For a moment Alice wondered who she was shouting at, then, before she could think of anything to say, the woman resumed shrieking into her face.

'I know what you and him have been up tae a' these years, everybody here knows, so don't deny it!'

Even then, Alice turned round to see if she was yelling at

Sadie, but she wasn't, Alice was her target. 'I . . . What . . .?' she stammered.

'I tried everythin' tae keep him away frae ye, but ye kept him goin' back, didn't ye? Ya slut! He was a married man, he was *ma* man!'

The woman was overcome with such a rush of grief that she couldn't say another word, for which Alice was selfishly grateful as she made her escape and headed for home, trying to keep her head high as the crowd muttered around her. Beth wasn't with her, though she didn't realise this till she had opened her front door and then locked it securely behind her.

Beth couldn't hear the tone of the woman's voice; she knew from the atmosphere that something dramatic was taking place, but not what, then her attention was drawn to a figure on the periphery. He looked like death, the yellowed skin of his face with flecks of dried blood dotted about, and prominent bones, his scrawny neck emerging from a shirt collar that was too large, and his eyes, his terrible eyes. He was a mourner, but this was more than grief, the man wasn't really there in any mean-ingful sense and he was slowly sinking to the ground. She was beside him in a flash, her arm under his elbow to support him. All around there were faces looking in the direction of what-ever was going on in the crowd, but she was with this awful-looking young man, the two of them standing in total silence and stillness.

She helped him to a low wall around what should have been a garden, where the metal railings had been removed for the war effort, and made him sit down. He didn't look at her, but his lips moved, so, taking him unawares, she put the fingers of her right hand under his chin and raised his face so that she had eye contact. 'I can't hear,' she mouthed, 'I'm deaf,' and she smiled. He nodded, breaking the contact quickly, then pointed towards where he lived, and without another word she helped him to his feet again.

Beth was aghast at how light he was, as, slowly, leaving the commotion in the crowd behind, she walked John Pollock home from his father's funeral.

In the weeks after the two murders a new normal began to emerge in Inchcraig and everyone had to get to grips with it. Things spun out of control so that no one but thugs walked the streets after dark. Soon Bernard's violence and cruelty would dim in their memories and all people would remember about him was that he had kept their streets safe.

If anyone had mentioned depression to Alice McInally she would've said it was only for weak people. Alice McInally coped by controlling herself and everything around her, it was the only way to be securely in the driving seat. If you lost sight of that you also lost the advantage, as Bernard Pollock had discovered. However, now Alice looked into herself and sank lower than she had ever been.

It had all been her fault, every bit of it, she decided. All those years ago, when the families had objected to their relationship, Liam had given her the choice of what to do, and, if she had told him it was over, that it was too much for either of them to shoulder, he would have accepted it. She was the one who had made the decision to defy their families, so she had caused everything that had happened from that moment on Shaw's Bridge. She had lost Liam his family, lost him Lough Neagh, and taken him to Glasgow, where he got caught up in a war that he could have avoided, and that had caused his death. She was responsible for Liam's death. Even Beth's conception, that was entirely her fault. He would have waited, but she had decided otherwise, and she had brought his innocent child into the world with a handicap that isolated her, and made her a bastard child through no fault of her own, but through her mother's and with a handicap that isolated her. And she had never explained about Beth's father, about Liam, she had brought his child up believing a lie. Alice told herself that the time had never been right, but she was lying there, too. There would never be a right time, so any time would have done.

Following on from that was the rift between the McCanns and the McInallys that had eventually lost Henry his livelihood, and, furthermore, who could ever be sure that Victoria's early death hadn't followed directly from what Alice had done? Had her mother lived, Matt would have been brought up in Belfast, which had to be safer than where Alice had taken him.

And poor Brendon, who had broken with his parents because of the way they had behaved; but they wouldn't have behaved like that if she hadn't behaved as she had.

Then she had brought the family to Inchcraig and defied all of Maggie's attempts to get her to move them out to somewhere better. Why had she done that, if not out of stubborn pig-head-edness? So she had caused Matt's death, too – if he hadn't been in Inchcraig he wouldn't have thought of becoming a criminal.

All her thoughts led to Bernard Pollock. She was so ashamed that she could hardly bear to think about him. His wife had thought there had been something going on all these years, an affair; and Alice had denied it. But there had been, that was the truth of it. She had been attracted to him, the tall, handsome, smart, gentle man who had people killed for getting in the way of his 'business'. The shame she felt overcame her every time she thought of it, the guilt of being attracted to a man like him, knowing full well what he did, what he was capable of. It was such a betrayal of Liam.

However, Bernard hadn't touched her, hadn't ever come close; though the Alec Caldwells of the world would never believe it, would laugh if they heard it. Bernard Pollock, despite the life he led and the ones he had scarred, was a man of strong moral principles. Even if he had touched her physically, she would not have allowed it, but there was something deep between them. No wonder his wife hated her: it was the hardest thing for any wife to handle, the thought of her man connecting emotionally with another woman in a way she couldn't, it must have been torture for her all these years. An affair could be handled one way or another, you could wait for it to pass so you could forgive and forget, or you could decide not to wait, leave and move on. What existed between Bernard Pollock and Alice was different, though. They bonded on a basic level, instinctively, almost addictively. And it wouldn't make any difference if she went to see his wife – not that the widow Pollock would see her – and reassured her that nothing physical had ever happened. It would only make her angrier and more resentful that Alice, the despised other woman, understood her pain; and that would have humiliated her even further.

All those years when Alice had fooled herself into believing she only tolerated him because she had to, but it was all lies. She wanted his company, needed to see him, as he had needed to see her: each of them fulfilling something that was missing in the other's life. Now she missed him so much that she dreaded each Wednesday coming round and didn't want to get out of bed. She wanted to hide there, pretend that Wednesdays didn't exist, so that his non-appearance wouldn't hurt as much. What a weakling, what a fraud! She had been such a failure, yet she had thought she was on top of everything.

★　★　★

Soon Alice didn't want to get out of bed on any day, and an increasingly worried Beth sent a message to Maggie asking for her help. Alice's memories of that time were of sparse, long stretches of black nothing with small bursts of logical, lucid thought. Maggie had taken her to Kew Terrace and looked after her for some time, she wasn't sure how long, before she had asked one day where Beth was.

'She's still in Inchcraig,' Maggie replied, 'for the moment.'

'But she can't stay there by herself,' Alice protested.

'Well she's managed perfectly well so far, dear,' Maggie laughed gently. 'And to be honest, for months before we brought you here she was looking after you as well as herself.'

'How long have I been here?' Alice asked, confused.

'Don't think about it, Alice, you have to get well, and you have to accept that will take as long as it takes. No use thinking in months.'

'Months?' Alice asked in alarm.

'Well, yes, months, dear, about three I think, so far.'

Alice tried to get up. 'I have to get back to Beth!' she cried.

Maggie gently but firmly pushed her back on her pillow. 'As I said, dear, Beth is doing very well. You brought her up to be an independent woman, and she is, and Maureen is keeping an eye on her.'

Then, before Alice could reply, the darkness descended again.

In Maggie's parlour a few weeks later, a family conference was being held. Louise was spending more time in Glasgow than she did in Belfast, and on this occasion Brendon had come over with her. They had come together with Beth to meet with a doctor Maggie had asked to see Alice. He was tall and very thin, with a small fringe of dark hair round his head and a patrician air about him.

'He must practise that attitude in front of a mirror,' Louise muttered to Brendon, 'for when he needs to talk to idiot children like us.' Louise didn't like tall, very thin men, they all reminded her of 'the Guthrie creature', even if they didn't have red hair and eyes that were too pale.

'I'm afraid I have to tell you,' Dr Murdoch said, with excessive sadness in Louise's opinion, 'that she really is quite ill and there hasn't been any great degree of improvement. It's as bad a case of depression as I've seen.'

'But why has she broken out in that awful weeping rash all over her body?' Louise asked suspiciously.

'That can happen in severe cases,' the doctor replied. 'Mental conditions can have physical effects.'

'And it's not the medicine you've been giving her?' Louise persisted.

'That could also be a factor,' he admitted.

Louise glanced at Brendon and raised her eyebrows. Her experiences with George's last illness had left her less than impressed with doctors.

'And you're proposing some other treatment?' Brendon prompted.

'Well, there is one. It's pretty new in this country, but it's been used in America since the early 1940s for cases like this. It's called Electroconvulsive Therapy, ECT for short.' He smiled at them as though he was offering to prescribe toffee three times a day.

'Well, what is it?' Louise demanded.

'Electrodes are placed on the head and an electric shock is administered,' he said calmly, still in his toffee-prescribing voice.

'And what does that do?' Louise asked curtly.

'Well, it induces a convulsion.'

314

'And this is a good thing?' Louise said, looking round at the others.

'Well, it seems to be,' Dr Murdoch replied happily.

'But the patient is under anaesthetic, of course?' Brendon asked, putting a hand out in Louise's direction to make her stay in her chair.

'Well, no,' Dr Murdoch said in a bemused tone.

They all grimaced as one.

'It hasn't proved necessary, apparently.'

'In whose opinion?' Louise demanded. 'Has anyone asked the patients?'

Dr Murdoch smiled condescendingly at her. 'Most of the patients who require this treatment, dear lady,' he said, taking off his half-moon spectacles and peering at her, 'are in no fit state to understand what is going on.'

'Or to object?' Louise asked, ignoring Maggie's growing irritation on the other side of the room.

'Sometimes only a few treatments are required,' he reassured them, 'plus more every four to six weeks, with drugs in between in case of a relapse.'

'Sometimes?' Beth mouthed to him.

'Well, there are cases that have required twelve to fifteen.'

Louise was squirming about, but controlling herself admirably in the circumstances. 'And the benefits of this are?'

'It can speed up treatment, though there are side-effects, of course, as there are with everything. Memory loss is the most common, but it usually returns in a month or so.'

'How does this treatment actually work?' Louise asked.

'Well, that's the funny thing, we don't know, precisely,' the doctor said with a little laugh, 'all we know is that it does, or can. The alternative would be to take her into a psychiatric hospital long-term.'

315

There was as long a silence as Louise could stand. 'Well, Doctor,' she said quietly and slowly, 'let me be clear about this. First of all, Alice will not be going into a psychiatric hospital.' She looked quickly at Maggie, who nodded firmly. 'She will be cared for here for as long as it takes. Second, we have decided to decline your kind offer. Mrs McInally will not be having your ECT either.' Then her fragile grip of self-control snapped and she stood up. 'You come in here and tell us that you want to subject her to sheer brutality, and, furthermore, you don't even know how this brutality actually works?' She advanced on the unfortunate Dr Murdoch before anyone could stop her. 'Get out now,' she snarled, 'while you still have the chance, you quack, you charlatan, you pompous shit, you creature!'

As Dr Murdoch hastily departed she grabbed his Gladstone bag from the parlour table and threw it across the room, hitting him solidly on the back of his head, then she picked up the poker from the fireplace and chased after him. 'Do you have piles, by any chance, Doctor?' she shouted after him. 'I think I have a new treatment, would you like to try it?'

When she turned back to the parlour, expecting to face her sister's wrath, Brendon, Beth and even Maggie were in a huddle, shaking with laughter.

'Oh, stop it!' she muttered angrily. 'I haven't put the poker down yet. Look, I vote we go upstairs to madam and tell her the position, no more pussy-footing, give it to her straight. At the end of the day she's the only one who can do anything about herself, isn't she?'

The others looked at Beth, who nodded.

'I mean,' Louise continued, 'she's had a breakdown, that much is clear.'

'No wonder,' Maggie said, 'with all that's happened. She keeps

316

everything inside, that's always been her trouble, just gets on with it.'

Brendon nodded, taking care of what he said in front of Beth. 'I don't remember her grieving for her mother or her brother all those years ago. She just went on, as you say, did what she had to do.'

Maggie nodded sadly. 'I think Matt's death was one step too far and now it's all caught up with her, all the other things that have happened over the years.' She looked meaningfully at Brendon.

'Well,' Louise said in a businesslike tone, 'no point sitting round getting melancholy, is there? We're all agreed that we can't let her go on like this, aren't we?' She looked sternly at them, one at a time.

'But is it the right thing to do?' Maggie asked.

'Well you've just heard the bloody choices from Doctor Quack, haven't you?' Louise shouted.

'Would that be Doctor Charlatan Quack, eldest son of the well-known Pompous Shit family of Creatures?' Beth signed, and they all laughed again. The departure of Dr Murdoch had been like lancing a boil, and suddenly they all felt a great relief that released their feelings of helplessness.

'Right, that's it settled then,' Louise announced. 'No time like the present, as they say. Follow me.'

The first Alice knew was the sudden appearance by her bed of the four figures as she fought not to come awake.

It was Louise who spoke. 'Listen, Alice, we have to talk to you,' she said conversationally. 'It seems you have to make a choice. Either the doctor wants you to go into some madhouse, from which you won't emerge for years, or he wants to send bolts of electricity through your brains.'

Alice stared at her.

'We've said no to both of those, so there are only two left. You stay here being cared for by Maggie for the rest of your life, or you recognise that this has gone on long enough and get yourself better.'

There was a long silence.

'So, what do you think?' Louise asked.

'Well, I think I might go for the last one,' Alice said finally.

'So I should bloody well think!' Louise replied.

It had taken the best part of a year to get to this point and Alice was doubtless ready to recover anyway. Louise had simply happened along with her choices at the perfect moment, having just buried George, whose death, although after a long illness, had come mercifully quickly instead of lingering. He had gone so quickly that their daughter hadn't had time to even think about coming back to Belfast, so that dilemma had been solved for Louise. She'd told no one till it was over, on the grounds that none of those based in Glasgow would be able to come to the funeral anyway, and even if they had, she couldn't have put up with all that blubbing.

Alice gave in to Maggie's constant nagging and decided not to return to Inchcraig to live. Beth would move into Kew Terrace as soon as possible, too, though she looked slightly anxious about that. Maggie was overcome with happiness. All of her children had married and moved out, and in the lull before grandchildren arrived she now had Alice and Beth to care for, to fill up the big house that had seemed terribly empty and quiet once again.

'But what about Tony?' Alice asked politely, as he sat with the newspaper glued to his face as usual. 'This is his house, maybe he wants it and his wife to himself. He doesn't want to be invaded by women, does he?'

The newspaper didn't even twitch.

'Don't be silly, dear,' Maggie said with a brittle-sounding laugh, 'Tony is barely here even when he is, he won't notice who's here and it will be company for me.'

Tony glanced across at Alice from behind his newspaper and grinned. 'What makes you think I have ever had any say in what happens in this house anyway?' he said in a stage whisper. 'I've been trying to get madam to sell up and move somewhere smaller, but she won't have it, throws a hissy fit and accuses me of forcing her to live in a tent. This way she wins.'

Alice wondered if this was what he really thought, or if that bitter edge to Maggie's voice was nearer to the truth about their marriage. She suspected the latter.

So it was decided. Alice and Beth would stay at Kew Terrace until they found somewhere else, though both of them had separately set their minds on the cottage in Port Bannatyne. Winter was approaching, though, no time to be setting-up home in a cold, unaired house across the sea; that would have to wait till the weather was warmer. In the meantime, Bella had continued to write to Alice at Inchcraig and Beth had taken the letters to Maggie, who replied, telling her that her sister had been very ill. Bella responded by inviting Alice to come to Canada for a holiday. Both of her children were married and so she and Billy, who had given up work after some health problems of his own, had moved out of Toronto to the countryside.

After a great deal of persuasion, Alice agreed to go and spend a couple of months in the comparative warmth of the Canada fall. Beth would be fine; Beth had Maggie to look after her, she was told, though Beth had other ideas.

Before Alice left there was the Inchcraig house to empty and things to sort out, things she wanted to sort out herself.

Whatever money had been borrowed from her wouldn't have to be paid back, she had decided that long ago, and she wanted to say goodbye to the neighbours. Sadie Duffy arrived before her mother, but with a child, a boy of about twelve months, and no wedding ring to be seen. It had been bound to happen, Alice thought.

'If ye'd been here ma mother would've asked ye for money for an abortion,' Sadie said. 'There's always somebody'll dae it for ye.'

'I'm sorry, Sadie,' Alice said.

'No, no, don't be,' Sadie smiled. 'Ah wouldnae have done it, anyway.'

'I don't suppose he would marry you?' Alice asked.

'Well, he couldnae, could he, Mrs McInally,' Sadie smiled sadly. 'He's lyin' in the cemetery, though my mammy thinks Ah don't know who the daddy is.'

It figured, Alice thought. In the mayhem that took over the Inchcraig streets after Bernard Pollock had gone there were bound to be boys and men caught up in it who wouldn't normally have been. Obviously the child's father had been one of them.

'But Ah dae know, Mrs McInally,' Sadie continued softly. 'He's Matt's.'

'Matt's?' Alice asked, shocked. 'My Matt's?'

'Aye. It was always Matt, Mrs McInally, since Ah was a wee lassie, the rest were just a bit o' fun.'

Alice sat down heavily on a packing box.

'But Ah don't want anythin',' Sadie said anxiously, 'don't think that. Ah just wanted ye tae know, that's a'. Matt didnae know.'

Alice cast her mind back to the two funerals and remembered noticing that Sadie was crying. She had put it down to the high state of emotion everyone in the area had been feeling at the time, but it hadn't been that, it had been Matt. She looked at the child, a little fair-haired boy. She had thought she knew Matt, but the more she discovered the more she realised how little she had known. The story of her life, really.

'Ah couldnae call him efter his daddy,' Sadie said, 'or ma mammy would've guessed. Ah've called him Harry. Matt said that was his daddy's name, and his grandda's as well.'

'But why don't you tell her?' Alice asked.

'Because she'll go oan aboot him,' Sadie explained, 'she'll call him every name under the sun, an' Ah canny dae wi' hearin' that. Ah don't want wee Harry tae hear it either. Ah'll tell her an' him one day, but no' noo.'

Alice hoped Sadie would make a better job of that than she had, but it was the girl's business, not hers. 'But how will you manage?' she asked Sadie, feeling a bond with the girl they liked to call 'a right cow'.

'Ah still work, an' ma mammy looks efter him,' Sadie smiled. 'He doesnae want for nothin', Ah see tae that. Except his daddy, of course,' she added sadly, 'but him an' me's in the same boat there, aren't we? You an' Beth as well, eh?'

After Sadie had gone, Alice sat in the house, silent apart from the odd echo that empty places have, looking around and thinking. She would tell Beth about Sadie and the child and they'd make some provision for them, she decided. She sighed wearily, wondering how she could ever have been so smug. She had known nothing, that was the truth, though she thought she had everyone and everything worked out. She hadn't even known about her own feelings, never mind anyone else's. Walking from room to room she heard the voices of the ghosts and listed what she hadn't known about them. Henry and his secret money and his collection of tat that had been worth a fortune. When Henry had died, Matt had moved into his room with his own secrets.

She wondered if the child might have changed Matt as it had Sadie, if the responsibility of being a father would have turned him in the right direction, made him concentrate on becoming an adult instead of a spoiled child forever looking for new entertainments. She doubted it, though, Matt was just who he was and what he was, and it no longer mattered anyhow.

Then there was Beth, who seemed as open as a book, but now Alice wondered. She was a grown woman, with a life of her own, confident, bright, dependent on no one, just as Alice had been determined to make her, and there was more than enough in reserve to make sure she wouldn't be short of money. But what went through Beth's mind, what did she think, and, more to the point, why should Alice think she had a right to know anyway?

By the old range was where those who wanted to borrow a few pounds had sat, those to whom the front door had been opened, and him of course. Bernard Pollock. She could close her eyes and remember his knock at the door.

Just then there was a knock. It was Marie Duffy, Sadie's mother.

'Just came tae say cheerie-bye,' she said awkwardly. 'We've missed ye this last while, but Beth kept us uptae date wi' how ye were doin'. Nice lassie, that, ye've a lot tae be proud o'. Where is she, the day?'

Alice recognised the oblique reference to Matt but chose not to respond. 'She's down in Bute,' she smiled, 'she loves the place, spends a lot of time there, though what she finds to do out of season I have no idea.'

'John Pollock goes there as well,' Marie said, looking round the empty house. 'So Ah've heard, like.'

'Yes, I think I remember that his father bought a place for him.'

'He's no' right, the boy,' Marie said sadly. 'Canny stand people near him, gets a' shaky if anybody even talks to him. Poor sowl. Looks like hell, tae, so Ah'm told, he doesnae go oot much. It's a helluva thing, war, in't it?'

'It is,' Alice replied, then, to change the subject, she said brightly, 'But you've a lot to be proud of, too, you know. Sadie's turned out fine, from what I saw, and the wee boy's lovely.'

'She paid ye a visit, did she?' Marie said sniffily. 'Ah don't think that's turnin' oot fine, a wean tae bring up by hersel'.'

'That can happen to the best, Marie,' Alice said quietly. 'But she seems different, somehow, it's not done her any harm.'

'Oh, aye, it's grounded her, right enough,' Marie conceded. 'Just a pity she didnae screw the nut afore she was left wi' somebody's bastard wean. Of course, he skedaddled, didnae he? Mind ye, she probably has a casta thousands tae choose frae, the only way she could come up wi' a name would be tae put them a' in a hat and pick wan oot. She'll be oan her own noo, that's for sure, who'll take her an' a wean noo?'

'Wait and see, Marie, you'll be surprised. It's not the old Sadie you're seeing now, you've said that yourself. And they tell me Annie Feeney's married again?'

'Aye, nice fella, took oan her three weans as well, but fellas like him don't grow oan trees, dae they?'

'If you see her, tell her I was asking after her, would you? And one day you'll be saying the same about the "nice fella" who'll take on your Sadie and wee Harry, you mark my words.'

With that, Marie Duffy sprang forward and hugged Alice, her voice choked with emotion. Normally Alice shrank back from shows of sentiment, but she had been taken off guard by this one. Even so, she was halfway to pulling away, then she smiled and returned the embrace.

'We're gonny miss ye,' Marie sniffed. 'An' that thing that Mrs

Pollock said aboot ye, we a' knew it wasnae true, she just wasnae thinkin' straight, that was a'.'

'Understandable, Marie, she had just buried her man,' Alice replied diplomatically.

'Aye, we tellt her that efter,' Marie said, dabbing at her eyes. 'Ah mean, you wouldnae be interested in a bad big bastard like him, would ye? Just because she was a mug, it was nae reason tae think anybody else woulda been, least of a' you, eh?'

As Alice was getting into Maggie's car at the close-mouth, there was a shout. She closed her eyes for a moment, hoping fervently it wouldn't be Bernard Pollock's widow, and, if it was, she hoped even more that she was about to deliver another abusive tirade; she could not have borne an apology. But it was Annie Feeney.

'Ah'm glad Ah caught ye,' she said, out of breath. 'Ah just wanted tae thank ye for yer kindness, Mrs McInally, ye saved me and ma weans efter the war, Ah'll never forget it.'

Alice remembered how hurt she had been when Annie had handed back her gift of 'tainted' money, but she smiled anyway. 'I hear you're married again?' she asked.

'Aye, Ah am,' Annie smiled. 'An' would ye believe it, we grew up together, he was ma first boyfriend, he'd waited for me a' they years?'

'Well, he knew he was waiting for a good thing, Annie. I wish you all the happiness in the world.'

For the second time in half an hour Alice was stunned to suddenly be enclosed in warm arms, and even more surprised to feel tears welling in her eyes. 'Look, will you do me a real kindness, Annie?' she asked.

'Anythin', Mrs McInally,' Annie replied. 'Just say the word.'

'Will you let me give you five pounds as a wedding present?'

Annie looked at her and blushed as she realised that she must have hurt Alice. 'Mrs McInally, Ah'd be proud tae,' she said gently. 'Ah never meant any insult, ye know, Ah'm sorry if that's how it seemed tae ye.'

'I understood, Annie,' Alice replied, handing over the notes. 'In fact, in your place I'd probably have done the same.'

As the car moved off there was a rap on the window, and a hand reached in and placed something on her palm. She was so busy waving left and right as the car gathered speed that she didn't look at what was in her hand till they had left Inchcraig well behind. It was a piece of newspaper shaped into a cone and twisted at both ends, and inside were six toffee balls. Paying customers only got three, she thought, blinking, she had no idea anyone liked her enough to give her six candy balls. All she needed now was a bottle of bleach to take with her.

21

The weeks on board ship were like a holiday in themselves; they were certainly a recuperation. She wouldn't have believed how physically ill she had been, and it was taking longer than she thought for her energy to return, so that she was constantly tired, no matter how long she slept for. On the boat, out of boredom, she got into the habit of taking frequent rests – an hour in her bunk, and that seemed to be the solution – so that when she arrived she felt better than she had for a long time, and she looked well.

Meanwhile, Beth was also on the high seas, if only eight miles of it, and so was John Pollock. The first time she had seen him after his father's funeral was on the ferry. She'd watched him being dropped off by car then boarding the ferry alone, but she hadn't approached him. The crossing was busy, with a crowd of schoolchildren on board who were out of their teachers' control. Beth couldn't hear them, of course, but she could see their speed as they raced round and round the boat, all of them feeding off each other's excitement and, inevitably, things started being knocked down: cups and cutlery went flying, bags went up in the air, the odd child was knocked for six. That's when she saw John get up and make his way shakily to the deck area at the back of the boat, with that same panicky expression he'd had the first time she had seen him. She followed him outside and found him sitting alone, trying to find shelter from the rain and cold in the lee of the boat, eyes shut, coat collar pulled up as far as it could go around his face.

At first she'd just wanted to check that he was all right, then she'd noticed that he was shaking, so she had watched a little longer, in case it was just the weather, but the shaking got worse and even in the chilly air she had seen that he was sweating and he looked as though he might pass out. She'd sat beside him and put a hand gently through his arm so that she was supporting him, and held tight. Eventually, when the shaking subsided, he opened his eyes and glanced at her, then nodded slightly, recognising her.

'It was the noise,' he said apologetically, after a while. 'And the people, all going so fast.' He'd tried to laugh, but she could see it had failed.

'It's OK,' she had mouthed back. 'We'll just sit here, and when it's time to get off we'll let everyone else off first.'

He had nodded, relaxing. 'I don't know your name,' he'd whispered eventually.

'Beth,' she mouthed back. 'Beth McInally.'

'I'm John,' he said.

'I know,' she replied.

When they had got off the boat she had insisted on taking him to his father's flat above the tea-room before making her way to Port Bannatyne. She didn't know what had attracted her to him, though she could recognise an underdog from miles away. Fellow-feeling, she supposed: someone like herself who wasn't quite involved in what was going on in the world around them; the sight of someone else who was isolated, though by what, in his case, she had no idea. She had never come across him as she had grown up: she had lived in Inchcraig, gone to the local shops, said 'Hello' to the neighbours in passing, but she hadn't truly been part of it. The world Maureen said she belonged in was the deaf world; her people were the ones she met once or twice a week. It wasn't enough, though. On the way to the deaf club she had seen other shops, other people. She didn't feel defined by her deafness, as many did, and she had wanted to see what else was out there.

Her deafness didn't embarrass her as she knew it did other people, and she understood that; but Aunt Alice had never treated her with kid gloves, she had insisted on her being independent, so if hearing people didn't understand, she made them. If signing puzzled them she mouthed the words, using exaggerated lip movements, or she wrote words down, or drew things, there was always some way of communicating. If you gave them time they usually understood, she found, and when they got over their own embarrassment most were quite nice, really, if you ignored the idiots who laughed as though you were a freak.

But John Pollock was much more isolated and handicapped than she had ever been. At the door of the Rothesay flat he had thanked her and seemed glad to shut the door on her. The man just wanted peace.

After that Beth met John on various crossings, and he always sat with her in some quiet place. She worked out that that was one of the attractions for him: she was supportive but she was quiet, although she could hardly be anything else. Then he had told her it would be his last visit, that his mother had sold the flat, and she jumped in with both feet. She was decorating a cottage to let out, she told him, and if he wasn't coming back to Bute he must come round to Port Bannatyne and see it.

Then she had held her breath. He was a fragile man, he wasn't up to company and flinched away from most human contact, so in all probability he would refuse. She had to steel herself to accept that with a smile. But he didn't, he nodded and agreed to go with her: he wouldn't be back on Bute again, after all, it would be his last visit.

Seeing him at 'Anneetermore' she had felt as though her heart would burst. He fitted it; it fitted him. He stood by the front door, under the name sign, and looked around, looked out to sea, and ten years dropped away from him; it was the first time she had ever seen him smile a genuine smile. Beth had taken her courage into both hands.

'Why don't you stay here for the weekend?' she'd asked, trying to appear off-hand. 'I mean, I'm planning to let it out, you could inspect the place, tell me if it's ok.'

He paused for a moment and she busied herself around the cottage, getting her smile ready for his refusal. He touched her shoulder. 'You're sure that would be OK?'

'Why wouldn't it?'

He shrugged and looked sheepish. 'I just thought, you know, the two of us here together . . .'

'That people might say I'm a hussy?'

He laughed. 'Well, that sort of thing.'

'To hell with them,' she said, looking straight at him. She could see he was laughing out loud and wished she could hear it. 'We'll spend the time writing out a pile of notes saying I'm your landlady, and if anyone finds out we've been here alone we'll hand them out. That ought to take care of my reputation, though I can't guarantee yours. How's that?'

'That's fine,' he said, and for the first time he met her eyes of his own accord.

★　★　★

329

When 'the Guthrie creature' met Alice as she came off the boat in Toronto she almost laughed out loud. What she had been expecting was a slightly older version of the Billy Guthrie she remembered; but though he was unmistakably Billy there had been changes. Not only was he even thinner than she recalled, accentuated by his height, of course, but all his red hair had gone completely. There wasn't even one grey or white hair to show anything had ever grown on his bald pate. He looked, she thought, like a very tall, emaciated baby. Alice always looked at people's eyes, and in his there was an expression she didn't remember. There were times when he was young – when they were both young – when she had thought she glimpsed a predatory look in his very pale blue eyes, but now there was something else. What was it?

Self-pity, she realised, a hard-done-to look, an invitation to see that he had suffered. But maybe she was jumping to conclusions, perhaps it was shyness – after all, they hadn't seen each other in a very long time and so many things had happened in those decades. Even so, she could hear Louise's voice cackling in her head.

There was no embrace and very little speech. Billy simply showed her to a red car and saw her safely installed, though she somehow felt that he wanted her to be impressed by it. It was like the big, flash cars in American films, and he gave off a feeling of great pride in it, smugness even, that made her smile. He was like a child showing off his toy.

'Isn't Bella with you?' she asked, slightly dismayed at being alone with him.

'Bella doesn't travel much,' he drawled, and she was immediately struck by the strength of his Canadian accent. She had spent more years in Glasgow than he had in Canada, but her Irish brogue was unmistakable, whereas his was undetectable.

'She has things wrong with her,' he said dismissively, 'and it's a two-hour drive.' He laughed quietly. 'Life wouldn't be worth living on a two-hour drive with Bella.'

Alice didn't know how to take this. Whatever 'things' Bella had wrong with her, she didn't want to start discussing her medical history with her husband here and now; and, whatever the 'things' were, she bridled slightly at his tone. Maybe she was taking him too seriously, though. She had just arrived; she could hardly jump out of the car and take the next boat home, declaring, 'How dare you speak about my sister like that!' Besides, she knew Bella could be less than inspiring company, for she had often said so herself, to Maggie's disapproval.

On the long journey to Bella and Billy's home near the Great Lakes, conversation was restricted to the scenery, with the odd grunt from Billy and a comment or two about his children, Sheila and Gary, though he was less than effusive about even them. They were now married with children of their own, he told her, no names given, which she thought strange: grand-parents were usually more than forthcoming on the subject of their grandchildren. They both lived in Toronto and had 'their own lives', which seemed to imply that he played little part in them.

Billy didn't ask about anyone, not even Matt, though he and Bella knew he had been attacked and killed. But she was judging him too harshly, Alice decided, he was obviously a quiet, even shy man who liked to concentrate on his driving, especially on a long journey like this. He had, she reminded herself, already driven for two hours to get to Toronto, and here he was, driving straight back. No wonder he didn't indulge in small talk. In fact, it was to his great credit, she decided, mentally saying, 'Be quiet, Louise!', that he was concentrating on the task in hand. Yes, he was being responsible rather than unfriendly.

Bella was waiting for them – at least she presumed it was Bella, from a slight distance it could've been anybody under a large amount of blonde hair. When she got closer Alice realised it was a wig, several sizes too large by the look of it, but Bella's features, suffused with deep lines, were still just discernible below it. She had shrunk, that was Alice's first impression; then she wondered what Bella's impression of her must be after all these years. Even so, Alice, nearing her six-tieth birthday, looked younger than Bella, who was in her early fifties. Maybe it was the sun, she thought. She had heard that constant exposure to the sun caused wrinkles; but it was more than that. As she hugged Bella briefly she could feel the bones of her shoulders clearly, and a birdlike body under-neath. Billy's references to her health had been right, then, but she was sure Bella had said some illness of Billy's had made them move to the country. Still, all would become clear, she supposed, although it happened rather sooner than she had expected.

'I'm sorry I couldn't meet you,' Bella said. She, too, had a strong Canadian accent without a trace of where she had come from, and she yelled everything – she had the loudest voice Alice had ever heard. 'I don't keep too well. I have this urine thing,' she explained. 'I can't travel more than ten minutes without having to stop, if you see what I mean.'

Just as Alice was thinking that one through, her sister provided more information at foghorn level. 'And I have this womb-prolapse problem, too, you know, and an irritable bowel. There are so many things I can't eat, I won't bore you with them.' The only trouble was that she then did. 'Nothing fried, no vegetables, no coffee, no cakes or cookies, no fruit and a whole variety of grains, so I have to have special bread.'

Alice had the impression that her sister was pausing for breath before coming out with an updated list, so she tried to divert her by commenting on the house.

'My, but that's a grand view,' she said, looking out at the surrounding countryside and taking a deep breath, whereupon she found herself coughing on cigarette smoke and, turning round, found both Billy and Bella smoking.

'I have to have special cigarettes, too,' Bella bellowed, taking another drag.

'Yes,' Alice thought, 'I'd have put money on that.'

Throughout this litany of maladies, Billy stood saying nothing, but there was a feeling of resentment, of boredom, that Bella seemed totally oblivious to.

Later, Alice soon found out that Billy and Bella kept rigid hours. At eleven o'clock at night the lights went off, with no exceptions, and at seven in the morning everyone had to arise.

'I'll just read my book for a while,' she said on the first evening.

'Why?' Bella asked.

Just as Alice was trying to understand the question, Billy got up, said, 'You can do that in the morning,' put the lights off and departed to bed, leaving his guest sitting alone in the dark in a strange house. As she stumbled her way to her own room she didn't know whether to laugh or protest, but luckily she was so stunned that she did neither. It didn't matter, she told herself, she would turn on the bedroom light and read till she felt like sleeping, but the moment she hit the switch, Billy's voice said ''Night', which she took as a strong hint to hit it again, making her wonder if he had been standing outside in case she had disobeyed orders.

The next morning she discovered that Billy had planned her day: she had many things to see and he would make sure she saw them. It wasn't what she had envisaged. She was recovering after a long illness and had intended to relax and perhaps get to know her sister again, especially as she had not known her particularly well when they were younger, but there seemed no way of refusing to follow orders. This meant spending long hours in the big red car, being driven across miles of countryside that looked remarkably similar to the miles before. Bella never went with them on these guided tours, which meant Alice was stuck with Billy's mainly silent company for long stretches, which she found more tiring than the travelling. Still, it would get better, she decided. It had to, and she was in their home, after all – maybe Billy even thought he was being a good host, so she tried hard to make conversation with him.

'Do you miss anything about Belfast?' she asked.

'What is there to miss?' he responded dully.

'Oh, I still miss it at times,' she said brightly, her heart falling. 'Though I suppose childhood memories get stronger and rosier with age, don't they?'

'Mine don't,' he replied in the same tone, 'but you had a better childhood than I did. I was dragged about by my mother, when she wasn't taking off by herself that was. I never knew if she'd be there when I came home from school or where I'd be sleeping, never had any money.'

'But there had to be happy times, surely?' she suggested, wondering how her simple remarks could have provoked this response.

He grunted.

'Your grandmother was kind to you, wasn't she? And you had a brother and sister.'

He grunted again.

A few miles on, Billy said, 'But you have to put it all behind you. If you keep thinking about it, it would make you bitter.'

'Quite,' she thought, wondering just when he was planning on putting it behind him.

She tried again by mentioning his children, saying he must be very proud of them. Another mistake.

'They don't bother with us,' he said bitterly. 'Sheila married a guy we didn't like and Gary just falls in with anything his in-laws want.'

'They're happy though?' she asked, feeling helpless.

'I guess. Sheila didn't need to marry that guy, she was fine on her own, and she knew we never liked him.'

And throughout the long hours of the trips he continued to chain smoke, lighting one cigarette from another, till Alice's eyes hurt and her clothes and her hair smelled of tobacco. There was nothing she could do about the smoking. Her sister smoked just as heavily as Billy and so the entire house was in a permanent fog, but it was their home, after all. During the enforced trips, though, she decided to stay as silent as possible, hoping that they would end soon, and she resolved to avoid Billy's depressing company at other times if she could.

However, day after day it continued, and if she wasn't standing by her bed at seven o'clock, he paced up and down outside her bedroom till he heard stirrings that indicated she was awake.

Everything about the household confused her. For instance, she discovered that breakfast wasn't a family affair. Billy made his own, with Bella waiting by the sink to instantly wash whatever he had finished using, item by item. When he put sugar in his coffee and stirred his cup, the spoon would be removed, washed, dried and put away, and no sooner had he buttered his toast than the knife was uplifted, cleaned and put from whence it had come, and the whole meal was like that. Then Bella made her own breakfast, leaping up to go through the same routine the moment she had used something. Alice, it soon became clear, was expected to do likewise, though she found it very difficult to eat with her sister standing by, waiting to wash everything the second it was no longer needed. When everything had been consumed, used, washed and put safely away, the table was swept for crumbs and the tablecloth either folded and put in a drawer, or, if it had a tiny spot of something it shouldn't, instantly washed. All meals followed this pattern, but by then Alice had noticed that the entire house was unnaturally spotless and in perfect order, not a cushion out of alignment, nor a chair slightly awry, and no newspapers and magazines were to be seen. She noticed that when she put a book down and got up to go to the bathroom, by the time she came back the book had been tidied away, and if she got up again the same thing happened. No speck of dust was ever allowed to settle either. Bella was on constant alert, duster in hand, and Alice found the regime hard to cope with and was always anxious in case she had put something where it shouldn't be.

There had to be something wrong with someone who constantly washed and cleaned, she thought, and wondered if Billy had even noticed his wife's abnormal tidiness, because he showed no signs of it. In fact, his way of dealing with Bella was to ignore her completely, though this couldn't have been easy, given her loud voice. At first Alice wondered if her sister might be compensating for being slightly deaf, then she realised it was how Bella communicated. Maybe there was a link with having nothing of interest to say and yelling it out loud to make it seem as though she did. Billy, on the other hand, when confronted with something he had to comment on, snarled at his wife or used sarcasm, though none of it seemed to make any impression on her.

When Bella was young she would attempt the crossword

puzzle in the newspapers at home, but the answers bore no resemblance to the clues. Bella simply filled in any word with the right number of letters. This had been a family joke and Alice was amused to see that she still did this, but when she looked at Billy she was shocked to see a look of such utter contempt and loathing on his face that she had to turn away. It was a look she was to see often. On one evening there was an American quiz show on the television, the first one Alice had ever seen, and it was announced that Bella loved it and everyone had to be quiet.

'Which World War Two army general is currently running for the office of President of the United States?' the quizmaster asked.

'Eisenhower,' Billy whispered.

'Albert Lincoln!' Bella squealed excitedly.

Alice didn't know where to look, but out of the corner of her eye she saw that glare of hate on Billy's face.

'Why is Florida called the Sunshine State?' was the next question.

Alice closed her eyes and Billy didn't reply, presumably because he, too, considered it too easy.

'It makes oranges!' her sister replied happily.

'Where does the Statue of Liberty stand?'

Under his breath Billy muttered, 'Liberty Island, New York harbour.'

'In the water!' screeched Bella.

It was Bella's crossword routine all over again, and she didn't seem in the least put out that her inane answers were always wrong; she didn't seem to notice that or her husband's naked contempt. But perhaps that was because they were rarely in each other's company. Billy had converted the basement of the house into a separate, fully equipped living quarters, while Bella ran the upstairs like a show home, sitting in her little palace, recounting her many illnesses. During the day their paths rarely crossed, and Billy seemed to take every opportunity to be out of the house, so Alice began to understand the long trips he insisted on taking. He was using her as his current escape route from his wife. In conversation it became clear that they had no friends, and there wasn't one human being who had a good word said about them in the Guthrie home – Alice was pretty sure she fell into that category, too, when she wasn't actually with them. When Alice, who was known for keeping herself to herself, mentioned that the people next door seemed nice, Billy muttered, 'These people aren't my friends, I just live near them,' which left Alice thoroughly confused.

But still, she had a niece and nephew to meet, along with their families. That at least would be a diversion, even if Billy and Bella had to be almost forced into it.

'I'll go to Toronto to see them,' Alice said, 'I'd like to see the city anyway.' Inside she was thinking, Please let me out of here! The haste with which a dinner at Billy and Bella's was then arranged made her wonder if they didn't want her talking to Sheila and Gary when they weren't there, and if that were the case she knew it was Billy's idea, her sister didn't have the intelligence to think of it.

And so they arrived: her niece, Sheila, a lovely woman who looked disconcertingly like Victoria, the grandmother she had never seen; and Gary, a tall, red-haired chap full of cheerfulness and enthusiasm. Sheila's husband, who wasn't liked, proved to be a pleasant and obviously long-suffering man who adored his wife and was treated with the barest civility by his in-laws.

For the whole meal Billy remained outdoors, walking about his garden, or 'taking care of chores', as he put it. He didn't mix with his family, far less break bread with them, and he had no interest in his grandchildren, which didn't seem to surprise anyone. Meanwhile, Bella waited to wash each item of crockery and cutlery instantly as usual, standing at the elbow of anyone she deemed to have taken too long, which meant that she too missed eating with her family. At one point, after Bella had repeatedly asked Alice if she was finished with a glass, she said, 'Drink it or lose it!' with a false-sounding cheerfulness. Alice was almost embarrassed for her sister, and caught the eye of the hated son-in-law, who smiled slightly at her from across the table, a smile that said, Yes, I know, what can you do?

No one asked anything about the families in Belfast. It was as though Billy and Bella had grown up as orphans without any knowledge of their parents. Alice couldn't fathom any of it: it was like entering another world, yet these people were her relatives. Then her nephew, Gary, asked if Aunt Alice would please spend a night with his family before she went back home, and with Billy outside it was left to Bella to try to dash the idea, and Bella wasn't fast enough. Alice was delighted. Her nephew and his wife seemed like charming people and they had three handsome, polite, happy children. She was sure that her nephew, who despite his resemblance to his father was a fine fellow, wanted to talk to her away from Billy and Bella, even if his sister didn't. Doubtless he was curious about the family he appeared to know nothing about. Then she saw a look pass between Gary and Sheila and understood that they talked to each other, and he would pass on to his sister anything Alice told him, as long as their parents didn't know about it.

Later, when the families had gone, Alice looked for Bella to ask if she could help in any way – she knew this would be refused, but she felt she had to ask – and found her in the kitchen, wolfing down a bag of doughnuts that the grandchildren had brought with them from Toronto. Alice didn't know what to think. This was the woman who had a long list of foods her various ailments stopped her from eating, who didn't let one meal go past without repeating the litany of items that would be poisonous to her system, and she was pretty sure doughnuts had to be high on that list. Then, feeling even more of an atmosphere – due, she was sure, to Gary's determined invitation – Alice tried to dispel it by congratulating Billy on his fine family.

'Sheila's OK,' he drawled, 'though she didn't need "him", but the boy's nothing great.'

'No, no,' Alice protested, her jaws aching from the fixed smile on her face, 'I thought Gary was wonderful, so smart and funny.'

'He only thinks he is,' Billy muttered. 'He's a bighead.'

'They do nothing for us,' Bella chipped in. 'Him and his wife are always running after her family, but if we ask for anything they never have time.'

Alice had no way of knowing if that were true, but if it were, given their attitude, was it any wonder? 'And your grand-children are such a credit to you,' she persisted, though she had long ago accepted that the horse had been well and truly flogged to death.

'Huh,' Billy grunted. 'The eldest boy's supposed to be smart, he's in an accelerated class, so they say. "Oh,"' he said, mimicking a child's voice, '"I'm so clever, I'm real smart!"', and the two of them cackled like a couple of witches. It was the only time they seemed united.

Alice was appalled. This little boy was their grandson. They should be able to take some pleasure in the fact that Gary and his family were doing so well; surely it reflected on Billy and Bella themselves that they were?

Everything she had seen so far was strange, bizarre even. Bella hadn't asked about her father and showed absolutely no interest when Alice tried to tell her about his life when he left Belfast with Matt. It was as though once she left Belfast and no longer saw him, he ceased to have any real importance to her. She wasn't even bothered about Henry's death. The reasons why Alice and Liam had left Belfast were never mentioned, there was just no interest, and Matt simply didn't exist on her map of the world. When Alice tried to tell her about him, she said, 'Oh, the boy who was killed? Was he nice? That was a shame,' then calmly lit another cigarette and picked up a cross-word puzzle to mutilate. By the time eleven o'clock came round each evening Alice found she was more than ready to be by herself, away from her screeching sister, morose brother-in-law, the weirdness and the incessant cigarette smoke.

22

Beth was reading by the fireside in 'Anneetermore', while John Pollock gazed into the fire. It was beautiful fire, the kind that late autumn brought, with embers that glowed richly rather than blazed, that crackled instead of spluttering. She watched him without lifting her head from her book, feeling happy and satisfied by his contentment, intent on doing nothing that would threaten the easy relationship they had.

This was a good day. When he felt bad he looked like no one, but when he was well she could see his father's features emerge, could see what Bernard must have looked like as a young man, handsome, with the same dark hair and deep brown eyes. He went walking alone by the sea every day, rain, wind or shine, and she let him go without a protest of hurt, understanding that he needed his own time and space; and gradually, over shared, secret weekends, she felt him relax. Sometimes he would seem tense and withdrawn in the mornings and she knew he had had a bad night, riven with nightmares, even though she couldn't hear his footsteps leaving his bedroom in the early hours and padding downstairs, or the cries that had awakened him. She asked nothing of him, not explanation, not confidences, she simply accepted him as he was. Nor did she try to encourage him, as she knew his remaining family did, or try to help him. He had to have his own space and time. If he wanted to go out, he did; if he wanted to sit by the fire then that was fine. There would be no questions until he felt able to give answers, and, as far as she was concerned, he wouldn't ever have to do that unless he chose to. She had no idea how she knew she should do this, but they were good companions to each other, that much she did know.

They had worked out an ingenuous way of avoiding detection. She no longer lived in Inchcraig, so no one would be aware of their comings and goings at similar times and then put two and two together and guess that they might be meeting. After John's mother had sold the flat in Rothesay he had told her he would keep spending weekends there, paying for bed and breakfast, and she had accepted that. At first Maggie expressed concern about Beth being by herself on Bute, but she had settled down to trusting that she was safe and could come to no harm on the island. 'It's not a centre for white slavery, you know!' Beth had teased her, and Maggie had laughed, at herself mainly. Though what she would have said if she had known that Beth was spending her weekends alone with the son of the notorious gangster she had so disapproved of, well, that was another story, a bridge to run across when the time came, if it did.

Gradually, the weekends stretched without either of them planning it or really being aware of it. Instead of arriving on Friday evening, they would arrive in the morning, then on Thursday afternoon; or journeys home on Sunday moved to Monday, sometimes Tuesday. Soon Beth was spending whole weeks there, waiting for John to arrive when he felt like it, with perhaps a day or two at Kew Terrace now and again to keep Maggie happy. There was so much work going on in the house, she told Maggie, and if she wasn't there to push the workmen on they might not do it as quickly. Ideally, she wanted it all finished by the time Aunt Alice came home from Canada, so that they could begin letting the cottage for the summer months.

'Any more word from her?' Beth asked, to deflect more questions.

'Funny you should say that,' Maggie replied. 'This arrived this morning.'

She handed Beth a telegram and Beth quickly scanned it. 'Living hell here. Stop. Big mistake. Stop. Please send telegram demanding my immediate return. Stop. Also arrange passage home as soon as possible. Stop. Depending on you.'

Beth laughed out loud. 'Must have cost her a fortune!' she signed, then giggled. 'What have you done about it?'

'I've sent a telegram saying there are some problems with the house only she can attend to, and can she possibly leave Canada sooner than she had planned?' Maggie told her guiltily.

Beth laughed again.

'I do wish you'd stop laughing, Beth,' Maggie chided her. 'I felt awful telling such a lie, but what could I do? She sounds desperate.'

'It was in a good cause by the sound of it,' Beth signed, reading the telegram again. 'Does Louise know?'

'Yes, I phoned her today. She laughed as well, so now you know what bad company you're in, my girl! She wants to be told when Alice is due to return, so that she can come over and hear what she insists on calling "all the gory details".'

'She's here so much these days I don't know why she doesn't move over,' Beth asked.

'She's thinking about it,' Maggie replied.

'Really?'

'It's funny, you know, she was the one who liked to annoy my mother, but she nursed her till she died a few years ago, never once complained about it.' Maggie stopped. The rift between herself and her mother had never been healed, though she was pretty sure Louise had nagged Bessie about it often. With her mother's death Maggie had had to accept that it never would be, and it still hurt. 'Besides,' she continued with a smile, 'since George passed away she has no family left in Belfast. She'd deny it, but I think she's pretty lonely at times.'

'Well I hope she does move over here,' Beth decided. 'It would be good to have her around.'

'Speak for yourself, madam!' Maggie replied. 'My sister can be a bit of a handful you know!'

In Canada, Alice was becoming more confused with each passing day. She had briefly escaped the attentions of her brother-in-law, saying she needed stamps for some postcards home, and had sent her telegram to Maggie instead. What had led to this drastic measure was a visit to a museum, which she might well have enjoyed if she'd had a different companion, rather than the one who had inflicted his morbid self on her. Afterwards he drove her to his daughter Sheila's house, explaining glumly, 'He won't be there, we don't go when he's there,' as though this were the most natural thing in the world.

When they arrived at the house they had found that Bella had driven herself there. The woman who couldn't travel any longer than ten minutes from home, due to her suspect innards, had driven over a hundred miles. Just as Alice was turning this over in her mind, Bella announced that she would just shoot off now, as though she were a neighbour who wanted to leave family alone together. Alice looked at Billy, who registered no emotion whatsoever and said not a word, but when his wife had gone out of the door, he muttered miserably, 'Thank God she's gone. We'll get some peace now,' and settled down on his daughter's couch and picked up a newspaper.

The only person who seemed to feel uneasy about any of this had been Alice, who had been walking on eggshells already but was now walking on eggshells she couldn't actually see. So she had sent an SOS to Maggie, hoping desperately that she would understand, fervently praying that she would think of something to get Alice out of this strange situation.

The thing was that Bella seemed to adore her husband, and she certainly repeated his every thought as though each one had been handed down from on high. But it was one-sided. Billy talked to her so harshly at times that Alice had to bite her tongue. If Bella asked if he'd eaten, he'd snarl, 'Mind your own business.' A polite inquiry asking if that had been the mail or the newspaper being delivered was met with, 'What's it got to do with you?', or on another occasion, 'If you're that interested, get up and see for yourself, but if it's mail, don't open anything.' To get rid of her he sent her into the garden to dig up dandelions, and when she returned to the house with something to say, he stopped her by informing her, 'You've missed some,' and redirected her outside again.

The worst of it was that Bella complied, never once seeming in the least put-out by his contempt or his directions. She seemed, in fact, totally unaware of what he was saying. And just as Alice was feeling sorry for her dim sister, Bella produced a battered jotter and handed it to her. Inside were lists and lists of books she said she had read, though Alice hadn't seen her lift a book and doubted if she had ever read one, and beside each title and author's name were written a few letters. 'B' was Bad, 'QG' stood for Quite Good, 'G' was for Good, and 'NBG'

346

meant No Bloody Good, though Bella was amazed that Alice had worked any of this out. Among those who had received the definite critical thumbs down were Charles Dickens, Neil Gunn, Ernest Hemingway and, Alice noticed with a start, John Steinbeck. In a sad attempt to connect with her clever husband, Bella, Alice realised, had picked up books Billy had read, and, not understanding them, had been forced to abandon them, branding the best of them 'No Bloody Good'. So somewhere she must know that Billy looked down on her, but she only had the intellect she had, there was nothing she could do about that. Alice, the jotter in her hand, looked across at Billy, who stared back at her with the expression his unwanted son-in-law had had: Yes, I know, what can you do? The only difference was that Billy's look wasn't one of reluctant and quiet acceptance, but of bitter resentment. Poor Bella, she thought, poor dumb Bella.

The sudden arrival of Maggie's telegram was greeted with great sadness, by Alice at any rate. How awful that she had to go back home after only three hellish weeks, but Maggie must have good reason for asking her to return. She had very little packing to do, having taken the precaution of already having it done, but it gave her a precious hour alone in her bedroom to work on not blushing. Then she checked every aspect of the bedroom from every angle, to make sure there wasn't anything a centimetre out of line, though she knew that the minute she left her sister would be in there, duster, cleaners and slide rule in hand. And no, she protested, she wouldn't hear of Billy driving her all the way to Toronto, thereby losing several hours away from Bella. She had wanted to see the countryside from a train while she was here anyway; if Billy would just be so good as to take her to the nearest station, she was sure Gary would pick her up at the other end and take her to the boat for her journey home. It would give her a chance to say her goodbyes to him and his little family, it would work out nicely.

When Alice left she gave many thanks and even more assurances that she would be back one day soon, and hugged her frail sister with the big hair, while trying to avoid the ever-present cigarette. She commented that now Billy would be able to get his life back, but when she looked at him she could tell by his expression that it was the last thing he wanted.

At the station the train was late and she told Billy brightly that she would be fine now, he mustn't sit there with her wasting his time.

'I'll just wait,' he said. 'There's nothing to go back to, only Bella.'

As the train pulled away from the station, the last sight Alice had of 'the Guthrie creature' was of his glum face, wreathed in palls of smoke, staring forlornly after the departing train, as her heart sang with joy at the prospect of never seeing him again.

As Alice had expected, her nephew was a delight. He was a clever boy, which had to have come from his father, and he worked as a chemist. He and his wife had a lovely home, a good lifestyle and were full of enthusiasm. They were a happy couple, as were their three children, and Alice was captivated. As she expected, Gary wanted to know about his family history.

'My folks' background,' as he put it, 'is a big black hole.'

'You mean you know nothing?' Alice asked.

'I know they came here from Belfast, that's it,' he grinned, 'and that he had an unhappy childhood.'

Alice's eyebrows shot up before she could stop them.

'So that isn't true?' he laughed.

'Well, those were hard times for a lot of people,' she said gently. 'I'm not sure I'd say he had any worse a time than most people, and maybe better than many. His younger brother and sister were farmed out to anyone who would take them – if anybody had a hard time, I'd say it was them.' She stopped. 'Do you want me to go on?'

Gary nodded seriously.

'Your father came into my family through the church. Your mother was very beautiful when she was a girl and quite besotted with him, and after I left Belfast they married.' Then she told him about the McCann–McInally relationship and her flight from Belfast with Liam, without mentioning Beth. There seemed no point really, it was very unlikely he would ever meet her, and it was his family she was telling him about, not her own. 'Neither family approved so we never saw our families again. This is the first time I've seen your parents since 1915.'

'That must've been tough,' he said.

'It was. I always hoped they'd relent, but they didn't, apart from Liam's brother. We were in our twenties, so we knew what we were doing, and, looking back, I wouldn't have done anything differently. Luckily I had a cousin in Glasgow who had done the same thing. Liam died of flu at the end of World War One, as did my brother and his wife, and they left a baby boy. Then my mother, your grandmother, died and my father brought the baby to me in Glasgow and we lived together. They're both dead now.'

Gary was silent for a long time, then he said a startled, 'Wow! And you never married after Liam died?'

'No, I never considered it.'

She let him take in the information, then he said, 'I married a Catholic, you know. I became a Catholic and the kids are Catholic.'

Alice put her head down and chuckled. 'I'm sorry,' she

laughed, 'I'm just thinking of the Billy Guthrie I knew having to swallow that one! It explains a lot!'

'My mother's very protective of him,' he smiled, 'says we have to make allowances for him because of his bad childhood, but we never knew what that meant. Not a lot, by the sound of it. He had a bad drink problem, did you know that?'

'I heard something about it,' Alice replied diplomatically.

'He was doing really well, then he started drinking and things just got worse and worse. He was a rotten drunk, nasty and threatening, it went on for years till he lost his job. He stopped drinking a couple of years ago, but his health has never recovered.'

'Well, that's to his credit,' Alice said gently. 'He did stop, after all.'

'Hasn't made him any happier,' Gary grinned weakly. 'He's permanently miserable, can't see any good in anything or anyone, me included. He doesn't actually like me, I've always known that.'

'At least you know he's not singling you out,' she said, feeling sorry for him. 'The minute I left he'd be muttering about me, too. It's just how he is, Gary, it has nothing to do with you, but I must say, he says some really hurtful things to your mother.'

'Oh, I'm sure he doesn't mean it,' Gary replied.

Alice smiled. She thought it was admirable that he defended his father when his father didn't deserve it. It said more about Gary than it did about Billy.

'But he is a bit of a grump,' he conceded with a sigh, 'always has been. When I was growing up I used to wonder if I had a real name. He just called me, "That stupid bastard" or "You stupid bastard".' He laughed, though she could see it had left its mark on him. 'I was never close to him because I challenged him, I guess. He likes to be in control.'

'I noticed that.'

'Did you know my father's younger brother made contact with him a few years back?'

'No!' Alice said, shocked that no one had mentioned it.

'A really nice guy, and that annoyed my father for some reason. He had done pretty well for himself and was cheerful and easy-going. He's only a year or so younger than my father and I remember thinking at the time, Hang on, they must've had the same childhood. How come my father's turned out like he has, hating everybody, resentful and miserable, and his brother is such a good guy? He was planning to move to Canada and we were really happy, we would have family for the first time in our lives, but the minute my father heard that he said he wanted nothing to do with him, said even if he moved next door he would never talk to him.'

Alice was aghast. 'Why?'

Gary shrugged. 'He's my father,' he said quietly. 'So who knows? Maybe there were things he knew his brother would be able to tell us that my father didn't want us to know. It's all we could think of. We never heard from my uncle again after that.'

'That's so sad, for all of you, I mean.'

'Yes, I thought he'd be good for my father, make him more human, you know? So there we were, back in that black hole of knowing nothing and having no family.'

On the boat back home, Alice could think of nothing but her sister's disastrous family set-up and she wondered how her niece and nephew had emerged from it as well as they had, though it was clear Billy still ruled them to an extent. She had told them both that they would be welcome to stay with her in Scotland and, she was sure, with Maggie whenever they wanted to, but deep inside she knew she would never see or hear from them again. Billy and Bella were the only family they had, apart from their in-laws, and to challenge Billy in any way would mean the children losing their grandparents, such as they were. And that, she reasoned, would be too much to lose to gain family so far away.

The more she thought about them the more despairing she felt. Billy had married Bella for their family connections, she was sure of that now – as sure as Louise had always been – and because of Bella's beauty and her clear, unquestioning adoration of him. Somehow, though, for all his cleverness, he hadn't realised that Bella was as dim as his mother, though her morals were presumably better, and she wondered at what stage that had dawned on him. Was that when the drinking started? When whatever early romance they had had in their relationship had inevitably worn off, and he had discovered he was stuck with a stupid woman after escaping from one? And by that time he would have been trapped, tied to Bella by their two children.

Billy was an intelligent man, so perhaps that was when he started ignoring Bella, too, when he knew he couldn't talk to her anyway, and so she had tried to gain his attention with illnesses. The trouble was that Billy ignored her illnesses as well, so in desperation Bella had kept inventing more, which he also ignored, only with each one he added another dash of contempt.

Alice remembered an incident when she had picked up one of Billy's books and remarked that she had read it. They were beginning to compare notes, when it was brought to a sudden close by Bella clapping her hands and singing in the corner of the room, a woman in her fifties behaving like an attention-seeking child of two, and Billy had stared straight ahead. Could that be the explanation of the loud voice? Was it yet another attempt by Bella to be taken notice of?

Who to feel sorriest for, that was what Alice wondered. Her sister or the arrogant self-seeking man who thought only of himself, who owned his family rather than loved them, keeping them away from anyone who might take his possessions by really loving them? He deliberately opened gulfs to keep people away, whether Alice or his own long-lost brother, the nice guy who'd been turned away for simply getting on with the children in ways Billy couldn't and didn't want to. And keeping people away had the added bonus of hiding his past from his family, so that they only knew he must never be upset because he had endured some vague hard childhood. Billy was so sensitive that he might crumple up and die before them if they upset him or asked questions, that was what they had been raised to believe, when all the time he was a man without emotions, a family tyrant who got his power by manipulating theirs.

Who to feel sorriest for?

All of them, she decided. All of them.

23

The plan had been to spend Christmas with Billy and Bella and travel home in early January, but Alice arrived home, happy and relieved, a fortnight before Christmas. The widow Louise was already in attendance at Kew Terrace, more, as Maggie remarked, for 'all the gory details' than for the Yuletide festivities.

'Where's Beth?' Alice asked, as they settled down in the parlour that had witnessed so many of their discussions over the decades.

'Oh, she's on the island,' Louise said impatiently. 'She'll just have to catch up later. So come on, tell all!'

'At the house? But why?' Alice persisted. 'It's winter, what has she to do there?'

'Well, people do stay there in winter, surely?' Louise said briskly. 'I mean, they don't shut the place down, do they? For heaven's sake, Alice, why does this matter?'

'What my impolite and downright nasty sister should have said,' Maggie smiled tightly, 'is that Beth is overseeing some building work, and I think she just likes the place.'

'Yes, yes, yes,' Louise muttered, 'kindly get on with it now, Alice!'

So Alice described her time with her sister and 'the Guthrie creature', her narrative interrupted by many 'Oh's, 'Ah's and 'I told you so's from both her cousins, and giggles from Louise.

'It sounds dreadful!' Maggie said, shocked.

'It was, it is,' Alice told her. 'He is so awful, bitter and twisted, and he really doesn't like women. It doesn't take long to work that out.'

'Well, when you think back to his mother,' Maggie said thoughtfully, sipping her tea.

'Yes, but he had his grandmother after that, didn't he? From everything I have ever heard she doted on him.'

'And he had your mother, who doted on him, too, and you and Bella,' Louise remarked. 'If he only had to contend with one rotten female apple in life, I reckon he got off lightly. I'm with you, Alice, I think it's him. And what is Bella like?'

'You wouldn't recognise her,' Alice said, grimacing. 'She's very loud, very thin, has deep lines on her face, a terrible blonde wig, she smokes non-stop —'

Louise fell back in her chair laughing.

'— she says she has every illness under the sun and can't eat, not till your back's turned, anyway, and she's no more intelligent than she was. And you would hardly recognise him. Remember all that thick red hair? Gone, not a single hair of any description on his head, and he's even thinner, even taller, if that's possible, than he used to be. And such a hangdog expression, everything about him is unhappy.'

Louise was dabbing at her eyes, overcome with mirth.

'Louise,' Maggie said sternly, 'you're showing your least attractive feature. It's very ungracious to wallow in someone else's sadness!'

'Oh, Maggie,' Louise said breathlessly, 'your primness is your least attractive feature, give yourself a break! Any more, Alice?'

'He's just a truly horrible man.'

'As I always said,' Louise muttered smugly.

'But what has he to feel so sorry for himself about?' Maggie mused.

'I keep asking myself that,' Alice said sadly. 'He has a lovely house in a wonderful location, they clearly have no money worries, even if he did lose his job. He did have a bad drinking problem, apparently.'

'Which I told you,' Louise chipped in tartly, 'and which was his own fault.'

'He sees himself as a victim, though, as someone who has suffered unfair horrors. And the rest of their family, well, they're really lovely people, but it's not just that he doesn't enjoy them, he doesn't like them, and Bella just takes her lead from him. I'm telling you, Maggie, if I hadn't been able to send that telegram, and if you hadn't acted on it, I don't know what I would've done.'

'And to think we sent you there to recover!' Louise laughed merrily. 'Little did we know Billy and Bella were far sicker than you ever were. Oh, I wish I'd gone with you, Alice, you lucky thing!'

'Talking of travels,' Alice said, 'what's this about leaving Belfast? I hear you're really serious.'

'Yes, I am, I'm going to be one of Maggie's children, just like you.'

'So what happened?' Alice asked.

'Oh, Alice, it's a long story, the long story of my long awakening, I suppose. You've no idea what it's like over there, the sheer hatred, the pettiness. I could take you to meet Catholics at home and you'd think they were the nicest people in the world, and I could take you to meet Protestants and you'd say the same, and you'd be right. Put them together, though, and they turn into beasts. I realised recently that I was listening to people talking and deciding their religion by how they pronounced the letter "h". "Aitch" is Protestant, "haitch" is Catholic. It's insane. I've always thought for myself, but even I've been brainwashed.'

'Tell Alice about the hairdressers,' Maggie giggled.

'I was getting my hair done and a girl was saying how unfair it was that Catholics were kept down so much. One of the others said, "You'd never take her for a Catholic till she says something like that." I got so angry that I walked out with my hair soaking wet.'

Maggie dissolved in floods of giggles at the thought and Louise glared at her.

'The girl was talking about fundamental rights, but as far as they were concerned if she thought Catholics should have any, she had to be one. I just found it very depressing – it isn't the Ireland I grew up in, for all its prejudices. In fact I could be attacked for even saying that. It isn't Ireland, it's Northern Ireland, forget that at your peril.'

Alice smiled, 'Beth says we're like Macbeth's witches when we're together.

'Then she'd better watch out,' Louise said tartly.

And so they spent Christmas together, a Christmas they hadn't expected to be together for: Alice, Louise, Beth, Maggie and her family, including Tony, who was very much outnumbered in his own home without seeming to mind very much. After the initial excitement of seeing Aunt Alice again, Beth asked if anyone would mind if she went back to Bute sooner rather than later.

'But why?' Alice asked, disappointed.

'I just prefer being over there to here,' she replied. 'I don't mean your house, Maggie,' she hurriedly assured her, 'I mean the city.'

'I know that, dear,' Maggie replied, a little uncertainly.

'And there are still things to be done in the cottage,' Beth explained. 'The best time to get them done is the close season, especially if you want to start letting next summer.'

'Yes, I understand that, Beth,' Alice told her, 'but you'll miss New Year. We've always been together at New Year.'

'Exactly!' Beth laughed. 'And you know what I think of New Year, a lot of drunks and nonsense!'

'But it isn't a time for being alone,' Alice persisted.

'It is if you want to be,' Beth told her firmly. 'The trouble is getting other people to understand that.'

When she had gone, Louise turned to Alice and Maggie.

'There's a man involved here,' she said, eyes narrowing.

'Oh, don't be silly!' Alice laughed.

'I'm telling you!' Louise almost shouted, looking at Maggie.

Alice turned to Maggie, eyebrows raised.

'Well, dear,' Maggie said nervously, 'I do think it's a possibility. She seems to spend more time there than bricks and mortar can justify.'

'She's spent enough time there to build a palace!' Louise giggled joyfully. 'Well, what are you looking so glum about? It's good news, isn't it?'

'I don't know,' Alice said quietly. 'Maggie?'

'Neither do I.'

'Oh, for heaven's sake, you two, be happy for her, she could finally be getting some rumpy-pumpy! Some good, healthy sex will do the girl the world of good!'

'Louise!' Maggie hissed. 'Kindly behave yourself, you have had too much to drink!' She turned to Alice again. 'Alice, I know we've touched on this before, dear, and you always thought the time wasn't right, but have you given any recent thought to telling her you are her mother?'

'I think about it all the time,' Alice said glumly. 'I don't know where to start.'

'It occurs to me that if she is involved with someone, she might well need her mother, rather than her Aunt Alice, if you see what I mean.'

'But this might be exactly the wrong time to tell her as well,' Alice suggested.

'Well, you know best, dear,' Maggie said gently, 'but just think on it, that's all I'm saying.'

Alice couldn't explain the many levels of her concern. Not that she believed it, of course not, but what if Louise was right? Beth hadn't any experience of the world, not of men, not in that way, and who could he be? An islander? One of the workmen? Who would woo a girl in her position unless it was for her money? It would be obvious to any man, from the sale of the house and the amount of work being done on it, that Beth came from a family with some money. Maybe some man had paid attention to her, and Beth, being unused to it, had been flattered and had gone along with it. In the end her heart would be broken, which, in turn, would break Alice's heart.

Maggie was right, she had to tell Beth now. It was one of those situations where it seemed crystal clear in the beginning, but if she'd had her time to live over she might well have come to a different solution. The right time to tell Beth would have been from her earliest years, before she could even understand, so that her identity would be who she was. But Alice had left it too late, she knew that now – from the best of intentions, but even so. What was the old saying? Beware of your best intentions for you will be punished for them. She would go over to Bute as soon as she could after New Year, she decided, and talk to Beth, tell her everything. That would be her only

New Year's resolution, to be honest with her daughter. It had to be done, so no time like the present. Like all best intentions, making a mess of one sort doesn't stop you running headlong into making an even bigger mess of the next batch in line.

It was a beautiful crisp, dry winter's day at the very start of a brand-new year. Her breath was like sharp clouds in the cold air, and the light was so clear that it made everything familiar look different and new, so that she wanted to keep looking, as though she'd never seen it before. As if all was not already perfection, there had been a fall of snow overnight on the island, highlighting a landscape that was already impressive and picking out ridges and paths that were covered by the greenery of summer. She had loved the island in spring and summer, but winter, she decided now, was her favourite time. At the pier she got in a taxi, one of the few waiting there, for Scotland did not hurry its New Year celebrations and most people wouldn't think of going back to work till the fourth or fifth of January. When she mentioned this the driver replied that he had been taking an expectant mother to board the boat Alice had just come off, or he wouldn't have dreamed of stepping away from his own fireside, which was, by coincidence, in Port Bannatyne. As they passed Pat and Molly Murphy's big house, she asked who stayed in it. It was a guest house apparently, though it had once belonged to a lawyer fellow from Glasgow, whose family sold it after he died.

Stopping at the bottom of the slight rise from the road at 'Anneetermore', he refused to take the fare, saying he was coming this way anyway. Another Scots New Year trait was that everyone loved everyone else, drunk or sober, so she insisted that he take a tip for his Ne'erday. Then they wished each other all the best, and before he drove off he pointed to a cottage a

360

few hundred yards away, and told her to call him when she wanted to go back to Rothesay.

Alice had planned it in her mind. The fire would be roaring, the house would be cosy and warm, and Beth would be sitting there, book in hand, a cup of cocoa beside her. They would embrace, then they would settle down together, and Alice would tell her everything. About her wonderful father, about their flight from Belfast and their near marriage, and about her conception in this very cottage, followed by Liam's death. She would explain why she had done what she had done, and how she had tried many times through the years to tell her the truth and how she was deeply sorry she hadn't done so, and she would ask Beth's forgiveness. It was best that it would be just the two of them. Maggie and Louise meant well, but this was between Alice and Beth, mother and daughter.

As she approached the door her mind was full of what she would say, the words she would use to explain that she hadn't been ashamed of her daughter, but had been trying to shield her from the harsh judgements of others as she was growing up – she'd had enough to contend with, after all. On the way to the door she stopped to look in the window and saw the scene she had imagined in her mind. Beth had her back to her, sitting on the couch before the fire, a book in her right hand, a cup of something hot on the table beside her. But her left hand rested on the head of someone stretched out beside her, his head on her lap.

Alice stood bolt upright, her eyes never leaving the scene inside. The man was facing away from the window, looking into the fire, his features lit by the warm glow. Bernard Pollock!

She pulled back from the window as though scalded. It couldn't be, he was dead, she knew that – yet it was, she knew Bernard Pollock when she saw him.

Suddenly she realised it must be his son, John Pollock. She had seen enough pictures of the boy over the years to recognise him. She could see another scene clearly now: the tall, handsome, deadly Bernard Pollock proudly passing over the snaps of his sons in her Inchcraig sitting room, Buster lying contentedly at his feet. She had often remarked that the younger boy, John, looked just like him, and Bernard had bristled with pride. But how could it happen that Beth was sitting in 'Anneetermore' with her hand resting on Bernard's son's head?

Alice didn't know what to do, didn't know what to feel apart from extreme shock. Should she barge in, full of anger, demand that Beth explain all and throw John Pollock out of her house – throw Beth out of her house as well, come to that? She felt deceived and humiliated. She'd thought she and Beth were close, but now she saw the girl leading a completely separate, secret life, and with this man, this man of all men. Louise and Maggie's suspicions had been right, but no one could have thought up this particular detail.

She had walked away from 'Anneetermore' towards the taxi-driver's cottage without thinking about it, it was just away. Then she stopped in the cold air that was suddenly much colder and decided her feet knew best. Funny how a winter's day could change from bright and crisp, and chill you to the bone in seconds instead. She had to get back to Glasgow and into the safety of Kew Terrace, back to the good counsel of her cousins without Beth seeing her. She didn't know how to handle this situation, but it had to be done right and she was in no position to do that. She had to think.

The taxi driver hadn't even taken his coat off. He looked at her, surprised.

'I'm sorry to trouble you,' she said, amazed at how normal

her voice sounded. 'I've obviously made a mistake with the date, the people I'm looking for weren't there.' She smiled. How could she possibly smile? 'I wonder, would it be too much trouble to take me back to the pier? I do hate asking you to come out twice, but otherwise I'll be stranded, you see.'

'Of course, of course, lass,' he said graciously, though she was old enough to be his mother. 'If we get our skates on the boat will still be there,' and he hurried her to his taxi outside.

When Alice saw the boat still at the pier she felt like crying with relief, then she rushed aboard as though she was being chased and settled herself inside, agonising over each minute the boat waited before casting off. The whole atmosphere of the day had changed in less than half an hour, the feeling of hope and light had disappeared as though it had never been, to be replaced by an empty weariness. She had done it again, she realised; she had got it all wrong. It could be the theme of her life. She thought she knew her family and Liam's family, thought she knew Matt, and all of it had ended in disaster, and now this.

It was early afternoon in Kew Terrace when she arrived back, and the snow had proceeded eastwards and had covered Glasgow. Although the light was already going, the streets were lit by an almost ghostly, white light. Maggie and Louise were surprised to see her, but, as she turned to take her right arm out of her coat, she caught a glimpse of their faces, flushed with expectation. When she turned again to remove the left arm, they noticed her expression, and she saw them exchange looks of confusion and alarm.

'Well, how did it go?' Louise asked with false brightness. 'You know, you shouldn't be surprised if she didn't take it as well as you wanted, she'll need time to . . .'

Alice could sense Louise catching Maggie's eye and, uncharacteristically, stopping herself.

They rushed her into the parlour, rubbing her shoulders out of sympathy for whatever had happened. They settled her beside the fire then sat down opposite her, their hands in their laps, waiting. Looking at them she wanted to laugh, but she found herself sobbing instead. It was some time before she could tell them she hadn't spoken to Beth, and what she had seen through the window of the cottage.

'But are you sure, dear?' Maggie asked. 'As you said yourself, the light wasn't good, you only saw him by firelight.'

'That's who it was,' Alice stated. She had never told Maggie about her friendship with Bernard Pollock. Maggie would have been horrified, as she had been herself, and, in a strange way, still was. 'I saw him growing up in Inchcraig, and I remember him coming back from the war. It was definitely him.'

'Does it matter who it is?' Louise asked distractedly. 'I mean, he may be his father's son, but he isn't his father, is he?'

'Of course it matters!' Alice said, shocked – even for Louise that was a stupid thing to say. There was no comment from Maggie. 'It does matter, doesn't it, Maggie?'

'I need to think, Alice,' Maggie replied quietly. 'It's not that I'm disagreeing with you, dear, I'm just so stunned by this that I need time to think, as you do yourself. I'm sure you did exactly the right thing in leaving without going into the house, though. The last thing the situation needed was hasty words spoken in anger.'

'It wasn't from wisdom, believe me,' Alice said sadly, 'I just didn't know what else to do. I took the coward's way out, I turned and ran.'

'No, no,' Louise said soothingly, 'as Maggie says, the right thing is to give it some thought. There was nothing to gain from confrontation.'

'Now I know I'm in trouble,' Alice smiled weakly. 'It has to be a bad sign when Louise doesn't advise charging forward.'

Over the next few weeks, and much to Maggie's concern because of the wintry weather, Alice walked where she had once walked with Liam, retracing their steps along Great Western Road and down Byres Road, reliving their conversations in the Botanic Gardens, remembering how she had thought she had everything sorted back then. As life had unfolded she had dealt with it as best she could, yet here she was now, in a mess. She mentally accused Beth of deceiving her, but, when she thought about it, she had deceived Beth all these years, so who was she to judge? There was nothing she could do, anyway, till Beth came back to Kew Terrace, and even then, what exactly was she to do? And all the while, Beth was at 'Anneetermore' with Bernard Pollock's son. It was unbearable; and without her cousins it would have been even worse.

'You know, dear,' Maggie said to her, 'I've been thinking. Beth is what – thirty-two? You've always said no one would marry her because of her deafness, and here she is, with a man who is at least interested. Can that be an entirely bad thing?'

Alice stared at her, shocked, and Maggie rushed to reassure her. 'No, dear, I'm not suggesting that she should take whoever comes along because she might never get another, I'm just saying maybe you should consider that she may now have a chance of happiness that you never thought would come her way.'

'But we don't know he has anything decent in mind,' Alice protested. 'She's been very protected – I've tried to make her as independent as possible, but she has still been protected. How can we be sure he's not just making use of her?'

'You're right, of course, dear,' Maggie sighed. 'I suppose I'm trying to find that silver lining we're always hearing about.'

'But let's suppose', Louise interrupted the gloom, 'that he is seriously interested in her. What exactly are the objections?'

'His family,' Alice told her. 'His father was a notorious gangster and criminal and his son was brought up in that atmosphere. I don't want Beth to be involved with a family like that.'

'Quite right, dear,' Maggie responded.

Louise looked at them. 'Have you two heard yourselves?' she asked. 'You two, of all people?'

Alice and Maggie exchanged bemused glances.

'Well, you can hear yourselves, but are you actually listening? You both had to run from home because of other people's beliefs, because of families who disapproved. Is that what you want for Beth?'

'But that was different!' Alice protested.

'Of course it was!' Maggie agreed.

'But it wasn't, it was just the same!' Louise insisted in an agitated voice. 'Look, we don't know what Beth's intentions are, we don't know what this chap's are either, all we do know is how his father lived, his father's beliefs, isn't that so? Yet here we are, worrying ourselves to a frazzle, examining every aspect of something that may not exist.'

'And what are we to do if it does exist?' Alice asked. 'Tell her it's quite OK to take up with a monster's son, to mix with his family, to bear his children? Maybe we should buy our outfits now and prepare to dance gleefully at the wedding? Louise, you can't expect me to approve of this?'

Louise put her hands in her hair and pulled great tufts, so that her head swung from side to side. 'Argh!' she shrieked. 'I don't know you. Which biased, selfish old witch are you? Victoria McInally, Bridie McCann or my own dearly departed mother?'

On Bute, John Pollock had wakened in the night in such terror that he had run downstairs. It was a noise that had done it, a noise he knew well. It was like that. He could go on for days, feeling more and more normal with each passing hour, he could even persuade himself that he was getting better, whatever better was, then something would trigger a response that pulled him back to that time he wanted to forget. It was such an insignificant noise, probably no one else would hear it, even if he pointed it out.

They called it Chinese Water Torture, though it wasn't, it had come from Italy of all places, in the sixteenth century, so he had been told after the war, as if it mattered. It wasn't their worst punishment, it was only one of many they thought fitting for soldiers who they believed had dishonoured themselves by surrendering, though he saw many Japanese soldiers do the same at the end of the war without feeling they deserved brutality in return.

You only had to look at a guard in the camp to be punished, often not even that: as a race they seemed to have a liking for torture. They had three versions of water torture and he'd seen all of them. There was the jolly jape of holding the head of some unfortunate 'offender' underwater until he almost drowned – some till they had drowned, he had seen more than one fellow prisoner die that way. One man, his body ravaged with hunger, thirst, disease and cruelty, had stated that he wasn't anyone's prisoner. 'I am', he said with quiet dignity, 'a soldier,' but the last sound he heard was the laughter of the captors who held him down till he had died.

Another involved stuffing a dry, absorbent rag into someone's mouth and dripping water on it till it gradually expanded and slowly suffocated them, and the third was the one they had used on John.

One of his friends had been put in a wooden cage for being so ill with dysentery that he collapsed while working on the railway. The cage was only big enough to sit in and the men were kept there for as many days as the Japanese felt like, suffering in the stifling heat without food or water. John had stood it as long as he could and had then taken the risk of trying to sneak water to his friend after dark; but the Japanese were cunning, they had a very good understanding of the western psyche, even if they despised it, and they were waiting for someone to help the soldier. If he liked water so much, they decided, they would give him water, and they tied John down and left a tap drip-dripping on his forehead. It seemed almost nothing when he thought about it now, but at the time it drove him to the edge of insanity. Lying there waiting for the next drip, and the next, hour after endless hour, as though it was wearing a hole not just in his skull, but in his soul, and he would have gladly died. He lost track of time, of day and night, but eventually he had been released, until the next time.

After VJ Day arrived, bringing the release they all believed would never come, a minister had advised the former POWs to try not to hate the Japanese, to forgive even if they couldn't yet forget, and John knew he would have killed him with his bare hands – if, that was, he'd had the strength to even stand. Now here he was cowering in the dark, because – he had finally worked out – in his sleep he had heard a tap dripping in the bathroom. He felt stupid and weak and sick, but he couldn't summon up the courage to simply go in and turn the tap off. Instead he had taken off downstairs and lain on the

couch, unable to hear it now, but still sure he could, too terri-
fied to move.

And then Beth appeared, alerted by some sense he didn't
have, as she always seemed to be, and she looked down at him
and smiled her soft smile. He signed to her, as she had taught
him, hoping he was saying 'Dripping tap upstairs', and she
nodded and went back upstairs to turn it off. Then she returned
with a blanket and put it over him, made him a hot milk drink
and left him with a touch of her hand on his forehead. He had
never met anyone like her. She didn't do things for him, she
helped him do them himself; and she never questioned him,
simply accepting whatever bizarre behaviour he presented her
with as though it was perfectly normal.

There was no feeling of anxiety about her, as there was from
his family. They waited anxiously for him to return to normal,
in their distress lacking the vision to understand that he couldn't
become who he once was. The John Pollock who had gone
off to war had died as surely as his brother had. Now he was
who and what they saw, and Beth, gentle, kind and quiet, didn't
ask anything, had no expectation of him, instinctively knowing
when he wanted to be alone without taking offence, and sitting
with him when he needed company. Lying on the couch, he
realised he couldn't be without her, that she was somehow part
of him now, and he of her, they mattered to each other's lives.
He drank his milk, listening to the sound of the sea outside
and calming down, breathing in slowly as the waves washed
onto the shore and then breathing out as they were swept off
again. He loved the sea – it soothed him as Beth did.

'The way I see it,' Louise said, 'we have to play it calm.'

Alice and Maggie nodded firmly.

'When she comes back here no one should ask her anything,

we have to wait till she tells us, and then we must react as though we hadn't a clue.'

Alice and Maggie nodded again.

The trouble was that when Beth did return and was safely seated in the parlour, Louise immediately said, 'So tell us, Beth, is it true that you've got a young man over there?'

Alice and Maggie almost choked on their tea and Paris buns.

'Well, I can't be bothered with all this pussy-footing around,' Louise protested. 'So, out with it, Beth.'

As Alice and Maggie tried to compose themselves they noticed that Beth was laughing.

'So what if I have?' she signed.

'Who is he?' Louise giggled. 'Some fine lusty peasant from the island?'

'I'm not telling you,' Beth replied.

'Why not?' Louise demanded.

'Because it's none of your business.'

'Is it serious?' Alice asked as casually as she could.

'I'm not telling you that, either,' Beth told her, 'and for the same reason.'

'But you have to understand that we're interested, dear,' Maggie cajoled.

'I daresay you are,' Beth teased, 'as it's true, you do look exactly like Macbeth's witches! But my lips are sealed, my fingers too, come to that.'

When she had gone upstairs the three women sat in confusion. 'She really can be very headstrong, you know. What do we do now?' Maggie asked.

'I have no idea,' Alice replied.

'Well, I'll tell you,' Louise announced, and they turned their full attention on her. 'Bugger all, that's what we do.'

'Louise, really!'

'Oh, do be quiet, Maggie, there's a dear. We do bugger all because there's bugger all to do. Plain and simple. She holds all the cards and she knows it.'

'I can't believe she's being so secretive,' Alice said in a hurt tone.

'Yes,' Maggie muttered. 'I wonder who she gets it from?'

And so the situation simmered along, with no one knowing what was going on, even though they knew who it was going on with. Then one day in May as they sat in Kew Terrace, Beth announced that the extension at the side of the house had been completed and she thought Alice should go over with her and inspect it. Oh, and it might be an idea if she met John at the same time.

'John who?'

'John Pollock.'

'Pollock?' Alice stressed. 'Not any relation to –'

'Yes, he's the son of Bernard Pollock of Inchcraig.' If Beth knew this would come as a shock she didn't let on.

'Beth, I can't believe this,' Alice told her. 'You must know that I have concerns.'

'I don't know why,' Beth responded.

'Because of his father. You do know what he did, don't you? I know you didn't mix much in Inchcraig, but you know the man was a criminal, don't you?'

'I don't care what his father did. What has that to do with John?'

'He was raised by Bernard Pollock, that has to have left its mark. How do we know he isn't like him.'

'He isn't.'

'But how do we know, Beth?'

'Because I tell you,' Beth replied.

The two women stared at each other.

'We're not living together, if that's what you think,' Beth told her. 'I stay here most of the time and he comes down when he can, and stays for a few days, most of which he spends sleeping or walking. We have separate rooms.'

'I wasn't worried about that,' Alice lied.

'Look, I don't need your approval,' Beth told her bluntly. 'I can live without it.' With that she turned to walk out of the parlour, then she turned back. 'You seem to forget that I met his father,' she mouthed, 'and where.' With that she departed, leaving Alice stunned.

Alice was suddenly catapulted back decades. She had had very similar conversations over her relationship with Liam and knew how it felt to be in Beth's shoes, but Beth didn't know this. She wished she'd managed to tell Beth everything, but adding that to what was happening now would only increase the tension. Even if she was serious about this man, and even if Alice approved, Beth would face opposition from his mother because of Alice's friendship with Bernard. The whole situation was impossible; there were too many layers of difficulty for a straight-forward solution, and she couldn't meet him, there was no point.

'But you have to, dear,' Maggie told her sensibly. 'How can you possibly refuse?'

'How would you have the brass neck to refuse?' Louise demanded. 'You of all people!'

'Louise, this isn't a religion thing,' Alice protested.

'It doesn't matter, don't you see that?' Louise replied, raising her voice. 'That's a red herring. The only point at issue here is that you don't approve of Beth and this man. There is nothing more to consider. I tell you, if you refuse to meet him, I'll tell Beth that I'd be happy to. The choice is yours, but I have to say I'm disappointed in you, Alice, I really am.'

'So you really expect me to go to my own house to meet this man?' Alice asked.

'What does it matter whose house it is?' Louise shot back. 'Where would you like to meet him?'

'I wouldn't like to meet him anywhere!'

'Exactly! There's the truth of it. Everything else is excuses, and you know it!' Louise cried triumphantly.

24

The last time she had arrived at 'Anneetermore' she had done so unexpectedly, so this time she told Beth she was coming, who received the news calmly and cheerfully.

John was in the garden at the back, Beth told Alice when she arrived; they'd look over the extension before she introduced them. So Alice did as she was bid, making appreciative noises about the new rooms, the workmanship, the decor, but she knew if anyone had asked her to describe those moments later she couldn't have. As they came to the front of the house again Beth glanced in the window and announced that John was inside. It felt the wrong way round. If anything, Alice should be waiting inside for some suitor of Beth's, approved of or not, to be brought in to be introduced to her, but she felt the roles had been reversed.

The first thing that struck her was how like his father John was. When Bernard Pollock had first entered her life in Inchcraig he was about this age, too, in his early thirties, a tall, dark, handsome man with warm brown eyes. The difference was in presence, she supposed. There had been about Bernard a feeling of power, a strength he knew he had and the confidence coming from that, as he politely, pleasantly, but very firmly warned her off harming his business interests. John had the looks, but that was all, there was no menace in this man and, as he shook hands, no great strength either.

Suddenly Alice could see why Beth had taken him under her wing. She had always had a weakness for underdogs, for obvious reasons, but Alice still wondered if that would be enough to carry them into a future. John was courteous, but she could see how difficult this meeting was for him, as Beth hovered beside him like a protector, ready to spring into action, she supposed, at the first unkind word. Alice decided there wouldn't be any, neither Beth nor John deserved that.

She looked at them and saw herself and Liam: the circumstances were slightly different, but in essence they were the same. Louise had been right all along. They had done no wrong to anyone, they were just two young people who had found each other, and whatever difficulties they faced she was sure, as sure as she had been when she and Liam had fled Belfast, that they would deal with them. No one else had any right to suggest they wouldn't cope; it was no one else's business.

'I didn't mix much in Inchcraig,' John told her over tea. 'I was a bit like Beth in that respect, only for different reasons. I went to school in Glasgow and all my friends were there.'

Alice already knew this, of course. 'I knew your father,' she told him. 'He used to show me pictures of you and your brother, he was very proud of you.'

'I know what he did, Mrs McInally.' John smiled weakly. 'I didn't know when I was younger, but I found out later. I still have difficulty believing it because he was never like that at home, but I know who he was.'

'He had another side to him,' Alice nodded. 'I think he had many sides to him, to be truthful – you saw what and who he needed you to see.'

'Yes, that's what I think, but I sometimes wonder if I think that because I need to believe it, if you see what I mean. I've heard some of the things he did and I wonder how I could've lived with this monster. But he wasn't, you know, not to us, and all we knew was that he was in business. As a child you don't question what you're told. He never talked about it, and I think that was because he didn't see us following him into "the family business", if you like. We had a good standard of living; we lived in a house rather than in the Inchcraig tenements; my brother and I had a good education. I now know how he afforded that, and it doesn't make me feel good, but it's something I can't change.'

'We're not responsible for our parents, John,' she said soothingly. 'You were a child, you could hardly have asked him where the money came from.'

'Well, if you're worried about Beth on that account, please don't be. I knew nothing about my father's business – it's as awful to me as it is to you.'

Beth, standing behind him, put her hand on his shoulder. 'That's enough for now,' she mouthed at Alice, 'he's tired.' Alice understood what an effort the meeting and the conversation had been for him.

As he got up John said to her, 'I'm sorry about this. Sometimes I need to rest, it'll get better,' and he went upstairs, leaving Beth and Alice together.

'There you are,' Beth told her. 'If you thought he was making use of me, you can see he hasn't the strength. He has never laid a hand on me.'

'I take it marriage is on the cards, though?' Alice smiled. 'But have you really thought this through, Beth? What if he never recovers? Have you thought of that?'

'This is the only way I know him. If he gets better than he

is now, he gets better. If he doesn't, so what? So if you have any objections –'

'No,' Alice interrupted, 'no objections. I like him, I like him a lot.'

She watched Beth trying to control her smile. 'Good,' she told her primly.

'You may have problems with his mother,' Alice warned. 'She had some mad idea about me and his father.'

Beth put her head down and laughed. 'Yes, we heard about that. I laugh every time I think about it!'

'Don't you dare laugh!' Alice chided her. 'I was quite a looker when I was young, believe it or not.'

'Yes, but you as a femme fatale, it's ridiculous!' and Beth laughed again.

'Well, even if you don't believe it,' Alice said, looking at her as though she was hurt, 'she still might. Just be prepared, that's all.'

'It won't bother us,' Beth stated simply. 'If she objects that's her problem.'

'But Beth, are you really sure? I know you feel sorry for the poor chap, but do you think that's enough?'

'Aunt Alice,' Beth sighed, 'I know you've never been in love, but trust me, if you ever had been you'd know that when it happens you don't mistake it for pity.'

Ah, Alice thought, the arrogance of the young. I remember it so well! But she said nothing.

'I could tell you the very moment I realised,' she said. 'His father had a flat here, in Rothesay, and after his father died his mother sold it. I met him on the boat and he said it was his last visit before the new owners took it over, so I asked him if he'd like to see the cottage, in case he might want to rent it. He stood on the doorstep under the name, and it was the oddest thing, but he just fitted, he looked right here. Do you know what I mean? No, of course you don't! Anyway, I knew then. I have no idea when he knew.'

Alice sat silently. *He fitted, he looked right here, though she wouldn't have any idea what that meant.* The feeling of Liam was so strong that they might have conjured him up between them. Liam had fitted, he had looked right here, too, and it only felt like yesterday.

'Where are you planning to live?' Alice asked, though she already knew the answer.

'Here, on the island,' Beth replied, an innocent look on her face.

Alice saw it hanging in the air. 'You must live in this house,' she said.

'No! It's your house, you're going to let it out.'

'Well, that was an idea, but it doesn't matter now,' she smiled.

The letting idea had gone many moons ago. She was staying at Kew Terrace while she looked around for a new home, but the truth was that she intended coming here, to 'Anneetermore', to stay.

However, if Beth planned to move here with John then she still had other options. Louise had now left Belfast, so they could look for somewhere together. It would never be dull sharing a house with Louise. When Alice thought about it she knew moving to the island, to this cottage, had been a dream, a way of trying to reclaim the life she and Liam would've had there, to salvage something, but it was far too big for her. It was a family home, it deserved a family. The bright, noisy, happy and free children she and Liam had planned wouldn't run around here, but their grandchildren would, and she knew he would be happy with that.

'You could stay here with us,' Beth suggested.

Alice shook her head. 'You wouldn't want an old woman with you when you start out on married life. It wouldn't be fair for one thing,' she smiled, 'and this old woman wouldn't want to live with a young married couple.'

'But there's the extension,' Beth insisted, 'it could easily be changed to make a completely self-contained little house.'

'You've been thinking about this, I can tell,' Alice teased.

'A bit,' Beth admitted, smiling to herself. 'He knew Matt, would you believe it?'

'Really?'

'Yes, but not well, mind you. They were in the same Argylls intake, or whatever it's called, but Matt was quickly selected as a marksman. He was deadly accurate with a gun, so he was sent elsewhere.'

'Good heavens!'

'John says that was tougher in a way, because when you had to shoot someone you often had to do it at close range, so you saw them as people, whereas the others fired at the enemy and it was like firing at targets.'

Alice was thoughtful for a moment. 'He had terrible nightmares when he came home, you know. He would scream the most awful screams, but when I asked him the next day how he slept he always said, "Like a baby."'

'I guessed about the nightmares. He looked terrible, it was obvious he wasn't sleeping. I recognised the same look on John's face when I first saw him, too. He still has nightmares.'

When Alice left she promised to think about Beth's suggestion that she could move in to the cottage with them, but they both knew she wouldn't, of course.

Maggie and Louise were waiting for her at Kew Terrace, rubbing their hands together, the other two Macbeth witches. 'It looks like we're having a wedding,' Alice told them. But if the family thought a grand occasion was in the offing, that idea was swiftly put down by Beth on her next visit. John wasn't up to a big do, she told them, and neither was she, though for different reasons – hers being that she didn't like a fuss. They would get married as quietly as possible at Martha Street Registry Office, close family only allowed, if they insisted, as long as no one got boisterous. Everyone looked at Louise, who stared back innocently.

As it was, there would be no rush – they weren't eloping, for heaven's sake – and it was more important that John should be allowed time to recover and get stronger. All they had done was clear the air about their plans, made the position clear, so there would be no grand announcements or gestures, everyone had to remain calm. Was that clear? To everyone? To Louise?

'She is quite something,' Louise said sniffily when Beth had gone. 'A right little madam.'

'Yes,' Maggie replied, both of them looking at Alice, 'as I've said before, I wonder who she gets it from?'

The discussions about where to live went on in Kew Terrace. Maggie didn't want Alice and Louise to leave. She enjoyed the company and looking after the 'younger' ones, who were now in their sixties. Her children were starting to produce grandchildren, but they had their own lives and, to be truthful, faced with the reality of the first screaming baby, she now found grandchildren too much to contend with for long stretches of time.

'They're all very well for a short visit,' she said, 'but it is quite wonderful when they go home and you have the place to yourself.'

'So why do you want us to stay?' Louise demanded.

'Well, it's nice to have someone of your own generation to talk to, I find, don't you?'

'Can't say that I do,' Louise replied. 'I feel eighteen most days, twenty on my bad days.'

'And you act it, dear,' Maggie said wryly, making Alice laugh, 'don't you worry about that!'

'You can see how Beth came up with her "Macbeth's witches" crack, can't you?' Louise said pointedly.

'I still wonder how Tony really feels about this, Maggie,' Alice said quietly.

'For heaven's sake, dear, we're not honeymooners, we got past all that many moons ago. Besides, Tony will go on in business till he drops, and I'm not a part of that.'

Again, Alice sensed a sadness there and exchanged a glance with Louise. Tony and Maggie had been happy, but Louise and Alice both thought Maggie had been a little disappointed in her marriage, that she would have liked more companionship from her husband, but she had settled for what she had. Later, when Maggie was out, Louise and Alice talked about it.

'I sometimes think the families did entirely the wrong thing all those years ago by opposing them, you know,' Louise said. 'I sometimes think that if they'd bided their time Maggie would've seen what a boring chap he was and ended it. Instead, they almost issued a challenge.'

'Louise, even by your standards that's a bit harsh,' Alice protested.

'Oh, I don't mean he's not a nice chap, of course he is. Maggie says he became obsessed with work and success to show everyone he was good enough for her, but it was never about that, was it? It was about the religion thing – who was good enough for whom didn't enter into it. I suspect if they'd been the same religion and they'd married, he'd have been the same, don't you? But if the families hadn't reacted with their usual hysterical outbursts, Maggie might've had more time to get to know him before they got married and realised what he was like.'

'But they've been happy,' Alice said. 'For all anyone knows she could've found that out and still married him.'

'Oh, please,' Louise protested, 'you're not going to tell me they were made for each other, are you?'

'I was thinking about it, yes.'

'And that there's one special person for everyone?'

'Yes.'

'Oh, God!' Louise shouted, slapping her forehead. 'A bloody romantic, that's what you are, yet you did your level best to come between Beth and John – a romantic hypocrite, that's what you are, Alice McInally!'

'Stop being so theatrical,' Alice complained. 'And you've over-simplified everything, as usual. Are you saying you were married all those years without feeling your husband and you were meant to be together?'

'Well, if you're expecting me to go all gooey-eyed just because he's dead, you're sadly mistaken!' Louise laughed. 'Why do you think we marry people who are nearby?' she asked. 'If it's all about finding that one special partner in all the world, why do most people marry the person round the corner? What law of nature says your one and only must live near you and not in deepest Peru, or Russia, or the Sahara Desert?'

'Now you're being silly, Louise.'

'I'm not, I'm just not being gooey-eyed, you silly romantic! I loved my husband dearly, but I always knew there were many people I could've, maybe would've loved, had I met them, and the same for him. Do you really think some power-on-high sits there pairing off people on earth? 'Oh, he looks the perfect

382

match for her, so we won't make him live in Paraguay, we'll put him in West Belfast.' If that were really the case that power-on-high should find another job – you just have to look around you to see that. In fact, all you have to do is think of Bella and the Guthrie creature, and you'll see that my point has been made.'

'Well, all I know is that I would have picked Liam from all the men in the world,' Alice said defensively.

'You only think that because it's what you want to think, you romantic witch,' Louise smiled at her. 'But it makes no sense all the same. Most of us make it work by compromise, and that's what Maggie has done, so you have to admire her for that. In her shoes I might've taken an axe to dear old Tony long ago, much as I like him.'

'Are you saying that we should do as she wants and stay here with her?' Alice asked, amazed.

'It might be a kindly thing to do. God knows, she's done enough kindly things for others all her life. She's right that Tony won't notice whether we're here or not, he's rarely here, and the house is so big that she'd rattle about in it on her own.'

'She was doing that when Liam and I arrived,' Alice recalled. 'She was doing all this charity stuff to fill her time and I remember feeling that she was actually rather lonely, though she pretended to be terribly busy all the time. When I left with Beth she had her first child on the way, so she was busy from then on.'

'And now they've gone,' Louise replied, 'and now she's in her seventies we're her children. Besides, she can be very po-faced, my sister. I see it as my duty to annoy the hell out of her from time to time. It's what she needs.'

And so the matter was settled to everyone's satisfaction, for a time at least. They were like girls again, shopping together, taking tea in Glasgow's many tearooms while they gossiped and argued, and going to the theatre. John Pollock was eventually adjudged well enough by Beth to be introduced to Kew Terrace's inhabitants and pronounced rather nice, and Alice was chided for being so negative at the outset. Then Maggie came up with the wonderful idea of having the wedding reception at her home, a very small wedding reception, she assured Beth, nothing too boisterous, as she had said, just tasteful and, well, if they must, small.

The date was tentatively set for the following May, more than six months hence, and the ladies went shopping for their outfits, there being not a moment to lose. In the process they stumbled upon, by sheer coincidence, the viewing of several wedding dresses that might suit Beth rather nicely. Not that they told her, there was time enough for that, but they couldn't have her getting married in the austere grey suits of post-war Glasgow. Brides tried their best, usually adding a blouse in a bright blue or pink underneath the tightly waisted jacket, with a bit of lace on the Peter Pan collar, but it was so, well, as it was, utility. Beth deserved better – they would deal with whether she wanted it or not at a later date.

Then a thought occurred to Louise one morning and she rushed to Alice's bedroom. It just came to her from nowhere: Beth's birth certificate, why had none of them thought of it? Alice still hadn't told Beth the truth, but Beth would need her birth certificate to put up the banns three weeks before the wedding and that time was approaching fast. They couldn't have the poor girl finding out all by herself. On the certificate it would state her place of birth had been Glasgow and her mother as Alice McInally, spinster; father unknown. Alice had to tell her now, there was no time to lose.

★   ★   ★

384

Never one for standing on ceremony or protocol, Louise was through the door as she was still knocking. Alice was sitting up in bed, a book in her hands. 'Alice, put the book away, I've just thought of something awful!' she called, rushing to the window and throwing the curtains open.

It was the silence that made her stop. It wasn't just that Alice hadn't protested, it wasn't the lack of speech, it was another kind of silence, a heavy, permanent kind, the kind you feel rather than hear. Louise stood facing the window, her hands still on the curtains, desperately not wanting to turn round, then she took what Alice would call the coward's way out – she ran without looking.

Maggie was in the breakfast room. 'Good heavens,' she joked, looking up from her newspaper, 'are you up ridiculously early or haven't you gone to bed yet?'

'Maggie, something's wrong with Alice,' Louise said quietly.

'No wonder, the way the two of you stay up half the night gossiping, turning night into day. I'll have something sent up on a tray.'

'No,' Louise said very seriously. She put her hand on her sister's arm as she made to get up. 'No, Maggie.'

Maggie stared at her for a long time, neither of them moving, not a word passing between them. If they moved from this moment then it was real, it was now, and the later they didn't want would still be in the future; stay in the moment and it wouldn't happen. Eventually Maggie sat down and stared ahead and Louise rang the bell and instructed the maid to send for a doctor.

Alice had been dead for several hours, he told them, hadn't known a thing about it. The book was still in her hands, the bedclothes were tucked tidily about her, she had very likely had no warning and there had been no distress.

'Her mother died very suddenly at about the same age,' Maggie said quietly. 'Her husband left her sitting in the kitchen in the morning and she was still there when he came home in the afternoon. They said it was her heart.'

'It was very likely the same thing,' he said.

'Her father died reading in the library,' Louise smiled sadly, 'but he was in his seventies.'

'It was in the family, then,' the doctor said quietly. 'We'll need her next of kin, there are formalities, you see.'

The sisters looked at each other.

'That would be her daughter, Beth,' Louise said briskly. 'We are Alice's cousins. Beth isn't here at the moment, she's on the Isle of Bute. We'll have to send a message to her. She's deaf, you see, we can't just call, and we can't ask anyone else to pass on this news.'

Maggie nodded. 'Maybe we shouldn't send a message, maybe we should go over there and bring her home.'

'Yes,' Louise said, her voice dull, knowing there would be so much more to the conversation and that there was no way of avoiding it. It wasn't in Louise's nature not to charge in, but on this occasion she would have given anything not to be here, not to have to face Beth. Just weeks away from getting married, this was the last thing any bride needed, but what they had to tell her, and all of it at once, would break the heart of anyone, and the person who would have helped her, should have helped her, was gone.

'I don't know how we're to tell her,' Maggie whispered, weeping quietly into her handkerchief.

'Well, people always cope with these things better than we think they will,' the doctor smiled awkwardly.

Maggie and Louise looked at each other. The doctor wasn't quite talking about what they were talking about. 'Well, thank you for that wonderful platitude, Doctor,' Louise said wryly. 'I can see a university education wasn't wasted on you.' She rang the bell. 'The maid will see you out, in case you get lost on your way to the front door.'

'Louise, really!'

'On this day of all days, Maggie,' she replied wearily to the familiar reproof, 'please give it a rest. And pull yourself together, we have things to do and we can't have you weeping all over the place.'

'Beth?' Maggie asked in a quiet voice.

'Yes, Beth. No time like the present, Maggie,' Louise said firmly.

When Alice's body had been removed from the house they tidied up the bedroom themselves. It wasn't something they would have wanted anyone else to do. Beside her bed were a few photos, all of Liam. Liam and Alice at Lough Neagh; on Shaw's Bridge; one of Liam in uniform looking hopelessly young and innocent; another of him standing under the sign at the cottage, 'Anneetermore', a wistful smile on his face. And there was a pile of letters out of their envelopes, letters from Liam when he was at the Front; Alice had obviously been reading them again.

Louise remembered a conversation she'd had with Alice and for once in her life had regrets and wished she could recall every word. They had been discussing whether or not there was a special someone in all the world for everyone and Alice had insisted there was. Louise had laughed at her and called her a romantic, and Alice had gone up to her room afterwards and taken out her photos of Liam, her one special person in all the world. The book that had been in her hands when she died lay with the photos now, Robert Frost's poetry, still open at the poem she had been reading: 'The Road Not Taken'.

They set out immediately for Bute. It was mid-morning when they arrived in Rothesay, and a taxi took them to 'Anneetermore'. They stood at the bottom of the rise, looking up at the whitewashed walls, then turned to the sea and looked out at the view. The attraction of the place was obvious, and it was so quiet in the early spring sunshine. They made their way up to the cottage and saw Beth through the window, as her mother once had, but this time she was alone in the little kitchen behind the sitting room. Louise waved to attract her attention before they went into the house.

At first Beth smiled broadly in total surprise, but by the time they had gone through the door to greet her, her face was solemn – that extra sense had added up the signs and she knew this was no social visit. Still, she looked behind them for Alice, hoping, then sat down slowly on the couch, wiping her hands on her apron. They waited till she raised her head to look at them and they saw she was ready for the news they had brought, but they had decided to tell her only the worst part and to keep the story of her birth till she was at Kew Terrace. It would be too much to spring it all on her now. It was then they understood how difficult it had been for Alice to tell Beth that same story, how the time was never right, just as this time wasn't, so it could wait. Beth had always been, as they often said, a bit headstrong, a right little madam even, but looking at her now they saw a child's eyes staring back at them, unsure and afraid. When they broke the news she flinched slightly, then got up, took off her apron and fetched her coat and bag.

'John,' she signed.

'Is he here, dear?' Maggie asked, looking towards the stairs.

Beth shook her head with an impatient frown. 'He's due down tomorrow, if I'm not here he'll worry.'

'We'll send a message to him the moment we get back to Glasgow,' Maggie assured her.

It was a silent, still journey, each of them lost in their own thoughts, tearless from the shock, and they were all relieved to arrive at Kew Terrace. Maggie wrote a note to John Pollock and sent the car out again to take it to his family home in Inchcraig.

'Is she here?' Beth asked. 'I'd like to see her.'

'No, dear,' Maggie told her, 'they took her away this morning.'

'Where to?'

Maggie and Louise looked at each other; they weren't sure.

'To the mortuary, I think,' Maggie said.

'Oh.'

'Would you like to rest?' Louise asked her.

'No, I want to know what happened.'

'I don't think we know that for sure,' Maggie said quietly. 'Louise went to her room this morning and found her. She'd been gone for some time, though. She was reading when it happened.'

Beth gave a little laugh. Aunt Alice and her books. 'What?'

'I said she was reading, dear,' Maggie repeated, enunciating more clearly.

'No, I mean, what was she reading?'

'Robert Frost, I believe.'

Beth nodded. 'She liked him.' She sighed. 'What happens now?'

Again the sisters looked at each other uncertainly.

'Are you sure you wouldn't rather leave this till another time, Beth?' Louise asked again, feeling ashamed of herself for wanting to put this off for her own reasons, not for Beth's.

Beth shook her head.

The maid came in with a tray of soup and sandwiches, put it down and left.

'Beth, we have some things to tell you,' Maggie said.

'What more can there be?' she asked.

'Beth, you're going to have to be strong, and you'll have to concentrate. You're her next of kin, you see, there are things you have to be clear about.'

'You're her cousins, isn't that at least equal to a niece?'

'That's what we have to explain, Beth,' Louise told her. 'You're not her niece, you're her daughter.'

Beth looked from one to the other. 'I know, she became my mother when my parents died, mine and Matt's.' She shrugged.

'No, that's what we have to explain – please bear with us, this is hard. Matt was her nephew, his parents were Harry and Mattie. He was their only child. You were Alice's child, you were born here in Glasgow.'

The world ground to a halt. 'I don't believe you!' she said out loud in the strange, muffled voice she only used in times of stress. Maggie put a hand out to her, but she pulled away, her eyes angry. 'Why are you saying this?'

'Because it's true, dear,' Maggie said, instantly dissolving in tears.

'I knew you'd blub!' Louise yelled. 'I knew I should do it!'

'It can't be, she would've told me,' Beth protested. 'She wouldn't have lied to me! Why would she?'

'Why would we?' Louise asked.

Beth put her arms around herself and hugged them tight, her head down, rocking slightly and very silent.

'We'll wait till you're ready,' Maggie said, though Beth wasn't looking at her. Maggie was thankful for the time to compose herself. She wanted to do this properly for Alice, and for Beth;

the tears were a distraction and she was as annoyed with herself as Louise was.

Eventually Beth looked up and nodded.

'Your father's name was Liam McCann,' Maggie said.

'McCann? Like Uncle Brendon?'

'Yes, Uncle Brendon is Uncle Brendon, he's your father's younger brother.'

'So he lied to me too?'

'Beth,' Louise said firmly, 'I think you have to stop talking about people lying to you.'

'No wonder you think that: you've both lied to me all my life as well!' she accused.

'If you can't be an adult about this, I'm leaving,' Louise announced, then sat down again at an angry glance from her sister.

'This is your idea of helping, is it?' Maggie demanded. 'This is your idea of sympathy?'

'Well, for God's sake!' Louise shouted. 'I'm trying my best. She has to help, too. This isn't exactly the best day of my life either!'

Then Beth put her arm out in a gesture of defeat and apology. 'Go on,' she signed.

So they told her the full story, stopping when she looked too upset to go on and waiting till she told them to continue. They told her about her father and a little of what he had been like, about the flight from Belfast, the near marriage, and the little cottage on Bute where they had planned to raise their family. 'That's where you were conceived,' Maggie told her, and handed over the picture of Liam taken under the house name when he was home on his last leave.

'It wasn't like today,' Louise explained. 'You couldn't go into the Registry Office, put up your banns and get married three weeks later, you see. Back then you had to have a church wedding, and neither of them wanted that, or you went to a lawyer, declared yourself married before two witnesses, then went to the Sheriff Court for a piece of paper, then to the Registry Office to have the marriage officially recorded. They did the first two, but the Registry Office was closed, it was a holiday, and your father had to go back to the Front a few hours later. He bought her the two rings she always wore.'

'I always assumed they had belonged to her mother,' Beth signed, looking at the other pictures that had been handed over as the tale unfolded.

'I have them here for you,' Maggie said, giving them to Beth.

'But why didn't she tell me? Matt always wanted a father, but I always wanted a mother, and I used to feel guilty about that because I knew what Aunt Alice had given up for us, for me. Now I find I did have a mother, but it's too late to call her that. It's so unfair! She should've told me!'

From the corner of her eye she caught a movement from Louise, who was sprawled in an armchair, sherry decanter in hand. 'And you can shut up!' Beth told her. 'I don't want you to tell me anything, you witch!'

'So we're of the same mind, you ungrateful brat!' Louise enunciated clearly. 'Cheers!' And with that she took a long slug of the sherry.

'You have to understand what it was like for illegitimate children at that time,' Maggie said gently, hoping a catfight could be avoided. 'It isn't much better now, to be truthful, but then they were regarded as something sinful, something to be ashamed of; and she wasn't ashamed, you know, she never was. They were bullied by everyone, not just other children but by adults as well. When Alice took in your grandfather and Matt she knew he would get treated much better than you would,

392

simply because his parents had been married. Think how that would've affected you as you grew up, especially as you had your deafness to contend with. It just seemed a good opportunity to make things better for you, especially when you had so much to cope with already.'

'She was always going to tell you,' Louise said.

'Then why didn't she?' Beth asked bitterly.

'She kept trying to, but the time was never right. Last New Year she went over to Bute to tell you, but when she looked through the cottage window she saw you canoodling by firelight with some strange man she knew nothing about, so she turned tail and ran.'

'I was not canoodling!'

'Yes you were!'

'So she knew about John?' Beth asked. 'You all knew about him?'

Maggie and Louise nodded.

'I can't believe you! Every member of this family is deceitful!'

'You were the one sitting in her house with a strange man's head in your lap!' Louise replied, and even if Beth couldn't hear her, she knew Louise was yelling angrily. 'I've had enough of this,' Louise shouted. 'You'd think she was the only one affected by this, the only one feeling bad!'

'She was my mother, Louise,' Beth shouted back in her odd voice. 'Have you any idea how much I wanted her to be my mother, and now I find out she was, but she pretended to be my aunt right up to the day she died!'

'And she was a bloody good mother,' Louise shot back. 'I wish Maggie and I could've had a mother like her. You should be grateful, you should try to understand the position she was in. Instead you're sitting here whining!'

'I had a right to know!'

393

'Goodbye!' Louise shouted, running out of the parlour.

Just then Brendon arrived from Belfast, summoned by a message from Tony. He had expected to find a household becalmed by grief, silent with shock. Instead, Louise strode past without a word, glaring at him angrily, and in the parlour Maggie and Beth were making furious signs at each other, their faces contorted with rage.

'What the hell's going on?' he asked in a bemused tone.

'Don't you start!' Beth shouted at him. 'You're as bad as they are!' She ran out of the room, leaving him staring at Maggie.

'I've never heard her speak before,' he mused, 'I didn't think she could.'

'Her voice makes people look at her, so she doesn't use it unless she's upset,' Maggie said wearily, 'and today, naturally, she's upset.'

'But what have I done?' he asked. 'I've just stepped in the door.'

'Please sit down, Brendon. We had to tell her Alice and Liam were her parents. There are formalities for the next of kin and the legal fact is that Beth is Alice's next of kin. Besides, she's getting married shortly: even without Alice's death she would have to have been told soon, she would've needed her birth certificate.'

'Oh. And that makes me part of the conspiracy?'

Maggie nodded. 'Everyone is. She isn't taking it very well – who thought she would? And Louise is being Louise, she rarely helps any situation. You know what she's like. She is very upset, too, of course, she found Alice this morning, then we both went over to Bute to tell Beth and bring her back. We are not in the first flush of youth and now we're both exhausted, that's the truth.'

The front door rang again and this time it was John Pollock.

'This is John, Beth's fiancé,' Maggie said hurriedly as she left the parlour and headed upstairs to her bedroom. 'John, this is Beth's uncle, Brendon McCann. Now, if I don't lie down I may fall down. Brendon, could I ask you to please tell John about what's been happening today, or as much as you understand? Ask the maid for anything you might want.'

Brendon looked at the younger man and smiled. 'It's nice to meet you, John,' he said, 'but I arrived here five minutes ago and in that time three women of my acquaintance have run out on me. I have no more idea what's going on in this house than you have, so perhaps we can just sit down and get to know one another?'

'Is Beth all right?' John asked anxiously.

'Well, she was one of the women I mentioned, and she seemed in the rudest of health as she passed, throwing abuse at me, as far as I could tell. I suggest we leave her alone till she feels more sociable.'

25

Beth lay upstairs in her bedroom, though she was rarely there these days. All her life she had felt isolated by her deafness, but the people around her had deliberately included her as much as they could, or so she thought. Now she felt betrayed, as though everyone had been pretending she was one of them, and all the time they were keeping this secret from her. And it wasn't just a secret, it was an enormous, life-shattering secret, so big that she felt she should have been aware of it without being told. They had all known, everyone in her family, and she'd been in the middle, like some fool, the only one kept in the dark.

When she thought of Aunt Alice – her mother – she was overwhelmed with a mixture of anger and grief, but it had nowhere to go, no escape. Clutched in her hand were the photos Alice had by her bed when she died. She looked at them, at the pretty young woman who smiled out from them, her mother, but not as she knew her, and her handsome father, so young, both of them, younger than she was now. She got up and went to the dressing table and, while she was brushing her hair, she looked closely at her reflection, then at the pictures. She could see herself in both of them, but more so in the young man. Then she went back downstairs and found Brendon and John in the parlour in deep conversation. She crossed the room, took John's hand and sat beside him.

'I hear you've been causing a bit of mayhem?' Brendon smiled at her.

'You could say that,' she replied. 'Just a bit.'

'And are you calm and rational now?' he teased.

'Just a bit,' she smiled back. She held up one of the pictures. 'Will you tell me about him?'

Brendon took the first one. 'That was taken on the banks of the Laggan, on Shaw's Bridge, by the look of it,' he said. 'It's still like this today. Tall beech trees, the Minnow Burn running underneath. I remember Liam had a camera with a delay, he must've taken this himself. They were hellish things,' he laughed. 'Always went off when you were nearly where you wanted to be, or just as you'd given up and turned your back.' Beth handed him another. 'And this one is on Lough Neagh. Both sides of the family came from there originally. Liam loved it; he learned to build boats there. You see that white building in the background?' He held the photo out so that Beth and John could see it. 'That's Nancy O'Neill's in Anneetermore.'

'Anneetermore?' Beth said out loud.

'Yes, the white gable of the house was a beacon for the local fishermen. They always knew where they were when they could see it.'

'But the house on Bute is called "Anneetermore"!' Beth signed, thrusting into Brendon's hand the picture of Liam standing at the door, under the name Alice had put there.

'That must have been why they called it that,' Brendon said quietly. 'It must have reminded them of Nancy O'Neill's on the Loughside.'

Beth handed him another photo, one of her own, of John standing under the same sign, his stance the same as Liam's. 'Look,' she signed. 'I took this one of John at the cottage.'

John squeezed her hand. 'Beth, you have to stop giving Maggie and Louise such a hard time over this,' he told her gently. 'Brendon's been explaining the whole thing to me, and they were only doing what your mother wanted, it wasn't their decision.'

'And give your mother less of a hard time while you're at it,' Brendon said. 'You can't judge her, Beth, she did what she thought she had to so that you wouldn't suffer. Think if it had been you and John instead of Alice and Liam – faced with those circumstances, what would you have done?'

'It wasn't out of selfishness,' John agreed, 'it was out of a need to protect this little girl without a father, who was also deaf.'

Beth nodded. She had more anger to express, but she couldn't do it at that moment.

'And she never wanted to marry?' she asked Brendon. 'After he died, I mean?'

'As far as I know, the thought never occurred to her. There had only ever been Liam for her and Alice for him. I can see them now as very small children, always together.'

'I suppose I feel cheated in a way,' Beth signed.

'Of course you do, but so was she, Beth,' Brendon replied. 'She was cheated by life.'

There was so much Brendon had to tell Beth, but the pressing matter now was the planning of Alice's funeral. It was decided not to have any religious service, then there was some discussion about where she would be buried.

'She should really be with my father, I think,' Beth suggested.

'Well, I'm the oldest living McCann,' Brendon replied. 'As far as I'm concerned, if you want her beside Liam at Derrytrasna, then that's where she'll go.'

'Oh, come on, Brendon!' Louise sighed, raising her eyebrows. 'With your mother and father already in residence? I don't think so! There is such a thing as a fate worse than death, and that's it, if you ask me.'

'I have to agree with Louise,' Maggie said thoughtfully, 'in sentiment if not in expression, but I don't think it would be quite appropriate to bury her beside her mother and brother either. Beside her father and Matt perhaps?'

Beth shook her head. She didn't know the right thing to do, but she felt Liam should be part of the plan. 'Was there somewhere she and my father went together?' she asked.

Brendon thought for a moment, then his face lit up. He picked up the photo of Alice and Liam taken all those years ago. 'Shaw's Bridge,' he smiled. 'That's where they used to meet. It's a beautiful spot, high beech trees, flowers everywhere, and there's a little burn running under the bridge.'

'Does it have bluebells?' Beth asked. 'She loved bluebells, you know.'

'That's probably why she loved them,' Brendon smiled, 'they carpet the banks of the Laggan in spring.'

'And this is spring,' Maggie said, clapping her hands happily.

'Yes, she did time it rather well, didn't she?' Louise muttered. 'Think what a difference it would've made if she'd been diffi-cult and died in winter.'

'Louise,' Maggie said stiffly, 'I don't think you should have any more sherry dear, it makes you very brittle.'

'It's a shame, though,' Louise said, pouring herself another glass from the decanter. 'She always wanted to go back to Bute, and now she'll never be able to do it.'

'I thought of that,' Maggie said, glaring at the glass in her sister's hand, 'but she wouldn't know anyone there, would she, dear? No, I don't think it would be fitting to put her somewhere she doesn't know the people round her.'

'Dear God, Maggie!' Louise muttered, shaking her head. 'Maybe she could have a get-to-know-you tea for all her neighbours in adjoining graves!'

'Louise!'

'Well, you really do bring it out in me, Maggie, you really do! The things you come up with!'

'If you two will stop bickering,' Beth signed quickly.

'And if you just slow down,' Louise suggested. 'Your fingers talk far too fast for the human eye to hear.'

'We'll have her cremated,' Beth signed, 'and scatter her ashes where Uncle Brendon suggests.' She looked round at each of them. 'Any objections?'

One by one they shook their heads.

'You'll all have to be there with me, of course.'

'No, no, dear,' Maggie replied, aghast. 'I can't go back to Belfast. After all these years? No, no, really, dear, I couldn't.'

'Why not?' Louise demanded.

'You know perfectly well why not!' Maggie said accusingly. 'Stop being so confrontational, Louise.'

'People don't say things like that, Maggie,' Louise giggled. 'I don't think I've ever heard anyone ever say "confrontational" in my whole life, but if someone had to say it, it would have to be my big sister!'

'You're being very rude, Louise,' Maggie responded. 'Again.'

'And you're being boring, Maggie. Loosen your stays for God's sake.'

Maggie decided to change the subject. 'I was wondering,' she said primly. 'Do we tell her sister in Canada?'

'I'd be careful there,' Louise retorted, 'she might come over – worse still, she might bring the Guthrie creature with her.'

'I doubt that, Louise,' Maggie said sharply. 'It would take weeks by boat, wouldn't it? And I doubt she'd fly over.'

'She's so stupid that if you suggested it she'd flap her arms and try,' Louise muttered. 'Besides, we all know she can only travel ten minutes away from home without her bowel or her bladder bursting, or whatever it was.'

'Yes, bring sensitivity into the proceedings, won't you?' Maggie said. 'And please don't have any more to drink, it doesn't bring out the best in you. I only wondered,' she continued in a hurt tone, 'if we should tell Bella at all. Would it be the right thing to do, that sort of thing, you know? Maybe we could just drop her a note afterwards?'

'Well don't put your address on the back,' Louise warned, pouring herself another sherry. 'Just in case. Cheers!'

The news had spread around Inchcraig and there were many of the old neighbours waiting at the crematorium, which surprised Beth. There had been so much happening that she hadn't thought of sending word to anyone and now she knew she should have and felt guilty. Seeing them there would have surprised Alice even more, she knew – the old neighbourhood come to say goodbye to 'Auld Nally'. As Beth passed in the big car she nodded to them, feeling very emotional. There was Isa from downstairs: another day when the children of Inchcraig would be without candy balls, she thought. And Annie Feeney, pregnant again, which was nice, Alice would've approved, with her husband beside her, of whom she had approved. Beside them Marie and Sadie Duffy stood with Harry, the little golden-haired boy, Matt's son. Another child without a father and whose father hadn't known about him before he died; she couldn't help feeling a bond with him. She had a promise to keep on her mother's behalf there, she knew, and on her own, and would see to it later.

It was a simple ceremony. Brendon said a few words, describing himself as 'Alice's brother-in-law'. Alice was Beth's mother, he told them, though most people there would know that by now, and he talked of Liam and the childhood he had shared with Alice. It was simple and fitting and there were no hymns, but a selection of Scottish and Irish music was played instead, ending with Robert Burns's 'Ae Fond Kiss', a song Beth said she liked. Brendon announced that everyone would be welcome back at Kew Terrace afterwards and Beth cursed herself again. She hadn't thought about the old neighbours being there and they wouldn't have transport, so she hurriedly asked someone to arrange taxis to take them there and back, determined to make sure they didn't feel out of place. Then they went to Kew Terrace for the traditional reception, that feast no one is ever in any mood to enjoy. Once the mourners relaxed a little, Beth and John mentioned quietly that they had decided to postpone the wedding and were immediately loudly set upon by Louise.

'Are you both mad?' she spluttered, spraying sausage roll everywhere. 'That is the single most insulting, crass thing you could say here today. How dare you!'

'She's right, dears,' Maggie said. 'I wouldn't have put it quite that way, naturally, but she's right. Think about what your mother would say, Beth, if she knew. Her of all people, making you stop your wedding.'

'It would only be till later,' John offered.

'That's what she said one Good Friday a long time ago,' Maggie reminded them, 'when she was seeing Liam off for the last time. The one thing she would not have wanted was for her daughter's wedding to be put off on her account.'

'Precisely!' Louise said firmly. 'And you should've thought that one out for yourself, madam!'

'Will you kindly behave?' her sister asked.

The next day they set off by train and then boat for Belfast. It was a beautiful day, with the heat in the new season's sun burning off a heavy frost in the places it reached, creating a striped landscape of green grass and sparkling silver. Beth, ever aware of John's still fragile state, had suggested he remain in Glasgow, and John, being a sensitive chap, did so, leaving the final rite of Alice's life to those who mattered most to her.

Louise was dressed in her usual oddly attractive style, in a wide midnight blue and mulberry patterned tapestry skirt with a heavy velvet jacket, which had a curved hem covering her hips, complete with knotted fringing all round. She had pulled a curl-brimmed velvet hat low around her ears, and wore black suede kitten-heeled shoes over black stockings. Maggie, meanwhile, wore a plain black suit with a straight skirt to mid-calf, so that she had to hobble on fashionably high heels while holding onto Louise's arm, much to her sister's annoyance. Underneath the suit was a high-necked white blouse with folds of lace, and her hat was a tiny crescent of straw and lace clamped on either side of her head. Round her shoulders, completing the picture of a lady of means and decorum, was a mink stole. The sisters bickered with every step, which was a welcome diversion for Beth.

'You just never get it right, do you?' Louise demanded.

'It's called fashion, dear,' Maggie retorted, 'and we all know that's something that passed you by.'

'Yes, it did,' Louise replied tartly, 'but style didn't. You either have it or you haven't, and if you haven't you have to rely on fashion, I suppose.'

'I think I look very elegant, if you must know, and you were the one who constantly attacked me for not keeping up with the latest designs,' Maggie replied, removing a hand from Louise's arm to pat her head approvingly, just where the natty little concoction that had her head in a vice-like grip was inducing a headache, though she would never have admitted it.

'And you're risking life and limb because you can't walk properly, you stupid woman!' Louise muttered. 'You'd think common sense would tell you to embrace the New Look, rather than encase yourself from head to toe in things that stop your blood circulating, not to mention that collection of poor dead creatures round your neck. Those shoes are killing you, too.'

'No they're not,' Maggie replied. 'They are very comfortable, if you must know, and far more respectable than those nasty little things you have on your feet!'

'And I'll bet anything you're still wearing corsets!' Louise said accusingly, suddenly grabbing at her. 'I knew it! I knew it!'

'Really, Louise, on this day of all days, you'd think you could be a bit more ladylike!'

'And you think it would bother Alice dead or alive, do you, whether or not I conform to your ideas on ladylike behaviour? At least I can walk by myself, and I can think for myself.'

'Are you accusing me of not being capable of thinking for myself?' Maggie demanded, trying to slow Louise down.

'Oh, you're capable, all right,' Louise replied. 'That's what makes your blinkers all the more infuriating: you have the capability, you just don't use it!'

But it wasn't just for Beth's benefit, of course; the two elderly sisters were distracting themselves, too. Here they were back in Belfast, where one had left in disgrace decades before, and the other had left in sorrow only recently, too recently for the sorrow to have dulled. They tried not to, but they recognised landmarks, places they had known in their younger years, some more changed than others, and they had mutually and tacitly agreed to get through the day the best way they could, by throwing jibes at each other – that way their minds could skim over what was too hard to notice and dwell on. They would not be visiting old haunts today, there would be no nostalgic visits to what had been their family home, church or school. They were here for a purpose, and when it had been completed they would return to Glasgow, to their chosen home; but even so, just by being here a few ghosts had been woken from their slumbers.

Shaw's Bridge was as they remembered it, though smaller, magnified by memory, and the Minnow Burn beeches were a little taller. The scent caught their attention instantly, that thick, sweet, fresh, unmistakable scent of bluebells, then there was a collective intake of breath as they saw the wide swathe of blue carpeting the banks of the river. Beth immediately walked to where her parents had stood to wait for the camera to click, looking a little way off to where the camera must have been, imagining the flex in Liam's hand as he waited to press the button once he was happy they were both in place.

'Can we please get on with it?' Louise muttered. 'Little do the rest of you know that there have been wanted posters all over Belfast offering large rewards if Maggie Doyle is turned in, dead or alive.'

'Louise, really!'

'She's a fugitive from Protestant justice – any minute now a bunch of coppers will descend on her and beat her to death with an orange sash, so we'll have to be quick,' Louise continued. She turned to her sister, her eyes narrowed. 'One thing, Maggie,

I must earnestly beseech you, please don't cross yourself, the world will instantly come to an end!'

'I wouldn't even know how to cross myself!' Maggie protested.

'Well, Brendon there will show you – on you go, Brendon!'

Brendon shook his head as the sisters continued to squabble. 'Can we just get on with this?' he said.

'What do I do?' Beth asked.

'Drop them over the side of the bridge and run!' Louise said merrily.

'I knew it, you've been drinking!' Maggie hissed at her.

'Oh, loosen your stays, Maggie!'

'I was just thinking,' Maggie said quietly, 'are we allowed to do this? Officially, I mean.'

'Don't suppose so,' Louise replied. 'Next stupid question?'

Beth eased open the lid of the urn and slowly let the ashes drop into the burn, and as they were carried away by the burbling water they all saw their reflections being carried with them, all the people Alice loved most. Even Louise was silenced, as she walked off to the side.

'We never brought flowers,' Beth mouthed. 'We should've brought her flowers.'

'Here,' Louise said to Beth, handing her a bunch of bluebells to cast on the water under the bridge, 'she loved bluebells, especially the ones that grow here.'

Beth married John a week later as planned, at the Registry Office where her parents hadn't managed to do so. Her wedding band was the one Liam had slipped on Alice's finger. Alice had worn it with the sapphire and diamond engagement ring till the end of her days, as their daughter would till the end of hers. The bride had wanted to wear something restrained, in lilac, perhaps, out of respect for her recently deceased mother, until Louise exploded right on cue, saying that she was, in fact, being disrespectful. A few short weeks ago, she lied wistfully, Alice had come upon a certain dress and had announced that Beth just had to get married in it. 'You could say', she said, 'that it was her dying wish.'

So the bride married in a full-length cream satin gown, with long, tight sleeves and a starburst of beading from neck to waist, though there hadn't been enough emotional blackmail to force her to wear a veil. She suspected, though, that for the rest of her life Louise would use her mother against her, and that there would be many more 'dying wishes' to contend with in the future. Still, she turned the tables by using John's health against them to have only close family see them marry, including John's mother, though no one sought her views.

As Beth was deaf an interpreter was needed for the vows. She could lip-read perfectly well, but the registrar wouldn't have been able to understand her seldom-used voice as she repeated the vows, or understood signing, so Maureen Murray, who had taught her as a child and become her friend and mentor, was proud to attend as interpreter and witness. Brendon was their other witness, because Beth wanted the name McCann on her marriage certificate in honour of her father. She wasn't allowed to have it on her birth certificate, but it would be on her marriage certificate, and that was the best she could do.

At Kew Terrace the bridal party walked into the agreed small, quiet reception and found they had more family than they thought they had.

'Just as you said, dear,' Maggie said brightly, 'close family only,' but she did have the good grace to add under her breath, 'and a few friends.'

'I saw that,' Beth replied. 'A few friends?'

'A few close friends of your mother's, Beth,' Louise said, frowning at her. 'It's what she wanted, she told me so herself.'

Brendon laughed out loud. 'The thing I've always admired about Louise,' he told Maggie, 'is that she went from outrageous young woman to eccentric old lady without the slightest pause.'

'If you mean without pausing for maturity,' Maggie said acidly, 'I totally agree, though I don't think the word "admire" is quite the one I would have chosen, Brendon.'

The young Pollocks didn't have a honeymoon. They went straight to their home on Bute that day. They wanted to escape from their families to be alone together, as newlyweds do. When she woke the next morning, Alice went alone to the shore in front of the house and thought about how much had happened in so short a time. She had thought of putting Liam's letters beside Alice in the coffin before the cremation. Such innocent letters, they were, full of love and hope for the future. She decided to keep them instead, so that her own children and grandchildren could read them one day and get to know the young couple who had been responsible for the island life they would have. As she watched, the waves gradually crept nearer as the tide came in, then she went back up to the cottage and stood looking out of the window at the sea. John came up behind her, slipped his arms around her and rested his chin on her shoulder.

'Look,' he said as she turned to face him. 'Bluebells.'

'Yes,' his wife replied, following his gaze. 'Bluebells.